DESTROYED

INVINCIBLE, IMPENETRABLE, INVISIBLE

BY

PEPPER WINTERS

Ded Amy ♥.

Thank you for the INSANE event. You kicked arse & we're so grateful for the hard work ♥

Published: Pepper Winters March 2014: **pepperwinters@gmail.com**
Publishing assisted by Black Firefly: **http://www.blackfirefly.com/**
(Shedding light on your self-publishing journey)

Editing: Chrystal
Cover Design: Cover it! Designs:
https://www.facebook.com/CoverItDesigns
and
Book Cover By Design:
https://www.facebook.com/bookcoverbydesign
Proofreading: Jenny from Editing for Indies
Formatting by: **http://www.blackfirefly.com/**
Images in Manuscript from Canstock Photos:
http://www.canstockphoto.com

For finding redemption in love.
For finding a second chance in hope.

Prologue

ROAN

I didn't believe her when she said she was complicated.

She didn't believe me when I said I had secrets.

I didn't understand the truth, even when she let me glimpse behind her mask.

She didn't understand that I couldn't live with the consequences.

I thought she was a saint.

She thought I was a sinner.

Too bad we didn't try to find the truth.

We both paid the price.

We destroyed each other.

One
 Hazel

If I knew now what I suspected then, I'd like to think I would've done things differently. I would've planned better, worked harder, stressed out on more important things. But I was young, naïve, and woefully unprepared for the big, scary world of life.

Now, I looked back on the past with a strange fondness. While I lived it, it seemed hard but now it seemed so incredibly easy. Especially now when the present seemed impossible and the future dire and bleak.

That was...until I met him.

Then it got worse.

"I don't think this is a good idea, Clue." The gothic mansion rose from gravel and soil like a beacon of doom. Gargoyles decorated plinths and overhangs; huge pillars soared to at least six stories high. I didn't know anything like this existed in Sydney, let alone in the rich and exclusive Eastern Suburbs.

My fingers hadn't stopped twitching for my knife ever since we stepped off the bus and headed toward a residential suburb instead of the party district in town.

Losing ourselves in a rabbit warren of streets, my heart never settled sensing this might be one experience that would end up killing us.

"Stop being such a worrier. You said you'd come. I need my wing woman," Clue said, her gentle voice edging to stern.

My mouth hung open, gawking at the intricate stonework, trying to see past the grandeur to unveil the tricks of such a place. It couldn't be real? Could it?

It seemed misplaced—as if it'd been transplanted from a long past century. It sent chills down my spine, conjuring images of insane, broken women and psychotic, sadistic men.

Huge double doors halted our entry. The thick wood, embellished with wrought iron accents in the shape of a fox on a wintry night, cracked open to reveal a black-suited bouncer with oil-slicked hair. His body jammed the doorway like a mountain while his face crossed somewhere between a bulldog and a shark.

His eyes froze me to the spot, capturing us with just one look. His pupils were black as the night behind us and held a cocky glint.

"You better have the password; otherwise you'll wish you never set foot on this stoop." His gaze swept to the concrete beneath us. A motto had been painstakingly engraved with a chisel into the stone. It looked hand done and rudimentary, but held a certain threat all the same.

Was that Russian? I couldn't make out the verse, but I inched to the side in my stupid kitten heels to avoid standing in the groove of letters.

"We were invited by Corkscrew. He gave us a one-night pass." For the millionth time since I'd showered, donned this ridiculous gold and silver dress, and coaxed my thick chocolate hair into some resemblance of curls and waves, I wanted to throttle Clue.

She was my dearest friend, closest confident, flatmate, babysitter, and non-blood sister, but I wanted to kill her for dragging me out tonight.

Clue and I had history—linked by shared dreams and hopes. We wouldn't let the other fail. And that was the only reason why I hadn't knocked her out and dragged her unconscious body back home.

She knew all I wanted to do was return to our crappy two bedroom apartment and avoid the world. She also knew I'd suffered so much in the past few weeks that I'd hit rock bottom, and I had no energy left to fight. Life had effectively pulled the rug, the flooring, and the fucking planet from under my feet. I didn't want to be here.

But as I grumbled and shed a tear on the couch, hugging my very reason for existence, she swore and cursed me. She reminded me that I might be in a bad place, but she needed me. That life goes on, solutions come, and tragedies happen. I couldn't change the future by either moping on the settee or dressing up like a hooker and going out with her. And as much as I wished I had a hacksaw in my cleavage, to threaten her to take me home to Clara, I didn't.

"Corkscrew, huh? What discipline?" The bouncer crossed his arms, raking his eyes over me. I'd lost weight from the stress of the last few weeks, but it didn't stop me feeling like an over-stuffed sausage in Clue's slinky dress.

My stomach twisted as I plucked the loaned attire that clung to me like a second skin. A web of lace covered my shoulders, but it couldn't disguise the sluttiness. My entire figure was on show, complete with perky nipples from the chill in the evening air.

Damn Clue and her fetishes for blingy, completely impractical clothing. She always forced me to wear the worst one. She said I was too serious; too focused; too obsessed with creating a future where nothing bad from the past could find us.

And she was right.

Clara.

Tears pricked the back of my eyes again, and I swallowed hard. *I shouldn't be here, dammit. What am I doing?*

"Muay Thai," Clue answered, her black almond eyes flashing with pride. Her latest acquisition, who I'd only met once, had successfully swept my commitment-phobic friend off her feet.

I didn't even know how they met or his real name. And Corkscrew, what the hell kind of title was that?

"Ah, great sport." The bouncer relaxed a little. "What's the password then, sugar tits?"

My mouth pursed. I couldn't stop the flash of fire; protective instincts rose to swell firmly in my chest. "Did you just call her *sugar* tits?" I'd never been one to stand by while another was ridiculed, embarrassed, or taken advantage of. I liked to think it was a strong character trait, but life had turned it into yet another flaw.

He chuckled. "Well, she has nice tits and she looks as sweet as sugar, so yeah. I did." His eyes narrowed. "You got a problem with that?"

Don't do it, Zel.

Clue patted my forearm, and I forced the retaliation from my tongue. My hands clenched, but I stayed silent. Giving him a verbal lashing wouldn't help us gain entry into this illegal club for Clue to see her man.

Dismissing me, the bouncer looked back at Clue. "Spit out the code or leave. I don't have time for this."

Clue cocked her hip, accenting the fluidity of her amazing figure. I had a small flash of awe, taking in Clue's perfection. Dressed in an equally slutty dress, she sparkled with red sequins. Looking part Geisha, part ninja warrior, Clue was one word: stunning.

"Thou may draw blood, but never draw life," Clue whispered, layering her husky voice with a heavy dose of allure.

Even if the password had been completely wrong, the bouncer was so spellbound he would've let us in. His cocky attitude left; replaced with a smitten smile. Clue had magical powers over men. She was the exact opposite of me. I seemed to repel men, which was perfect considering my situation.

"Well, what do you know? You're in." He swung the door wide, spilling warm light into the darkness of the night. "Head down to the end, then to the left. The main arena is there. Don't go into the other rooms unless invited."

Clue smiled and brushed past him, deliberately letting him gawk at her cleavage. "Thanks so much."

He nodded dumbly, letting me sneak past without fanfare.

My heart raced, taking in the ridiculously wide corridor. The heavy doors latched behind us, and all I wanted to do was run home to her.

You left her alone. With strangers. For this.

For this? This decadence, this richness, this mockery of everything that I needed in order to save her life. Instead of tears, anger filled me.

Whoever owned this monstrosity had so much more than they deserved. If only life had been kind enough to give me a way out. Give me a way to save her.

I can't do this.

"Clue. I've had enough. I'm sorry, but I'm leaving."

Clue spun again, grabbing my hands. "You're not, Zel. And I'll tell you why."

My temper rose further.

Her thumb caressed my knuckles, trying to calm me, but just riling me up even more. "You're not going home. Mrs. Berry will take great care of her. Life hasn't ended outside our apartment. You need to remember why you fought so hard to get to where you are." Her voice softened. "I'm losing someone I care deeply about and my best friend, too. You can't die with her, Zelly. I won't let you." Her eyes tightened, full of grief.

The fucking tears that seemed to be a constant companion these days shot up my spine in a tingling wake. I squeezed my eyes to stop them from spilling.

Clue gathered me into her arms, whispering in my ear. "You'll find a way. I swear. I know in my bones you'll save her. Just like you saved me. You'll have a lifetime together, and she'll drive you nuts when she's older." Her voice thickened. "But you have to get out into the world to find a solution. You won't find it hidden in the cereal box in a dingy flat you haven't left in weeks."

I shoved her back. "I couldn't care less about the world. It took everything from me. And now it's taking Clara, too." My heart squeezed, causing me to rub the centre of my chest. Funny how emotional pain could create such physical pain—it didn't matter I was healthy and fit and only suffering from tragic news—my body made it real.

Clara would end up killing me, because I cared too much. My heart would stop when hers did.

Clue tensed. "Remember who you are. You're a fighter. You didn't overcome your past to give up now."

I'd relive it all over again if it meant fate wouldn't steal her.

Damn fucking fate. My anger rose again, heating my blood like lava. "My daughter is dying, and you think I'm giving up?" My voice wobbled, and I stormed forward. I couldn't have this conversation anymore.

I couldn't rewind to the old Hazel: the twenty-four-year-old woman who'd been on the cusp of happiness. I'd had a great job—legal and law-abiding—which was new for me. I'd been healthy and content. And I'd had a daughter who made me a better human being.

You have *a daughter. Not past tense. Not yet.*

But Clue was right. I'd overcome so much already. I couldn't give up. I wouldn't lie down and let my daughter leave me—I had to find a cure, and to do that I had to face the world and keep fighting till the end.

I will find a way.

Slapping back the helplessness and tears, I fanned my anger until I thrummed with energy. Whatever this place was, I was done being walked over.

Stalking forward, I called over my shoulder. "You win, Clue. Let's go."

Her heels clicked on the stone-work of the corridor, catching up to me. "Don't hate me for making you remember how to fight. She's fine. You haven't told her what's wrong; there's been no relapses other than—"

I held up my hand. "I don't want to think about it." I needed to keep the image of Clara's seemingly harmless asthma attack out of my mind. The fucking doctors and their misdiagnosis. Now, when I thought of them, rage came first rather than tears. It'd taken three weeks and walking into an illegal fight club to find my inner strength.

Embracing the shift, I felt calm and in control for the first time since the ambulance ride. My own life no longer mattered. It would be collateral to bargain for hers, and the freedom that gave me filled me with adrenaline.

I would no longer taunt myself with 'what ifs'. I would focus on doing anything, absolutely *anything*, to extend my daughter's life. Including selling my soul to whoever could offer redemption.

Linking her fingers with mine, she murmured, "Tonight will give you the boost that you need. You'll see." Adding some bounce into her step, she added, "After all, we're going to watch men beat each other bloody. If that doesn't inspire you to get revenge and punch the world in its fucking face, then I don't know what will."

I forced a small laugh, but she was right. In so many ways.

The empty corridor went on for ages, past huge swathes of material and massive nonsensical artwork of blizzards and forests, of darkness and wolves, of a violent world. Sculptures made of bronze and iron guided us like sentinels. A mix of modern art and intricate lifelike animals. All large, imposing, and entirely too real.

The atmosphere in this place set my instincts on high alert, searching for danger.

Grunting and panting came from behind a large door as we

passed.

Clue cocked an eyebrow, staring at the door as if she had x-ray vision. "I wonder what goes on in the private zones. More fighting, or do you think the victor steals a woman from the crowd and makes mad passionate love to her?" Her voice turned dreamy. "He'd be hot and sweaty and slippery with blood, but his kiss would make the girl forget. She'd let herself be consumed by the man who proved he was strong enough to protect her."

I shook my head, smiling indulgently at my dreamer-best-friend. Clue had been the result of an illicit affair between a Chinese diplomat and a Thai prostitute. Born out of wedlock, she'd been thrown away like rubbish when she was just two weeks old.

We met three years ago when I saved her from being raped and mutilated in a rural Sydney suburb.

Clue batted her eyelashes, blowing me a kiss. "You can't tell me you don't want to be ravished by someone who just fought a battle to win you? I know you don't have physical needs like the rest of us, but that has to turn you on."

This time I laughed with my heart and not just out of requirement. "I have needs, you know. I just have more pressing responsibilities than chasing a man who isn't interested in a mother with baggage." I refused to dwell on urges that woke me up in the dead of night. Craving a release, begging for another's body—too bad I never found anyone I wanted—not even Clara's father.

"But think of it, Zelly. Muscles, gruffness, barely restrained violence—a man who kisses with possession and gentleness." She fanned herself dramatically. "I'm turning myself on just thinking about it."

I rolled my eyes. "You're way too much of a romantic for these times. You should've been born six hundred years ago if you want men who kill and women who swoon."

She grinned, showing perfect pearly teeth. "I *was* born six hundred years ago. That's why I hanker after it so much. Men these days who work in offices and eat pies for lunch need to get in touch with their sword-wielding forefathers."

"You're getting worse." I smiled. Clue had two fascinations in life: men and past lives. She swore she'd lived countless times before, and as much as I liked to joke and pluck holes in her tales, I couldn't ignore the fact that she knew things. Things she shouldn't know for a discarded child with no education.

"You're an old soul too, Zel. I can tell. I haven't figured out where you're from, but I will."

I didn't have the heart to tell her she was wrong. I acted old beyond my years, because I'd had enough bad fortune to last me forever. If I had lived before, I must've been a witch or a murdering psychopath to warrant the trials I'd endured.

I squeezed her hand as we turned left at the end of the corridor and promptly slammed to a halt.

"Holy mother of God, where have you brought me?"

Dropping her fingers, I moved forward, almost in a trance.

The double doors had been crafted from metal. One side depicted a fairy-tale: a young man faced away from the viewer, standing surrounded by piles of coins, sunshine, and young children. Fantastical turrets of a castle rested in the distance.

My heart hurt as I looked at the next door. If the first had been heaven, this one would definitely be hell.

The young man now faced the viewer, but his features were blank. No nose or eyes or mouth, just a smooth blank oval. Behind him wolves fought while lightning and storm clouds brewed. But what killed me was the children who'd been laughing in the other portrait were now in pieces, scattered on the ground in melting snow.

"Whoa, that's a bit morbid," Clue said, reaching out to touch a severed leg.

I snatched her hand back and pressed the other door to open it. I wanted away from the scene; it came too close to home.

Don't think of your troubles. Tonight, pretend to forget.

Troubles.

I could never forget about them. They were a noose around my neck; a guillotine waiting to fall. But I was done moping, so it didn't matter.

The instant the door cracked open, noise assaulted us. A potent mixture of fists hitting flesh, grunts of pain, lilts of feminine laughter, shouts of encouragement, and the smooth beats of music.

We entered a cavernous dark room—either a converted ballroom or a specially designed arena. It welcomed us with thick black velvet covering four story high walls. Lining the perimeter, a grandstand held black couches, La-Z-boys, and luxury daybeds. Each one had its own podium with side table and a small lamp, looking like fireflies in the dark.

"Oh my," Clue murmured, focusing on the main event.

Every apparatus of fighting existed: a Mixed Marital Arts cage, a boxing ring, a Muay Thai ring, mats for close combat, and bare floor for other barbaric blood sports. Each space was crowded with men either bloodied from a fight or bouncing on their feet ready to meet a new opponent. I'd never seen such a display of masculinity—raw and unbridled.

Sweaty towels hung off chairs and modesty was non-existent as men changed from torn work-out gear into loose fitting cool down attire. Water stations and medic booths rested between each arena.

My breathing came faster, dragging in scents of disinfectant, beer, and the clean smell of hard work. I couldn't focus on just one thing. A fight had begun with a bombardment of fists and scary determination in the Muay Thai ring, while another fight in the MMA cage had just finished—the victor pranced around his unconscious foe waving his blood-smeared fists in the air.

Everywhere I looked men grinned, audience members encouraged, and people throbbed with vitality. My body sucked up every ounce of liveliness, storing it.

What the hell is this place?

A huge banner hung from the ceiling directly above all five fighting rings.

Fight with honour, fight with discipline, fight with vengeance.

Goosebumps rose on my arms. The words were poignant, holding a promise of more than just violence—a whole new world I didn't know existed. Despite myself, I wanted to find out more. Clue was right—seeing a man fight awoke something deeper, darker, less tame inside me. We may be refined and socially acceptable on the outside, but at heart we were still animals. All my life, I'd fought my own battles, but now I wondered what it would've been like to have someone fight beside me.

"I think I died and went to man heaven," Clue whispered, her almond eyes the widest I'd ever seen. Her cheeks flushed with colour as a man in the boxing ring took a hit to the jaw by a fighter glistening with sweat and crimson.

Every man held an edge of eager pleasure—even those black and bruised joked and watched comrades get beaten while sipping on icy bottles of water.

The atmosphere in the room wasn't feral or violent like I expected. It had an old-world class about it. An exclusivity. A richness. An unwritten code that said they'd try to win, but would never kill. I found the restraint reassuring but weirdly annoying at the same time.

There were so many fighters I had no idea how Clue would find the man she'd come to see.

The music changed tracks from sultry to pulsing. Not so loud to distract the fighters, but it added yet another element to this strange, illegal club.

Arms suddenly slinked around Clue, dislodging her from my side. I blinked as a tall man with cropped black hair and ebony skin gathered her close. His arms were cut and defined, wrapping around her with propriety but also tenderness. "You remembered the address and password. I'm impressed." He nuzzled her throat, sending Clue into a flurry of lusty giggles.

My heart fluttered for her. I loved seeing her smile. I didn't think I'd seen her so infatuated before. Ever since I took her home that fateful night and put her broken pieces back together, I'd been afraid she wouldn't ever trust a man enough to let him get close. Hence why she called herself Clue. She wanted to be a mystery that no man could solve.

My eyes flickered between the two; my heart thudded sensing the spark, the need between them. If lust could be seen they'd be wrapped up in a cloud of erotic colour.

Where Clue was an Asian beauty, this man was an African Adonis. If they ever made it to procreation, their children would be spectacular.

The thought of children sent mine reeling back to Clara. Her pretty, eight-year-old face filled my mind. Her long hair, so similar to my own, and her dark brown eyes made my heart weep knowing our time together was running out.

She looked nothing like her father which I thanked the universe for every day. She was mine. All mine.

Not for much longer.

The memory shattered and a rush of vertigo grabbed me. After weeks of barely any sleep, constant stress, and a body humming with a mixture of anger and tears, I suffered a momentary lapse of motor control; I stumbled.

Clue's man grabbed my forearm, steadying me with a strong grip. His touch was warm and comforting—brotherly compared to the obvious spark between him and Clue. "You okay?"

Clue untangled herself from his embrace to support my other side. I thought I'd turned a corner walking in here. I wanted to fight. Not wallow.

Standing tall, I smiled and waved a hand. "I'm such a floozy. I shouldn't have skipped lunch today, that's all." I couldn't ruin Clue's fun. I had no right. Not after everything. "Thanks, though."

Taking a step back from them, I forced animation into my voice. "So, you're Corkscrew? Clue has told me a lot about you." *She's told me nothing about you.*

He looked me up and down making sure I could stand unassisted before he laughed. "That's my fighting name, but yes. Tonight, I'm Corkscrew." His black eyes twinkled as he leaned closer. "My real name is Ben. Clue's told me a lot about you, too. It's a pleasure."

The unassuming kindness of his deep voice and the normalcy of his name helped settle me; I grinned. "I like that. Two identities."

Just like me.

Up until recently, I'd had two personas. I'd spun tales and weaved stories as effortlessly as if it were the truth. I wrote my own story with a magical pen called lies.

And it worked.

I survived.

Clue asked, "What's this club called? I couldn't see any name on the building." Her eyes danced around the dark space, drinking in the blows and parries of half-naked men.

My interest spiked and my damn heart flurried. I didn't like to admit it, but the virile energy of this place called to something deep inside. It made me want to embrace my inner fighter—to become someone dangerous. It gave me equal measures of unhappiness and hope.

I hated the wealth dripping from every statue, but at the same time, I never wanted to leave. I wanted to steal all the positive energy and strength that existed and bottle it— create an elixir to cure Clara.

Ben smiled, his skin looking like polished jet. "This is the best place on earth." Spanning his arms, taking in the club as if it was his own, he said, "Welcome to Obsidian."

TWO
ROAN

I never asked for the hand life dealt me. I never wanted to be a ghost or a buried soul from society. But I learned from a very early age that choice was an illusion and freedom was a farce.

I no longer cared about that bullshit.

My past was my past, it sculpted me. My actions and wrong doings were my penance. My future and aspirations my vengeance.

I surveyed my empire, taking in the multiple fights, and the men and women seated in their plush spectator seats. If I allowed myself to feel, I would indulge in a little pride. I created this. From nothing.

For a dead man walking, I achieved more than I'd hoped, but I still wasn't fucking happy. Never had been. Never would be. Not with the shit living in my skull.

My eyes flew to survey the boxing area. Nestled between the MMA cage and Muay Thai ring, it gleamed red and black with padding and ropes. Giant spotlights hung from the ceiling, sending washes of light on all platforms while leaving the decadent seating around the perimeter in the dark.

Emotions were foreign to me, but if I had to guess at what burned in my chest, I would say survival.

Survival to become more than what I was. To create a life where I could hide in plain sight.

My back creaked as I leaned my elbows on the glass banister. Considering I hadn't yet hit thirty, my body believed I was a pensioner.

That's what you get with a life full of violence.

Most major bones had been broken at least once; I'd shed more pints of blood than flowed through my veins; I'd been trained in a skillset that only a few elite ever learned.

I had a past that made all of this possible. A past that would never leave me alone.

My eyes settled on the boxing match below; a glint of silver flashed just before a punch landed on the jaw of a well-built man with long hair tied in a knot.

The man went down.

Fast.

His body bounced on the springy floor, and the referee blew his shrill whistle, signalling the end of the fight.

My body switched from relaxed to revving in a second flat. *Goddammed cheaters in my fucking club.*

"That cocksucker just signed his death warrant." My muscles bunched in pleasure, arching with energy at the thought of violence. It'd been a full week since someone cheated, and it was high time I taught someone a lesson.

Egotistical bastard to think he could come in and cheat. No way. Not in my house. My thoughts raced, shading everything with bloodlust.

You're going to pay tonight, and I'm going to love making you scream.

"Death warrant? Nah, you're mistaken, mate. He had the crap beat out of him. He's just a little pussy. Can't take a real man's punch." Oscar, my second in command, kept his eyes on the fight and reached to pat my shoulder.

The second his hand landed on my blazer, he stiffened then wrenched his touch away. "Shit."

Yes, shit. I gritted my teeth, riding through the muscles spasms, barely keeping control. Locking eyes with him, I said, "You've worked with me for a full year and yet you still haven't learned. Maybe I should throw *you* in the ring tonight." Anger rippled through my veins, hot and swift—taunting me with images of pain and power. For a moment, I hoped he *would* touch me again, then I'd have an excuse. I could break one of my many laws and enjoy a bit of recreation. I could give in.

He dropped his arm quickly, fingers opening and closing. "Sorry. It's hard not to when it's second bloody nature. Everybody touches, mate—either in violence or love." He frowned. "If you're going to re-join the human race anytime soon, you have to get used to people patting you on the back or shaking your hand."

My hands curled, wanting so much to punch someone. I needed a victim—someone I could pour all this shit inside, so I no longer had to live with it. I might have escaped my past, but I hadn't escaped the memories. Oscar thought it was second nature to touch—not for me. My second nature had been reprogrammed so efficiently it overruled every conscious thought.

I may be human on the outside, but inside…inside I had no control.

"You're heading into the shut up or get fucked territory again, Oz. Don't say I didn't warn you. Do it again, and I'll make sure you damn well remember to keep your hands to yourself."

Oscar rolled his eyes, muttering, "You're such a drama queen. God knows why I put up with your theatrics."

A full year and I still hadn't gotten used to his lack of fear around me. It wasn't natural—not where I was from. It was why I kept him around to help maintain the illusion that I was like everybody else.

I forced the black thoughts away. "And you're a cocky bastard who thinks he's above harm."

When I re-entered society, I did so on my own terms. I wasn't there to make friends. I wasn't there to take a wife or breed. My life path was one I'd trampled for far too long to deviate.

Not that I wanted any of those things. The only thing I craved was the thrill of the chase, the satisfaction of the hunt. And that's why I could never be free.

Oscar shrugged. "I've told you time and time again. Go for a surf, mate. All that shit inside your pretty little head will disappear."

Too fucking bad I didn't know how to swim.

Spinning around, I refocused on the floor of Obsidian. Spread at my feet, housed in a cavernous room of the residence I'd built based on a childhood location, sat a ten million dollar investment.

I'd learned pretty early on that men were basic creatures.

Take away their suits and wives and jobs and responsibilities, and you're left with a beast. A beast who wanted to spar and maim—to embrace their inner savage.

I offered rebellion and a chance to find themselves.

I gave them a place to fight.

The day I opened to exclusive members, I'd been prepared for a few interested parties. But I hadn't been prepared for the overnight success or the worship of so many.

To be a part of my world, I requested three things:
Obedience.
Discipline.
Utmost secrecy.

Not to mention the obscene membership fees every month.

Oscar moved beside me, scanning the floors. "Don't do anything idiotic. Everest won't take accusations kindly. You know what happened last month with Praying Mantis."

Last month Praying Mantis, also known as David Gorin, had cheated and ended up with a jaw vacant of teeth and a concussion. I'd only hit him once.

Oscar drummed his fingers on the glass balustrade. "If you go cursing and pointing blame, you'll only bring—"

"Bring what? The wrath of the Wasps MC? Fuck 'em. They can't do anything worse than what others have already done." I tensed. I hadn't meant to say that. I'd meant to say I'd kick his ass and toss him from my club forever, but Oscar glanced at me sideways.

"If you told me what they'd done, then maybe I could agree. But seeing as you like to keep your aura of fucking mystery, I don't have a clue what you're talking about, and the veiled hints are really starting to grate on my bloody nerves."

I cracked a rare smile. I liked that Oscar, with his blond hair and baby face, could stand up to me. Not many did.

In fact, I could list two men in my life who'd ever made me cower. The rest I didn't give two shits about, and in turn, they feared a cold-blooded instrument who lived in the grey area with no right or wrong.

Oscar grinned, flexing his arms. "Knew I'd get you to smile eventually."

Cricking my neck, trying to lubricate long abused joints, I muttered, "It's time for me to have a little chat with the so-called unbeatable Mount Everest." I'd hit my limit with his bullshit. I'd been looking for an excuse to throw him in the ring, and he just gave me one.

The only time anyone was allowed to touch me was during a fight. A punch to the gut didn't hurt nearly as much as a tender touch to the cheek. I could handle that. A wallop was medicine; a caress was a curse.

"You never chat. You just hurt." Oscar shrugged his blazer off and threw it onto the black couch behind us. The mezzanine level held a small bar, black sofa, and coffee table. Most nights were spent here overseeing and commanding. My office was kept strictly for me—locked and impenetrable— away from patron's curious eyes.

"It's what I do best. What I was made for." Smoothing a

hand through my longish hair, I startled when I found length and not a buzz cut. All my life I'd been forced to have it short—like a cadet. The strands had been red once upon a time, but as I grew older they turned to copper then to a bronzy black until nothing existed of the little boy I remembered.

"First etiquette lesson of the week. He owes me more fucking respect." My fingers cracked as I clenched my fist.

Oscar nodded. "True enough." Giving me a smile, we headed off down the black carpeted staircase. Every step had a silhouette of a fox embossed in silver thread. "You have a habit of demanding respect by the aid of physical abuse."

Oscar was right. People owed me respect because I'd damned well earned it. Every scrap, every shred, I'd pulled with my bare hands from men who thought they could wipe the floor with me. I'd shown them I might live in a body scarred to shit, but I'd earned every single scar. Each one spoke of what I'd done, of what lurked in my past.

The sound of music disappeared as the howl of artic wind and icy prickles of snow stole me from present to past.

"Kill him, Operative Fox."

I'd never disobeyed an order till now, but I shook my head. Already shitting myself at the retribution such a refusal would bring, but unable to pick up the blade and stab the kid in front of me.

Just a kid.

Just a kid.

I was just a kid myself. Barely into my teens and yet I was a seasoned killer.

"You know what we'll do to you if you refuse."

I knew, but it didn't change anything. I slammed to my knees in the snow, hating the shrieking winds and negative temperatures. Tonight would be a bitch.

"Throw him in the pit until he learns his lesson."

The memory exploded into splinters, stabbing my brain with an illusion of the present and past mixing for a brief moment.

Shaking my head, I turned to Oscar. "Call Dawson and his security team. I want Everest and his minions hauled out after this."

We paused at the base of the stairs. "Will do." Oscar raised his hand for me to high five. "Here's to dishing out respect."

Idiot.

I didn't move, just switched from personable to my old self; the self that'd been trained and sculpted by hatred and discipline.

The click from normal to killer happened instantaneously.

Oscar hastily withdrew. "Crikey. You need to get over that shit, Fox. It ain't natural."

When did I ever say I was fucking natural?

Ignoring him, I strode from the shadows and into the organized chaos. The rings were operating at full capacity tonight. Waiting lists hung beside the scoreboard with many a denied request for a session.

The Muay Thai ring had been reserved for the evening by the Stingrays. A group of men who looked tough, but had the art of a real group of fighters. They weren't there just to draw blood but also to improve their craft.

I wanted to go head-to-head with their top guy, a man named Corkscrew, but I hadn't found a reason to get him in the ring—yet. But I would. It was only a matter of time before he pissed me off.

As I passed, my eyes narrowed on the very man I wanted to fight. He stood with his arm around a stunning Asian woman while touching another delectable creature dressed in gold and silver. Women meant nothing to me. I neither wanted them nor needed them. But the instant my eyes landed on thick mahogany waves draping over porcelain shoulders, I wanted with a ferocity that I'd never felt before.

It was as if all the coldness in my blood suddenly erupted into fucking steam, hissing through my veins. My back locked as I fought the urge to stare. In a flash, I memorized her face, catalogued her weaknesses, archived her mannerisms. Medium height and lithe muscles, she had just enough curves to entice, but not enough to call her voluptuous. She held herself stiff while her face split into a smile, hiding her true thoughts.

The longer I looked the more I noticed: weakness, anger, strength, resilience, but beneath it all, the same raging confusion that lurked inside me. The same helplessness for a life we couldn't do anything about.

I didn't need my training to taste the sheer hatred she hid so well. I recognised it as a twin to my own. My eternal anger would never die—directed at a past I could do nothing to change.

Fuck. I hated the burst of connection while salivating at the thought of more.

There wasn't anything unusual about her apart from her obvious beauty, and yet, there seemed to be a cloud over her. Her body introverted, eyes glossed with unknown sadness.

I want to know why.

I stopped short. *No, you fucking don't.*

I didn't care. Not in the slightest. She was a woman, and I didn't succumb to their charms. I found relief in other addictions.

Pain mainly.

I'd wasted enough time acting like a moron. Making a deliberate effort to ignore the woman who'd sparked something deep inside, I glanced around the room. Everywhere people moved silently and respectfully. The hired women who earned more working for me in a week than a year on the streets moved sexily, serving patrons in classy outfits. Drinks were free, but hardly ever accepted by fighters, only the audience.

If someone wanted a private fight or a room to fuck in, the whole bottom floor of my residence had spaces for hire. Nothing was cheap, and everything was exclusive.

I'd never been around wealth until recently, and I had to agree, the warmth and shelter money provided was a damn sight better than shivering in the snow while waiting for something to kill me.

Two ends of the spectrum.

Two lifetimes that could never mix.

The scar on my cheek twinged like an old enemy, reminding me that no matter who I created from the ashes of my past, I would always be the kid who killed.

"Ah, fuck, he's back again." Oscar nodded at the well-known trouble-maker in the MMA ring. The guy sneered, raising his taped-up fist in a mock salute. "He's one step away from an ass-raping at the local jail. I heard he runs a meth lab down in Coogee."

Kissing his fist, he bared his teeth and laughed.

Slamming to a halt, I pinned him with my stare. With one steady finger, I dragged it from the top of my right cheekbone all the way down my face to my chin. I barely felt it—the scar tissue desensitized to anything but brutal force. Once I'd traced the contour of the scar, I dragged the same finger across my throat in the universal sign of 'you're dead' and pointed at him.

"He may be a douche, but he's a client." Oscar groaned. "Fox. Stop that. You can't scare off all the clientele. What sort of business model are you following?"

Muttering under my breath, I answered, "A damn good one if I don't have to deal with little shits like that."

Oscar sighed. "Whatever, mate. He'll fuck himself up without your help. Who do you want to go after? Him or Everest? You can't do both."

I didn't need to think. A jacked up meth-head wouldn't last five seconds against me. At least Everest had some small chance of hurting me. Not bothering to answer, I bee-lined for the boxing ring.

Fighters parted for us like I was the messiah, and they were a rolling tide. Looks of awe and fear lit their eyes even as their ripped, sweaty bodies tensed in preparation.

It seemed my reputation preceded me. Again.

I summoned every rage existing in my blood and slammed to a halt in front of the mountain of a man. My heart beat faster as I embraced the part of me I pretended didn't exist.

"We need to fucking talk." I crossed my arms. I wasn't small, but this man made me look up. His arms were bigger than mine, his torso thicker. Everything about him screamed sloppy and fake, whereas me? I seethed with reality. Mess with me and pay the consequences.

Everest, also known as Tony from the Wasps Motorcycle Crew, wiped his mouth with the back of his hairy hand. "Well, if it isn't Scarface and his bitch, Barbie." Sniffing in distain, he added, "Come to congratulate me? Come to get some pointers perhaps?"

A couple of men behind Everest snickered. He always came with an entourage—never comfortable on his own. A complete joke considering he cultivated a rumour that he killed men on a daily basis. I knew killers and this fucking idiot wasn't one of them.

My spine stiffened as my body soaked in adrenaline. Oh, I would enjoy this. A whole fucking lot.

I looked to the right where the man who'd fought and cheated counted his winnings. Another one of Everest's little minions. Fisting a pile of hundred dollar bills, his grin was full of greed.

Nodding at the evidence, I said, "Pity your plaything didn't win on merit and not on fakery. Didn't realize times were so tough you had to cheat to pay your bills." Stepping closer, I snarled, "You and your idiots on bikes think you're the law, threatening my club for payoffs, cheating under my fucking roof. Guess what? I've had enough. I'm calling your debts, Tony. And I'm done having your filth tainting my rings."

Obsidian was a registered business. It didn't matter that documents lodged with Inland Revenue said it was an upscale recreational gym. The government didn't need to know about the illegality or the fine line of bribery we walked to keep local enforcers away. However, I refused to pay a cent to MC's and mob members who wanted to acquire it.

I wasn't a pussy, and I'd done far worse than any of those

fakers had ever done. I'd like to see them try.

Everest rippled with anger. His eyes darkened until his pupils looked gigantic. "You're a fucking dead man, Fox." Shoving a hand in the direction of the man holding the cash, he snapped, "That there? We earned that fair and fucking square. Go back to your throne and enjoy your last night of sleeping without having to watch your back."

I threw my head back and laughed. It wasn't merriment or intimidation—it was cold and calculated. Everest glared, then tensed as I locked eyes with him. "It's not me who has to watch their back. You. Me. In the cage. Now."

Everest slapped his legs with meaty hands. "Ha! You think I'd demean myself by entertaining a little wannabe in the ring? No chance in hell, Scarface. I'm not fighting you. Leave. We've got another set to win."

"To cheat you mean."

He spluttered, sending his large neck wobbling with indignation. The fucker had a receding hair line, looking like a juiced up freak past his prime.

I took a step toward him. "I saw the knuckler duster, you asshole. This isn't a negotiation. Get in the cage."

"Better listen, Tony. Fox doesn't make idle threats," Oscar said. His arms stayed tightly crossed, flanking me like a bodyguard.

Everest puffed out his large chest, standing to his full height. His body threatened with impressive size, but I'd long ago lost the ability to fear.

"You want to repeat that, Fox?" Anger blazed in his eyes, looking like he wanted to hammer me into the ground like a rusty nail. "I. Don't. Fucking. Cheat."

Loud bass and sombre beats of music pulsed through the club, intoxicating my blood for violence.

Goddammit, I needed a fight.

A punk kid, who stupidly didn't see my scorching anger, sidled up close. "Wow, I didn't know you were here tonight." He bowed his head looking star-struck. "It's an honour to meet the legendary Obsi—"

Everest snorted. "Oh, give me a fucking break."

I glanced at the kid. Half-naked, he had traces of blood coming from his mouth. Someone had decked him hard.

"Leave kid. Go get another role model." My voice didn't rise, but it didn't need to. It reverberated with reprimand. I *hated* being fawned over. Fawning led to affection which led to attachment which led to death.

He frowned, brushing back long blond hair from his forehead. "Umm, sorry. I'm just a huge fan. Your reputation is what brought me here."

I bared my teeth forcing him back a step. This was why I stayed on the mezzanine level in the dark. No one understood. Fighters wanted to be me; losers wanted to run from me. But no one wanted to know my past. If they knew, they'd hand me over to every law enforcer around the world for my crimes.

Everest smirked at the kid. "Take a good look, boy. 'Cause after tonight he's a dead man walking." Everest leaned toward me. "Get that motherfucker? Me and my crew are gonna take this joint and leave you in the dirt."

And there it was. Freedom. He'd fucking done it.

Tonight had just got interesting. I'd planned on taming myself. One fight that ended with no broken bones. But Everest's stupid power-trip had earned him a first-class trip to the ER.

The kid ceased to exist. A shot of energy filled me more thrilling and intoxicating than any illegal substance. "I was going to promise you'd walk out of here on your own two legs, but that offer just expired. You obviously haven't listened to the rumours." I tutted under my breath, shaking my head. "Big mistake. Big, big mistake." My voice didn't rise past a threatening purr.

Looking Everest up and down, I dragged my fingers through my shaggy hair. The warm wax sent a whiff of chocolate into the air. "You're going to be handed your own ass, and then you'll go back to the morons in your MC and tell them if they so much as come near my club, they'll end up being fertiliser in my fucking garden."

Everest roared and lunged. I sidestepped before his hands connected with any part of my body and pummelled his kidney with a fist. One hard, fierce wallop. I relished in the slight twinge of pain in my knuckles. *Give pain to receive pain. Receive pain to give pain.* A lesson I would never be free of.

Gasping, he held his side. "You'll pay for that! No one fucking touches me!" Everest snarled, revealing gold-capped teeth. "You better walk away, Fox, or I'll deliver the ass-whooping of your fucking life."

I let him rant and rage, basking in his anger, feeding on it, drinking it in.

"I'm done arguing." My temper vanished; replaced with the coldness I lived with, the vacancy that I'd never been able to lose. "Get in the cage."

The rows upon rows of high wattage spotlights boiled us from above. A trickle of sweat rolled down my lower back beneath my black shirt. The only embellishment was the silver fox on the breast pocket.

I pushed forward until we were almost nose to nose. Inhaling his cheap cologne, I wanted nothing more than to bite off his nose and go rogue on his ass.

My reflection gleamed in his black eyes: a vague outline of a man with no soul left and a raw scar disfiguring his cheek.

The scar terrified most people, but my eyes unsettled them more—so grey, they were almost colourless.

"I'm growing bored of your disobedience, Tony. Make me ask again and I can't promise you'll remain alive. You had your boy use a duster. I have proof. You can squeal and deny all you want. Evidence doesn't lie."

Leaning down, Everest entered my personal space. "Your little threats don't work on me, Scarface. Everybody cheats."

"Not in my club, they don't." I cracked my knuckles. "This is *my* club. And you obey *my* rules. If you disobey those rules, consequences must be paid." Lowering my head, I glowered from under my brows. "I won't tell you again. Get. In. The. Cage."

For a large man who spoke like a killer, he took a pussy step back. Finally a thread of apprehension filled his cocky gaze. "Fuck off. I'm not fighting a piss-ant like you." His anger siphoned away, leaving a blathering idiot. "I'll give you ten grand for the loss of winnings for whoever bet wrong on the fight."

Oscar stepped forward, cracking his neck. The tension in his muscles sent more eagerness through me. "You can't bribe your way out of this. Saying no to the boss of Obsidian is not an option. It's in the rules. He wants you in the cage. You get in the fucking cage."

I shuddered in pleasure.

Obsidian. That was mine. My creation. The one thing that gave me something to live for and focus all my inhumane cruel tendencies into. It was ironic that the one place I'd been running from all my life had become my future.

Thoughts raced in Everest's eyes. Finally, he glared. "This isn't the end of this, Fox. You may've won tonight, but I'll pay you back with a whole lot of interest. Just remember me when someone pops a bullet in your brain." Everest shrugged off his large shirt, uncovering a torso full of muscle blanketed in a layer of pudge. He used to be cut, but now he was soft around the edges. "I'll make you pay, asshole."

I didn't say a word. I didn't need to. He'd dug his own grave.

"Boy, pass me those fucking gloves." Everest held out his hand for the rookie to place a pair of blue boxing gloves in his grip.

I snapped my fingers. "No gloves. No boxing. Get in the cage."

Three
Hazel

I'd always prided myself on being strong enough to handle anything life threw at me. I promised that no matter what, I would win. And until three weeks ago, I lived that promise like a law. I achieved things that seemed impossible; I overcame things that seemed un-survivable, but then life decided to teach me a new lesson.

It taught me that prices must be paid and sent me reeling from strong to weak. My outlook on life went from determined and fierce to wallowing and negative.

But the moment I walked into Obsidian, the taste of violence rejuvenated me—reminding me I was a fighter, and I would win. I just wished I could've avoided the catalyst that destroyed me.

Him.

Obsidian Fox.

The bastard who gave me so much but stole everything.

"What's going on?" I whisper-hissed into Clue's ear. We

hadn't budged from the Muay Thai ring but the atmosphere in the club changed from well-mannered and excited to restless and electrically charged. I couldn't tell what started the switch, but it built slowly until the room thrummed with excitement.

Clue's eyes were glued on Corkscrew. He ducked and swung, looking part god as he easily overpowered his opponent. His match had begun a few minutes ago, but it seemed the audience was more interested in the men having a conversation by the boxing ring. Steadily whispers wafted on the warm air; people shifted excitedly in their chairs.

"I don't know what's going on, but doesn't Ben look delicious all gleaming like onyx and fighting like a warrior?" She smiled. Her eyes glowing with an infatuation that'd doubled from interested into obsessed. They'd only had a few dates, but she'd skipped right back into the mind-set of a swooning woman lusting after a man who would no doubt claim her and mark his territory the moment the match concluded.

Tearing my eyes away from Corkscrew's fight, I focused on the crowd crushing together, subtly drifting toward the boxing ring.

My eyes flickered over to the man dressed all in black, barely visible through the throng of people. I didn't know who he was. Something about him unsettled me—further amplified by the force of danger he possessed. I wanted to keep my distance, but was drawn to him nevertheless.

He'd passed us not long ago and the moment his eyes fell on me, I'd felt a shift. A spark. An awareness. Call it fear or acknowledgement of a virile male, it caught me by surprise. My entire body shot into hyper alert—heart racing, breath quickening. My body prepared to either fight or flee. I didn't understand why he invoked such a reaction.

When he prowled past, I had the opportunity to stare at his retreating back, and I wished I hadn't. He was tall, moving with the elegance of a man who had almost regal bearing. His back flexed beneath a tight fitting shirt while dark, bronze hair gleamed under the spotlights. He carried an air of power, of discipline, and of certain unpredictability. Everything about him sent a frisson of heat racing into my stomach.

Eight long years had passed since I'd suffered the sickly prickle of physical attraction. Sickly because when I last succumbed, all I'd earned was illness and tragedy.

It changed my life forever.

I didn't have time for attraction.

Clara was the result of my last infatuation, and I'd been stupid. So stupid.

A wave of excitement crashed over me from the building crowd. I grabbed Clue's hand as anxious energy unspooled in my blood. Spectators gathered tighter; heads bobbing, trying to catch a glimpse of the two men by the boxing ring.

Clue glanced at her hand in mine, then met my gaze. "Feel free to watch other fights, Zelly. I'm sure there are plenty of sexy men you could have fun with."

I rolled my eyes. "I'm not interested in finding a bed-mate, Clue. I'm interested in why everyone's acting so tense." The hair on the back of my neck prickled. I couldn't stand there and not discover the source of the energy. My instincts said to run but my mind said to stay. I needed to understand it. Had to see it, feel it, so I knew how to defeat it.

Danger.

I'd always been able to taste when danger was near—when something drastic was about to change my life forever. And I felt it now.

Ignore it and go home to Clara. This is pointless.

Pointless, but addicting. Unwrapping my fingers from Clue's, I murmured, "I'm going to figure out what's going on."

Clue was so enthralled with Corkscrew that she only nodded. Leaving her safe, I moved away from the bright halo of lights surrounding the Muay Thai area and headed toward the boxing ring.

Weaving my way through the crowd, whispered words met my ears. "It's him. He's going to fight."

"Whoever pissed him off isn't going to be happy when they

wake with a concussion."

I inched forward with the crowd, steadily growing thicker as more people drifted down from their La-Z-boys to mill around the ring.

Breaking through the swarm of people, I couldn't understand what warranted the crowd's building excitement or my nervousness. No threats or raised voices were heard. My skin prickled again.

You know what's causing it.

It was all to do with him.

The man who seemed more than human; the man who set my teeth on edge.

My eyes zeroed in on him dressed all in black. He emitted an energy, infecting everyone.

He stood chest to chest with a huge brute who looked like he'd killed a few men himself. He didn't move or speak or make any gesture of violence, but he simmered with raw energy.

My mouth went dry for no other reason than I sensed him as a terrible menace.

The other man didn't cower, but he lacked what the man in black possessed: a rigidity, a confidence—the sure knowledge he would win, and there was nothing the other man could do.

The man in black bared his teeth, glaring at the taller guy. Their lips moved but I couldn't hear what was said.

I ducked closer to the side of the ring as the wash of excitement from the spectators built into a crescendo. People pressed closer; the atmosphere thickened with visible tension.

I blinked and missed what started the scuffle, but one moment the men were talking, the next they exploded into a squirmish that subsided almost as instantly as it began. A few more terse sentences and the man dressed in black pointed at the cage beside them.

The referee in the cage, who'd been watching the interaction, blew his whistle, stopping a fight mid-way. The fighters looked to the side, saw the man in black and nodded, leaving the cage as meekly as school children facing a strict headmaster.

My heart pitter-pattered as the man in black spun around and caught me staring from my place by the rigging.

His gaze glued me into place; I couldn't move—not even to breathe.

He frowned; colourless eyes darkened with annoyance. His teeth clenched as he reverberated with energy. His square jaw looked powerful while his slightly crooked nose spoke of previous violence. His cheekbones were almost too stark for his muscular body. And I didn't need to see beneath his clothing to know he didn't have an inch of fat on him. He wasn't just a man—he was a walking weapon.

He was just…more. More in every way. More man. More danger. More threat than I'd encountered in any male, but it was the scar that made him unique. Jagged, irregular, it transformed half his face from perfection to sordid story. Half of him seemed approachable while the other steeped in hell.

The doors.

The depiction of heaven and hell on the doors was perfect for the man before me.

I didn't know him—I knew nothing more than he suffered some terrible past that made him into whoever he was, but my heart beat faster. I wanted to know, wanted to learn.

That was before he dismissed me with one look and snapped his fingers at the large man behind him. Whatever brief connection existed between us was snuffed out, leaving me with a chill.

Together they made their way to the cage and climbed the small stage to enter. Once secure inside, the man turned and locked the door.

The crowd went utterly ballistic.

The large guy ran hands over his face, speaking to the man in black. Another tense standoff happened, but finally the scarred man shook his head, snapping his fingers at the referee.

Nodding, the ref pulled a wireless mic from his back pocket

and faced an audience that had turned from sedate to mob worthy.

"Ladies and gentlemen, do we have a treat for you!"

The volume on the crowd's enjoyment dipped, holding their excitement in eager bodies. Impatience filled the large space as they tried to quieten.

My heart raced harder; blood pumped thicker.

I wanted to run. I couldn't move.

The man in black morphed before my eyes. Bouncing on the balls of his feet, rolling his neck, he gathered every bit of energy from the room until he positively glowed with violence.

"It's a special event—unplanned and never to be seen again. Between two ruthless contenders, please put your hands together and give a rip-roaring welcome to Mount Everest!" The referee pranced around the large shirtless man, reeling off facts. "Weighing in at two hundred kilos, Everest is well-known for his stable of elite boxers and an all-time winning streak of seventeen to none. Semi-retired, he makes his living off training other impressive fighters but is still a fearful mountain of muscle. This is the first time he's been in the cage in over six months. Let's make him feel welcome...Mount... *Everest!*"

The crowd clapped and whistled while a flurry of cash was transferred from one palm to another while bets were placed. I stayed stiff, trying to become invisible by the rigging.

Everest held up his hands, grinning with gleaming gold teeth. His bravado couldn't hide the sheen of sweat or pallor of fear.

The crowd screamed harder.

I grimaced. He seemed juvenile even though he was older than his opponent.

The man dressed in black shook his head, saying something that caused Everest to growl in anger.

The referee put the mic back to his lips and the applause faded away. "And now, ladies and gentlemen, let me introduce the fighter who will be going head-to-head with this well-known opponent."

Screams rose from the crowd. I cocked my head, straining to hear. I wanted to know his name. I wanted to know why he enticed and made me fear all at once.

The ref carried on, "I'm sure this man doesn't need an introduction."

The crowd went positively bonkers. Feet slammed against floors and women squealed.

"Fox."

"Fox."

"Fox."

The man in black held up his arms, letting the audience rain him in misplaced affection. He didn't smile. He didn't encourage; he wasn't there to be adored, unlike the other man. He was there to fight—pure and simple.

Spectators cheered, adoring a man who looked like the devil himself—a man about to indulge in illegal blood sport.

The referee laughed, shouting over the manic crowd. "That's it everyone. Our very own! The owner of Obsidian! Please put your hands together for...Obsidian...*Fox!*"

My hands twitched to clamp over my ears. I never thought such a sedate crowd, all sequestered in the dark, could conjure such mayhem.

The moment the ref finished introductions, Fox launched himself at Everest. No hesitation. No pause.

The fight began with vengeance.

Fox pummelled a fist to his opponent's temple. Everest reeled away, thumping with large hands, trying to strike Fox's head. But he dodged every one, raining punches on Everest's jaw and chest.

The pure precision and cold calculation made me hate the spiral my life had become. I valued strict rules and prided myself on planning—I recognised the same discipline in the man in black.

My body grew hot with anger, absorbing the fight—letting it energize me. I didn't know what came over me, but the man who owned this place, the man now putting his life in jeopardy just for some masculine power play, had everything I never would. I hated him for being reckless. For causing bodily harm when he had wealth to help find a cure for disease. He could be a saviour; instead he flaunted and abused. Instead he hurt others. For what? A show of ownership or pride?

I hated him.

I hated that he invoked such strange feelings inside me.

I hated that he had so much while my daughter would never live to see her teens.

I hated him for no reason at all. He was purely the vessel to funnel my hatred into. It didn't make sense—it wasn't rational, but my fists curled as I finally acknowledged the deep sense of helplessness I suffered. For three weeks, I'd hidden from it, pretended I could cope, but it took an illegal fight to show me just how twisted my emotions were—just how broken Clara's diagnosis had made me.

If I had less sense, I would've charged into the ring and hit him myself. I wanted to hit him. I wanted to bite and lunge and inflict as much pain as I felt.

I wanted to go to war and battle and come out a victor, so I could save Clara.

Everest snapped and charged. Tackling Fox, they wrestled, yelling obscenities into each other's ear.

Fox swung and connected with Everest's abdomen.

Everest stopped, gritting his teeth before swinging and aiming with a sucker punch.

Ducking, Fox wheeled around and thumped a fist into his liver. My eyes never left Fox's face. He winced in pain as his fist made contact, but then smiled, growing bolder, angrier as the fight went on.

He was completely in his element and fear threaded through me for Everest. He may be larger, but Fox had something he didn't.

No remorse.

No respect for life.

The crowd booed as Everest landed a fist to Fox's head.

Instead of dancing away and preparing another strike, Fox laughed. His voice rang around the club, weaving with base notes from the music, sounding almost psychotic.

Everest shouted, "You're a fucking crazy son of a bitch."

Fox didn't reply. Moving within hitting distance, he delivered four punches in quick succession. Instead of going down, Everest sprawled forward, forcing Fox to back up as his large fists connected with his sides and cheek.

Everest went for the cheek.

The scar.

The one place I'd never be brave enough to touch. It seemed almost sacrilegious.

Then Fox stopped. Dead still, he dropped his arms, leaving his body unprotected. His lips moved, and Everest froze.

My feet moved forward on their own accord, needing to be closer, needing to hear. I'd never been so wrapped up in a fight before. Even though I deplored it—hated the waste of pain and stupid need for domination—I couldn't look away.

"You want to knock me out? Be my guest and fucking try it." Fox's voice sounded rough and angry. Accented. He swallowed certain words and accented others in a way that made me shiver.

Everest exploded forward, waving his fists like clubs. One struck Fox's cheekbone, the other his gut. But instead of curling over in pain and backing away, Fox did the opposite.

He stood taller. Squeezing his eyes, he seemed to drink the pain, feed off it.

One moment he seemed utterly content, the next he tackled Everest, and they fell in a tangle of body parts to the ground. Legs wrapped with legs; arms twisted with arms.

In one sharp kick, he shattered Everest's kneecap.

Everest bellowed and bucked, squirming like a child instead of a mountain of a man. "Get off me, you bastard!" Genuine terror laced his tone.

In a blink, Fox slammed Everest's face against the floor, breaking his nose before kicking him again and wrapping an arm around his neck. Tightening his grip, he slowly throttled him.

All thoughts of fighting disappeared from Everest. I knew the switch from fighting to surviving. I'd been victim of it myself numerous times.

Kicking with one useful leg and one broken, he scrabbled. He tried to dislodge Fox's arm, but he fought an already lost battle. Fox used his momentum to jerk Everest's left arm behind his back.

The crowd chanted as Fox leaned back, taking the limb with him.

My heart pounded, sick to my stomach.

"Crush him."

"Gut him."

Fox didn't pay attention, only choked his opponent harder, all the while jerking his arm further and further backward.

Everest gave a small groan as his shoulder dislocated, and he fell unconscious—a limp body on the floor.

The moment he passed out, Fox climbed to his feet and acknowledged the crowd with a nod. Wiping the blood trickling from his nose, he frowned at a tear in his shirt.

For the first time, I noticed he remained fully clothed the entire fight. He'd rather ruin his clothing than fight shirtless.

Why?

Fox waved once; the roar of appreciation took the roof off.

This man was loved or feared or hated—maybe a combination of all three.

Staring at him, once again the prickle of interest and fear sent my skin scattering with goosebumps. Something told me the crowd wouldn't be so welcoming if they knew what he kept hidden behind those colourless eyes. He'd been inhuman while fighting—dishing out revenge with no thought or compassion.

Wiping his forehead with his sleeve, Fox brushed past the referee and left the cage to an uproar. "Obsidian Fox! Obsidian!"

I didn't care for the glory of winning—it seemed neither did

Fox. He moved smoothly, ignoring everyone. The crowd kept their distance, sensing they could look but not touch.

The wash of trepidation filled me again as he came closer. I didn't want to be any nearer—not after seeing how dangerous he truly was.

Time to go home. To return to my normal life. *And your dying daughter.*

The thought fisted my heart. Shit, would the memory never stop sucker-punching me?

I turned to leave. I needed to be away from this all-consuming madness.

The crowd dispersed, and I made my way slowly toward the Muay Thai ring.

Four steps, five steps, before strong fingers bit into my upper arm, spinning me around.

I looked up, a curse on my lips, but all words evaporated into shocked muteness.

I was prepared for a small shock at having a stranger touch me—a hint of newness and uncertainty, but I wasn't prepared for the electric bolt that whizzed from his flesh to mine, resonating like an epicentre in my chest.

My eyes widened, and I swallowed, trying to get my brain to work.

Fox made a sound in the back of his throat, tightening his fingers. He glared, looking ready to murder me. "Who *are* you?"

When I didn't respond, he swiped his face with his other hand. His forehead furrowed while his expression turned pissed and stormy. "You think I didn't see you watching? You had your eyes all over me. Answer me. Who the fuck are you?" His deep, accented voice stiffened my nipples even as the thrill of fear jolted through me.

My temper gave me false courage. "I'm not in the habit of answering such rude questions."

His jaw clenched; fingers bit deeper into my arm.

All I could think was: run. His eyes looked almost white. His face sheened with sweat, and the small smear of blood from his nose smelled metallic. The scar on his cheek screamed that he wasn't a nice man. This was a man who lived with no rules or laws. This was a man to fear.

"I'm not in the habit of touching women, and yet, I am." He shook me to emphasize his point. "Answer me. Who the fuck are you and where did you come from?"

I couldn't move as he leaned closer, eyes delving deep, deeper than anyone had gone. I felt exposed, defenceless, and completely trapped.

Raising my jaw, I glared. "Let me go."

Shaking his head, sending strands of bronze everywhere, he demanded, "What are you doing so close to the rings? Girls are meant to be either flat on their fucking backs in the private rooms, or mingling in the crowd." Fox's eyes left mine to trail down my body. "Unless you're not an employee but a spy. My patience is on a very thin leash; I suggest you answer my question."

Every fear and hardship in my life seemed inconsequential as he jerked me closer. His body heat filled me with need and loathing. This wasn't a man. This was a stone-cold killer.

Twisting my arm, I rolled my shoulder to force his hand to drop. Problem was he followed the motion and his fingers unlatched only to retighten once I'd given up fighting. The effortless way he kept me prisoner sent my heart whizzing around my chest. I hated my betraying body for acting more alive than I'd ever felt. I hated the challenge he presented. But most of all I hated the intrigue, the puzzle.

"I'm not a spy. What are you James Bond? Get your hands off me. I'm done being interrogated."

"Not until you tell me how you got into my club. What is it about you?"

"There's nothing about me."

"You're lying. There's something different." His attention turned inward for a brief second. "You make me feel—" Cutting himself off, he glowered. He smelled of earth and smoke and power with a trace of chocolate. His hand was hot and tight on my arm—deadly. "I've never seen you before, and I don't like strangers. I'll ask one more time. Who the fuck are you, and why am I drawn to you?"

My heart skidded to a stop. *He's drawn to me?*

He felt it, too. The strange compulsion, the unknown need. Maybe it was purely lust—two bodies who recognised a person with similar wants and urges. If it was, I'd never been affected so violently.

Everything I'd felt while watching him fight bubbled to the surface. He'd hurt with no remorse. He'd acted as if shattering a guy's kneecap was nothing. How could I let some stupid chemistry in my body override my self-preservation?

I curled my hand, ready to punch him and run, but I paused.

He made me feel *alive.*

He made me feel like a woman and not a mother or friend or failure.

He made me feel powerful and submissive all at the same time.

I felt as if I'd lived my life in a haze. Trudging through day to day, always putting other's needs before my own. For the first time, my own needs made a very strong appearance, and I embraced the awareness, the connection, the simple infatuation by a total stranger.

But then responsibilities bulldozed the fleeting attraction away.

Clara.

Destitution.

Ruin.

How could you let yourself be consumed by him when you shouldn't even be here?

I no longer hated him. I hated myself for being so weak— he'd made me forget for the briefest of time.

Freezing, I looked directly into his eyes, ignoring the snarl in my stomach. "You're mistaken. You're not drawn to me. You've never seen me, and I'm leaving so you'll never have to see me again. Let go of me."

His eyes rested on my lips; his face hardened, blocking off the interest I'd seen before. "I'm never mistaken." He unclenched his hand. Pins and needles rushed to the spot where he'd gripped me. "And I never settle until I figure out what I don't understand."

My heart lurched. *He's the same.* He had the same need to understand. To figure out the unknown before the unknown could hurt him.

"Go away before I regret letting you leave," he muttered. With fists clenched by his sides, he looked over my shoulder as if searching for a way to run. Gone was his dominating air, replaced with heavy acceptance. Without his potent gaze on me, I scrutinised him.

I didn't like what I saw. Something heavy lived inside— something squeezed until he trembled with more than just anger. He used the scar as a deterrent, but behind all that lived something else. Something darker, something…sad.

My heart thudded, sending a flood of compassion into my veins.

Oh, no you don't.

Gritting my teeth, I closed my eyes and forced all interest and empathy to die a quick death. I couldn't afford to suffer such idiocy. I was searching for reasons behind his surly attitude, seeing a heavy penance in his scar. *You can't get swept up in the need to help, protect, and listen.*

Dragging hands through his longish hair, Fox glared. "I let you go. Why haven't you left yet?" The faint foreign accent lurked behind a cultured Australian voice. He may have studied hard to sound like a local, but he couldn't hide his roots completely. Just like he couldn't tame the wildness in him—the savageness beneath the cool façade.

He didn't belong here. He belonged in the wilderness, hunting in the dawn, just like his namesake, the fox.

It was my turn to suffer unavoidable curiosity. "Who are *you*?" I tried to relax, reminding myself he couldn't harm me, not with so many witnesses. "You trap me and demand answers to your questions, but it works both ways. You want to know something about me?" Twisting to point behind me, I said, "I'm here with a friend. We were invited by Corkscrew and he's an expert Muay Thai fighter. I didn't want to come here. I hate what I'm wearing, and you drive me crazy because I can't read you. You're dangerous, and I think you have some serious issues."

Fox pierced me with white-grey eyes. "You're right to think I'm dangerous." Ignoring my other comments, he muttered, "Finally, I have a reason to get him in the ring. He can't flaunt the rules and invite whoever he damn well pleases." A hard smile stretched his lips.

My skin prickled at the thought of Fox fighting Corkscrew. I liked Ben. He was kind and looked at Clue as if she were a precious gem. There was no way I wanted this lunatic hurting him.

"Stay away from—"

"Everything okay here?" I jumped as a man solidified beside me, appearing from the thinning crowd. He flicked me a curious glance before looking at Fox. "What did I overhear? An excuse to get who in the ring?"

Fox stopped smiling. "Corkscrew invited people without paying for their admittance. I have my reason." He cracked his knuckles, looking determined and not a little scary.

The blond haired man shook his head. "Oh no you don't. One fight is enough. Bugger off. Let me run the floor for the rest of the night."

The air crackled as Fox pierced the new man with a look. In one second Fox asserted authority and in another dismissed it. "Fine. Take over. I'm done being around people for the evening." His grey eyes landed on mine, letting me know he truly meant me.

"Good choice." The newcomer frowned, pushing long blond hair from his eyes. He looked as if he should be in an ocean with a surfboard and not an illegal club. "Who are you?"

He assessed me, pursing his lips. "I thought all girls had to wear a uniform, so their services weren't confused?"

Girls? Shit, is that what the waitresses were? Prostitutes?

My hackles rose. My frayed nerves reached snapping point, and I lost all decorum. "Stop asking who the hell I am. I'm done being manhandled, cursed at, and being mistaken for a whore. I've had enough." I pushed past the blond guy only for him to lasso a hand around my upper arm.

Eyeing my breasts, he added, "If you don't want to be mistaken for a whore maybe you shouldn't wear such a slutty dress." He dropped his head, breathing me in. "I can particularly see your nipples, and I know you're hot for my boss. You can't hide the flush, princess. You're wasting your fucking time. He's onto women like you."

"Fuck you." I raised my hand to slap his cheek, but Fox beat me to it. His fist landed on the man's jaw. Oscar dropped his grip, and I stumbled backward.

"She's not a whore, and I'll say if she's wasting her fucking time, Oscar. Goddammit, you're pissing me off tonight."

Oscar rubbed his chin, blue eyes sparking with anger. "You're a son of a bitch."

Fox rippled with rage. "Go back to work."

"I am working—I'm keeping you from killing someone."

I laughed once at the madness of this place. Seemed everyone was infected with whatever disease lived within these huge black walls. "Oh, my God, you're all crazy. I'm leaving." I spun around and took one angry step before strong fingers latched around my wrist. My heart raced as once again electricity shot from his touch all the way to my traitorous core. Everything about him drew me and repelled me at the same time.

My body thrilled at the primal possession while my mind laughed at my weakness.

"Let me go." I glared at the scarred hand wrapped like a handcuff holding me captive. I raised my eyes, latching onto the colourless gaze of the man who was swiftly becoming my nemesis. "I'm done playing this stupid cat and mouse game."

He clenched his jaw, eyes blazing. "Not yet. I'll say when you can go, and I revoke my earlier permission." He bowed his head, whispering against my ear, "I'm not letting you go until I understand you." His breath tickled the fine hair behind my ear, and I fought an uncontrollable shiver. Everything inside me liquefied.

"Permission? You think I need your *permission?*" A cocktail of anger and lust flurried my heart. I hated it. I loved it. I'd never wanted to run or kiss someone so much.

What the hell is happening to me? No wonder lust was such a dangerous thing. It made me forget my problems, my troubles—it ceased every concern apart from the urge to fight with him. To give in to him.

"Eh…" The blond man cleared his throat, forehead wrinkling. "Uh, Fox? What exactly are you doing?" His eyes dropped to my wrist where Fox steadily squeezed harder until my blood thrummed in my fingertips.

Fox never broke eye contact with me, keeping me prisoner in more ways than one. "I'm learning. Go away."

Learning? He didn't need to learn how to pretzel my insides or turn my thoughts against me. He was a flipping master at it already.

The blond guy chuckled, but his eyes darted between us warily. "Learning?" He took a step closer. "Look, mate, I'll take care of her."

My eyes shot to his. Egotistical wanker. "Take *care* of me? Like I'm a hooker or the rubbish you have to leave on the side of the road?" My voice rose and I squirmed against Fox's hold. "I don't want to hear anymore. I'm done. I'll ask one last time. Let me the hell go."

Fox growled under his breath, glowering at blondie. "You're making it worse, Oz. Go away." Jerking me closer, he hissed as my shoulder bumped into his. His body heat enveloped me, along with the faint smell of rust from the fight. "Stop fighting. I'm not letting you leave, so you might as well get used to it."

"You can't hold me against my will. If you think you can, you're a bigger idiot than I thought." My heart beat faster, pushing adrenaline through my system. "Don't make me hurt you." I hadn't lived the life I had without learning how to protect myself. I would hurt him. I would get free.

Oscar took a step back, reluctantly obeying Fox's order to leave.

Only once he'd gone did Fox bow his head, eyes staring icily into mine. My stomach squeezed, and my legs turned from firm to flimsy. The effect he had on me wasn't fair. Never had someone turned me on by making me fear them.

"You would never be able to hurt me, *dobycha*."

My ears pricked at the exotic word.

His eyes widened, then narrowed in annoyance. He'd slipped—used a non-Australian word—it pissed him off.

"Is that a challenge?" I whispered, unable to tear my eyes away from his silver scar. *Someone managed to hurt you. You can't ignore the evidence.*

His lips twitched. "It's a promise."

In that case, I had to teach him a lesson.

With my free hand, I slinked my fingers through my curled and carefully styled hair. My heart thudded harder as I pulled the single clip free and brought my arm down. Keeping my hand hidden by my side, I opened the clip with practiced fingers and slid the blade into locked position. Palming the knife, I smiled. "Don't make promises you can't keep. And never hold a woman against her will again."

Confusion flickered in his eyes, followed by a burst of understanding. He shoved me away but was too late.

In a quick swipe, I dragged the small, sharp blade across his forearm. Not too deep, but not too shallow either. Instantly, a well of crimson showed in the tear of his black shirt.

"You should've let me go when I asked nicely."

He sucked in a harsh breath between his teeth. Grabbing me again, his fingers flexed around my wrist. "You think pain affects me?" His eyes flashed. "It only makes me worse."

The burn of satisfaction was nothing compared to the biting throb of Fox's fingers. His touch seemed to zap me with a million volts. My mind swam with contradictory things.

I wanted to run.

I wanted to kiss him.

I wanted to hurt him.

I wanted to touch him and bite and drag sharp nails down his back as he entered me.

Shit, Hazel. What are you thinking?

Fox sneered, twisting his scar. "You cut me." His eyes found mine again, glinting with smoke and smog. "That means you owe me."

I'd reached the end of my tether. I couldn't let this man warp my brain and play my body like a puppet. "I owe you *nothing.*"

The last few weeks caught up with me, and all I wanted to do was attack him. He deserved it for detaining me, antagonising me, and proving that a life on my own was no life at all. I'd been kidding myself when I said I didn't need to share my bed with another.

The last few weeks I would've given anything to have a guy to lean on, to cry in their arms, and share the burden of Clara's future. Clue was incredible, but I as much as I would deny it, I wanted a different kind of taking care of.

Fuck this man for making me crave. Fuck him for showing me how weak I truly was.

"Zel?" Clue appeared from the gloomy shadows. Her eyes popped wide seeing me trapped by a scarred stranger dressed in black. Sympathy glowed in her eyes as she sensed just how close I was to losing it; then they filled with fiery rage.

"Hey! Get the hell away from my friend." She charged forward like a mini torpedo. "Let her go!" Grabbing my other wrist, she pulled hard, causing me to lurch forward only to be yanked back by Fox. I became the toy in a game of tug-of-war.

"Clue." I tripped sideways as she pulled harder. "Clue." My

hand tightened on the knife as my shoulders screamed in pain. "Clue. Stop!"

She froze, breathing hard. Glaring daggers at Fox, she captured my face with her gentle hands. She conjured so many memories touching me that way. Considering we both grew up with no affection, we often touched and hugged.

She helped ground me even while tearing me into pieces. How many times had she touched Clara the same way? The same love and adoration glowing in her eyes. I hadn't stopped to think how hard this would be on her. She was losing a part of our family, just as much as me.

"You're okay. I'm here." She dropped her hands.

I smiled. "Thanks."

"And who the hell is this?" Fox asked, his voice low, deceptively smooth. Looking Clue up and down he muttered, "You're interrupting. Leave."

Clue placed her hands on her dainty hips. "I have no intention of leaving. I'm her friend. Let her go."

Fox shook his head. "Not till I get some answers. Plus, she cut me so she owes me a small debt."

Oh, God. A debt? Images of him extracting a toll from me made my core clench despite my anger.

"Clue?" Corkscrew appeared. His black eyes widened taking in the scene before him. He'd obviously just finished his fight—and most likely won judging by the lack of injuries.

Clue stepped toward him. "I'm glad you're here."

In a lightning move, Fox wrenched the knife out of my hand and pressed it against my side. He'd stolen my blade so fast no one had seen.

I went desperately still. Ice-cold fear siphoned through my blood. *Shit.* A second ago I battled attraction and lust. Now, I fought the urge to scream and run.

"Is everything okay here?" Corkscrew puffed out his chest, looking entirely terrifying with chiselled muscles and dark skin.

Clue waved at us. "This idiot won't let my friend go. Make him." She smiled coldly at Fox. "You haven't had the pleasure of meeting the top ranked champion of the Stingrays."

Fox nodded at Ben. "I know of you. You're good, but you don't want to get in the middle of this."

Corkscrew paused, head cocked to the side. Then a burst of excitement filled his eyes. "Wait. You're Mr. Obsidian. Wow, it's an honour, sir." Gone was the angry vibe, replaced with interest.

I couldn't believe it. This man was like a rock star with fans and crowds screaming his name. The entire time we'd argued not one person had come near him. Eyes never stopped watching, but everyone preferred to keep their distance.

Clue's mouth hung open. "*That's* the guy you were talking about?"

Corkscrew smiled. "Yep. Undefeated in every fight. Sets the bar high."

My stomach fluttered then turned to stone as Fox smiled thinly. "You're correct. Undefeated." He stressed the word. "Now, if you'll excuse me, I have unfinished business with this woman." He angled the knife deeper into my side, threatening heat and pain—entirely too close to puncturing my skin.

I glared, wishing I could knee him in the balls. We didn't have unfinished business. I wanted my freedom.

Clue shook her head and came closer. "You don't have to go with him, Zel. Doesn't matter if he owns this joint or not." Her almond eyes sparked when she looked at Fox. "Come on. Let's go home."

I wanted to tell her about the knife in my side. I wanted to run home and hug Clara. I wanted to scream bloody murder, but Fox twisted the blade until I winced, shattering everything I wanted and leaving me with the only thing I could do.

"Just a chat. That's all," Fox whispered, so low only I heard.

The fact he'd willingly kidnap me at knifepoint just to 'talk' made my protective instincts swell to protect Clue. I needed her safe, so I didn't have to worry about anyone while I laced into this maniac.

It was time to show Fox he'd captured the wrong woman to

interrogate.

Plastering a convincing smile on my face, I said, "No, it's fine, Clue. I'll go and talk. I'll see you back at home, okay?"

Clue shook her head. "No. I'll wait. Whatever he wants to talk about can't take very long."

"You'll leave," Fox snapped. "I have a lot of questions to be answered. I'll make sure a car sends her home when we're through."

Clue glared at Fox, her eyes full of fire. She never took orders well. Coming closer, she whispered in my ear. "Blink twice if you want me to kick his ass."

I almost did it. Almost.

But this was my fight—not hers. I needed her gone so I could win. Plus, if I couldn't go home yet, I would rather Clara be cared for by her Auntie rather than a strange babysitter.

"I'm okay. Honestly." I forced my eyes to stay wide, hoping she saw a relaxed and willing conversationalist. I didn't want her to see just how terrifying Fox truly was. And not just because he was a lunatic. I didn't trust him. I didn't trust myself with him. I didn't trust what would happen if he took me away from the public eye.

Fox didn't just want to talk. The awareness bound us together—a static charge vibrating ceaselessly where we touched.

I tried to make myself care that the moment he got me behind closed doors, I expected we'd both give in to more than just talking.

And I hated myself for needing a small dirty moment where I was nothing more than a woman seeking a release with a menacing man.

After a tense moment, Clue nodded. "Don't worry about Clara. I'll take care of her." Squeezing my hand, she murmured, "I'll wait up for you."

Corkscrew gave me a concerned look. "You're sure you're okay?"

His concern flurried my heart. He was a good man—

worthy of my best friend. "I'm sure."

Clue narrowed her eyes. I had no doubt she'd harass me for every detail of whatever was about to happen.

I stifled my groan as Corkscrew wrapped an arm around her, and they disappeared into the crowd.

Fox murmured, "We'll go to my office. It's quiet, and we won't be disturbed."

My heart rabbited.

Office. Undisturbed.

He should've said dungeon, and then I would've believed him.

A steely resolve came over me. It helped me ignore the spark smouldering between Fox's body and mine. Clue was gone. She was safe. Now I could worry about how to free myself from this crazy idiot stabbing me with my own knife. I'd had a moment of weakness, entertaining thoughts of forbidden sex, but now I was clearheaded.

"I'm not going to sleep with you, you know," I muttered as Fox pushed me toward a wide set of stairs leading up into the dark.

He huffed. "I said I wanted to talk. Not to fuck."

Such a crude word.

I hated that it turned me on.

A shudder travelled the length of my spine. His voice was perfectly level, restrained and controlled, but beneath his careful tone lurked lethal potency.

Climbing the wide stairs, he said, "I expect answers. I want to know who you are. I want to understand why you're different."

My stomach erupted with fluttering winged things. "What makes you think I'll answer? Having a knife pressed against me doesn't make me very eager." I sucked in a breath as he twisted the blade once more before withdrawing. Holding the knife up, he tucked the blade away and slipped it into his pocket.

"There. Now, you'll talk."

No, now I'll lie.

Four

ROAN

I'd learned from an early age to use people's weaknesses against them. Taunting the fragile, mocking the littler. Instead of being told no, I was encouraged. Given the tools to excel in murder, and browbeaten into being the perfect obedient machine.

The moment I set eyes on her, I tasted a delicious combination of fear and strength. Weakness and bravery. Sadness and resignation.

Instincts and needs that I'd buried and ignored volcanoed to the surface. I lost control. I broke every rule and didn't give a fuck.

She woke a part of me I didn't know existed—a man not layered in ice and coldblooded disassociation. This new man ached with every inch; he craved heat and fire and lust.

And so I stole her.

And I took her.

Over and over again.

Shit.

How the hell had this happened? This *never* happened. Never in my life had I submitted to a bodily craving. That sort of thing had been tortured out of me. I didn't suffer from a lack of discipline.

Ever.

Until now.

The instant I saw her I lost a part of myself. I became drunk on a new sensation. Something about her drew me. I didn't lust or fuck or need. To be close to another filled me with horror not joy. So why the hell did I want to know her? Why were my thoughts full of nakedness and heat? *What the fuck am I doing?*

I glanced at her. With her shoulders back and chin thrust forward, she looked like she was headed to war not a conversation. Every step was calm and brave; every motion full of confidence and poise.

The stolen blade hung heavy in my pocket, thudding against my thigh with every step. I'd lost control and kidnapped someone at knife point. Not just anyone—a woman I touched.

I fucking touched her!

I never touched anyone voluntarily unless it was in a fight. It just wasn't done. My entire life I'd avoided every iota of touch and contact. And yet the instant I wrapped my fingers around her arm, my entire body shuddered with some unseen power filtering from her to me.

It intoxicated me. It bewitched me. It fucking scared me.

Only when I looked directly into her eyes did I taste just how much passion, fear, strength, sadness, and rebellion lived inside her. She was like an unlit firework—contained and neatly packaged on the outside, but a hazardous explosion on the inside.

"I want my knife back," she murmured, her eyes connecting with mine. All I could think about were emeralds and every green gemstone I'd ever seen. Her eyes mocked my own—whereas I had no colour, she had every spectrum.

"You're not getting it back till I say you can." *Until I*

understand this insane drive to touch you.

"You're not my owner," she snapped. "This isn't a discussion. It's my property, and I want it back. I don't know who you think you are, but I'm not playing your crazy mind games anymore."

The familiar strength and rage shot up my spine. Tearing my eyes from hers, I strode faster up the steps.

She took the steps two at a time and brushed past with a cold look. Her shoulder grazed mine. My vision turned red, muscles locked down, and the familiar command to hurt made me tremble. My jaw locked as I fought the orders.

Shit. She isn't different after all.

My fucking heart sank. I'd chased her, trapped her, and dragged her up here because I'd dared to hope. Dared to believe that I was drawn to her because she might be impervious to my training. That I might be able to touch and be touched.

Turned out I could touch her without falling into old patterns, but she couldn't touch me.

My heart hardened in disappointment. So she wasn't my cure after all. I'd hoped—

You'd hoped it was fading. That you could finally live a life where you wouldn't automatically punch someone in the fucking face or slam a dagger into their heart.

Tough shit.

I doubted I'd ever be free, and that just made me fucking homicidal.

Reaching the top of the stairs, her lips parted as she took in the large landing. Skating her eyes over the table and black couch, she drifted toward the glass perimeter. From here, the arena looked like a modern day version of the coliseum. Men fought in cages and rings, unconscious bodies were tended to by medics. All that was missing were the lions and other exotic animals the Romans used to kill unlucky slaves.

I shared a certain bond with those unfortunate souls.

No one would look at me and think I was slave. But I had

been. I still was. I probably would be forever.

I didn't say a word as she pushed off from the balcony and moved toward a statue of a twisted and gnarly tree.

The sculpture took me eighteen days with barely any sleep to finish. I'd warmed the metal just enough to twist and distort. I turned a pristine lump of bronze into a tortured piece of art. The tree looked like it was heralded by demons and designed by masochists. Its branches only suitable for carcass-eating vultures to perch.

But I liked it. In fact, it was one of my favourite pieces. It represented nothing, but at the same time, everything.

It was me. Bared raw.

Slowly, almost hesitantly, she ran her fingertips over the cold metal. The instant she touched it, my cock lurched. It fucking lurched for the second time in my sorry existence.

Heat. Delicious wanting heat blazed in my blood. Lust. So unknown and almost unrecognisable. It grabbed me around the balls, making me hard, filling my cock with new life.

My dick knew better than to act on its own. It'd been taught to never react. Thoughts of release and sex were beaten out of us at a very early age. And if we disobeyed—well…

The fear had kept me impotent, but this woman—this magical infuriating woman—had graced me with a fucking hard-on. I gritted my teeth, revelling in the sensitivity as I swelled, thickened, and ached with unfamiliar need. The flush of heat boiled the ice in my blood, leaving me steaming, angry, and on the cusp of something entirely alien.

Two years I'd waited for the thawing, and for two years it never happened. But tonight. Tonight, all thanks to one woman, I might've found the chink—the weakness—in my brainwashing.

She bent her spine, investigating the artwork closely. My balls drew tighter, throbbing.

Her body beckoned me. She was different, elusive, *unobtainable*. And my cock wanted unobtainable. For the first time since my life of slavery began, it came alive between my legs.

I didn't think I could stand the craving. It was too strong—too demanding.

I trembled for an entirely different reason. I wanted to scream at her for having such power over me while at the same time bow at her feet for freeing me from the cage I existed in.

Then came the fear.

The anxious sweats at misbehaving, the knowledge I'd disobeyed a direct order. Punishment would be horrific.

They're not here.

I closed my eyes, trying to get a grip—re-centring myself.

"Hey. Umm, are you okay?"

My eyes flew wide only to be trapped by her half-angry, half-concerned gaze. Her scrumptious body wrapped in gold and silver chased away my fear and my mouth watered at the thought of taking her.

Pity filled me. Pity for her because now that I'd tasted what she could do for me, I wasn't letting her go. She wouldn't be going home tonight. Or the next or the next or the next. She'd be in my bed. She'd open her legs and I'd—

Goddammit, I'm acting as if I'm fucking fifteen.

Trouble was I had a lifetime of lust fizzing and bursting inside. Two orgasms I'd enjoyed since I hit puberty. Only two. I was fucking desperate for a third.

"I'm fine. Why?" I eyed her provocative dress, drinking in her gentle curves; filling my mind with images that any man starved of sex would imagine. I wanted to run a tongue down her cleavage. I wanted to taste her skin before sinking deep, deep inside her.

I'd never felt this way. Never.

She stood taller, baring her shoulders with fearlessness and a fine edge of resentment. "You're shivering. And frankly you look sick." Waving her hand, she scowled. "Not that I care if you're sick, of course. Look, I'm done with all of this. Give me back my knife and let me go." One hand went to her side, rubbing where I'd placed the blade. "You're a bastard for forcing me against my will. If Clue hadn't been there, such a tiny weapon wouldn't have stopped me from ripping off your balls."

First image into my head was her tiny hands cupping my aching balls.

Second image was the ludicrous suggestion she could even touch me without my permission.

I couldn't stop it. Cold laughter erupted from my mouth. I froze, cursing this woman. Cursing myself for these new, strange feelings. I *never* laughed. I *never* touched. I *never* got hard. I *never* wanted to fuck.

She was a witch. She was magical. She would fix me.

"How much was Corkscrew going to pay you for tonight?"

Her nostrils flared. "Excuse me?"

"How much? To fuck you?"

She shuddered. "*That's* what you think I am? I thought you were joking before." She shook her head, a low noise coming from her throat. "Unbelievable. You're a bastard *and* an asshole. For your information, he's my best-friend's boyfriend. He's a nice guy—unlike you." She paced on the landing, her dress whispering around her legs with every step. "Fucking unbelievable. I want to leave. I'm done talking to you."

My muscles shivered, feeding off her temper, letting her spirit clash with mine. Another lesson I'd been taught: leech the feelings off another before stealing everything. It allowed me to feel their fear, live their terror—the only thing I could get in those days.

Dragging my eyes over her body, my fucking cock hardened to a rock. Her breasts were squished inside the lace of the dress, her waist so tiny I could crush the life out of her with just my hands. Her legs...

Shit.

The moment my eyes landed on her legs, memories swamped me.

"See her? The prima ballerina?"

My eyes had trouble focusing through the binoculars, but I could make out a girl in a tutu with legs that looked matchstick thin and so easily breakable. "Yes."

"She's the target tonight when her father and mother are asleep."

I'd long ago stopped asking why. I never got a reply, only a swat around the head, and any fear that my soul was destined for hell had been purged from me in the early days of training.

"Okay."

The pat on the back made me curl in horror. I hated people touching me. It always brought pain to me or pain to others.

"Stay here until 3 a.m., then proceed."

"—and just because you own this illegal place doesn't give you the right to hurt me!" Zel snapped.

I blinked, trying to seem like I'd heard the entire string of obscenities she'd no doubt thrown my way.

Dragging hands over my face, I said, "I'm not going to hurt you." *Much.* My voice was deep and gravelly. I hated flashbacks. They came at the worst times. Ironically, my body had been trained to perfection—I could kill in hundreds of different ways. I could mutilate and massacre with an artistry only learned from a lifetime of tutelage, but the weakest part of me was my brain.

Try as I might to block the nightmares and visions, they broke through randomly, shoving me back into horror. However, this one had done me a favour.

I was no longer hard.

What the fuck were we talking about?

Ah, yes. "Ten thousand is the going rate for a woman of talents. Not a bad income for a night's earnings." I licked my lips. "I could be persuaded to go to twenty thousand if you're so repulsed by me."

Her eyes flickered to my scar. "I told you. I'm not a whore. You can keep your money as there's no way in hell I'm letting you fuck me." She backed up to the balustrade, her face paling from cream to white.

The hair on my forearms stood up. I inched forward, trapping her between my body and the glass. A metre existed between us, but the air hummed, arching and spitting with the same delicious energy I'd felt when I'd touched her.

"Fine. You're not a whore. But if you were...inclined...to agree to a one off deal. To let me, as you eloquently put it, fuck you—what would you charge?" My heart raced at the thought of peeling the lace off her shoulders.

I took another tiny step forward. "I'm warning you now, I won't take no for an answer. I haven't wanted a woman, any woman, as much as I want you. I'm going to have you, so stop dancing around the fact, hoping you can get free, and agree to a figure."

My cock thickened again at the thought of touching her— relishing being allowed such a simple, but miraculous thing. I would savour every inch of her skin. I'd caress her with every fingertip, my tongue, my entire fucking body.

Zel shook her head, loose curls haloing her head. "Nothing. Because there is no deal. Back up and let me leave. Go and sleep with one of your employees. You don't need me."

Her denial made me want her all the more. It was torture. It was heaven. "You're wrong. I do need you. I wasn't lying when I said you were different. I don't understand it, but I'm fucking done pretending to be human when I'm not. I need you to let me be free. I need to fuck you."

Her skin flushed and she moved suddenly, darting to the side to reach the stairs. She was fast, but I was faster. I placed myself squarely in her path, gritting my teeth ready for consequences. If she touched me we'd both be in trouble.

She careened to a stop, unsteady in her high heels. "Move."

"No. Not until you agree." I took another careful step toward her. My mouth watered at the thought of kissing, licking, biting. I'd never been so irrational or so sure. Something about this woman made my lifeless cock sit up and fucking beg.

"There's always a deal. For the right price," I whispered, slowly closing the small distance between us.

Zel's neck rippled as she swallowed hard. "I'm not for sale."

The slight tremor in her voice stroked my need, making me burn. She lied. She might not know it, but she'd just admitted she would sell herself. To me.

My stomach flipped, filling me with edgy thirst. Thirst to have her.

I murmured, "I have a gift. A gift that tells me secrets that people think they hide so well. Call it sixth sense, or a hunter's perception, but I know things about you already. I know when you're lying."

She bit her lip, eyes flashing with defiance. "You don't know anything about me."

Bowing my head, I inhaled her soft floral scent. Lily of the valley. A plant we cultivated at the facility—a pretty little flower whose berries were poison. A convenient method of killing with anonymity.

If I tasted her would she poison me?

"I know you have two weaknesses." I'd catalogued them, committed to memory just like I'd been trained. It wasn't a gift, mainly just good observation. I knew what would bring out the ultimate amount of pain if I ever needed to.

One: she had a silver scar, long since healed, marring her beauty directly beneath her right eye. It'd been deep and long, but sewn together neatly, so it was barely noticeable under the makeup she wore.

Two: her right ear had been torn. Healed and stitched, a small triangle of cartilage was missing from the top.

The imperfections made me frown. I wanted to know who hurt her. I wanted to kill them.

She huffed, inching along the balcony to avoid my advance. "You can make up stuff all you want, but you're wrong on one count: I'm not for sale." She bared her teeth. "Back off."

"No." I crowded her against the glass. "I want you, and I always get what I want."

She stood taller, arching her back, looking like she'd sprout wings and take off from the mezzanine at any moment. "Well, unless you're in the habit of rape, you won't get what you want this time." Her hands flew up to shove me back, but I dodged to the side. Fear overrode my need, beating a fast tattoo in my chest.

I couldn't risk her touching me.

Her eyes fell to my scar again, making me very aware of her perfection compared to my grotesqueness. Of course, that's why she'd refused. If I'd been whole and not disfigured, I doubted she would deny me. I might know nothing of women, but I knew she suffered the same pull, the same need.

I captured her elbow, quivering thanks to the charge between us. "Would you fuck me if you didn't find me so repulsive?" My entire body erupted from the single contact. It twisted my gut, scrambled my brain.

I would never be good enough. Not for this flawless creature who had the power to free me.

But that was a lie. She did have flaws.

She portrayed a woman who had everything and needed nothing. Someone strong and independent, but that was false. She was damaged. I might wear my mistakes for the world to see, but it didn't make hers any less visible.

The anger on her face disappeared, replaced by tenderheartedness for just a second. "Is that what you think? That I'm refusing you because of your disfigurement? You aren't repulsive."

I decided then and there I hated her compassion—I preferred her anger. I deserved it. I didn't deserve empathy.

"I'm refusing you because you're an overbearing psycho who can't take no for an answer and stole my freedom and my knife. Your scar has nothing to do with it."

My temper built. "I know you need money for something. The way you look at the wealth around us screams the truth."

She froze.

"I'm guessing you need a sizeable sum." I glared harder, deciphering the greed and hunger in her eyes. She didn't seem the type to want frivolous things. It was for something deeper…something….

The answer appeared from nowhere—like it always did when I let myself delve deep.

"You need it for someone you care about. I'm also guessing you'd do almost anything to get it." I delivered it like a threat, a curse. "All I'm asking is for you to let me fuck you. And I'll give you what you need. Name a figure and it's yours to spend however you fucking want."

My lifeless heart stuttered as her fight faded and her green eyes shimmered with tears. "You arrogant prick." The spark and intense awareness between us shifted from lust-filled-competition to grief-ridden. "You don't know a thing about me. You don't deserve any part of me."

Shit.

I didn't know what to do. Standing there like an idiot, I offered no condolences as she sniffed and gritted her teeth. No tears fell, but the glossy look never fully disappeared. "You truly are a bastard. For your information I felt what you did. I found you intriguing and don't mind admitting I entertained the thought of what it would be like to kiss you. You could've had me. All you had to do was be a gentlemen and ask me on a fucking date. But you ruined it, and now you've used my one weakness and made me feel like shit." Her shoulders fell, and I knew I'd won.

I'd won, but I didn't feel victorious. I felt like fucking scum.

Being able to read what people tried to keep hidden meant I could intimidate and influence. Up till now, I didn't give a rats-ass about hurting anyone, but this woman… this woman….Shit.

Sighing, I muttered, "Tell me about your ear, then maybe I'll let you go." *Give me one piece of you.* I placed my hands in my pockets and backed off a little, giving the illusion of freedom and safety.

She shook her head, balling her fists. "What sort of mind games are you playing? Why do you want to know anything about me?" Her voice was soft but strong, lyrical but brave. Something twinged deep inside, recognising the fight in her—

the same fight that lived in me.

Spreading my arms, I said, "No games. You were honest with me, so I'll be honest with you. I've lived a lonely life—not through my own choice—and for the first time I connected with someone. I like the lust flowing in my veins. I love the anticipation of fucking you. And I love your fierceness." I waited for her to look up—to make eye contact—but she never did.

"If I tell you about my ear, you'll let me go?" she asked softly.

I stifled my growl. After my honesty, admitting I was drawn to her, all she wanted to do was leave. Fine. I crossed my arms. "I said maybe."

Silence pulsed between us, thickening with tension. The ache in my cock was overshadowed by an ache for something different. I needed pain. I needed a fight. Only pain could eliminate the confusion and give me room to breathe. I hated suffering such intense emotions, all while hoping they'd never leave.

I felt *alive*. And annoyed and horny and frustrated.

The fight with Everest had done nothing. His fists hadn't hurt; he'd been too easy to defeat. Arrogant bastard hadn't lived up to his boasting and now I'd have to find another way to self-medicate with pain.

I didn't think Zel would answer, but finally she said, "It was my foster-sister. They were my ninth foster family, and I was more like a feral cat than a little girl. For the first day, I was a novelty, same as always, same as before, but then by the third or fourth day, I was the toy that got pulled apart. Her and her brother coaxed me into the garage, saying they'd seen a kitten running around.

"I related more to animals and only the thought of having a feline friend made me follow. Once we were there, they threw me to the ground and duct-taped my legs and arms."

She paused, unconsciously tracing the piece missing from her ear. "They used their father's tin-snips to cut me, saying I should be tagged like a wild animal seeing as I would never be a real girl. Afterward, they left me to bleed until their father arrived home from work. Instead of rushing me to the hospital, he attempted to sew it up himself. If child services had found out his own children hurt me, he would've been taken off the list for carers and denied the weekly paycheque.

"Thing was, he did such a bad job, I ended up looking like I'd been mauled by a dog." Her body tensed, morphing from victim to fighter. "That night, I ran. It was the first time I ran away. I had no money or idea where I was going, but it was the best thing that happened to me. Running, that is."

I hadn't noticed my fists had curled and every muscle tensed. The urge to find pain mixed with the urge to take retribution on those bastard's children. I had no qualms about hurting minors. "How old were you?"

"Thirteen."

My respect for her increased. Not only was she a strong woman, but she'd been a strong child, too. A bit like me in a way. I ran, but unfortunately ran in the wrong direction.

I wanted to ask about her other flaws. I needed to know every secret but I wanted to savour them—try and unravel them before learning the truth from her. And I would find the truth because she wasn't leaving.

"Thank you for telling me."

She raised her eyes; the green was darker, more forest than grass. "Now will you let me go?"

I smiled, forcing the scar on my cheek into a grimace. "No. I have no choice. I can't let someone go who intrigues me this much. Who makes my cock ache this hard. I don't even know you, yet you invoke more questions and urges than anyone before." Shrugging, I encroached on her space, pushing her back. "I won't let you go until I've had you, and there's nothing you can do to stop it."

She looked at me as if I were the devil asking for her soul.

My stomach roiled with sick satisfaction. Too long I'd been the one being used. It would be nice to use someone else for change. To use her body, her mind, her soul to fix everything inside me.

Zel took a step back, eyes flashing with green embers. "You're unhinged. Do you honestly think I want you after that? Whatever attraction I felt has flown away thanks to your caveman demands. You're an imbecile, and I'm done. Let me go."

I ghosted forward, heart racing with the thought of taking her against her will. *You can't do that. You know what it feels like too clearly.*

Standing still, I straightened my shoulders. "How much?"

She slammed hands onto her hips glaring as if she could incinerate me with her gaze. "Are you fucking deaf? There *is* no price. There *is* no deal. I'm leaving, and you can't stop me." Her face tightened; her lithe body trembled. Everything about her made me want to taste.

Balling my hands, I winced at the small cuts on my knuckles from the fight. "What's your full name?" I decided to go a different tact—confusion. Wear her down with insinuations and endless questions.

Scowling, she exhaled heavily; anger flushed her cheeks turning her skin from cream to roses. Her eyes darted around the space—over my shoulder, at the statues, toward the stairs. Every flick of her gaze cut me off from seeing her thoughts.

Goddammit, look into my eyes. I'd never realized how much I relied on seeing into someone's soul. It gave me clues and insights I couldn't get otherwise.

"If you're looking for a weapon you won't find one, and I doubt you're strong enough to throw a fifty kilo statue at my face." I patted my pocket where her knife lay. "Agree to a sum and as an act of good faith, I'll give you back your blade."

She froze as deliberations played over her face. "Let me get this straight. You want to pay me to fuck you, even though you own a monstrosity of a mansion and could get any woman into bed if you actually learned some tact and charm." Her perfect pouty lips quirked into half a smile. "Rather sad when I think about it. Shame I don't sleep with men out of pity or for money or for any reason so shut up and let me leave."

My eyes couldn't stop looking at her condescending half smile. Mocking me. Belittling me. Half smiles were lazy. They were fake. Either smile with your fucking soul or don't bother.

Probably why I hadn't smiled since I was six. My soul was dead.

I'd had enough. Anger frothed in my blood, and I needed her beneath me. No more fucking games.

"I don't just want any woman. I want you. So stop fucking me around. Name your price and I'll pay it."

I may own a mansion and a tempting club, but I hadn't shared my bed with anyone. Sure, I'd fucked before, but never had the responsibility or pleasure of sleeping beside another. To sleep with someone was the sign of ultimate trust. To be defenceless in the presence of another? No. It wasn't an option with my past.

Zel pursed her lips, not saying a word.

"Give in. This is one business transaction I'll win, *dobycha.*"

"Whatever you're calling me. Stop it," she snarled, her eyes lighting with green fire. "Don't call me that."

Her strength and blatant disregard of my request stoked my temper until my body ran hot with feral energy. I wanted this woman to fear me, yet she stood regal and taunting— untouchable.

My eyes fell to her breasts, rising and falling rapidly. "This could've been so simple. I'm not asking to hurt you. I'm asking to give you pleasure while taking my own and pay you a handsome sum." I licked my lips loving the tightness in my belly and pangs in my cock. "I need to fuck you, and the more you fight the worse it gets."

I moved forward and captured her chin, holding her tight. The intense spark between us returned like a lightning bolt, whizzing and searing, turning my fucking thoughts to mush.

Goddammit, I wanted her.

Her skin glistened, mouth parted. The angry flush faded

only to be replaced with colour full of erotic need. I dropped my hand from her chin to her breast.

She froze even as her back arched, forcing more flesh into my palm. Rage battled with flaming lust in her eyes, and I forgot how to fucking breathe as I fondled her, completely consumed by the way her nipple hardened and peaked.

The argument and refusal only hiked my need. My head filled with images of how wet she'd be, how soft she'd feel, how sweet she'd taste.

I couldn't take it anymore. "I'll pay you one hundred thousand dollars."

Her mouth plopped wide; she didn't breathe.

I had a sudden psychotic urge to kiss her. Every second I spent touching her brought me back to life, wrenching me from the bones and ashes of my past. She was ambrosia, utopia—a cure.

Fuck, I couldn't wait much longer. I'd take her over the balcony in full view of the fighters below if she refused. Closing my eyes briefly, I muttered one word but it throbbed with everything I needed. "Please…"

Zel sucked in a shaky breath, her breast still hot in my hand. "One hundred thousand dollars? To do what exactly?"

I had no idea.

Suck my cock; let me do untold things to you. Let me touch you. Fuck you.

A plan formed rapidly in my head. I could keep her for a certain amount of time. By locking her into a contract it would give me time to figure out what the fuck I was doing.

"One month. You'd stay here. With me."

A thrill of fear shot through me at the thought of her sleeping beside me. Precautions would have to be taken, but it was doable.

Her eyes dropped to my scar, before looking away, denying me access to her thoughts.

That pissed me off. I dropped my hand, letting her breast go. "Scars aren't contagious, *dobycha.*"

She shook her head. "Scars aren't contagious, but your craziness is. What makes you think you can wave money in my face, and I'll spread my legs for you?"

I crowded her against the glass; my hips pulsed needing to collide with hers.

"Because you feel it. If I touched you right now I'd probably find you're wet for me. And even though I'm crazy, all I want to do is drive deep inside you—I want to worship you in my own way. I want to adore you by touching you, kissing you, biting you." I dropped my gaze to her lips, loving the swollen pinkness, the tempting glisten. "Forget about everything but how your body feels. Do you want me? Do you want me to release your anger with my tongue?"

Her eyes met mine swimming and slightly vacant with desire. "You're messing with my head." She raised her hands to push me away, but I dodged her touch. "You turn me on, I won't deny that, but I'm not staying here. I can't."

"You can because you need the money. I won't be satisfied with just once. I need to know I can take you whenever I damn well want. I want to own you for thirty days with no limits."

She wrapped arms around her body, rolling her shoulders. "Why did it have to happen this way?" She looked up to the ceiling as if she could smite fate for landing her in my path. She looked desolate, confused, and sad, so terribly sad.

My heart jerked; I ran a hand through my hair. I was right. She was like me. More than I knew.

"Life hasn't been kind to you, has it, *dobycha?*" The angry dominance left my voice, edging toward soft curiosity.

Zel froze. Her teeth clenched; her sadness was replaced with coldness. "That's none of your business. And stop calling me that."

"Tell me your name, agree to my terms, and I'll call you whatever you want."

She tilted her chin upward. "Fine, if you want to know so badly. My name is Hazel Hunter, and you're right. If you touched me now you would find I'm wet for you. Wet for the promise of what you offer, for the anticipation of what it would be like, but it doesn't matter because one, you're an asshole, and two, I can't stay here for a month."

My cock lurched, picturing the dampness between her legs.

I didn't like was her refusal yet again. It was getting fucking tiresome.

My stomach twisted at the thought of taming this woman. She wasn't walking away. She would stay here a month, and I would get rid of this overwhelming obsession and go back to my sexless lonely life.

"Two hundred thousand." My voice roughened, already imagining her naked to feast on. "I'll give you two hundred thousand for one month of pure access. I want to buy your obedience, your body, your mind. But most of all I want to buy your secrets."

I expected her to scream, tighten her tiny fists, and smack me in the face. Instead, everything stilled. The noises of multiple fights downstairs and the soft notes of music faded as Hazel hypnotized me by sucking on her bottom lip. Nervousness etched her face as she cocked her head. "Two hundred thousand?"

I sensed her weakening and knew I'd finally found a figure she'd sell for. "Payable in cash at the end of the month."

Her eyes lit up as thoughts raced over her face, then faded just as fast. "You truly are desperate."

My heart stopped. Slamming me back to reality where a perfect goddess like Hazel would never sleep with a gargoyle like me.

Fuck this. Why was I bothering? I could choose any whore to service me and not have to fight and cajole. I switched from wanting her to wanting to throw her to the ground and make her swallow her words.

Her eyes zeroed in on the jagged scar on my cheek. "I'll tell you what I think of you, Obsidian Fox. Just because you excite some stupid part of my brain and make me want someone for the first time in years doesn't mean you can act the scarred villain and scare me into your bed. I'm not in the business of selling my soul or fucking strangers for money, but it so happens you're right. I do need the cash, and I'd be willing to do almost anything, but what I won't do is put up with a vainglorious asshole. I've dealt with enough of them for several lifetimes."

I never took my eyes off her. An aura of anger shimmered. Vulnerable but fierce—a potent combination for the killer inside. I wanted to break her all while letting her shine.

She laughed suddenly. "You're insane." Then she muttered under her breath, *"I'm* insane."

My stomach twisted as she locked her spine and turned the full force of her green gaze on me.

"I can't believe I'm doing this, but try to be less of a bastard." Her hand came out, palm facing upward ready to accept something. "Give me back my knife and ask me politely, gently. Don't give me a reason to want to use it."

My heart forgot how to beat, stuttering over itself. Respect braided with lust and I fell further into her trap. Somehow she'd ended up with the power, and I hated it.

Slipping a hand into my pocket, I removed the blade and held it out. My hands clenched. *She's fucking up my life already.* My body trembled with the need for pain. I needed to be on my own. I had to find relief from this horror. What was I thinking?

"You'll stay for one month."

She nodded, eyes latching onto her knife.

"You'll let me fuck you however I please."

Her body tensed but slowly she nodded.

"You'll stop arguing and answer any question I have?"

Her gaze met mine, a flash of ire in their depths. Finally, she nodded.

I dropped the knife into her waiting palm, careful not to touch her. I doubted my self-control could handle more stimulation at that moment. I felt like I'd been to war, came out bleeding, and not entirely sure who won.

The instant the knife fell into her grip, she wrapped her fingers tight around it and hugged it to her body.

I sensed the moment she came to her conclusion. Fire lit her face and resolution strengthened her body. "You mistreat me, and I'll make sure you'll be dickless for the rest of your life. Treat me with respect and desire and I'll stay."

Brushing a strand of hair curling around her cheek, she murmured, "I accept your offer, Obsidian Fox. Don't make me regret it."

Five
Hazel

My favourite saying was: the beauty in this world was hidden by filth and lies while evil was painted in beauty and smiles.

It had become a testament I lived by. A rule I never broke. Because I no longer trusted beauty and smiles. I learned the hard way.

I learned to scratch the surface and search for truth and realness, all the while protecting myself in lies.

But then a man, who was neither beautiful or a liar, made a proposition. With fear and stupidity, I sold myself to him. Sold myself to a fighter who could sense my lies as easily as a fox senses a rabbit.

I regretted it.

I revelled in it.

It destroyed me.

A second after I sold myself, a rush of horror smothered my heart.

What the hell am I doing?

I regretted it instantly, but I'd told Fox the truth. I would do anything for money, as money had the power to save Clara. She was the only thing worth fighting for. The only thing that would make me do such horrendous things.

If it meant she'd live another day, a month, a year—I would sell myself to countless men or work in a mine or even deal drugs out of my tiny apartment.

I sold my dignity. My body. My very fucking soul for money. All because I had no other way. No other assets, no hope apart from trading myself like some possession at a garage sale.

But with horror came relief. Half an hour ago I had no hope, but now I had two hundred thousand wishes to find a way out of heartbreak.

Fox stood tall, watching me warily. He seemed as shocked as I was with what happened between us. I hadn't lied when I said he could've had me for free. If he'd been cordial and kind—I would've willingly gone on a date and even slept with him.

He's an asshole but you like his arrogance, his iron-will, and demands.

I wanted to scrub my brain from such stomach-churning thoughts. I wasn't a woman who bowed to the wills of men. I was a woman who shoved them down and trod all over them, leaving them in my dust. But Fox…he was angry but damaged. Scary but lonely. Demanding but requesting.

I couldn't make sense of him at all. And that made me nervous. How would I know he would pay?

How will you stay for a month?

I gritted my teeth. That was one part of the bargain I would break. I wouldn't stay for the month. I would sneak out and see Clara. I would find a way to see my sick daughter because I could never live with myself if she thought I'd abandoned her. And I wouldn't put up with such stupid demands to keep me prisoner. A revision of the terms would be addressed, but not yet. Not until I gave him a little, so I could take a lot.

Cocking my head, I asked, "How can I be sure you'll pay?"

His hands clenched as a burst of energy filtered through him. He smiled, but it didn't reach his white-grey eyes. "I'll pay. I promise."

"You promised I couldn't hurt you, but I did. Like I said, don't make promises you can't keep." My eyes fell to his torn shirt, searching for the small cut I'd delivered.

"Alright, I see trust is a big issue for you. Just like I gave you back your knife in good faith, I'll pay you half up front." He raised an eyebrow. "Does that settle your nerves?"

Holding my head high, I said, "Yes, that would be appreciated." The moment I had the cash I would take it home to Clara. As tempting as it would be to break the rest of the contract, I wouldn't. I gave him my word.

My stomach fluttered at the thought of him touching me, thrusting deep inside. The money was for Clara, but the sex—I wanted that for me. I wanted to see what people wrote sonnets about. If the sparks between Fox and me were any indication, when he finally took me it would be worth the mild discomfort of accepting his money for a service rendered.

Fox came closer and I steeled myself against his overbearing presence. His scent of smoke and metal surrounded me, playing havoc with my thoughts. My knickers were damp from fighting with him, and my nipple still tingled where he'd cupped my breast.

His hand landed on my hip. A thumb circled my pronounced hipbone beneath the gossamer material of my dress. If I thought an innocuous touch on my wrist resonated with connection it was nothing, *nothing*, compared to the burst of hotness, the euphoria of his fingers stroking my tender flesh.

"I can't wait to see you naked, *dobycha.*" His head bowed to run a nose through my styled hair. "I want your hair loose so I can hold it while I take you from behind."

My core melted, my heart thrummed. I had nothing to retaliate with.

His gaze fell to my lips. "Don't move." Time slowed as his hand came up and cupped my braless breast again. "Tell me what you like so I can make this good for you, too."

I shuddered as he brushed a thumb over the highly sensitive nipple. I swayed forward, willingly giving him access. "I like that." A strange kind of peace settled over me. Gone was the embarrassment at selling myself. I would get more than just money from this. I would unlock hidden desires I never knew existed. I'd done the right thing and fate hadn't forgotten about me—it had listened to my screams for help. It had given me Obsidian Fox.

His grip suddenly went from caressing to possessing, and I bit my lip, swallowing back a moan.

He sucked in a heavy breath, pinching my nipple with strong fingers almost as if testing himself, pushing boundaries I didn't understand. "Do you like that?"

My head was suddenly too heavy for my neck; my body too floppy to stand. I wanted to press against him, encourage more of the aliveness to filter.

.My cheeks heated at the thought of admitting I liked it rougher, but then I embraced the fighter he brought out in me and looked up through my eyelashes. "Yes. I like that."

"As much as you fight, you like to be controlled." His head dropped and the tips of his shaggy bronze hair touched mine. "I can't wait to find out what else you enjoy."

My stomach clenched, sending thrills of fear and need into my core. Shit. He did have a gift. Yes, he could sense things only a highly in-tune person could know, but he also had a power over me. His unnerving presence made me forget everything but him. He took over my world. He was an eclipse.

Dropping his hand, he murmured, "Get in my office. Now." His gaze caused the swirling lust and temper to bubble once again in my blood.

He stepped back and the low illumination glittered on the silver of his scar. It ought to make him hideous, but it only made it that much harder to ignore him.

Taking a step toward the stairs, I said quietly, "I'll come back tomorrow. Once I've given my excuses and packed."

In one insanely fast move, he barricaded the stairwell. He moved like a black ghost—silent, deadly, just as unnerving. "You're not leaving. You agreed."

My forehead furrowed, battling the call from his body to mine. "I agreed, yes. But not starting now. I need to go and see my—" I cut myself off.

Don't tell him about Clara.

I found him sexually potent and secretly craved the dangerous unpredictably he presented, but I didn't want him knowing about something so fragile and innocent.

Never.

Iciness replaced the heat he invoked. "I'll come back tomorrow."

A sliver of worry stabbed my heart. What if I left and he had second thoughts? What if he followed me home and found out I had a dying daughter? Buying a woman for sex was one thing, but it was an entirely different matter buying a mother.

Now the cash was in my reach, I wouldn't give it up.

Fox shook his head, advancing toward me. My heart stuttered with his every step. "You're not leaving until the month is up. Deal's a deal." He pushed me backward, not touching, just manhandling me by his sheer will. "I told you I wanted you. And I'm going to take you tonight. You're nuts to think you can leave here without letting me sample what I've bought—especially after you made me work so hard to earn it."

A trace of chocolate and smoky metal surrounded me—his scent was a contradiction. He wore authority like one would wear an aftershave—reeking of anger and power.

He'd already won the argument, but I loved the thrill of fighting with him. It made my dampness turn to wetness. It turned warmth to hot. It made me crave him. "You can't expect me to stay here with no preparation. I have to arrange everything. I have to change my clothing. I need a toothbrush for heaven's sake."

He smiled, the scar on his cheek twitching a little. "I have a spare toothbrush that I'll give you. As for clothes, what makes you think you'll be wearing any? You said you'd give me a month. I didn't say where you'd spend that month."

My heart shot out of my chest and exploded through the ceiling. I wanted to squeeze my legs together at the indecent desire he conjured in my veins. But then images of being chained in some torture chamber bombarded my mind. Bondage and pain and submission. I was better than that. I wasn't a submissive. I was his equal, and I wouldn't—*couldn't*—let someone abuse me.

I wanted him. But I wouldn't give up my rights as a human being. "Just so we're clear, I'm not agreeing to any torture, or pain-play. I'll let you take me, and I'll let you decide what I wear, but I will not let you bind me or hit me." My breathing quickened in a mixture of lust and terror.

Fox slammed to a stop. His large shoulders rolled and he looked as if I'd said something blasphemous. "You have my word I won't use whips or any other equipment on you. Unless you change your mind." His face twisted with some strange afterthought. "However, bondage will have to be addressed."

"What? No. That wasn't agreed—"

"Agreed or not you gave me your word. You're bound now." The way he spoke resonated with past emotion. As if he'd learned that the hard way. A contract was a contract. And in this case, unbreakable.

"I promise I won't hurt you. Stop pissing me off by doubting me." His eyes narrowed, delving deep into mine as if he could expose every lie I'd ever spun. I'd shocked myself when I told the truth about my ear. I hadn't told anyone. But I had no choice. A man like Fox could smell a fib like a pheromone. He would've known.

Oh, God. That was another thing I'd suffer—not having the protectiveness of my lies. I couldn't mask my sadness through fakery; I wouldn't be able to gloss over the truth.

Sounds of flesh hitting flesh and grunts of violence rung in my ears from down below as a fight reached a pinnacle moment. The burst of noise stole me from the small world I'd existed in with Fox and reminded me he owned a place of fighting and encouraged blood to flow. If he loved to hurt others, how could I trust that he wouldn't hurt me?

Regret and worry swarmed in my skull like angry hornets. There was no way out of this deal and no way I wouldn't be stung.

Fox kept a careful eye on me and moved toward the wall to his right. He stepped elegantly through the shadows as if he was a shadow himself. Punching in a code on a keypad lock, he swung open a door I hadn't seen, camouflaged by the black décor. Inclining his chin, he said, "Now that's cleared up, shall we?"

The stairs were open and beckoning. I could run and forget tonight ever happened. But I'd never get an offer like this again. I'd always wonder just how alive he could make me—just how fierce he would make me become.

This was my only chance to help Clara—unless I wanted to rob a bank, or came up with some equally reckless notion.

Gritting my teeth, I stalked into his office with all the bearing I could muster. Fox didn't move and his body heat scorched all my reservations to ash. My skin tingled as a slow curl of attraction rose. My nipple throbbed remembering his touch.

It's been too long.

So long since I'd been touched and cherished. I shook my head. I was spinning lies—I'd *never* been cherished or adored. I'd been used and thrown away. I'd been shown the illusion of being desired for a very brief moment only to learn a valuable lesson: nothing was sacred, least of all my virginity.

Fox locked the door behind him and came toward me. I locked my knees together so I wasn't tempted to step away. That would be a weakness, and I wasn't weak. It also stopped me from doing something dangerous like demanding he touch me again.

He moved like a master—a man who knew how to fight and wasn't afraid of forcing another to do his bidding.

What would he say if I told him I was a mother? Would he despise that I pretended to be a sexual creature, but really was practically a virgin? One prick to take away the title of inexperienced, and one prick to land me with Clara. Hardly counted as life-altering.

I captured my bottom lip between my teeth. I finally let myself be truthful. I was hungry. Really hungry for something true. A connection; a sexual awakening. My body wanted Fox while my mind wanted to fight him on every subject. The combination threatened to create an addiction that not even money could break.

"You've gone whiter than normal." Fox leaned closer, nostrils flaring as if he could taste my panic. His eyes dropped to my throat. "Your heart is pumping wild, and your scent is stronger." With a tentative hand, he brushed away the loose curls resting over my shoulder. The whisper of his skin against mine had me battling lust-heavy eyes, fighting the overpowering need. "What's wrong?"

It didn't matter if I was inexperienced. Sex was primal, instinctual, animalistic. I felt like a world-class courtesan. A woman who'd seduced men and been seduced in turn.

Fox was every erotic fantasy I ever entertained. *And he's paying to fuck you.*

The thought should've turned me off, but it made me wetter.

Sucking in a breath, I whispered, "Nothing. Nothing's wrong."

Fox cocked his head, frowning. "Remember, I can smell lies."

I met his gaze—the icy grey made me feel as if I stood in a hurling snowstorm.

The more we stared, the more my body heated, the more I wanted. Until coming to this cursed club, I'd been satisfied. I didn't crave a man, or need a pleasurable release. I had too many things consuming me without the complication of romance. But the moment I set eyes on Fox, I knew he was different. He was a man I could lust after.

It wasn't his looks, or skill in the ring, that drew me. It wasn't his scar or element of ruthlessness.

It was everything.

Obsidian Fox was so much male it was terrifying. Not only handsome, he wore his flaws for the world to see and offered no apology.

Breaking eye contact, I glanced around his office. The only light came from small LED strips highlighting more metal sculptures and artwork. I'd joked about his office being a dungeon, but it was close to the truth. Black painted walls, carpet, furniture, even light fixtures.

All black.

A large graffiti artwork of a fox, hunting under the glint of the moon, graced one wall.

Peering closer, I noticed a nasty scar deforming one side of the fox's face, just like its owner. He seemed to love symbolism. Either that or he took himself way too seriously.

Fox inched nearer until the hairs on my arm stood up. Being so close made me yearn for his touch and fear it at the same time

I stifled a shiver as Fox stopped beside me, staring at the same graffiti. From this angle, his left profile was untouched. Smooth cheeks, smooth neck, angry desolate grey-white eyes. He held himself tight and alert. Primal, untamed, yet so disciplined and remote.

"Admiring Oscar's handiwork?"

Oscar. The blond idiot who spoke about me like I was hooker trash. I bristled, hating that the douchebag had talent. Every feather and sweep from whatever method he'd used spoke of a true artisan.

"It's good," I muttered. "Talented." I glanced at Fox. He looked wild as if he didn't belong in manmade rooms—they were cages, no matter how he decorated.

I wanted to ask why he had an obsession with black. His club name, his furniture, even his wardrobe. Did he believe he deserved no colour in his life?

Fox made a noncommittal noise, his attention turned inward. The back of my neck pricked as his body tensed.

I fell deeper into the trap of wanting to know him. "Why do you try and hide where you're from?"

His body locked down, eyes tightened. "Don't ask questions you won't like the answers to."

His reluctance only made me more intrigued. "You can't expect me not to ask questions in return for my secrets. I can tell you things I've sensed already. You never know…I might be as intuitive as you." My voice was soft.

Fox glanced at me, his fists curled. "You're confusing me with someone who gives a damn. I don't care what you think about me. You're mine to fuck, not to talk to and share my past." He moved quickly, bringing the heat of his body close to mine. "Believe me, *dobycha,* you would not like what I have to say."

I didn't believe him. He wanted more than just sex. Cursing my rapidly thudding heart, I whispered, "You think I'm stupid, but I'm not. For instance, I know you use it as a weapon. Your scar."

He scowled, facing me head on. His fingers twitched by his side.

"You were made to fight, that's probably why you started this club, but you haven't found peace yet. You're angry and bitter and torn up inside and if you think you can pour all of that into me, you're mistaken."

He smirked, but it looked odd on his scarred face—an inhuman sneer that didn't seem natural. "You think you're smart? I'll tell you something—you agreed to do the stupidest thing in your life when you accepted my offer. Not only do you think you can read me, but you're silly enough to get swept up in the romantic notion that I'll find redemption."

He seemed to grow larger, more intimidating. His scar

shone silver and weathered in the gloom. The air in the office thickened until it pressed heavy all around us, trapping me with a male who glared at me with hatred. "I don't use the scar as a weapon. I use it as a warning." His eyes flashed. "You may be able to hide your fuck-ups and mistakes, but I don't have that luxury. My scar is a talisman. I don't need to remember my sins—it's visible every time I look in a fucking mirror."

My stomach rolled as his energy buffeted me. His eyes locked onto mine, staring so hard I felt a twang deep inside when he plucked on my stupid heartstrings. "I'll learn your sins before the month is out. But you won't learn mine. And that's a promise."

Yet another promise you won't be able to keep.

My lips parted as I sucked in an apprehensive breath. Violence tainted the air, turning it dark and smoky. It reminded me of a forest fire after it had incinerated everything in its path.

I had no intention of being in Fox's path. His path to destruction.

I wanted to retort that he wouldn't know my sins, but I knew the truth. He would. Normally, that would terrify me—to have another know absolutely everything about me—but in Fox's case, even my worst sin probably wouldn't compare to his.

A small noise sounded in my throat as Fox splayed a large hand possessively on my lower back and jerked me closer. I shivered as my hips connected with his hard and fast. The hot steel in his trousers branded my belly only for a moment before he pushed me non-too-gently away.

Grabbing my wrist, he yanked me across the room. "We'll discuss the fine print at my desk."

I slammed on the brakes.

I had a good mind to scream and kick him. I hated the way he manhandled me. How he expected me to obey implicitly. He proved he had no concept of how to treat a woman at all.

Rules.

"We need rules. You need to know the dos and don'ts

around me, and I need to know them for you." My eyes narrowed. "Rule number one. I don't appreciate being corralled or forced to do something I don't want to. It never worked for anyone in the past, and it won't work for you."

His silvery eyes glinted with interest. "Sounds like we have more in common than I thought." Giving me a small nod, he let me go and rounded the desk to sit in the black chair behind. "Rule number one for me. Don't disrespect me. If you have something to say, be eloquent. I don't respond well to profanity or ridicule."

Crap, he was right. We did have things in common.

I fumbled for my next rule. "Rule number two. I'm not a belonging you just stole and have the right to treat like dirt. If you ever pull a knife on me again, you won't be a man anymore. You'll be a eunuch." My hand holding my blade reached up and re-secured the clip into place.

His lips twitched. Placing his palms on the desk, he leaned forward. "Rule number two for me. If I ask you to do something, you'll do it. Think of the next month's pay as a salary for being my employee. It doesn't matter that sex is in involved. I want more from you than just the pleasure of sinking between your legs." His voice roughened, eyes glowing with white hot lust.

My stomach flipped at the mental image of him taking me. Fucking me. Despite my best efforts to remain aloof, a tingle darted to my core, and I had the sudden urge to sit down. Clearing my throat, I sat in the only chair in front of his desk.

Tension curdled as Fox stayed frozen, watching my every move. I crossed my legs, pressing my thighs together against the throbbing desire permeating the room.

Announcing our rules had suddenly become more than just talk about business, it'd become layered with unspoken attraction and frightful uncertainty. I'd never had to fight my body's reaction before. I'd never come across a man who I wanted to strip to the bone and discover everything he kept hidden.

Not even Clara's father.

Not that it would be considered a love affair. He'd taken my virginity behind the toilet block in Hyde Park. It'd been messy, awkward, and a little painful. It wasn't rape, but it wasn't exactly consensual either. I'd been a stupid, reckless fifteen-year-old who thought she could tease and not pay the consequences.

Fox shattered my reminiscing. "Rule three for you?"

The stress in my body returned, mirroring the anxious strain in the room. Fox never took his eyes off me, effectively pinning me against the chair. I no longer focused on my surroundings. This man had the power to steal my every thought.

"Rule three," I began, my voice huskier than before, "umm, I expect you to treat me as more than just a sex toy. I need mental stimulation and would appreciate if you spoke to me kinder rather than like a giant gorilla who thinks he's top authority."

My mind raced between the threat of sex and the allure of money.

What sort of mother am I?

Fox's lips flickered into a quick smile before he smoothed his features.

He tilted his head in vague agreement. "Rule three for me, I'll give you the mental stimulation you need, but in return I expect everything. I ask a question—you give me the truth. I ask you to do something—you do it."

Snapping his fingers like I'd seen him do on the fighting floor, his voice darkened. "While you're in my house under my protection, you'll forget about the outside world. Your friends, your family, your entire life no longer exists. Just me."

My heart bucked as true fear rushed back and doubt crept in. I'd learned how to sneak and stay hidden from my childhood—I just hoped I could use those skills to disappear at night to see Clara. Fox would never have to know, and I could hug and kiss my daughter while making sure she stayed happy and well.

I nursed my own deception even as I accepted his rules.

"Do I need a medic to run a sexual health test on you? Are you on the pill?"

I should've been prepared for that question. Of course, he wouldn't want to wear condoms for a month. But I hadn't rehearsed my answer.

Old pain rose as memories tried to cloud me.

Fox sat forward. His eyes narrowed, sensing my reluctance.

I dropped my gaze. My fingers swooped up to fiddle with the matching star necklace Clara and I wore. The familiarity of the silver helped calm me.

I'd been eighteen. A struggling mother with a bratty two-year-old, working all hours of the day to support us. I'd been so wrapped up in my worries, I hadn't heard the footsteps behind me.

"Give us your money, bitch."

One moment I stood on two feet, the next I kissed asphalt.

Four pairs of legs surrounded me, all male, all young, and full of something to prove.

Without a word, I fumbled for my bag and gave the thirty dollars and twenty-five cents that I had in cash.

"That's it? Where's the rest of it?"

What followed hurt too much to relive. I'd been lucky, I supposed. I wasn't raped, but there were only so many kicks to the stomach that a young body could sustain until infertility occurred.

I'd spent a week in hospital while my precious toddler had been looked after by an elderly woman who lived above us.

"Tell me. What are you thinking?" Fox growled.

A chill eased through my blood, helping me remain cool and unfeeling. "I'm clear from diseases, and you don't need to worry about contraception." My voice hardened. "I'm not going to sleep with you until I know your history, too. As part of my rules, I need to know you're clean."

His shoulders tightened and jaw ticked, but he nodded

slowly. "I'm clean. You have nothing to fear from me." Darkness shadowed his eyes for just a moment followed by a flippant hand gesture. "I'm taking sleeping with bastards for cash is a new thing for you?"

My mouth hung open. "There you go again. I thought we'd made progress—that'd I'd judged you too harshly, but nope. You're still an asshole." Swiping a hand through my tangled hair, I snapped, "I've already told you I'm not a whore, and I'm not answering anything that's disrespectful. I promised I wouldn't disrespect you, so don't do it to me."

His body rippled with energy, everything about him poised to attack. Slowly, he rolled his shoulders, dismissing the build-up as quickly as it'd come. "You're right. At least we have the formalities out of the way."

My legs itched to stand up and walk out the door. Everything about this agreement was wrong. But the bribery of two hundred thousand kept me glued to the chair like a puppet, and his mystery kept me from hating him completely.

And your desire for him makes you wet.

I shifted, feeling cheap.

He ran a forefinger over his bottom lip. The lighting in the room didn't illuminate much, leaving me with the sensation of being cut off from everything. Alone in a private world with this scarred stranger.

"I'll have Oscar arrange the first payment and send it to wherever you want, but if you leave without my permission you will owe me every cent." The leather of the chair creaked as he sat higher. "Don't expect a generous lover in me. I plan to take everything you have to give." His voice came out low, husky, almost inaudible.

Nerves fluttered in my stomach. His eyes captured mine. "That's hardly fair."

He spanned his hands. "That's the deal. I'm buying you for *my* pleasure. Don't forget that."

"How can I forget?" I muttered.

Fox sniffed at my flippant remark.

I said, "You won't let me leave for a month, but you'll let me use the phone. I need to call someone."

His forehead furrowed. "One phone call."

"One?"

I can't believe this. It's like being in jail.

"From now on, you have to ask permission to do anything. You've handed over your rights to me." Fox smiled grimly. "Welcome to my world, *dobycha*."

Goosebumps spread at the foreign word.

Sighing, I thought about what I'd agreed to. For someone who'd never had to answer to anyone her entire life, it would take a lot of getting used to.

"And the other fine print?" I asked.

He stood and came around the desk to face me, trespassing on my personal bubble. "You let me do what I want to you."

I held up my hand, ready to cut him off, but he snapped, "Let me finish."

"I have free reign over your body. You let me treat you like a possession, and I promise I won't hurt you."

Questions flew wild in my head. He was asking me to give up my freedom, to bow to him, to relinquish all thoughts of belonging to myself, and obey his every whim.

Two hundred thousand suddenly wasn't enough.

The word 'no' danced on my tongue. He might intrigue me, seduce me, and offer a chance at saving my daughter, but a month was a very long time.

In a lightning move, Fox grabbed my arm and hauled me upright. I teetered on my stupid heels, cursing the pinching pain of blisters. My eyes came to his mouth, and I gulped as he licked his lips.

"Your first order is to put your hands behind your back." His breath tickled my eyelashes, smelling faintly of chocolate and mint.

I frowned.

"Do it," Fox demanded.

Slowly, I brought my arms behind my back and linked my

fingers. The moment I'd locked them against the small of my back, he hooked his finger into the dip in my dress and dragged me forward. My chest collided with his—my breasts against his hard muscle. My stomach rose and fell, brushing against his chiselled one.

"Don't unlock your fingers." His voice acted like fuel to the fire already licking my core. I shivered as his fingers trailed from my hips up to my waist. The pads of his thumbs tickled the sides of my breasts as he worked his way upward.

Slowly. So, slowly. Softly. So, softly.

My vision darkened; I went lightheaded all thanks to the heat he invoked inside me—turning my craving into a lunatic obsession.

I needed his touch. I needed to be petted and pampered and adored. I'd never been a sexual creature, but now I understood why people hungered for it. Why the thought of being taken and worshiped had such maddening appeal.

Shamelessly, I felt wetness building between my legs.

Fox bowed his head, his eyes never leaving mine. Green to grey, vivid to colourless. My lips parted on their own accord; my breath grew shallow as my legs shook.

Inch by inch he came closer, bringing with him the scent of smoke and metal.

I tensed for a fast kiss. A hard kiss. But Fox held himself still, hovering over my mouth only a fraction away from touching. My lips tingled and ached; my tongue wanted to dart out and lick him.

If he was using my body against me, it was working.

A small noise sounded in his chest, and I looked harder into his eyes. Instead of raw passion there, I saw utter confusion. My heart stuttered and once again my protective instincts rose. He shouldn't be confused. I would kiss him in that moment even if I had to do it for free.

I'd never know who crossed the last millimetre of distance, but I moaned the instant his lips touched mine. Our eyes snapped shut, and nothing else existed but taste.

I kept expecting him to break. To drag me closer and plunge his tongue into my mouth, but he did the opposite. With perfect pressure, he coaxed my lips apart and the very tip of his tongue entered my mouth. His taste intoxicated me, and I strained forward, rubbing my breasts against him.

He stiffened, but didn't stop kissing me, keeping up the maddening softness, exploring deeper with a gentle tongue. My head swam as I forgot to breathe; my fingers loosened until my hands fell to my sides. All I could think about was touching him, dragging him closer, forcing him to be rough, to end his infuriatingly slow assault.

Something switched in him and his lips pressed harder. Confidence filled his touch and he dragged me closer, hips thrusting just enough for me to feel the hard heat in his slacks. I tipped my head, allowing him better access, wanting him to kiss me deeper.

But he didn't take advantage.

Slow and soft and coaxing.

It was the best kiss I'd ever received, but also the worst. It sparked lust and need in every inch of me. My lips wanted more, my tongue wanted savagery. My skin wanted to bruise because he needed to touch me so badly.

All my thoughts disappeared as I nipped at his bottom lip. He flinched, but a second later he copied, his sharp canines piercing my oversensitive flesh.

I moaned.

I couldn't take it.

My hands flew up and gripped his shirt. Yanking him toward me, fireworks whizzed in my fingertips; my heart galloped toward exploding with lust. I'd never been so drunk on someone before.

Then I landed flat on my back.

The crack of my skull jangled my teeth. The thick carpet did little to cushion me. My eyes flared wide and I grunted in pain. Fear, hot and terrible, swamped my lust in a dampening wave.

"Top rule. *Unbreakable* rule. Don't. *Ever.* Touch. Me." Fox kneeled on one knee beside my head, breathing hard. His hand noosed my throat, pressing my spine into the carpet. His eyes were cold and lifeless, looking like a hunter intent on blood.

I gasped, struggling to breathe. I couldn't unfog my brain.

"Never touch me." His hands tightened, crushing my windpipe.

He's going to kill me.

Hot terror erupted and I scratched at his grip. Scratching, prying, trying to unlock his incredibly strong fingers. Clara flashed in my mind, bringing hot tears to my eyes.

He bent further, squeezing harder. "What did I just say?"

I thrashed, needing air. My eyes felt too big for my sockets; my ears roared with blood. *I need to breathe!*

My thoughts were scrambled, but one thought trumpeted: *Don't touch him.*

Stop touching him!

It took all my strength to obey. Every instinct boycotted when I forced myself to let go—to allow him to willingly strangle me.

Dropping my hands to my sides, I locked my elbows, keeping them dead straight. I shuddered uncontrollably, battling the instinct to fight back.

Only once I'd gone completely still, with no threat of touching him, did he unlock his fingers and stand. The instant he let me go, I rolled onto my side and hacked and choked, dragging oxygen into greedy lungs.

He stood staring, his face black and terrifying.

I thought I knew what I agreed to, but I hadn't. I hadn't factored in his volatile mental state. He was more than just an asshole. He was unhinged—deranged—and every agreement we'd made seemed incredibly idiotic.

He groaned under his breath, sounding like a wounded animal before dragging hands over his face. He paced away, stalking from one end of the room to the other.

By the fifth or six lungful of air, I sat up. But I was too afraid to stand. I liked being down here, away from his murdering fingers.

Fox prowled, muttering under his breath. His eyes flashed from deadly to contrite to weary. Stopping behind his desk, he snarled, "I didn't mean to do that." His fists opened and closed with unspent energy. "You provoked me. At least now you know what happens. Don't disobey me. Next time, I might not have the strength to stop."

His mouth tightened into a grimace. Anger rolled off him, buffeting me across the small distance between us. My heart raced, and I couldn't look away. He entrapped me with his stare, wreaking havoc on my emotions.

I flushed, dropping my gaze. "I'm sorry," I whispered. Nervously I climbed to my feet, kicking off the stupid heels to stand barefoot on the silky strands of the carpet. Better to run. Better to flee. "I didn't mean to disobey."

I wanted to curse him for hurting me rather than apologise, but his remorse was real. It echoed in the room, vibrating in his muscles. He watched me warily as if I'd run at any moment. It was his fault for kissing me so sweetly, so gently. For a man who wore violence as his true identity, my mind couldn't come to terms with how softly he'd kissed me.

Running a shaky finger over my bottom lip, I tried to forget. Tried to ignore the awkwardness, the strange determination, and sweet eagerness that'd been on his tongue. If I didn't know any better, I'd say that it'd been his first kiss.

Testing, learning, figuring out how to do it.

My eyes widened, staring at Fox. The concept of him never kissing anyone seemed completely absurd. This male didn't kiss. He plundered and took.

So why did I kiss a completely different man than the one standing in front of me?

Once again my heart popped with little bubbles of despair. The tenderness of a motherly instinct rose quickly. I wanted to tear through his inner turmoil and give him a person to confess to, lend an ear and nod in concern—to share his burden.

Because he was burdened. Heavily.

His gruffness and scar didn't scare me. He spun a lie and the stench of untruths never worked on me.

Flashes of emotion appeared in his eyes.

My heart raced, bashing against my ribs. Taking a careful step forward, ignoring the bruising around my neck, I asked, "Are you alright?"

His eyes popped wide and he laughed. "You're asking if *I'm* alright? Shouldn't I be asking you that?"

I shrugged. "We all have triggers. I believe you when you said you didn't mean to hurt me."

He froze, staring as if I confused the hell out of him. "If we all have triggers, you must have one. What's yours?" His voice stayed deceptively quiet.

I wasn't being baited into revealing more of my secrets before I was ready. Shaking my head, I said, "That doesn't matter. What matters is I promise I won't touch you again. I can see it's an issue for you. I've learned my lesson."

And I'll figure out the reason behind it.

Fox gritted his teeth. For a second, I wondered if he'd order me to leave—that he no longer wanted to buy me.

Finally, he nodded. "In that case, let's proceed."

Six

ROAN

There were certain things in life that made sense and others that made no sense at all. Most of my life didn't make sense—I had no freedom, no right to my future. I obeyed orders: slept when I was told to sleep, ate when I was told to eat, and killed when I was told to kill.

But my ruthless conditioning, the coldness that imprisoned my life, had cracked and splinted and begun to thaw.

And it was all because of one person.

One person who didn't fear me. One person who pushed me beyond my boundaries and helped me find a way to wellness.

One person who could make it better.

I knew it was only a matter of time before I ruined it. But I wasn't strong enough to stop it.

Tonight, I did the one thing that made the least sense of all.

I bought a girl.

And I would never let her go.

I couldn't meet her eyes.

I couldn't look at the red marks on her neck without being crippled by guilt. There was no correct etiquette of what to do after throwing someone to the ground and strangling them mid-kiss.

My first fucking kiss and I fucked it up.

You should've done what you were ordered. I should've believed them when they said there would be no going back.

There were no guidelines, or manuals on how to break what had been drilled into me for twenty-two years. They created a machine and everything of who I'd been had ceased to exist. That kiss just proved it.

I've bought a woman, and I'll probably kill her before I've even noticed.

My heart squeezed at the thought. I didn't know her, but already she'd given me something incredible. She'd kissed me with nothing barred; she'd poured every need and dream into her tongue and licked me with passion. Her body pressed against mine, her heat sent my cock rippling with the first pre-cum I'd enjoyed in my life. Everything overwhelmed me and I over thought the kiss, trying to understand how to tilt my head, how hard I could go without clashing teeth. It'd been consuming, amazing.

My hands curled with hatred for myself. I'd expected too much—I thought she'd offered me a miracle.

I let my guard down and broke my feeble control. One touch. One simple touch to send me hurtling back to who I'd been and using second nature against me.

Zel rubbed her neck, nonchalantly bringing her thick hair to cover her shoulders, hiding the majority of the bruising. "It's okay, you know. I accept your apology. You don't have to look as if someone will come and beat you."

How did she guess?

I snarled, pacing away. "You don't know anything. Stop trying to figure me out."

I hated that I was supposed to be in control but every time

Zel stole it off me. Either with her temper, her understanding, or her strength. I was one step behind and fumbling like a fucking buffoon.

I wanted to scream at her to let me inside—to give me power over her, but at the same time I needed her to remain strong. I needed her courage if she had any chance of surviving me.

Deciding to focus on the kiss rather than the aftermath, I stopped pacing and faced her. "What did you feel kissing me? I want to know."

Her cheeks flared. "I don't need to tell you. You know."

"What do I know?" I knew her taste still lived in my mouth. I knew my cock hurt with how much I wanted to plunge inside her, but I had no fucking clue what she thought. I wanted to know she was as affected by whatever existed between us as me.

Because if she doesn't it'll prove that you're fucking unlovable.

The thought came from nowhere, and I sucked in a gasp. Fuck me, was this what rehabilitation felt like? Ripping myself apart, tearing away the pieces I wanted to be free from, flushing remnants of addiction from my veins. There was no doubt I was in withdrawal—not from substances, but from a conditioning that owned me body and mind.

Hazel murmured, "When you kissed me I felt everything. I loved the slipperiness of your tongue. The heat of your body. I could feel—" She paused before carrying on, "I could feel your cock against my belly, and it made me want you. The kiss whispered of promises, and my body melted for you. Does that answer your question?"

Goddammit, it made me rock hard and drooling.

Zel was so different than the last woman. She was a comet, blazing through my dead world.

I'd screwed a total of one woman. She'd been like me: a belonging. We sneaked out of the establishment one night and indulged in what we'd seen people do on television. It hadn't been great, more like a life experience I needed to get over with, but it'd given me a brief taste of connection. We hadn't kissed. We hadn't hugged—touching apart from the essentials was out of the question.

Afterward, we went back to our cells and never mentioned it again.

Two weeks later, we all graduated, and she left for her assignments and I left for mine. The rest of my life had a large stain over it, and I didn't like to go swimming in memories.

Why did you buy her? You know it's not going to end well.

I didn't fucking know. It'd been spur of the moment, an urge I couldn't disobey. I *had* to keep her. I had to know if she could cure me. I couldn't describe the insane idiocy of dragging her upstairs. The connection made no sense. I'd never been interested in anyone the way I had locked onto her. It wasn't logical for a man of my past to even care about another human, let alone suffer lunacy at the thought of letting them go.

The kiss had been too distracting. Dropping the tight grip on my control, I focused on her heat and texture. I memorized every nip and sweep of her tongue. I didn't notice she'd unlocked her hands.

Big mistake. Huge fucking mistake.

It couldn't happen again.

Scowling, I settled stiffly into my chair, thankful for the large expanse of wood between us.

She moved to the chair opposite and sat down. My eyes narrowed on the shadows on her neck. As much as I thirsted for the connection, as much as I wanted her to touch me and find solace from a lifetime of pain, I couldn't.

The closest I could come was using her callously. Never letting her get too close, never sharing any of my thoughts or past.

It was best she knew nothing about me.

I told her not to touch me. It's not my fault I hurt her.

That was bullshit.

It seemed other precautions would have to be taken to make sure she didn't disobey again and make me kill her.

Her eyes met mine and my heart lurched. *Run. Leave me. No amount of money is worth staying with a monster like me.*

Needing to dispel the wariness between us, I muttered, "I'm sorry."

Zel nodded, wincing a little from her sore neck. "I know. You don't have to mention it again. Call it a learning curve." Her eyes held forgiveness along with fierce determination.

I snorted. She thought she could fix me, and I wanted her to. Too bad it would never have a happy ending.

Sighing, I grabbed a piece of paper and my favourite fountain pen. Bowing my head, I scribbled:

Contract between Obsidian Fox and Hazel Hunter.

The vague agreement wouldn't stand up in a court of law. I only bothered so I had something to hold over her if she suddenly tried to leave. I might want her to leave for her own safety, but I was a selfish man and would use her for as long as I could.

Hazel agrees to obey Fox implicitly for the agreed amount of time of one month. In that time she will go where he wishes, do what he wants, and offer no argument or disrespect. In that time, Fox agrees to treat Hazel with respect and won't make lavish demands. Hazel agrees to be available to Fox at any time, night or day for his needs, and will obey any order that's given. Fox agrees to keep her safe, not cause any pain—

Stopping, I scratched out the last line. I'd already caused her pain by body-slamming her to the ground.

Fucking idiot. Fucking machine.

My handlers had ruined me for life. The automatic maiming from being touched had been so ingrained, it would never leave. I was a moron to think it ever would.

The heaviness in my soul grew as I accepted the inevitable: I would never be free.

I'd been able to break other commands, but touching had a

special hold on me. After all, they'd gone to a lot of trouble to make it my first instinct.

The cane came from nowhere, walloping me around the back of my knees. My hands flexed around the knife as I faced the target of bundled hay dressed in kid's clothing of dungarees and green t-shirt.

"Stab it, Operative Fox."

They struck me again, and this time it was instant. The moment pain radiated in my joints, I stabbed the dummy with all my strength.

Again and again they hit me until the hay and clothing were a shredded mess at my feet. Sweat ran under my thick winter jacket even as snow flurried around us from the icy Russian winter.

Pain equalled pain. To be inflicted meant to inflict. Touch meant to kill. Simple.

It was freeing to obey such a basic code.

I shook my head, frowning at the piece of paper. Damn fucking flashbacks. They came more often when I was stressed.

Returning to the paper, I finished writing:

Fox agrees to pay Hazel one hundred thousand up front, and another one hundred thousand dollars at the end of one month. If Hazel leaves without Fox's permission before the time is up, the contract is null and void and no money shall be exchanged.

Scrawling my illegible autograph, I looked up.

Zel hadn't moved, her eyes focused on my scar. Interest and pity etched her face.

I growled, "Another rule I forgot to mention. Don't you dare pity me. I don't want your pity. I don't deserve your pity. Understand?"

She flinched, but didn't look away. "It's not pity. It's curiosity." Her hand flew up to spin a delicate chain around her throat. I'd noticed it before. A single star.

The way she touched the silver in reverence hinted that it held a tender history. It meant a lot to her.

It made me jealous.

"I'm just trying to understand you. That's all." Her voice

was firm and not in the least bit scared of my minor episode of throwing her to the floor. She was so damn strong. Idiotic hope sparked once again. Was she strong enough to withstand me?

My lips tingled, remembering her taste. Remembering the brutal need in her—the summoning from her body to mine.

My heartbeats changed from low and measured—how I always was when I slipped into conditioning—to fast and hard with need.

I wanted her.

Shifting, I rearranged my fucking hard-on. Her lips curled just a little, almost as if she knew what caused my discomfort.

It was her. All her. Damn woman.

"Sign this." Shoving the paper across the desk, I motioned for her to come forward.

In bare feet, she stood and padded closer. Perching on the edge of the desk, the gold and silver dress hitched up, showing a split to mid-thigh.

Goddammit.

My stomach twisted as my cock lurched, growing hotter and thicker until I was sure it would self-combust.

With slightly shaking fingers, Zel took the piece of paper and read it. Her eyes narrowed and she nibbled on her bottom lip. I expected an argument, but she only nodded and looked up. "I need your pen."

Silently, I passed her the fountain pen and held my breath as she signed with a pretty flourish. I felt like a full-blown asshole. I'd made her submit for money. What sort of bastard did that? It couldn't be helped that she really had no concept of survival. Selling herself to a stranger for a month? What woman did *that*? We were both as bad as each other.

The thought had a strange appeal.

Keeping my face completely neutral, I took the signed contract from her, keeping my fingers well away from hers, and placed it into the top drawer and locked it.

A smidgen of relief filled me. She was mine for exactly thirty days. It was time we got acquainted.

Her eyes swept upward, connecting with mine only briefly before dropping to the scar. Her pouty lips thinned while thoughts swirled in her green eyes.

The scar had been a punishment—a reminder of just how deep I'd fallen. It'd been retribution for not obeying.

I couldn't even think about that night without breaking into a cold sweat.

"I'll show you where you'll be sleeping." Checking the time on my phone, I added, "What time do you normally go to bed?"

She paused, surprise written on her face. "Same as everybody else I guess. About midnight, get up at about six or whenever Cla—"

She snapped her lips together, avoiding my eyes.

"Don't do that—cut yourself off mid-sentence. Whatever you were going to say, I want to know." I hated her keeping things from me. Even though I had full intention of keeping everything from her.

She pulled her shoulders back, fighting me with her gaze. "I was going to say when Clue gets up for work. She has a range of jobs, and some days she's up very early."

The lie rained from her lips like the truth, but I knew different. The decibels of her voice were odd.

Shaking my head softly, I whispered, "I know you just lied, but after what I did, I won't push it. But next time…it better be the truth."

She held her ground even as a flash of apprehension filled her gaze.

I cocked my head, drinking her in. "Where are you from originally?" I guessed Europe—Spain perhaps. I'd become quite an expert on guessing nationalities. Another hazard of my previous employment.

She shrugged, eyeing me warily. "I don't need to lie about that. I only knew my father. Or at least, I think he was my father. He looked after me until he just disappeared one day. I think I was five when he left. I vaguely remember him speaking another language, so it's entirely possible I'm from overseas and not Australian originally."

I didn't have a retort to that. Seemed we had yet another thing in common. Missing lineage. Missing pieces from our past.

She glanced at the phone in my hands.

"I want that phone call. I need to arrange something."

Shit, I'd forgotten about that. I didn't want her talking to anyone—spilling the details of what we'd agreed to. It wouldn't paint either of us in a good light.

Reluctantly, I dropped the phone into her waiting palm. "I'm not giving you privacy, so don't bother asking."

She huffed, but didn't argue. Pressing a sequence of numbers, she paced toward the graffiti artwork, chewing her bottom lip.

"Come on. Please, pick up," she whispered.

It seemed an age before she slouched and sighed heavily. "I thought you weren't there. Did you get home alright?"

The concern in her voice sent a sharp bolt of jealousy through me. I didn't like that she cared so deeply for another. Someone had the privilege of living with her, learning her secrets.

"No, it's fine. I've got it under control." Zel frowned, listening to whoever existed on the other end of the phone. "No. I'm good. Listen, I have to do something you're not going to understand, but don't freak out, okay?"

She nodded, twirling a piece of hair around her pinkie. "I know. I feel awful to do this to you and…well you know, but I won't be home for a while."

She threw a glance my way. My hackles rose, unable to determine why I suddenly felt on edge.

"I'll be away for a month," she finally said.

I gritted my teeth. She hadn't lied, but she hadn't been entirely truthful either. I narrowed my eyes. If she thought she could leave, she had a surprise coming. She didn't know what I had in store for her. It wouldn't be simple matter of walking out the front door.

A screech came from the phone and I wished I knew what the other person said.

"I have my reasons. It'll mean a lot to us financially if I stay. Don't get upset. I'll explain it better soon." Her eyes dashed to mine again before she cupped the mouth piece. "Clue, don't. I can't tell you. Not yet."

My body clenched. She refused to speak honestly in front of me. How could I trust her with anything she might say in the future?

"No. Don't put her on!" Zel whisper-yelled, then her shoulders rolled and she went to the corner of the room, trying to get as far away from me as possible. "Hey, sweetheart."

Sweetheart? Fuck, did she have a lover? What the hell?

"No, I'm okay. Do you think you can be good? Take care of Clue for me?" Her naked shoulder blades hunched as she curled around the phone, almost embracing it. "I miss you, too. But I'll be home before you know it. Just be safe and don't get too tired, okay?"

She nodded a few times before whispering so low I almost missed it, "I love you so much. It's going to be agony not holding you."

My heart exploded inside my chest. Fuck. *What did you expect? That she wouldn't have anyone at home?* Not only was she selling herself to me, she was cheating on someone who undoubtedly loved her.

My hands curled and the rage I'd tried so hard to keep away came back with a vengeance.

She sniffed and hung up. She stayed facing the wall for a moment, before spinning around and stalking toward me. Holding out the phone, her eyes mixed with regret and sadness. Doubt flickered in her gaze before she swallowed, forcing residual emotion from the phone call away.

If I was less of a bastard I could've just given her the money and sent her home to whoever she loved. But I wasn't. So I didn't.

The thought of her arms around someone else made my stomach roll in anger. "I hope you're not planning on breaking our agreement so soon. It won't be that easy to revoke your signature." My eyes flickered to my desk, already using the contract to bind her to me.

"I'm not backing out." Her jaw tilted upward defiantly. "But I'm not going to be held hostage either." Zel shed her tenacious resolve and something heated entered her eyes. "Besides, despite a learning curve of you throwing me to the ground, I enjoyed kissing you. I can think of worse things to do for two hundred thousand dollars."

My heart thudded, stuttered, then hung confused in my chest. I didn't know if I should be insulted or grateful. She'd forgiven me entirely for hurting her while putting me in my place once again.

Damn this fucking woman. Who the hell *was* she?

You just made the worst decision of your life.. There was no way a month would be long enough. She could turn out to be a conniving manipulator, and my cock would still beg for her.

I snapped my fingers and strode toward the door on the other side of the room. "Come on."

She didn't ask any questions, only padded barefoot toward me, leaving her shoes on the floor. Her body came within a hair of brushing past mine, and I tensed every muscle I possessed, just in case.

Slinking past, she caught my eye. My balls tightened as I sucked in her scent of Lily of the valley. Every part of me throbbed—it was painful in a way, and so fucking sweet knowing I was minutes away from taking her.

I couldn't stop the weird palpitations in my chest or the twisting of my gut.

While I was struck dumb, trying to keep a hold on my desire, Hazel headed down the corridor the wrong way.

"This way," I ordered. "You'll get used to all the doors." The house had been built like the establishment I'd been trained in. For some fucked-up reason, even though the place ruined my life, it was the only place I felt truly safe.

We headed down one long corridor with multiple rooms veering from it. No open spaces, apart from the fighting arena downstairs. Each room was private, self-contained, a cell for all intents and purposes.

We didn't say a word as we walked over the thick black carpet toward the south end of the house.

The corridor led to my private wing. Only Oscar and the occasional cleaner were allowed up here. Pin-pad locks rested on every door, adding more to the prison-like appeal. Shit, Zel would have to learn the combinations to move anywhere in the house.

The repercussions of sharing my life with her finally decided to make themselves known. I hadn't thought through how my sleeping patterns and habits would affect her. How my needs for certain types of release would freak her the fuck out.

Goddammit, this is a bad idea. Such a bad idea.

My room had a door I'd specially designed. Made out of composite metal, reinforced with rebar, and titanium hinges, it was practically bombproof. It offered some peace of mind that I'd hear them coming if they ever decided my vacation was over and came back for me.

Hazel stood beside me looking perfect, despite her crushed hair, smeared lipstick, and the shadows of bruising on her neck. Her perfection ridiculed me, highlighting once again that I'd never be good enough. That I'd always be who I was.

"Am I sleeping in your room or do I get my own space?" Zel's melodic voice stayed hushed as if afraid of startling me.

I scowled. "You'll sleep with me." Stupid question. "I just made a deal with you to use as I see fit, and you think you'll have your own space?" I didn't admit that it would be best if she did. I made promises I couldn't keep. I knew I'd end up hurting her. "This isn't a vacation, *dobycha*, more like a sentence."

Her forehead furrowed slightly. "Let's just get something straight. I'm here willingly. I signed your stupid piece of paper;

I agreed to let you take me however you want, within reason. You don't have to keep dropping hints about sentences and making it sound like I'll regret this."

Her hand came up to land on my chest but I lurched backward. She shook her head. "Sorry. I forgot. I was going to say, if you fuck me like you kissed me, I won't regret spending the month in your bed. What I will regret is killing you if you break your promise that I'm safe."

I laughed coldly. "You think *you* can kill *me*?" The absurdity of such a notion. Not even a highly-trained swat team could dispatch me—I knew—they'd tried once or twice.

Zel leaned forward, bringing a cloud of floral air. "You're forgetting that by sharing a bed with me, I'll have full access to you while you sleep." Her voice dropped to a husky whisper, "Sleeping with someone is a huge admittance of trust. If I wanted to hurt you I'm the only one close enough when you're at your weakest to do so."

Shit. Shit. Shit.

How did she know I'd avoided sleeping with another because of that same fear?

I wanted to wring her neck for her implied threat all while contemplating how to avoid such an inevitability. Lowering my head, I growled, "Thank you for pointing out yet another hole in this arrangement. I'll make sure to rectify it."

Her eyes popped wide.

Focusing on the keypad lock, I stabbed the combination. "The code is 11453. You'll need to remember that if I send you back here without me."

She nodded. Her heart-shaped face and flawless complexion glowed beneath the corridor lights. Her lips moved silently, committing the code to memory.

Swinging the door wide, I let her enter first.

Automatic sensors switched on, spilling illumination from two bedside lamps and subtle lighting around artwork and sculptures. Just like my office, the entire space was black. Again, not a matter of choice, but necessity. Drilled into me by a past I couldn't shake. It was ironic that I hated the dark, yet surrounded myself in it.

Zel gravitated toward a sculpture. Reaching out to touch it, I held my breath as her inquisitive fingertips caressed the brutalized metal. I'd finished it only a few days ago. It wasn't anything special. Just a hunk of metal that I'd welded and twisted and deformed.

Along with the iron, bronze, and silver, it also held my blood and sweat.

I fed my designs with everything that I was—including the stuff flowing in my veins. In a way, it made me immortal—morphing me into pieces of metal—hopefully finding peace by hardening my heart just like the statues.

"You mentioned Oscar did the fox mural. Who did the sculptures?" Zel twisted to look at me, her eyes green diamonds in the gloom. "Whoever did these has a heart-breaking story to tell. They're full of pain." Her voice dropped to a murmur. "Did you do them?"

My spine tickled with equal parts gratefulness and utter rage. Grateful because I'd finally found someone who saw past who I portrayed, and rage because she made me frustrated and weak— showing just how fucking messed up I was.

"If you can see all that; do you really need an answer?" I snapped, stalking toward the bed.

Zel followed me with her eyes, stroking the twisted piece. "No. I don't need an answer." She removed her fingers, looking at the hunk of metal wistfully. "It tells me more about you than you ever will. It redeems you in a way, enough that I can overlook your surly assholeness."

I ignored that.

Watching her carefully, I kept my muscles on a tight leash, just in case she triggered another relapse. Drifting from one statue to another, she kept surprising me by only showing interest in the deformed pieces. Humans were taught to run from imperfection. She should've been interested in the perfectly designed and flawlessly executed wolf sitting on the sideboard, but she wasn't. She couldn't care less, and I didn't know what to make of that.

She turned to face me, taking in the room as she did so. She didn't look like she wanted to run or try to fix me. She accepted the scar as if it hadn't damaged me, as if it just…was.

Acceptance.

Something wrenched painfully in my chest, dragging foreign emotions from depths I didn't understand.

I was right about her. She was magical—casting a spell over me, entwining me deeper into her web.

I suddenly had an overwhelming urge for pain. I needed it. I thirsted for it. Only pain would help me see clearly again.

Giving me a small smile, she moved silently toward the bed. Black sheets, black covers. Everything black. I wasn't comfortable in any other colour. I deserved no other colour. Black was the colour of evil, of death. Black was me.

The room was large. A seating area existed to the right, a bathroom to the left, and a huge bed on a raised platform in the centre. The bed looked like it'd come straight from a haunted forest. Wrought iron and bronze had been hammered into the illusion of branches and twigs, cocooning the bed in eager ghostlike trees.

The instant Zel sat on the mattress and looked across the room, I knew I'd made a big fucking mistake.

I couldn't sleep next to this woman. I would kill her.

I couldn't let her touch me. I would maim her.

I was a fucking idiot to think otherwise.

It wasn't a matter of if or how or maybe. It was as certain as the motto engraved on my doorstep. As rigid and unyielding as the conditioning I drowned in.

Thou shall steal life because that is thine only purpose.

My only purpose. The only reason why I was still alive.

Curling my hands, I backed toward the exit. "Stay there. Don't leave the room."

Zel sat up, her mouth opened in question, but I didn't wait. Striding out the door, I left, locking her inside.

My haven was a bunker buried amongst the foundations of the house. Here I could relax—as much as I could—and generally pretend the rest of the world and my problems didn't exist.

I breathed deeply as I unlocked the door and entered the familiar space. Smells of metal shavings, tools, and the stench of grease and paraffin welcomed me back. It was basic, rudimentary, but it fit me better than any of the grandeur upstairs.

I wasn't carved from money and gold. I was carved from ice and stone. I'd slept in a pit more nights than I slept in a bed all because I'd been chosen.

They say chosen. I say stolen.

Having a place like this underground with its unfinished walls and low ceilings gave me a respite—gave me a den.

Shoving aside a half-finished statue of a decapitated woman, I tried to remove Hazel from my mind.

Her dark hair, her knowing green eyes, her air of courage. I couldn't stop thinking about her—moving around my space, touching more statues, figuring out more of my history that I wanted to keep buried.

She might leave. You've left her all alone.

I didn't trust the locks would keep her in if she truly wanted to go. The steel inside her matched the steel inside me, and the knowledge I couldn't force her to stay fucked with my head.

My vision faded a little on the peripheral, warning me tiredness and stress were starting to take their toll.

Shit, what was I doing? I should be up there taking what I'd paid for. I should be plunging deep inside her and searching for some resemblance of happiness. I shouldn't have run like a fucking pussy.

I picked up hammer, squeezing the wooden handle in my fist.

Do it. It will help.

The enabling voice inside coaxed—like it did every time—promising sweet relief.

Splaying my hand on the bench, fingers flat against the well-used surface, I stared at it for the first time in a while. Crisscrossed with tiny scars, punctured with small holes of silver, my hand looked ancient and brutal. The urge to slam the hammer onto one of my knuckles consumed me until I shook with need for pain and a droplet of sweat rolled down my temple.

Breaking the spell, I slowly lowered the hammer and turned my hand over to look at my palm.

The moment I found freedom two years ago, I spent days with a scouring brush and abrasive soap washing off the mark.

Washing, sandpapering, scrubbing to remove the three small symbols of what I was. Only a fellow operative would know what they meant; would know I was a creature whose only purpose was to fight and destroy.

Faded now to a few indistinct lines, they filled me with bone-deep hatred and fear. Both palms held the mark: the Roman numeral III.

My body tensed, wishing Mount Everest had done a better job of hitting me tonight. It meant I'd have to service that need before fucking Hazel.

The reminder of why I was down here pulled me from my thoughts, and I surveyed the shelves and barrels full of metal to use.

I had to solve the problem of her touching me, but how?

No matter what designs or solutions I came up with, the outcomes I envisioned all ended badly. I couldn't trust her to obey. That meant I had to restrain her. Put her on a leash like a pet I'd bought to use. But if I restrained her, the neurons in my brain would think she was prey.

She is prey. Dobycha.

I'd slipped and used a word from my mother tongue. I'd called her prey in Russian. The intensive dialect classes I'd crammed when I first arrived in Sydney abandoned me for a moment. I couldn't use my first language anymore. It wasn't safe.

My heart raced thinking how easy it'd been to fall into old languages—how imperfect my life was.

Shit, at this rate I'd probably end up paying her tomorrow to get her the hell away from me. I didn't like these thoughts. These weak as fuck thoughts that dragged up my past.

You'll never be naked around her.

You'll never feel her hands on your cock.

You'll never be able to have full body contact.

You'll end up snapping her neck.

I was a fucking idiot.

I wish I never set eyes on her.

Prowling to the crucible with a lump of previously melted bronze in the centre, I cranked the furnace and set the tool into the licking flames.

Deliberately throwing myself into work, I ignored thoughts of how fucked-up my life was and flicked switches for sanders, drilling equipment, and buffers. Unravelling a length of silver chain I'd been using on an intricate custom piece, a concept came to mind. A blueprint to somehow keep Zel safe—or as safe as possible from me.

Minutes ticked by as I worked. It calmed my mind, granting a small illusion of peace.

Hours inched past as I toyed with metal and fire and sweat. Working with such unforgiving materials was a reminder that no matter how set in stone we seemed, we could always change. We could mould and adapt and become something new, even a hunk of iron.

I had to hold faith.

I could change.

Over time.

Settling on a stool under a large halogen, I turned my thoughts off and proceeded to turn a piece of chain into a prison.

The sun tinged the horizon with its pink and golden welcome by the time I'd finished. Climbing the stairs from my lair, my creation tight in my fist, I sighed heavily with relief.

Through the glass roof along the central spine of the house warm rays of sunlight spilled. The familiar tension left my body.

Night was over. Day was back.

With every step toward my room, I clutched the silver harder. I hoped like hell this worked. Opening the door quietly, I made my way across the carpet, deliberately walking in bright patches of morning sun. There were no curtains on the massive bifolds. No way to block out the glare.

That was another thing Zel would have to get used to. I *never* slept in the dark.

Night had been work hours—full of terror and terribleness. Day was my one chance to be in the light—the small window where the memories were forced to leave.

The night belonged to my past. The day belonged to my future.

The form of a sleeping woman lay burrowed under my sheets. Blankets tugged up over her shoulders, her hands shoved under the pillow beneath her cheek.

My heart thudded hard. She was in my space. Smelling my covers, sleeping on my side of the bed.

I wanted to tear the protection off her and touch her. I needed to find that spark, the energy that existed between us.

Remember why I was insane enough to try this.

But I couldn't. Not yet.

First, I needed purging.

Entering the bathroom, I shed my clothes and left them on the floor. Placing the item I made on the vanity, I stepped into the black-tiled shower. Turning on the tap, hot water rained instantly. I twisted it on as far as it would go.

It hurt. It burned. It scalded a layer of skin. But I didn't mix the temperature with cold.

The raining fire did something for me that nothing else achieved. It was my drug of choice.

I'd read somewhere that self-harm was a cry for help. A sure sign an individual needed counselling. And they were right. However, I wasn't crying out for help when I forced my body to stand under a torrent of boiling water. I found salvation.

Pain helped. Inflicting agony gave me a tiny bit of peace. It erased a little bit of badness. It was my version of meditation or relaxing music. It stopped me from exploding.

My skin turned lobster-red, and I shuddered with the urge to dart from under the pinpricks of agony, but I stood and accepted the punishment.

Five minutes passed eternally slowly, but I never once looked down. I never once ran hands over my flesh, or touched the new ridges of injuries and scars. I knew every inch of my violent past and wished it wasn't so evident on my skin. I never fisted my cock or sought to find a quick release.

I'd been conditioned to feel nothing but the will to obey.

My body wasn't mine to touch or look at. It had belonged to them; it *still* belonged to them.

With a shaking hand, I wrenched the cold water on and groaned as icy droplets soothed my burned flesh.

It layered the pain with two intense reactions, doubling the relief.

After blasting myself with ice, I turned off the water and stumbled from the shower.

Avoiding looking at myself in the mirror, I wrapped a towel

around my waist and entered the dark bedroom. Making sure Zel was still asleep and wouldn't catch me naked, I slinked soundlessly through the sunlight.

Entering the walk-in wardrobe, I let the towel fall and quickly yanked on black cotton pants, followed by a black t-shirt. Even on my own, I never slept naked—never ran the risk of being unprepared.

The moment I had clothing on again, I relaxed. Along with hiding certain things, my scars were cloaked, too. Hazel didn't need to see self-inflicted injuries as well as ones earned in duty.

She didn't need to know anything about me.

Padding over to the bed, I watched her sleep. Her long brown hair fanned the black sheets looking as if she'd become one with the mattress.

Her breathing was so shallow I had to strain to make sure she was alive. She looked so pure, so undamaged, so unlike me.

My eyes fell to the soft curves of her figure below. My cock twitched at the thought of what I could do to her. What she would let me do for two hundred thousand dollars.

I would fuck her and taste her and use her in every way possible.

In this private purchased world, I could do anything I wanted.

She was mine.

Her mouth parted as she rolled from her side onto her back. One arm flew above her head, thudding against the pillow. Her face scrunched up, eyes fluttered. Either a dream or a nightmare danced behind closed eyelids.

What did normal people dream of? Love and happiness?

"No," she murmured sleepily.

I froze, waiting for her eyes to fly open. When they stayed closed, I let myself drink in her parted lips, the flush on her cheeks. My thoughts filled with images of her mouth around my cock and her tongue licking me, tasting me.

I was hard at the thought of a release. I'd forgotten what an orgasm felt like. I had no recollection of the pleasurable explosion I'd felt only twice before.

Zel would teach me to remember. Zel would cure me of my sins.

And I was about to take her.

Linking the chain through my fingers, I leaned down and touched her.

Seven

Hazel

One terrible mistake ended up giving me the best gift of my life.

Every day was harder, every trial more stressful, but I wouldn't change a thing.

Before her, I didn't care about anyone or myself. I stole, I cheated, and I lied. I existed on a downward spiral with a grave for a destination. But she changed me.

Clara.

I used my skill at bullshitting to earn well-paying jobs. I studied relentlessly, teaching myself—a homeless ragamuffin with no education—to qualify for certificates and diplomas.

I forged my past to create a positive future, and it worked. The corporate world opened their doors; a regular income filled my bank account. I earned every penny from hard work.

But then I was fired, and every saved penny went to Clara's treatment. I existed on the fine edge of destitution.

I sold myself for two hundred thousand dollars to a man I didn't trust.

To a man who would hurt me more than anyone ever could.

I thought I could save him.

Just like I could save my daughter.

I was wrong.

"You like that? There?" Fox *murmured around my nipple. His hands coasted up and down my body, spreading fire, coating me in delicious sensation.*

My hands tangled in his hair, massaging his scalp, pressing his mouth harder against me. "Yes, there. Like that."

He pulled back, white eyes looking soft as snow. "Touch me."

I dropped my hands and followed the contour of his back, revelling in every ridge of muscle.

He groaned and grabbed me closer, kissing me with everything bared—rocking into me. Rocking, rockin—

"Zel." Something poked my shoulder, shattering the lust-filled connection. My dream disintegrated into smoke.

"Wake up, you're having a nightmare."

I wanted to argue. It wasn't a nightmare, more like a fantasy. I couldn't remember the last time I'd had such an erotic dream. I fought against losing the kinky comfortable nothingness of sleep; not wanting to return to the world of worries and uncertainty.

The first person to spring to mind was Clara. Her pretty seraphic face, pink with health and youth, smiling happily. But beneath the glow of vitality existed the life-stealing illness that I couldn't fight.

My heart squeezed, and I struggled to suck in a breath. It never got easier facing the possibility of death for my child.

"Wake up," Fox growled. His tone banished my sadness, recreating the passion from my dream. My mind entertained thoughts of his arms around me, lips kissing mine. My core throbbed in time to the delicious rocking he'd interrupted.

He had issues, and I would never trust him, but I couldn't deny the affect he had on my body.

I opened my eyes.

Sunlight!

Shit, I'd spent the entire night? Regret swamped me at the thought of Clara waking up without me. Of Clue explaining that her hooker of a mother was off spending time with someone else.

I'm a terrible mother.

My mind whirled with repercussions. I needed the money, but what was the point if money couldn't cure her? I'd be wasting a full month of being without her all for nothing.

I can't do it.

The morning sun brought a new reality, and my heart felt like it'd been ripped out of my chest. I'd never forgive myself if something happened to her while I allowed a stranger to control me.

The soft pleasure from my dream sharpened and twisted in my gut. Fox stood tall, dark, and brutal. His grey eyes glowed; his jaw clenched tight. "You're awake."

My stomach fluttered drinking in the ferocious male beside me. I knew three things instantaneously in that moment.

One, I would let him do whatever he wanted because I'd lived a life caring for others for far too long.

Two, I would leave the moment his back was turned. I needed to see Clara.

And three, he would end up hurting me more than anyone, and I would either hate him for eternity or kill him.

Fox glared, no doubt trying to figure out my thoughts. "What were you dreaming?"

Oh, God. A question I didn't want to answer and a lie he would be able to detect. My heart bolted around my chest. "Nothing."

"You're flushed. It's not nothing." Towering over me, he gave me no choice but to look straight into his silver eyes. He stood like a statue he'd created. "Tell me. Keeping secrets is non-negotiable."

My cheeks flushed recalling the dream. The need. The way he'd thrust into me hard and ruthless. Biding for time, I sat up and tucked the black sheet under my arms before it fell off my naked breasts. A curtain of hair covered my shoulders, providing some semblance of decency.

"Tell me, woman." Fox opened and closed his fists. "I won't ask again."

A thrill of fear licked my stomach. "You want to know, I'll tell you, then perhaps you can deliver. I dreamed of you." I tucked a strand behind my ear. "You licked my nipple, and I wrapped my fingers in your hair. I stroked every inch of you and when you thrust inside me I almost came just from the dream." Narrowing my eyes, I murmured, "Happy? Are you pleased to know I want you? Because I do."

And the sooner I can seduce you the sooner I can find a way home.

Fox stood frozen. His mouth parted as fiery lust exploded in his eyes. "You dreamed of me fucking you?" His voice rasped with need. "Why?"

I frowned. "Why? You've taken over my life in the last few hours; it's natural for my brain to be consumed by you."

He stiffened. "You're consumed by me?"

My eyes dropped to the rapidly growing erection in his trousers. I bit my lip as all the heat from arguing with him last night and my saucy dream cindered in my core. "Yes. And I know you're consumed by me. I know you want to sink deep inside me. You're making me wait, Fox, and it's only making me hotter."

"Fuck me," Fox groaned. His hand tightened around something glittering in his fist. "You're destined to ruin me." He bent over quickly, his eyes latched on my mouth. I parted my lips eager to accept another kiss, but he stopped and jerked backward. "Not yet. Not till it's safe."

My heart spiked, zeroing in on the chain he held. "What are you planning on doing?" For some reason my throat slammed closed and I fought the urge to scoot away.

Fox cocked his head. "Why? Are you afraid?"

"Depends. What's in your hand?"

He raised his fist, looking at it with a mixture of hope and hate. "It's for you."

A shiver darted over my spine. *He said he wouldn't hurt you.* "Do I have to take it?"

He cocked his head. "You agreed to the terms and proved you can't be trusted not to touch me. So yes. You do." His eyes fell to the precarious sheet. Dressed all in black, I had a hard time seeing him as human and not a life blotting shadow.

His eyes shone as he bent down and held out his palm. The item sparkled like silver tinsel. Jewellery?

He thought bribery would stop me from touching him?

"See, nothing to be afraid of," he murmured.

I sat taller, tucking the sheet tighter beneath my arms. I hated being half-naked while he stood fully dressed. Clothing granted power. It didn't matter that he'd see me naked very soon; I wanted to maintain as much equal footing as possible.

Fox had a way of drawing nerves and anxiety, along with lust and attraction—it was a potent combination. Shaking my head, I said, "There's always something to be afraid of."

His nostrils flared as his eyes widened. "Who exactly are you?"

"I'm the girl you bought for sex."

He chuckled.

My eyes widened. I didn't think he would be the type to laugh—he seemed too serious, too conflicted all the time.

Fox suddenly moved, destroying the tight awareness between us. Sitting on the edge of the bed, his hip pressed hard against my leg. His face was hard and stern, his scar particularly vivid. "Once I put this on, you're not to take it off."

I refused to agree to anything that related to my freedom. I wasn't a prisoner. His damp hair and smell of fresh linen told me he'd already showered. Changing the subject, I asked, "You never came to bed last night. Did you?"

He pursed his lips, fingers clenching around the gleaming silver in his palm. "That's another thing we need to discuss. I only sleep during the day. I sleep from sunrise till midday. You'll follow my routine."

In my real life, I would've been up for an hour by now, preparing Clara's breakfast and lunch for school. I would be dressed and amped on coffee, ready for another day.

Opening his grip, he let the silver slither from his hold and into my lap. My eyes widened, taking in the long length of chain pooling on top of the sheet. "What is it?"

"I made it for you. It's a way to make sure you don't touch me."

I swallowed, peering harder. I reached out to touch it, but Fox leaned forward and scooped the metal back up. His knuckles brushed between my legs, and we both froze.

My lips parted as the lingering heat from my dream came back in full force. My blood carried sticks of dynamite through my system, ready for more ammunition, ready to explode.

Fox cleared his throat, keeping a careful distance. His body stayed tight and disciplined as he ordered, "Lean forward and hold up your hair."

Ah, dilemma.

If I put my hands up, the sheet would fall. My nipples hardened at the thought of being exposed to him. As much as he turned me on, I wasn't comfortable baring myself completely. I stupidly felt that once he'd seen me, he'd know more of my secrets, understand just how much I kept from him.

When I didn't obey, he snapped, "Do it. I won't ask again." His eyes roved down to my lips, across my exposed throat, to the swell of my small B's. "I want to see. Show me."

The husky interest in his voice teased, granting me a small amount of power. Taking a deep breath, I slowly gathered my hair into a messy ponytail. Somehow, I managed to keep the sheet tight under my arms.

Fox scowled. "Let go of the sheet."

My heart flew into my throat. Gritting my teeth, I unclamped my arms and gasped as the sheet whispered down my body, kissing my nipples before dropping to my lap.

Fox sucked in a breath. Keeping my back straight, I tried

not to show what his fixed look of fascination did to me. Every inch of me burned, loving the single-minded obsession in his gaze.

Just like his body held remnants of his violent life, so did mine. I hadn't come away unscathed from a few incidents including a shallow scar along my left side and another deeper scar just above my pubis.

His hand cupped my right breast, his thumb skating over the nipple bar pierced right through. "You willingly deformed yourself?" His voice was different, strangled. "You mutilated your body? Why?"

The pleasure of him touching me evaporated. "I don't consider it deforming. I consider it my right. I can do what I want. Just like you adorn yourself in scars; I can add some decoration."

He exploded upright. "You think those are *willing*. You think I allowed those to happen?" Pacing away, he dragged hands through his hair before cursing under his breath.

His temper evaporated as quickly as it'd come and I sat exposed, wondering what the hell I should do. Was it my job to soothe him as well as fuck him?

Coming back to sit on the bed, he gazed at the barbell as if it was blasphemy. I didn't like the turbulent look in his eyes—gone was the strong, bossy stranger. In his place sat a man with issues deeper than I could ever imagine.

Swallowing, Fox morphed again and blocked everything off. "Lock your hands together and lean forward."

Not saying a word, I obeyed and shivered as his hands went around my neck. Fox's scent of smoke clouded me as his body moved closer to mine. The chain glittered in the sunlight like a living thing, but burned my skin like ice.

"What is it?" My voice wavered. Nerves lived in my stomach with frantic wings. My fingers grew white as I locked them tighter.

Don't touch him. Don't touch him.

"I told you." Fox's breath tickled my collarbone. He

fastened the necklace and drew back. A long length of chain dangled down the front of my body, puddling on the sheet. Concentrating, he positioned the cool silver in the valley of my breasts and down the centre of my stomach.

Every sense in my body sprung to attention. I wanted to lean into his touch and invite more, but at the same time I wanted to run. If a simple touch could make me wet, how would I cope when he finally took me?

"Keep your hands locked." He eyed my lap as if I planned to touch him at any moment with no warning. Eyes drilled into mine. I nodded.

Seemingly satisfied, Fox bent forward again. Gathering the remaining chain, he split it into two lengths and wrapped it around my waist. His fingers were gentle, worshipping. I froze as he fumbled behind me, securing it somehow.

The result was one chain around my neck, one around my belly, and a length running down the front of my body.

"Perfect. It fits."

I eyed the jewellery. It looked like a normal silver chain, but slightly thicker. More robust than an average necklace, yet delicate enough to be feminine.

Fox leaned back, nodding. "Hopefully it will work. At the very least, it will give me a warning."

I looked down, plucking at the silver between my breasts. "And I have to wear this all the time?"

He grunted. "You're not to remove it." His eyes hardened. "Every morning before bed, you're to let me secure the final part. Every time we have sex, you'll let me attach this to the necklace."

"Attach what?"

My mouth went dry as he pulled another chain from his pocket. This one had a small padlock on two sides. Motioning for me to hold out an arm, he secured the heavy duty silver around my wrists before snapping the padlock closed. He looped the length of chain through the one around my stomach before wrapping the last part around my other wrist and pressing the lock tight.

He'd effectively trussed me up like a fucking turkey.

"You didn't say anything about bondage."

He shook his head. "It isn't bondage. It's protection."

Fear thickened as I looked into his eyes. "Protection? From what?"

He stood, his colourless gaze ripping me bare. "Me."

Oh, holy God.

Reaching into his pocket a second time, he revealed a thick leather cuff with matching silver padlock. He murmured, "Every time we go to sleep, I'll wear this. If I forget to put it on, you must tell me."

I didn't want to ask why. *Don't ask why.*

"Why?" I breathed.

His eyes flashed. "Because if you don't, I can't promise you'll wake up alive. What I did to you in my office was nothing. I have no control when someone touches me, so make sure you don't."

My heart stopped. The way he said it so matter-of-fact chilled me to the bone. He wasn't dramatizing it—it just simply was.

I tried to hide my fear, locking it away beneath iron-willed control. "Okay."

"This agreement between us is to fulfill one need only. And I don't need the uncertainty of you being able to touch me whenever you damn well please." He looked sleek and ruthless. A thrill shot through me.

"What makes you think I want to touch you willingly?"

He frowned, clenching his jaw. "I don't care. This way, you can't."

We glared at each other. Coming forward, he overpowered me as his persona changed from angry owner to interested predator. My breath quickened in response.

In one fast move, Fox grabbed the sheet hiding my legs and tore it off. I flinched in shock, but didn't care about modesty; all I cared about was the desolate resolution in his eyes.

"I've wanted you since I set eyes on you, and I'm going to take you."

His large hands grasped my hips and flipped me over. I cried out as he propped me on hands and knees with effortless strength. "I made another promise I can't keep," he murmured, dragging his nose along my spine. "I thought I could do it, but it's not possible."

His hot breath tingled my back as he reached below and grabbed my breast with harsh fingers.

I shuddered, cursing my body warming for him, melting for him. I should hate the roughness, the lack of humanity in his touch, but he'd ignited the dynamite in my blood with his harsh, unloving commands.

"What promise?" I whispered, already panting.

His fingers hooked onto the sides of my knickers, pulling them down my hips until they rested around my knees on the bed. He groaned as he pushed my legs apart, exposing me.

My head lolled forward as he climbed behind me. The rustle of clothing being removed made my mouth go dry and my heart stop beating.

His finger traced the crack of my ass, dipping lower, following my heat until he found wetness. "Fuck me," he muttered before swirling the tip of his finger around my entrance. "God, you're wet."

My back bowed; my limbs trembled. I'd gone from tense to needing him in one second flat. The tip of his finger entered me before swirling back up to press against my clit.

"I promised I'd make you enjoy fucking me as much as I'd enjoying fucking you." He bent over, smothering my back with his torso. His teeth grazed my neck as the thick hardness of his cock nudged my core. "To do that I'd have to touch you. I'd have to let my guard down. I don't have the strength."

One hand grabbed a fistful of hair, jerking my neck back while another secured my hip, pinning me in place. His erection rocked against my outer flesh, hot and hard.

I wasn't ready.

I'm not ready.

Fear lit up my heart and I wiggled, trying to dislodge his hold. "Wait. No—"

"I'm sorry, *dobycha*," he groaned, thrusting violently, coldly, viciously into me. My elbows gave way and I fell headfirst into the pillow. My bound hands couldn't support me.

Everything burned. Everything hurt.

I gasped for breath, sucking in material as the searing, frightening pain of being taken violently made me cry out. Hot tears were absorbed instantly by the pillow as Fox rammed into me again. He lost himself, turning inhuman as he rode me. My scalp screamed where he held me captive by my hair.

Gone was the lust; the sparks of need in my blood. All I felt was used and nothing more than trash.

I bit my lip till I drew blood as he withdrew, only to slam into me again. "Yes. Fuck." He sounded far away, no longer with me mentally.

His fingers gripped my hips, holding me in place as he savagely thrust. Every pound sent shockwaves of agony through me. His hipbones dug into my ass, adding more bruises to the internal ones.

If there was any blessing in being taken so horribly, it was how soon it was over. Fox thrust harder and harder, driving me deeper and deeper into the pillow. He filled me to the brink until I thought I'd split in two.

But then he froze, jetting hot wetness deep inside me, groaning. The second the last pulse of his release filled me, he pulled out and climbed off the bed.

My entire body trembled with adrenaline and unhappiness. I didn't dare move until the sound of the bedroom door opened and closed, as Fox left me. With a ragged gasp, I flopped to my side and curled into a tight ball.

The stickiness of his come smeared my inner thighs, and the chain cuffs dug into my wrists, but I couldn't bring myself to move.

I couldn't bring myself to think or curse or run.

Yet again life proved I was an idiot. A greedy money-grubber who thought she could see something dark and troubled in a man. Who believed in the fundamental goodness of people enough to let herself be used and tossed away.

It'd happened before. It'd happened again. I hadn't learned my lesson.

I lay with my eyes wide open, watching the slow journey of the sun from sunrise to high noon to sunset. I couldn't bring myself to think how to fix this or even to think of Clara.

I'd besmirched myself, tarnishing my hope with reality.

Fuck two hundred thousand dollars. Fuck him.

When twilight fell and I'd had enough of wallowing in the filth I'd created, I stood gingerly and hobbled to the bathroom.

Avoiding looking in the mirror, I focused on the silver around my wrists. With gritted teeth, I yanked them with all my strength, sweating with effort until a link pried open, allowing me to get free.

I couldn't remove the necklace or belly chain, but at least my hands were free. Free to shower, get dressed, and walk out the fucking door.

Obsidian Fox had messed with the wrong girl. I would leave, then I would come back and make him regret ever hurting me.

I would teach him that even though he might be haunted, it gave him no right, *none,* to hurt others.

I would be his nightmare.

Eight

ROAN

Life was never easy.

I learned that thanks to a rigorous training program that left me mostly dead and fumbling for a way back to life.

I didn't make excuses for my behaviour. I knew what I was.

But I found a way to deal with the blackness in my brain. I found unwilling victims and gave them my pain. It was a trade-off and it worked—for a time.

I thought I could wipe my violent past free all thanks to the cure I'd found in one woman.

I piled all my hopes and pleas and prayers into a miracle, and it fucking ruined me when it turned out to be false.

Instead of treating her kindly, I slipped back to the past and lost.

I raped her. I hurt her. I made her run and leave me.

I should've known inviting a fierce woman into my life would only make it worse.

She succeeded in being my personal hell.

She made sure to break me.

Fuck.

I couldn't believe what I'd done. I couldn't believe I'd taken her so rough with no fucking remorse or thought to her safety.

The instant she was bound, instead of being soothed by being in control, it made me snap.

Fuck!

I was the biggest bastard alive.

I couldn't stand to be around her—knowing I ruined everything. I did the only thing I could do to protect her.

I ran.

I returned to the basement to pummel my anger into a piece of bronze. I fucked up by taking her so fast. I forced myself on her and was no better than rapist scum.

Bastard!

I cowered away and leeched my pain by branding the sole of my foot with a hot piece of iron. The stench of burning flesh helped purify my thoughts, giving me a respite from the monstrous things I'd done.

Only once I could think straight and resembled a human rather than a beast, did I search for her to apologise. I turned my house upside down, searching.

I couldn't find her.

Anywhere.

Everywhere I looked, it was empty. Every room. Every space.

I'd damaged whatever existed between us, but I hadn't expected her to abandon me.

You fucking raped her, you idiot!

I'd done to her what I'd sworn never to do again—I took someone's free will and made them do something against their wishes. I was no better than *them*.

She was gone.

Gone!

The club opened at nine p.m., and I waited for Oscar at the top of the stairs, quaking with helplessness and rage. The moment he showed up, I roared, "You let her fucking leave?"

Oscar climbed the last stair with the stiffness of preparation for a fight. His shoulders tensed, face darkened.

I clenched and unclenched my fists. How dare she disappear! I couldn't let it end like that. I had to make her forgive me. I had to apologise. I needed a fucking second chance.

He glared bloody murder, blue eyes tearing into mine. "What the fuck was I supposed to do? She's a free woman, not a captive! She asked for a lift a few hours ago and I agreed." Coming closer, he seethed, "What the hell did you do to her last night, Fox? She walked out of here as if she'd been used by a fucking stallion." His gaze shot me with bullets of rage. "I hope you got your money's worth because I doubt she'll be coming back."

This was the same prick who'd scorned Zel last night. The same man who looked at Zel as if she were a succubus out to steal my soul.

"That's none of your fucking business. She was mine. We had a deal!"

"A deal? What? Where you were allowed to destroy the poor girl? Don't make me laugh."

My rage morphed into white-hot anger. Oscar couldn't point fingers. Fucking hypocrite. He had more women than I'd ever met. He used them and cast them aside with no thought to their feelings.

"At least I've only hurt one." I narrowed my eyes, daring him to argue.

Oscar's mouth hung open. "Screw you. I fuck women who *want* me to fuck them. I don't kidnap them and then rape them. For God's sake, we'll have the police here if she decides to lay charges."

The thought of being touched by many, of being handcuffed and trapped in a cage, undid my shaky sanity even further. I was done living in cages, belonging to others. I was *done*.

I couldn't speak. Anger closed my throat as I stood precariously close to the edge I was always one-step away from plummeting off.

"I fucked her. So what?"

Oscar came forward. "Please tell me she wanted it or so help me. We may be business partners, Fox, and I don't know what shit you dealt with in your past, but if you raped her, I'll kill you myself."

The switch deep inside—the one I always struggled with keeping off—flicked on. The compassion I'd fought so hard to cultivate disappeared in a puff of smoke. Every lesson I'd ever learned, all the pain I'd suffered, all the blood I'd spilled swamped me in a cloud of contamination.

"You think you could kill me?" My voice never rose past a whisper, but it throbbed with a threat.

The noise of fighters pummelling each other in Obsidian below pricked my skin with energy.

Violence. Blood. Pain. It was my DNA. The only reason I was born—the only reason why I was still alive.

I took one step toward Oscar. His healthy tan faded as fear whitewashed his features. Instead of backing down, he stepped forward until only a foot separated us. "I think you need some serious fucking help, Fox. The way you were with that woman last night, it was obsessive. You seemed completely different. Good different." His voice lost the angry edge. "You seemed human for the first time since we met. You need to apologise if you have any hope of fixing it."

A Ghost never apologized. A Ghost was there to obey. A Ghost was nothing and no-one. We existed above the law.

You have to destroy evidence.

You have to kill her.

The conditioning doused my body in a cold sweat.

"What address did she give you?" Images of squeezing her throat, sucking her soul plundered my mind. It was the only way.

She knew about me. I showed her too much.

Oscar looked over his shoulder at the fighters below. The Muay Thai ring held an eager duo going at it with wild ferocity. No one looked up here, no one paid attention to the stand-off between us.

The longer he kept me from her, the more pissed off I got. She was mine. I had the contract to prove it. Every minute that ticked past cost me one hundred and thirty nine dollars of the two hundred thousand I agreed to pay—she owed it to me to be here. Fighting with me. Letting me do what I wanted.

His jaw clenched. "I'm not giving it to you." Taking another step back, he rushed, "You don't know what life she leads. What about the woman who was with her last night? The black dude? You can't go charging over there in your condition. It's professional suicide. Do you have any idea what kind of shit-storm this could bring?"

My temper flared into nuclear. "That's none of your fucking business."

Storming toward him, I shoved him out of the way of the stairs. Instead of going willingly, Oscar slammed to a halt and braced himself on my shoulder.

The moment he touched me, I lost it.

My world swooped like a bad time machine, shooting me from present to past.

"You've passed the first test of three. Congratulations."

My handler, and only person who I was allowed to talk to, came close and gave me what I so craved: food. Damn, I was hungry. After two weeks in the pit with just scraps for nourishment, they'd broken my will, and I'd done what they'd ordered.

My throat closed around the piece of chicken, remembering what I'd done only an hour before. I'd broken into a home—complete with Christmas decorations in the window and a fire flickering in the hearth. I'd sneaked up the stairs on silent toes and stood over a woman sleeping soundly in her bed.

I'd stabbed her in the heart while her husband slept on.

Then, I left.

I choked, throwing the chicken away, staring at my hands. Traces of blood coated my fingers, glowing bright with damnation.

"Well done, Fox. Well done for killing your mother."

"Fox?"

"Fox! Goddammit, stop!"

A fist to the jaw shattered the flashback, and I hurled myself at the stupid culprit. I'd kill them. I'd kill them for making me murder my mother.

"Fox!"

My vision cleared from blood-smeared thirteen-year-old fingers to a bulging eyed Oscar.

His hands clawed at mine around his neck, his feet dangled off the floor. The burn in my shoulders spoke of the weight I held almost unconsciously. It was so easy. I didn't know why I fought so hard. This was all I was good for.

Death.

Oscar spat in my face. His warm spit landed in my eye, and I threw him to the side disgusted.

"Snap out of it." He threw a crystal ashtray at my head. It bounced off my temple, knocking sense back into me.

I blinked, bringing into focus his torn shirt and bleeding lip. Fear stank around him.

Shit. Shit. *Shit.*

Backing away, I looked down at my hands—at the symbol III tattooed into my palms. How could I ever let myself get so weak?

Pain.

I need pain.

I needed deliverance. I needed an escape.

Turning on my heel, I bolted. Adrenaline pumped thick and fast, chugging my broken heart.

Bulldozing my way through the fighters on the floor of Obsidian, I already knew where I would go.

I didn't look back.

Twenty minutes later, I screeched to a halt outside Dragonfly. If Obsidian was exclusive and upmarket—created for skilful fighters who wanted prestige—Dragonfly was its sinful baby brother. A place where a disclaimer had to be signed and lodged just in case you didn't make it out alive.

My favourite place for medicine.

I'd found it purely by chance. When I moved to Sydney, I didn't know anyone. Cast out of the only world I knew, I fumbled in society. With no guidance or rules, I had none of my usual tools to stay together.

The only way to keep my temper at a manageable level had been to ambush. Most nights I hid in dark alleys, just waiting for random, clueless prey to stumble upon my trap.

The moment they were close I taunted and teased, hurting them just enough for them to hurt me. Then I'd force myself to stop—to give them the winning hand. Every strike helped ease my pain, and I welcomed the throws.

Only once they'd given me enough to exist another day did I knock them out and run. Leaving them to be found by another—keeping my identity hidden thanks to the tricks I'd been taught by my owners.

For weeks it worked, until one night I picked a guy who owned the Dragonfly and he gave me the beating I'd been searching for. He tore into me like he channelled a fucking velociraptor. He cleared my head completely of the mess inside.

A fight was mere aspirin, whereas Poison Oaks was my morphine.

His fighting name fit him perfectly—built like a thousand-year-old tree, his arms were the size of trunks, and his temper was poisonous. No one pissed him off. They knew better.

Double parking my black Cayman, I jogged down the dark

alley before taking a sharp left.

A glowing dragonfly was the only signal the club existed. No garish signs, no hint of existence. Just like Obsidian, both clubs worked on referral and secrecy.

Knocking on the door in the correct code sequence, I glared at the bouncer who cracked it open.

The gloomy, smoky world behind him set my teeth on edge. I needed to get in there and fight. Then maybe I could clear my head before searching for Zel.

To track her down and take her home like a kill that was rightfully mine.

"Poison Oaks? Is he here?" My voice lost its fake Australian accent and slipped into Russian. My eyesight pulsated with greys and whites, almost as if my vision clouded and fogged.

I hadn't been this close before. Not since two years ago.

The bouncer held out his hand, pointing toward the back. Stepping aside, he let me pass, knowing not to touch me.

I didn't say a word as I made my way through the heaving crowd, careful to keep a wide berth. The boxing ring in the centre of the club was the only fighting arena. Every discipline was allowed and the dark stains on the floor, along with the tattered rigging and ropes, spoke of battles won and lost.

My heart thudded faster, preparing for a fight.

I found who I needed sitting with a half-naked woman with fake breasts on his lap. His tanned skin and tattooed arms tensed, bouncing her weight like a pet or a child on his knee.

The instant he saw me, he froze. "Not tonight, Fox. I'm not up for your bullshit."

It took everything in me not to slap the woman off his lap and haul him into the ring.

"Ten thousand. Give me everything you have."

He shook his head, his bald scalp shining thanks to the neon lights in the shapes of dragonflies. The ceiling had been painted with a thousand of the fucking bugs, transforming the entire room into an insect ridden cage.

"I'm not in the mood to go to the hospital again, Fox. Fuck

off."

The woman giggled and kissed his cheek, rubbing her nipples against his groping hand.

The woman was tacky and cheap; my cock showed no interest in her fakery. Only Zel had power over that piece of my anatomy. She proved it still worked. Too well.

"I won't touch you. You have my word," I lied, but so what. I had to get him in the ring. My body felt like it would explode at any moment. I had to get this evilness out of me. I had to find my way back to the man I wanted to be and not the man I'd been trained to be.

I needed to be punished.

Poison's brown eyes narrowed. "You expect me to believe that?"

"You can bind my hands. I don't care." My eyes dropped to his fingers stroking the woman's thigh. I knew how deadly they could be. I'd suffered pain. Great pain. Pain I wanted again.

After a never-ending minute, he sighed. "Fine." Looking over my shoulder, he motioned to a large guy with a black goatee. "Get some rope and bind his wrists."

The man nodded and disappeared into the crowd. He returned a moment later with a length of heavy-duty twine.

I was well-versed in the art of knots and rope. It was a perfect weapon: silent, portable, undetectable.

"Hold 'em out." He chewed loudly on some gum, waiting for me to obey.

It took a lot to spin around and present my wrists. My jaw locked as I deliberately and obediently held the submissive position.

Looking over my shoulder, I demanded, "Don't touch me. Just wrap the rope and tie it tight."

"Dude, how the fuck am I not supposed to touch you?" He popped his gum, glaring at me like I was an idiot.

Touch me and see what happens, cocksucker.

"Do as he says, Geoff. You don't want to know what

happens otherwise." Poison Oaks shifted the woman off his knee and stood to his impressive six foot four height.

I kept my eyes locked with his, trying hard to ignore any quick touches as Geoff bound my wrists. My heart raced as the twine rubbed against my skin and pulled taut.

Once the knot was tight, he mumbled, "Done."

Poison cocked his head at the ring. "Come on then, you psycho. I don't have time for this bullshit." Together we moved toward the ring. He added, "You really need some therapy. This isn't the kind of shit you should need."

I didn't answer. My body had ceased to exist; all I thought of was finding peace. The fear of being bound couldn't override the delicious expectation of what was to come.

Poison looked across to the DJ in the corner of the small overly packed room and dragged a finger over his throat. The music cut out and people stopped talking instantly. "Anyone who wants to see a brutal bashing, gather 'round. You—" he pointed at the men in the ring "—out."

The guys slid through the rigging. I climbed up with the aid of an angry push from Poison. The moment we were in the ring, a buzz filled me. The knowledge I would get my ass kicked and everything would be okay.

"See how we manipulate you, Fox? You might as well stop fighting us. We win. Every time. You're ours, and you need to remember that."

The vision popped into my head just before Poison's fist collided with my gut. My lungs gasped for air as I doubled over—shock and pain quaked through my torso. The moment the agony pulsed through me, a small bit of torture left. The blackness in my brain cracked, letting light shine.

Music clicked on, raining from the speakers; reggae with a touch of drum and bass. My body twisted, anticipating Poison's next move. I was there to be purged by pain, but it didn't mean I'd make it easy for him.

He thought he was safe with my hands tied. Fucking idiot.

"Get 'em, Oaks!" someone shouted, just as Poison flung himself off the boxing ropes and torpedoed toward me.

Darting to the side, I brought my knee up and slammed him in the stomach.

Oaks bent to the side, breathing hard. His tanned skin flushed red with anger and pain. "Oi, motherfucker. I thought you said you wouldn't retaliate." He charged, pushing me back with well-aimed strikes. Fist after fist landed on my jaw and chest. Every wallop brought more light. More space to breathe.

I felt lighter, more human.

I smiled as he slugged me with a right hook, and I fell to my knees. Stars and bright lights danced in my vision, dispelling the white fog that'd crept over me. I was on the mend.

I'd found what I needed.

My teeth clanked together as Poison kicked me in the chest. My lungs slammed closed, stopping any air from entering.

I lay on my side, gasping like a fucking dying fish as Poison delivered kick after kick to my ribs. I kept my body clenched against the onslaught, protecting bones with thick muscles.

Confusion and memories—the mess in my brain— evaporated, giving clarity.

When Poison's leg came in grabbing distance, I reared up and head-butted his chest. He went down just like a giant oak tree, bouncing on the springy floor. "What the fuck, Fox?"

Climbing to my feet awkwardly, I kicked him once. "I said I wouldn't put you back in the hospital, not that I wouldn't try."

"That's a lie. You said you wouldn't touch me. Period."

I smiled, feeling a trickle of hot metallic drip from my nose into my mouth. "Oops."

He charged upright and lunged. His shoulder connected with my chest, driving me backward to collide with the ropes.

I closed my eyes as he trapped me and welcomed the flurry of fists to my sides. Every bruise sent pleasure and relief. Every agony helped me inch toward bliss.

Poison danced away, fists held upright, protecting himself. I advanced, arms tied behind my back. Breathing was difficult. Seeing was difficult. Every movement screamed with pain. But I couldn't stop yet. Not yet.

"Fox. Do—" he shouted just as I sprung and roundhoused his ear. Victory thudded swift and hot even as my wrists grew slick with blood from the twine.

Poison stumbled to the side, holding his head where I'd kicked him. His bald scalp showed a massive swelling building under the skin.

"You'll pay for that," he growled.

"Come and get me." I stood taller, leaving myself wide open for a free shot to my jaw.

He wasn't stupid. He sensed the trap and backed away, searching for a weakness. His hands flexed as he plotted his next manoeuvre.

I knew the moment he made a decision and jumped as high as I could go as he charged. The moment he rammed into me, my legs wrapped around his waist, and I used my skull to crash against his.

He stumbled, falling to the floor, landing on his side with me clinging to him. More stars flashed in my eyes, but I didn't unlock my ankles.

He walloped me in the side, sending dull agony through my lower back. Another fist connected with my solar plexus, collapsing my lungs, so I couldn't catch a breath.

Then he did a cheap shot.

An elbow landed in my groin. My balls shot inward, yelping in excruciation. Fire licked right through me. My legs let go on their own accord, and he pushed me away with an angry grunt.

The crowd's chants and encouragement for Poison clanged in my ears. The agony of the junk shot sent nausea building in my gut.

Fucking cheater.

I rolled to my knees, bowing over bent legs, gasping through the wash of pain.

Poison stood, breathing hard. A cut spewed blood from his forehead, tracking on either side of his nose. "Done, Fox?"

"You're never done. No matter what condition your body is in. You always finish the objective." My handler stood above me with the all too

familiar crowbar. He'd beaten me bloody enough times for me to shudder whenever he came near. I was right to fear him.

"Answer me, operative."

"Yes, sir." I kept my eyes downcast as he patrolled around me. I stood steadfast, not letting him see my fear. Out of nowhere, he thwacked the crowbar on my thighbone. It snapped with a horrible crunch.

I bit my lip so hard it bled like a waterfall in my mouth, but I didn't move from my position. I didn't make a sound.

Shoving a gun with a silencer into my grip, he pointed toward the horizon where a compound full of diplomats and informants rested. "Go finish your mission, operative. If you succeed, then we'll fix your leg."

I nodded once and clutched the gun as if it could give me pain relief. I hobbled off to work.

"Never done, Oaks," I growled, launching myself upright. Dropping my shoulder, I knocked him off his feet and went down with him. He punched my jaw and my cheekbone, until a few teeth rattled, and I could no longer see out of my right eye.

Only when I let all the fight out of my body and flopped to the side did he stop punching me. "Done *now*, motherfucker?"

I grinned, no longer in my broken and bruised body, but floating in a sea of calmness. Peace, serenity—a drug of oblivion.

"Yes. Now I'm done."

"You need to stop him from coming here. I'm done giving him his fucked-up therapy."

I left my pain free haze, where no thoughts or flashbacks existed to pay attention to the rumble of male voices. A car door slammed, blocking off the noise of street life and night time comings and goings.

My body ached liked I'd been run over by a fucking train.

"Got it. It won't happen again," Oz's cultured voice drifted quietly.

Goddammit, why had Poison called him? The one man I didn't want to see. The man I owed an apology to. I could've driven home after I slept off the worst of it.

Swallowing, I winced. Okay, maybe I would need longer than just to sleep it off, but that's what I loved about Poison Oaks. He gave me what I needed.

And I'd desperately needed an ass-kicking.

If you're not careful you'll turn him into your handler. Be a fucking man and own your own life.

I would if I knew how. How was a rogue killer supposed to exist in a world of hierarchy if he had no orders to follow?

They gave you the pill to end it. You know that's what's expected of you.

The cyanide pill they'd given me rested in my safe hidden in my wardrobe. I hadn't done what was expected as I wanted to live.

I wanted to see what everyone else had—to live a different kind of life.

I twisted a little on the backseat where I'd been laid. The pain resonated through my body, keeping me focused and present. Smiling, I sighed.

Tonight was a good night.

Tonight had purged me enough to be safe around Zel.

Tomorrow, I would find her and beg for a second chance.

"Wake up, you idiot. We're home."

My left eye had swollen shut and the one that was still operational had a red haze over it from the blood oozing from my hairline.

Oscar opened the car door, glowering.

I glared back, squinting against the lights of the house illuminating him as he stood with his hands on his hips like a disgruntled father.

Bet he was glad he wasn't my true father.

I killed him.

Swallowing hard, I focused on the aches and pains, so as not to remember last night. I couldn't think about raping Zel—about the monster I'd become.

Groaning loudly, I pulled myself upright and practically fell out of the car.

Oscar grabbed me under the arm, hoisting me to my feet. This time I didn't care that he touched me—his fingers held violence not companionship. I was used to that.

Instead of helping me into the building, he shoved me forward as if he couldn't bear to look at me. "Get some rest. I'll send up a medic."

I stumbled and weaved forward. My ears pricked as he muttered, "God have mercy on your fucked-up soul."

Giving him the one finger salute over my shoulder, I continued my swaying and shuffling journey toward my home.

My body creaked and complained, but slowly remembered how to move.

My blurry eyes peered at the horizon. Heavy black velvet blotted out all the stars and moonlight. I estimated the time was around two in the morning.

Shit. All I wanted to do was crash and sleep, but I couldn't.

The sun would be missing for another four hours.

I would have to wait for my one and only friend to appear and protect me from nightmares.

My vigil for daylight had begun.

Nine
Hazel

I'd always prided myself on being strong, on not taking life's nonsense lying down, but that changed when I was told Clara only had a few months left to live.

The illusion of power over one's destiny was a lie. The biggest lie of all.

Her immune system was her enemy and for that I hated life with an ever burning passion. I lost faith in humanity, in fairness, in myself.

I let my weakness put me in a situation where a man took brutal advantage of me.

But in his violence, he made me remember.

He reminded me of my past, my temper, my courage.

He gave me back my backbone and I would never let it go again.

I would teach him why I'd christened myself Hunter.

The hunt had begun to make him pay.

"Zelly, is that you?" Clue popped her head from her bedroom, black hair tussled from sleep.

I quietly locked the front door behind me, sighing. "Yes, I'm back."

I hadn't expected Oscar—the opinionated idiot who worked with Fox—to bring me home. When he spotted me sneaking through the semi-empty fighting floor just before sundown, I worried he'd throw me over his shoulder and take me back to Fox.

Instead he'd smiled and apologised for being a dick the night before and offered to take me wherever I wanted. We didn't say much on the way back, and we fell into a companionable silence that smoothed over the animosity between us.

The drive from the Eastern Suburbs to Inner Suburbs took longer than I wanted with traffic, and the lack of sleep caught up to me. All I wanted to do was curl up in a familiar bed and forget.

About everything.

Clue glanced at the door opposite hers and made sure it was shut tightly against inquisitive ears of my daughter.

Shuffling forward in her pink unicorn slippers and matching huge t-shirt, she looked about fourteen years old. "I thought you said you'd be gone for a while?" She slapped a hand over her mouth as a yawn caught her unaware. "What happened?"

The apartment smelled of oregano and basil from whatever Clue had cooked for dinner. The second-hand couch was covered in a daisy-print fabric, and our mix-match coffee table was an entirely different world compared to the sleek black violence of Fox's mansion.

This place resonated rainbows thanks to Clara's bright artwork blue-tacked to the walls and an odd assortment of knick-knacks. Fox's place was morbid in the use of nothing but midnight. No wonder he seemed so lost and alone. He lived in the never ending dark.

My hands closed around Clue's dress, hating that my mind kept skipping back to him. I toyed with the idea of never going back, but he deserved a piece of his own medicine and I still wanted the money he'd promised.

Every time I moved the bruises in my core throbbed, reminding me I'd been so stupid to think he'd be gentle. I let lust cloud my judgement.

Last night had been a mistake. I let him sweep me away by playing with my needs. Tonight he would have no effect on me as it was purely business from here on out. I would shut down my desire and forget about anything but scratching off the days on a calendar. Counting down the hours before I never had to see him again.

"What are you wearing?" Clue came forward, eyeing the stolen black trousers and t-shirt. I'd raided Fox's wardrobe. I didn't want to travel home looking like a hooker or doing the walk of shame. Not that they fit me very well—the trousers were too loose and the t-shirt too long.

Clue crossed her arms, raising an eyebrow. "So...are you going to tell me what happened? Explain why I had to tell Clara her mum wouldn't be home?"

My heart squeezed at the thought of how that conversation must've gone.

"Change of plans." I hid my stress with a smile and moved forward to join her in the centre of the small lounge. Her skinny arms came around me, squeezing me tight. I kissed her cheek, wrapping myself tight against her. This little Asian woman had been an island of refuge for me just as much as I'd been for her. The thought of her leaving if things worked out with Corkscrew hurt me deep. I wasn't ready to let her go. I wasn't ready for our little trio to change.

It'll change when Clara dies. The inevitable doom sucker-punched me.

After a moment, she pulled back. "She's going to be so happy to see you."

I looked toward the door where Clara and I shared a room. We both had single beds, pushed against opposite walls. When we first moved in, even though it was against the landlord's rules, I'd asked what paint she'd like to decorate with.

Probably a bad idea as I now lived in a purple and pink room with horses stencilled on the walls.

"I know the feeling." My arms ached to cuddle her and apologise for last night. Throwing Clue's dress on the arm of a dining room chair, I muttered, "I've only been gone twenty-four hours, but it feels like an eternity."

Clue rubbed my arm. "I must admit, I missed you. Why did you go and talk to him, Zelly? What did he promise to make you stay?"

Promises.

Every promise Fox made he broke.

"Baby?" a masculine voice grumbled from the doorframe of Clue's room. Ben stood dressed in a pair of blue boxer shorts with polished onyx skin and tight black curls.

I shot Clue a glare. "He's staying here?"

Clue moved to Ben's side, fitting into him like the matching puzzle piece. "I wanted to ask you. Ben's between homes at the moment and needed a place to crash for the week." Her eyes grew round, pleading with me not to get angry. "I figured with you gone…I didn't want to be alone. I love Clara like my own, but if something happened—"

Something like rushing her to the hospital or another episode. My heart sank. I'd let them both down.

I held up a hand. "It's okay. Really."

Ben gave me a sweet smile. Vague swelling puffed up one cheek, but the deep ebony of his skin meant I couldn't see any bruises from his fight at Obsidian.

Obsidian.

My heart rate picked up thinking about Fox. He seemed inhuman. He needed help.

All day, I'd flipped between never wanting to see him again, to wanting to torture him as much as he'd tortured me.

A plan formed loosely in my head, mainly thanks to Oscar. I'd asked him what *dobycha* meant, and he shrugged but tossed me his phone. Thanks to Google translate I found out what had Fox called me.

Prey!

The scalding heat of anger kept me company all the way home. The nerve of him. The egotistical nerve.

Prey. Me! Fox thought I was weak and malleable. He thought he could play with me like a cocky killer who had no mortal enemies.

Well, he'd made an enemy in me. And I had claws.

At least I could thank him for one thing. The Hazel I thought I'd lost—the woman who always won—was back, and I was ready to fight.

Fight for my daughter. Fight for myself. Just fucking fight.

Clue's eyes fell to my throat, frowning at the extra chain resting on top of the silver star. "Where did you get that?" She disengaged from Ben. Her hand came out to poke and prod. Plucking Fox's t-shirt from my frame, she asked, "What happened, Zel? You seem... withdrawn." Cocking her head, she said, "No, that's not right. You seem pissed off."

Ben came closer, smiling crookedly. "Uh oh, I know that look." Holding up his finger, he said, "Hell hath no fury like a woman scorned." He chuckled. "What did that bastard do?" His tone stayed jovial and upbeat, but his face fell when I didn't reply.

My nostrils flared as a slight twinge between my legs reminded me exactly what that bastard did.

Fox's snowy eyes popped into my head, full of arrogance, but also a strange contradiction of helplessness.

Clue sucked in a gasp. "Oh, my God, did he hurt you?" She grabbed my hand. "What did he do?"

The fear of being hurt by a man ran deep for both of us. The difference was I bottled mine deep, forcing it to brew with all the other bad memories I'd rather not think about.

Clue, on the other hand, slipped back into the broken creature I'd saved the night I found her. She would never know what happened between Fox and me. I didn't need her fearing for my sanity or running over there with the police.

Quickly shaking my head, I muttered, "He didn't do

anything to me that I won't pay him back for." Stroking her cheek, I smiled. "I came to see Clara, but I'm going back tomorrow. We have a new agreement. One that allows me to spend days with him and nights here."

So help him if he doesn't agree to my terms. I'd make him wish he never set eyes on me.

Clue opened her mouth, but Ben draped an arm around her shoulders. "Your friend has a plan. Let's hear about it in the morning, baby doll. I have to be at the job site in a few hours."

My body went from lithe and strong to utter fear lockdown. Fox asked me last night what my trigger was.

My trigger was so stupid it was inconsequential. A pet name shouldn't have the power to hurtle me from safety to hell.

But it did.

Baby doll sent me to a pit of darkness I could never remove from my soul. Clara had been the result of my one and only— until last night—sexual intercourse. But there were many means of inappropriate touching. So many other ways to break a nine-year-old's spirit.

Baby doll.

It'd been crooned with false love and accompanied with rancid fingers and breath.

I'd learned to run when a man softened his voice and murmured those words.

I'd learned to kill when they trapped me, so I couldn't flee.

Black clouds swamped my mind, but rather than curling into a ball like I used to, now I just shoved the clouds back. Back into the recesses of my compartmentalized brain where locks and chains kept my bad history archived and secure.

Clue stood frozen to the spot. She didn't know much about my past, but she knew my issues with those two words. She'd seen me explode and almost shank a man in a bar for groping me and whispering, "Can I buy you a drink, baby doll," in my ear.

Ben stood there, looking between us. "Did I say something wrong?" His large, black eyes held genuine remorse.

My spine unlocked and I slouched. Flashing a reassuring smile, I murmured, "No. You didn't do anything wrong. But please, call Clue anything you want, but avoid that one pet name. I'd really appreciate it."

He swallowed, frowning. "Um, sure. Consider it done."

Walking past Clue, I grabbed her hand and squeezed before disappearing into the shadowed world of my bedroom and shutting the door.

I woke to sticky hands gathering my hair to plait it. I smiled, heart winging as I opened my eyes.

The epitome of a gorgeous girl sat on the edge of my bed. Her long, chocolate hair stood up in clumps with frizz from her pillow. Her apple cheeks were flushed from happiness. Everything about her screamed healthy and strong—but it was all a lie.

"I thought you weren't going to be here for a little while. Aunty Clue said you had to help someone." Her eyes sparkled as she tugged a lock of my hair, twisting it into a braid.

I scooted upright before grabbing her with tight arms and flipping her onto her back. She squealed in my ear, giggling as I tickled her.

"Stop! Mummy, stop it." Her laughter was rhapsody to my ears.

But then she coughed.

Scrambling upright, I hoisted her into a sitting position as her face turned purple scarily fast. Her dark eyes bugged as her throat closed.

No. No. *No.*

Shoving her aside, I dashed across the small space of our bedroom and grabbed the emergency high dose inhaler. I'd told her that it was a special formula the doctors gave us for her asthma. In reality, it had some sort of trial drug only available to those who met a certain criteria. Unfortunately, we'd only been able to meet that criteria once. Thanks to me cleaning out my bank account and handing over every scrimped penny and saved dollar I'd earned.

If it wasn't for Clue paying my share of the rent until I could find another job, I would've had to file for bankruptcy.

Holding the back of her head, I placed the inhaler in her mouth and Clara let me press the depressor. She sucked in hungrily.

Slowly the medicine worked its magic and a rosy colour replaced the blue-purple ringing her lips. Giving me a wobbly smile, she hiccupped once. "Sorry."

My stomach flipped, hating her apology—wishing I could give her a solution.

Fighting my trembling limbs and calling fate every dirty cuss word I could think of, I said, "I must remember that you hate tickling so much. You'll go to any extreme to avoid it."

She giggled once, her lungs rattling as the attack faded, leaving her short of breath. "Yep. You really should know by now. Your tickling sucks."

I plastered an annoyed look on my face. "Well, I'll just have to find another way to torture you."

Her eyes flared wide, then we laughed, bowing our heads together. My heart ripped out of my chest and lay thudding, bloody and dying in my daughter's hands. She literally held my every happiness in her failing body.

How am I going to survive without you? How will I find the courage to tell you you're leaving me?

Fox popped into my head, shoving back the weakness and sorrow. His eyes, filled with his own demons, helped give me the strength to stay together. Just the thought of granting retribution for what he did gave me the fire I needed to nurse my strength to keep fighting.

"I wish I didn't have to go to school today," Clara moaned,

snuggling into me and making my heart skip a beat. I rested my chin on her head and rocked, inhaling her fruity shampoo and soft, innocent smell. "You like school. Didn't you tell me Mrs. Anderson allows you to pretty much pick what you want to work on?" Like me, Clara had the uncanny ability of photographic memory.

She seemed to be inattentive in class, but she absorbed everything. It was both a blessing and a curse as it meant I couldn't get away with anything. She sensed lies as easily as I did, but she had a knack at reading further. Almost as if her eyes saw past the restraints of a body and saw right into a person's soul.

No matter what I tried to keep from her, she knew. She always knew.

"She's super nice. I like her. We're designing a sculpture of Romeo and Juliet today."

I ignored the sculpture comment as it reminded me too much of Fox and his crazy collections all around his home. I frowned. "Isn't a tragic love story a bit too heavy for a class of eight-year-olds?"

She rolled her eyes. "We're mature, mummy. I know about death and stuff."

I froze, but she didn't notice. Her body bounced up and down, wriggling out of my grip. "I'm going to use a dead rose that I found on the sidewalk and dip it in glue to make it hard and then I'm going to paint it black and red and then…" she reeled off her project in intimate detail, charging around the room. Shedding her pink My Little Pony pyjamas, she diligently dressed in the drab greys and greens of her school uniform.

I couldn't do anything but sit and stare at the whirlwind of life that was my daughter.

It wasn't until I stood at the school gate, watching Clara disappear amongst a sea of matching uniforms, that the sharp pang of loss made me double over.

Rushing away from the school grounds, I hid in a bush as I balled my hands and shoved them in my mouth.

I screamed and screamed until my lungs ached, and the helplessness was expunged.

My body racked with silent sobs, purging the mourning already blackening my soul.

Only once I could breathe without wanting to murder someone did I step from my prison of brambles and plan my next step.

Clara would be occupied for the next seven hours. Clue had agreed to collect her after school. That meant I had a full twelve hours to return to Fox and show him exactly what I thought of his broken, secretive, non-touching ridiculousness.

It was time to make him pay.

"You again." The bouncer with the face between a bulldog and a shark eyed me up and down. "Where's sugar tits?"

Fox's mansion loomed above me. The gargoyles and block work somehow looked more menacing in sunlight than it did in the dark. It spoke of abandonment, of misplacement. No other house in the family affluent suburb looked so disturbing.

A chill darted down my back.

Why exactly did you come back?

Fox's silver eyes entered my mind again, tugging me against my will, bringing me back to finish what we started.

My hands clenched, but I forced myself to smile sweetly. My skinny jeans, suede boots, and grey shirt were a polar opposite of the monstrosity I showed up in last night. At least all my extremities were covered and not on show to gawk at.

"She isn't coming. Just me." When he didn't open the door wide enough to let me pass, I snapped, "Let me in."

He shook his head, slouching against the frame. "Nuh uh. Club doesn't open for another eight hours. Unless you're a VIP who has access to the facilities prior to opening, you're shit outta luck. Come back when the moon rises if you want to get laid by a champion." He thrust his hips like an ignoramus. "Unless you want a freebie here and now?"

I rolled my eyes. "I would rather stab myself in the eye."

He clutched his chest dramatically, staggering as if I'd shot him. "Cruel bitch. You sure know how to wound a guy."

Standing as straight as possible, I demanded, "Call Obsidian Fox. He'll let me in. I guarantee it." Crossing my arms over my chest, I flinched as the silver chain around my stomach pinched my flesh.

I'd honoured Fox's command to keep it on. I'd been tempted to find a pair of pliers and tear the jewellery off, but if my plan worked, I needed it. It was yet another weapon in my arsenal. My temper being my first artillery. My tongue was ready to give that man a lashing.

He needed to know just what I thought of him. And how I would *not* put up with his bullshit.

He'd promised me two hundred thousand dollars. I wanted my daughter to survive, and he was my only hope.

The bouncer scowled. "He's not to be disturbed." He pointed to the sky with a chubby finger. "The bossman sleeps like the nocturnal. No sluts till club hours."

It took every inch of my self-control not to pull the small blade free from my hair and stab him in his jugular. "Just call him, will you?"

He crossed his muscular arms, shaking his head. "Nope."

There was only one thing left to do. Pulling my large handbag around to my front, I rummaged inside, pushing aside an extra set of underwear and spare blouse. Pulling out the black t-shirt I'd stolen from Fox's wardrobe, I found the embroidered silver emblem and shoved the whole thing in the bouncer's face. "What's this?"

His forehead furrowed, squinting at the fox stitched into the shirt. "Hey, that's—"

"Your boss's clothing? Yep." I dropped my arm. "I took it

from him last night after we made an agreement. I'm staying with him for a month. He let me run a few errands this morning, and now I need to return to him." The lie spilled effortlessly from my tongue.

The bouncer scowled, gnawing on his lip in deliberation. "I dunno…"

Shoving the t-shirt back into my bag, I snapped, "What do you think he'll do if I tell him I had to wait on the doorstep for eight hours because his lunatic bouncer didn't get the memo?"

His eyes widened, dilating with anxiety. It seemed everyone had a fear about their capricious boss. Finally, he shoved the door wider and motioned me in. "If you're telling lies, I'll make sure to pay you back."

His tone didn't scare me—Fox had reminded me that fear wasn't in my repertoire.

Storming down the long corridor, I ignored the artwork and statues. For a house painted all in black with black upholstery and haberdashery, the sun had a strong-willed determination to warm every crevice. The glass ceiling above meant it was as bright inside as it was out.

Making sure to only touch the metal door with the child in wonderland and not the child with dead body parts at his feet, I entered Obsidian's fighting floor.

I slammed to a stop. I'd expected the arena to be abandoned—to have the place to myself, but the boxing ring was occupied by four men, pairing up to spar. The cage held a man in a spandex body suit practicing jabs and throws at an imagery opponent.

A cleaning crew worked industriously around the fighters, disinfecting floors and wiping down rigging. Even medics stood attentive and waiting at their stations, watching the preliminary warm-ups, no doubt ready to receive a patient.

Keeping my bag tucked close to my side, I bee-lined for the black carpeted stairs. Even though members were early, it didn't mean the boss would be ready to work. The large clock on the wall said it was only midday. I knew where I would find him.

In bed.

Vulnerable.

Hopefully asleep, so I could have the pleasure of screaming him awake.

Walking straight and with purpose, I refused to make eye contact with anyone. I cursed the bruising between my legs. Every step made my heart race, knowing I was about to face the man who hurt me.

I passed the Muay Thai ring, but slammed to a halt when a large man stepped purposely in my way. I didn't know what he wanted, and I wasn't in the mood.

"Move, please," I said, glaring.

He chuckled, stroking his five o' clock shadow. His body flexed with thick muscles and tribal tattoos. "That's no way to be polite." His voice sounded like a drum full of gravel. "I didn't know entertainment arrived early." He stepped closer, forcing himself into my bubble. "You fancy serving a winner after his fight?" He licked his lips, dragging icy blue eyes up and down my figure. "I'll fuck you *real* good."

"No thanks." I sniffed, keeping calm. "I'm busy; please let me pass."

He chuckled. "Oh, you used the magic word. Was that *please* let me suck your dick, baby doll? I think that's what I heard." His arm came forward, landing on my shoulder. His touch didn't scare me, but the use of the pet name did.

My body tensed, looking for a weakness to exploit. "Get. Your. Hands. Off. Me."

His bushy eyebrows slammed into a frown. "That's no way for a Fox Girl to talk to a paying client. Do you know the fucking fees I pay to come here? It's extortion."

I shrugged. "What you do with your money is your business. Now leave me the hell alone."

Shaking his head, he muttered, "You're not getting it, baby doll. I pay fees and included in those fees are the use of certain pleasurable activities." His fingers slithered off my shoulder, dropping to my chest.

I flinched as he grabbed my breast hard and twisted. "Get in a private room. Now."

Reaching automatically into my hair, I fumbled for my knife clip. My anxious fingers touched the blade, palming it discreetly.

A rush of power filled me holding the weapon. "Lay another finger on me and I'll make you regret it."

Two fighters nearby stopped towelling off and looked up. They murmured something to each other, watching our altercation. Their eyes dropped to my figure, glowing from confusion to interest.

Oh, shit, how could I get out of this without it turning into a bloodbath?

Deciding deception was the best way to go, I forced my body to relax. Placing a hand over my captors, I slipped into seductress and whispered, "Not here. You want me? You can have me, but your eyes only." *The moment I get you alone, I'm cutting your balls off.*

He grinned, showing yellowing teeth. "Knew you'd come around, baby doll."

A strong arm suddenly wrapped around my waist, yanking me backward into hard muscle. "What the fuck are you doing here?"

My nose swam with scents of sun and salt and wind. Whereas Fox smelled of the underworld he'd been birthed from, Oscar smelled of freedom.

"I came back as I made a deal with your boss." Nodding at the guy in my way, I added, "This lunatic thinks he can order me around."

Oscar breathed hard; his muscles pressed against my spine. I never relaxed even as his hard heat seeped into my body. I didn't like how firmly he held me.

I squirmed a little, testing his hold. Oscar grunted. "Stop moving. I know Fox wants you. I didn't deal with his bullshit last night for him to kill me today if he found out I didn't return you. It's your funeral for being stupid enough to come back."

Where did Fox go last night?

My mind raced as Oscar clutched me harder. "Spiderweb, nice to see you so early. You know the rules. You want a fuck; you have to wait till official opening hours."

Spiderweb bared his teeth. "I see a perfect little bug in front of me. She was all for it, weren't you, baby doll?"

I couldn't stop the shudder. I would never get over my hatred for that name.

Oscar stilled, a gust of hot air from his breath hit my neck. "She's not for sale."

My back stiffened, but I let him talk about me as a possession. He was trying to protect me after all.

"Whatever. Fair's fair. She's on the floor. I saw her. I want her."

Oscar tugged me harder into him, staking a possessive claim with his hand on my hip. I couldn't see him, but his voice seethed with authority. "She's already bought."

My temper flared. I wanted to disagree. I wasn't a pet or a piece of crockery to be bought and traded. I'd agreed to sell something to Fox in return for hope. What we'd agreed to wasn't just sex.

You want him as much as you want his money.

The reminder came from nowhere, bringing with it the heat simmering in my stomach. I'd wanted him before he took me so callously. The attraction was still there, frothing beneath my anger.

Spiderweb crossed his arms; his muscles jumped, making his spider tattoos seem like they were alive. "By who? I'll pay extra. I want that fine piece of ass." He blew me a disgusting kiss.

I bit my tongue against saying anything. Oscar's muscles bunched behind me, rippling with energy. "By the owner of this fucking club. So beat it."

Spiderweb sneered. "The owner can have anyone he

wants." Anger glowed in his eyes. "I want that one." Pointing at me, he grabbed his crotch. "She'd feel real good. I can tell."

I squeaked as Oscar grabbed my left breast. *What the hell?*

His breath blew hot on the side of my neck as he snapped, "See this?" Letting go, he added, "His. Not yours. His."

His voice held an accent—American perhaps, even though he looked like a true-blue Aussie with his tanned skin, bright blue eyes, and salt-bleached hair.

Whispering in my ear, he said, "Why did you come back? I thought he hurt you?"

"He did hurt me." I wanted to leave it at that, but I needed Oscar on my side if I had any chance of achieving what I wanted. "But he's hurting more."

Oscar didn't say a word. Shit, I said the wrong thing. I was incorrect to think he cared about his boss.

Oscar muttered, "If you think he'll change, you're delusional, but I won't stop you from destroying yourself."

Spiderweb took a hasty step toward me. "Hey! Stop sweet talking my girl. I'm taking her."

My temper exploded. I'd had enough of idiotic male testosterone. Shoving Oscar off me, I hissed, "I'm not yours. I'm not his. I'm mine. Now excuse me, Neanderthals, I came back for a reason, and I'm not done."

Stalking away, I dashed up the stairs and thanked my one bit of luck: Fox's office door stood open. Securing the knife clip into my hair, I entered.

I'd drawn my fair share of blood and hated the aftermath. The tremors, the constant questions, the wondering if I could've handled the situation better. I second-guessed every decision, looking for ways I could've prevented whatever happened.

The shakes began. They always did after a tense situation. My body, drenched in adrenaline, still wanted to fight.

My eyes fell to the carpet where Fox strangled me last night. My fingers flew to my neck, pressing lightly on the tender bruises. The memory of his hand around my throat made my heart pound harder.

He'd switched so quickly from worshipping kisser to crazed psychopath. There was no helping someone with such deep-rooted psychological issues. I should just turn around and forget about all of this.

Even as I thought it, I knew it wasn't an option.

Clutching my bag closer, I took a few deep breaths, forcing the build-up of stress to filter away. Only once my fingers were steadier and I could move without jumping did I traverse the office and open the parallel door.

Looking left and right, I held my breath. The length of the corridor held no one—empty as a gravesite.

Once again, the sensation that my life was changing occurred. I'd felt it when I first locked eyes with Fox—the pull, the gravity between us. It tugged me in a direction I hadn't known existed until him.

Fate had brought us together because we could help each other. I didn't believe in fairy-tales, but I did believe in serendipitous encounters. Fox could help me with Clara. I could help him with his demons.

After I hurt him.

My mind swam with Clara. The crushing weight of missing her kept me glued to the carpet. I would never forgive myself if I failed her.

Swallowing hard, I tiptoed toward Fox's bedroom. Pressing copious amounts of codes on the keypad, I finally figured out the right one. Turned out I hadn't memorized it very well.

The lock clicked open, and the door handle turned easily in my hand. The moment I entered the room, there was no turning back. I would tell the truth. I would force him to listen. And I had no clue how he would react.

What are you doing, Zel?

I honestly couldn't answer that question. I truly didn't know. The risk of coming back to a man as unstable as Fox was suicidal. It wasn't just the allure of money that brought me back. Yes, my heart never stopped bleeding at the thought of losing Clara, but something else drove me, too. Something, I didn't like. Something, I couldn't ignore.

Pushing the door open, I strode in, eyes zeroing in on the bed.

Empty.

My heart raced as I moved forward. The black decorated room was vacant. Sun danced on bronze and iron, glittering off statues of wolves and faceless boys. All around me I felt the threat of pain held tight in the metal sculptures.

A shield hung on the wall to my left, glinting with symbols and careful etching. The markings summoned me, whispering of a story—maybe a key to Fox.

Every chisel line looked angry, too deep, too filled with violence. Three Russian words caught my attention, scratched with no finesse, looking angry and sinister.

Letting my bag fall off my shoulder with a soft thud, I reached with inquisitive fingers to trace the foreign letters. I wished I understood what they meant.

The hair on the back of my neck stood up; my heart galloped. There'd been no sound, no hint that anything dangerous had entered the room, but my senses knew.

I stepped back from the metal shield, looking toward the bathroom door.

Wide open, with a cloud of steam billowing behind him, Fox stood glaring at me.

My stomach twisted drinking in his tight posture, the dampness of his hair. He didn't say a word—he didn't need to. His gaze was so intense it pummelled me from across the room. So many questions, so many accusations lived in his snowy depths.

I thought I'd never see you again.

Our deal is broken.

Leave.

Run.

I don't want you here.

I tried to communicate just as silently, showing him just

how pissed off I was, but that I understood, too.

You hurt me, but I came back.

You owe me for what you did.

I hate you, but I want to help you.

The silent conversation ended with Fox standing taller, drawing my eyes down his fully clothed body. His messy dark-bronze hair dripped moisture onto his shoulders, but his toned body was encased in a black sweater and black cotton trousers.

He dressed even thinking he was alone—why? I could understand physical shyness—even though he had no reason to be shy with his physique, but I couldn't understand the need to hide whatever existed beneath his clothing.

I spoke before I consciously made the decision to communicate. "What happened to you?"

His jaw was swollen, and one eye had a large cut beneath it, all puffed and purple. Blood crusted his hairline and he kept an arm tight against his side, protecting either his organs or ribs.

I balled my hands, fighting the urge to nurse him as he shuffled from the doorway toward the bed. He never took his eyes off me.

The energy in the room sparked and fizzled with awareness. I'd never been so in-tune with someone before—regardless if I lusted for them or hated them.

I bit my lip as he hissed in discomfort, lowering himself from standing to sitting on the bed. Despite his obvious pain, there was something different about him.

Gone was the fine edge of…I didn't know… power, hatred, poise maybe? He lacked the tense fierceness, the tightly reined control. Before, he looked like he could reap Armageddon, now he looked…relaxed. He looked tired.

The man before me was… content. A strange conclusion for someone bleeding and breathing shallowly, but his white-grey eyes weren't haunted. They were clear and focused and angry.

My heart fluttered, drawn to the damaged, magnetised to the need in him. Seeing him vulnerable wilted away my anger.

Carefully, he swung his legs onto the bed and reclined against the black fluffy pillows. His eyes trailed over my body, taking their time, branding me.

The bruising in my core turned from aching to throbbing. *You came here to scream at him. Don't fall into the trap of attraction.*

Sucking in a determined breath, I stomped to the end of the bed and clutched the gnarly tree bed-end. The cold metal gave me something to focus on. I glowered. "You hurt me last night. I came back to tell you exactly what I thought of you—to inflict some pain in retribution, but I see karma works fast and someone beat me to it."

His jaw worked, but he didn't reply.

Fine, if that was how he wanted to play. "Want me to guess how you came to be bruised and beaten? You want to know the truth about me…well, I want to know the truth about you. If I had more sense I would never have come back, but lucky for you I care about someone more than myself, and I'm doing this for them. I'm earning the money for their future."

"Well that just makes you fucking selfless then, doesn't it?" Fox snarled. "I don't want to hear about your reservations and regrets returning to me. If you feel that strongly just piss off."

I rolled my eyes, my temper heating. "You think I would willingly come back for abuse? Don't kid yourself. You practically raped me, and I should feel what exactly? I'll tell you what I feel: lust for the money you promised. I made a mistake thinking I could enjoy my time with you. I wasn't mentally prepared for you taking me because I'd hoped I would find satisfaction, but you taught me yet another lesson, and I won't make the same mistake twice."

Fanning my arms, I snapped, "I'm here. I'm here for your enjoyment, and I don't expect anything in return but your cash. I guess I truly am a whore."

His eyes flashed. "You're not a fucking whore. And I get it—you want to hurt me by saying you no longer want me in any capacity but to pay you. Congratulations, I understand completely."

"Good."

"Fine!" His face twisted, bruising and redness on his cheek highlighting his scar. "At least this way we know exactly where we stand."

I nodded. "Precisely."

Fox's eyes lost the flash of anger filling suddenly with tiredness. "Anything else you wish to scream at me before I pass out?" He looked defeated—smaller and vulnerable.

My heart thumped, diluting my anger with compassion. Running my finger along the top of the bed-end, I asked, "What happened to you? Where did you go last night?"

He scowled, shaking his head. "I went nowhere and nothing happened." He winced a little as he shifted on the bed. "Oscar told me he dropped you off last night, but he refused to tell me your address."

Relief siphoned through my blood. There was no way I wanted Fox knowing where I lived—not while Clara was there. "And he beat you up for asking?"

Fox laughed, holding his side. "As if." His eyes narrowed. "I got someone else."

My mouth plopped open. "You asked for that to happen to you?"

His lips twisted, refusing to answer. His eyes fell to the necklace he'd put on me last night. The silver disappeared down my cleavage, tickling my stomach whenever I breathed.

I sucked in a small breath as his eyes flashed to smouldering. Ignoring the burn in my belly, I pointed at the split in his lip. "Did you go searching for pain?"

His eyes flared and he winced. "Shut up."

My heart thudded knowing I was on the right track. "I'm not going to shut up until I know the truth." Pacing at the bottom of the bed, I added, "You're bleeding. If you didn't ask for this, then what happened? Did someone mug you?"

He sighed heavily. "Something like that." His gaze latched onto mine. "You're forgetting our deal. You agreed to answer my questions, not the other way around." He flinched as a wave of pain went through his body. "It doesn't matter anyway. You left. Our deal is void. Get out. I don't want you here."

I scowled. "I left because you hurt me. You promised me you wouldn't. It wasn't me who broke the rules—it was you."

He snarled. "I got what I wanted. I fucked you, and I didn't have to pay. You're the one who walked out the door and left—you're the one who decided I wasn't worth two hundred thousand dollars to stick it out for a few weeks." His hands balled on either side of his body. "Don't you get it? I got what I wanted. I fucked you and now I'm over it, so do me a favour and leave. I don't want you here." He clipped every word, layering them with hostility.

My pissed off mood deflated. I should've been offended, annoyed, or jilted, but instead I just felt sad. Sad for him. Sad for his lies.

The more I looked, the more I saw, and the more my heart went out for him. He was like a rabid dog, snarling, frothing at the mouth, guaranteed to bite my hand off if I got too close, but in his feral eyes lurked a plea. Something that said: don't give up on me even if I bite.

Narrowing my eyes, I snapped, "You're rude, but it won't work."

"What won't fucking work?"

I moved from my place at the foot of the bed, inching closer to him. He stiffened, glaring at my every step. I stopped at the side of the bed just out of touching distance. His body never unwound. If anything, his muscles bunched harder.

"You're pushing me away because you're a coward. You don't want me to leave as I'm the only one strong enough to put up with your bullshit."

His face went stark white. Eyes flashed with livid rage. "*What* did you just say to me?"

"You're a coward. You hide behind violence. You dish it out. You invoke it to happen to you, but really, you're lost and alone and you're drowning." My mind collided with so many things I wanted to say. "Something's destroying you inside.

You're looking for a way out but you can't find it. That's why you surround yourself with fighters. It's a world you know. The only world you can breathe in."

His teeth ground together; his body vibrated. "Get. Out. *Get out!*"

Ignoring him, I rushed on. "I think you bribed me to stay, because I'm the only one you have ever felt any connection with. I think chemistry and attraction is completely new to you and instead of asking me out on a date, you stole my knife and kidnapped me. I don't know what's going on in that brain of yours, but I'm beginning to understand."

He sucked in a harsh breath, his muscles shuddering with anger. "You think you know me? You think you can wave a fucking magic wand and *fix* me?" He moved to get off the bed, and I backed away. His feet touched the floor, but he didn't stand up, almost as if he forced himself to stay seated, to stay away from me. "It was a mistake to fuck you. It was a mistake to let you anywhere *near* me. You're crazy with your stupid conclusions. I'm not a pet project for a girl scout to fix. Get the fuck out and stop boring me."

"I'm boring you? Oh, my God, you're completely backwards. If you were bored you wouldn't care what I thought. You're not bored, Fox, because you know I'm right. What do you want from me? What were you hoping to achieve?"

From my place in the centre of the carpet, I balled my hands. "Did you think you'd win my affection by raping me? Or how about making me swoon with your fucked-up inability to be touched? I wanted you—I've been honest about that right from the start—but what I don't want is a man who's so far off the realm of sanity that I can't understand or predict. If you gave me the money right now, I'd leave, and I would never think about you again."

My throat closed on the lie.

Fox clutched the edge of the mattress. "Don't let me keep you, *dobycha.* Congratulations on fucking hurting me more than the injuries I'm suffering. You just proved how shallow you are. You never truly wanted me—if you did, you'd want more than just what my bank balance can give you!"

My entire body hummed with anger. "I'm the shallow one? How about you? You think you're one-dimensional; you provide a scarred scary persona who owns an illegal fight club, but that's not the truth. Want to hear my version of the truth and then you can see if I'm shallow enough not to care?"

I didn't wait for his reply. "You can't be touched. I would never be able to guess why that is but it left me wondering—why did you buy me for sex if you never undress and seem to abhor the very idea of being near anyone? You wear clothes as if they'll protect you from something. You sculpt and work with metal because you have control over the destiny of the piece that you're creating. You're screwed up and confused and—"

"Shut up! Get the fuck out." I leaped back as Fox stood upright. He roared, "Stop it. Just leave me alone!"

My ears rang from his fierceness; my heart bruised my ribs it thudded so hard, but for the first time, I sensed a crack. He wasn't Mr. Obsidian in that moment, he was just a man with a primal temper. A man on the verge of losing it.

"No. You're going to hear me." *I'm going to break you.*

His teeth ground loudly sending shivers scattering over my back. Swallowing hard, I demanded, "Had you kissed anyone before? Before me?"

He glared daggers, piercing my skin with his hatred. "What does it matter? Have you ever been so badly abused every bone was broken in your body? Have you ever gone days without food or had so much blood on your hands you wanted to kill yourself?" His chest heaved under his sweater.

We froze.

His nostrils flared. He didn't mean to slip—he'd said something fundamental—a huge insight into his past. I wouldn't let him retreat now. Taking a step forward, I pushed him, kept prodding, as if he were a cornered animal.

"No, but you have." I couldn't handle this. It hurt to think about Fox's past—what he kept hidden. He'd almost killed me. He'd taken me against my will. I owed him my hatred, not my pity.

But how could I fear someone in such emotional pain?

The scar on his cheek glowed bright red, looking as if it wept with fresh blood. Colour flushed his neck line, highlighting faded scars I hadn't noticed before. He seemed to throb before my eyes—changing from a zombie, a lifeless creature still going through the motions of life, to a man craving freedom.

"I know you're not Australian, and I know your scar was a punishment. Tell me."

He shook his head, damp hair flying. He bared his teeth. "Let me figure this out. You think you know me? You think you can read me and figure out what shit lives inside my head? You think you have superpowers?" He threw his arms up. "What other things do you think I happen to be, *dobycha?* A cutthroat murderer? A drug dealer? How about a rapist?" Running a harsh fingertip down the redness of his scar, he laughed. "Hang on, I guess I am a rapist after last night. Everything you think you know about me is tainted because of this. This scar—it makes you pity me and fear me."

His shoulders bunched as he took a step forward. "You think you can guess how I got this? What I've done? Stop spinning your lies and fabricating stories. You're so far off you're in the realm of fantasy you're embarrassing yourself. Do us both a favour and fuck off."

His lips snapped shut. A metre separated us, keeping me safe from his seething rage.

Not once had he moved to grab or hurt me. Not once had he dropped his guard. All the while hating me for making him face the truth, he protected me by staying away.

Fatigue hit me and I sighed heavily. "You don't trust yourself at all do you?"

He blinked at my whisper, so quiet after yelling.

My eyes met his, and I gave him a tiny smile. "Any normal person would touch and squeeze and manhandle each other in an intense argument, but you—you keep your distance. It's not me you don't trust—it's yourself."

He didn't say a word, trembling in the wake of his terrible anger. Despite the colour flushing his neck and rage glowing in his eyes, he withheld his strict self-control. What would happen if I touched him? What would he do if I opened my arms and hugged him?

You'd die.

I knew it. As sure as the sun would set and rise again.

Silence fell between us, and my eyes dropped to his forearms. The jumper he wore had been pushed up, revealing corded muscle and scars.

Scars. Scars. Scars.

More than I could count. Some faded and silver, others red and healing. But it was the four straight and perfect lines seeping with bright red crimson that caught my attention.

I'd seen marks like that before. On another. I'd witnessed first-hand the fractured mind of an individual who sought pain to help remove the build-up of agony inside.

Clue was a self-harmer.

Over time, I'd helped her stop, but I would never forget walking into the kitchen one night and watching her drag a sharp blade over her skin. I'd shuddered in horror, but she'd breathed heavily in relief.

I hadn't judged. I hadn't said a word, but through friendship and support I helped her channel her pain into exercise and less destructive methods.

"You self-harm because you can't deal with whatever lives inside you," I murmured.

He choked on a swallow. Tense seconds ticked past before he took a small step toward me. His joints clicked from abuse past and new. Standing to his full height, he hissed, "Leave now before I do something I'll regret." His eyes flashed as he took another step toward me.

I stepped away, keeping out of touching distance. My anger came back swift and hot. Waving at him, taking in his furiousness, I growled, "You think you can scare me? You're wrong. I've dealt with worse than you. You're kidding yourself with your dramatics."

Fox exploded from tightly coiled weapon to shrapnel bomb. "Get the fuck out! Now!"

"No!"

"Leave!"

"Not until you hear me out."

"There's nothing to hear!" He gripped his head, tugging his hair. "Leave now. Leave! Fucking go!"

Every survival instinct in me wanted to obey, but I'd pushed him this far. "I understand you, more than you think."

He laughed manically. "You? Miss perfect—the woman who has it all? Don't make me prove how ridiculous you are. You're a fucking chameleon with your lies and secrets."

Cocking his head, he stared harder, going deeper inside me than anyone had before. I didn't like how weak and insecure he made me. I didn't like feeling that my house of lies would come tumbling down at any moment. I didn't like being a specimen under scrutiny. "You think I don't see you? You have a past, same as anyone—but it's darker. You've done things others wouldn't understand, but it doesn't mean you know me. I don't trust you, Hazel Hunter." Moving forward, he pointed at the door behind me. "I won't ask again. Final warning. Get the fuck out and leave me alone."

I'd pushed hard, but I didn't win. I'd done my best. Backing away, I narrowed my eyes. "You want me gone, fine. But you owe me. You owe me for whatever connection sprang between us last night. You felt it—same as me. You forced me to agree to your terms as you couldn't ignore the call. What if that connection was the one thing that could help you? What if I'm the one person you've been searching for?"

I hadn't meant to say that. It was presumptuous. It reeked of high-handed righteousness. I didn't know if he felt the same draw. The same strange pull.

He reared back, knuckles going white from clenching his fists so hard. "Who the fuck are you to think you know me? You know nothing. *Nothing*! I don't need your help. I don't need your cure!" His voice changed from unrepentant anger to a slight thread of confusion. He stressed the word 'cure', slipping from Australian accent to something guttural, foreign, something that suited him far more than the falseness of his Australian twang.

I saw the truth. Clear as day. Everything I'd said had been real. Everything he tried to keep hidden came to light. "I'm not the only one lying. You are." I tilted my head, eyeing him closely. It was as if answers came to me from nowhere. Seeing through his shadows and secrets, latching onto small snippets of truth. "I think you're hiding from something and live in fear every day."

Fox bristled and seethed and stewed.

All the caring, stupid instincts swelled, hoping he'd crack, wishing he'd let his walls down. This man didn't need a woman to warm his bed. He needed a psychiatrist. I didn't want to be near someone so toxic, but I couldn't walk away either. "You owe me to let me help you."

Fear suffocated my throat as he seemed to grow larger, adopting an icy exterior that gave no hint of remorse or humanity.

I froze, locked in his ferocious stare. Trouble was I couldn't read him in that moment. He'd shut down, so all I saw was a cold man with a vicious streak amplified by the wicked scar.

He shuddered as his entire body went into lockdown. Muscles bunched beneath his clothing, his aura trembled with aggression and rebellion. "I owe you nothing," he spit.

My heart raced. Truth screamed loud and clear. Somehow he earned the facial scar thanks to a debt gone wrong. He wasn't a free man. He was owned by someone who either kept him on a tight leash, or abused him so much it wouldn't take much more for him to snap.

Hardly breathing, I dropped my eyes to his trembling body. I wanted to figure out the dark damage lurking in his eyes.

My God. What happened to him?

My gaze zeroed in on his as if I was a compass needle and he was my north. I'd never suffered a phenomenon such as this. Never been so tuned to another. Perhaps we were kindred souls—linked by something past the realm of understanding. Kismet.

It's too much. Too intense. Too dangerous.

I had Clara to protect and save—I had no reserves left for someone so deeply broken. It was time to cut him loose and forget—not just for my sanity, but my future as well. I hated that for the first time in forever, I felt weak. Weak because no matter how much I wanted to help him, I wouldn't be able to. He was unsaveable.

Exhaling heavily, I let it out—forcing all my questions and curiosity out of my mind. My life was already complicated enough. I didn't need to think about adopting a lost stray with a bite that would undoubtedly leave me in pieces.

"Forget it." Dropping my voice to a whisper, I said, "I'll go. But you should know I came back to give you a piece of my mind, but also to continue our agreement. I refuse to stay here for a month, but I was willing to spend my days with you. To give you what you wanted. Despite what I said—I did want you. I felt the same pull."

His back rippled with tension. The air seemed to crackle and weep around him with a mixture of regret and self-loathing. For a moment, I thought he would throttle me. Reach out and grab my throat in his large hands and wring the air from my body. But then his anger diminished, flickering out to be replaced with utter coldness. "I don't care. I never wish to see you again."

Fuck him. I was done.

Whirling around, I stalked to the door. My anger crashed over me in a wave. I gave him my passion and offered a lifeline, and he threw it in my face.

The moment I walked out the door I never wanted to see him again. I wouldn't be able to stand it. I needed to make sure the goodbye was final.

"Don't ever come near me again, Fox. If I see, or hear, or find out you've come near, I won't just hurt you.

"I'll kill you."

Ten

ROAN

The day I completed the final phase of training, two things happened. They tattooed me with the mark of the highest operative, and I was informed of my inheritance. For years I'd lived in a cell inside a giant manor; I'd been told what to eat, told who to kill, and when to speak. I lived in the same black clothes all the recruits lived in. I followed the code.

Then they told me who I'd been before they stole me on my sixth birthday.

I wasn't a pauper or a bum off the street like some of the other kids. I wasn't middle class from a generic family.

Oh, no.

Turned out, I was twenty-fourth in line to the throne. My ancestors had been kings and queens; my family God-fearing and respected.

They told me I was to inherit a multi-million dollar fortune of property, jewellery, and cash.

My real name was Roan Averin, but none of that mattered.

It didn't matter as I was a royal heir to a succession that no longer existed because I'd killed every last person from my bloodline. No one knew I was alive. No one knew I existed.

There was no one left.

Just me.

And I belonged to them.

"I'll kill you."
"Do it or I'll kill you."
"Obey or I'll kill you."
"Slaughter them or I'll kill you."
"Kill and sever and decapitate or I'll kill you."

The threat resonated in my head over and over and over. Zel's parting comment threaded with my past. *"I'll kill you."*

The small hold I had on my conditioning disintegrated, hurling me head first into darkness. My brain swam with memories of my faceless handlers. All I saw were waterfalls of red and slicing blades through flesh.

The urges sucked me deep and dark until I forgot I no longer lived that life. I was theirs. A nobody with no feelings or hopes or dreams. Worthless.

I'd been able to control myself while arguing with Zel thanks to the pain in my joints. The beating Poison Oaks gave me kept me sane—barely. I'd kept my distance—hating her perception, her correct guesses all the while saving her from myself.

Her passion turned my cock stiff as a fucking pole. My blood raced to take her again—to make promises—to swear I could do better. To promise the next time I took her I'd be strong enough to touch her sweetly. But the pain wasn't enough and every lash of her voice made me tremble, fighting my past.

I screamed and cursed for her own protection. I wanted her gone forever so I never had to worry about harming her.

But then she used the one sentence guaranteed to hurl me back in time.

"I'll kill you."

I groaned as the room swirled like a black hurricane,

propelling me from safety to horror. The aliveness in my blood switched from wanting to protect Zel to wanting to kill her, and I could no longer ignore the call. The conditioning was too strong, too ingrained, too deep to reject.

The rules I'd been made to live by compounded in my skull, pounding with an insane headache. She was a weakness. She was an enemy. She knew too much.

She has to die.

My jaw ached from clenching so hard, and I howled like the wolves who'd kept me company all those lonely nights. The last of my humanity filtered away. I was about to kill the only person who might've had a chance at saving me.

And I couldn't stop it.

Icy cold obedience flowed in my veins.

I launched at the woman intent on ruining me—intent on ripping my past and secrets from my broken corpse. She had the audacity to say she could fix me. There was nothing left to fix. I was a highly trained Ghost. She had to go.

Soon, she wouldn't be a threat. Soon, she'd be dead.

She screamed as I grabbed her from the door and shoved her face first into the carpet.

My knees slammed against the floor on either side of her body; my hands wrapped around her throat. The unprotected muscles of her neck were an aphrodisiac to my need to obey. My need to kill.

I revelled in the power of my fingertips as I dug them deeper and deeper into her flesh. The pain in my body from the fight diminished, blocked off just like I'd been trained—allowing me to focus entirely on the mission at hand.

"Fox! Stop it!" Her voice wobbled and wavered before I squeezed harder, cutting off her air supply. She made a pitiful wail in her chest, thrashing beneath me.

Her arms flew back, fingers desperately scratching at my forearms. Her nails drew blood, slipping with red, losing traction. The coppery stench of blood filled my nose.

Her hands struck my thighs, my elbows, flailing around,

hitting anything in reach. Her body convulsed as the terror of dying hit her central nervous system.

Her fingers locked around mine; her touch only made it worse.

The fog returned to my vision, turning everything blizzard white. I no longer knew where I was. All I knew was I had to kill her before my handler found out. He'd punish me if he knew someone had guessed my secrets. He'd find more victims for me to maim.

She was a liability. She was detrimental to my mission.

"You always were reliable, Fox."

My heart raced in pride. My coach, my trainer—my father for all intents and purposes—smiled, but didn't pat my back or shake my hand. Unnecessary touching wasn't allowed. "I think you're ready."

My heart thudded for a different reason. I wasn't ready. Never ready.

Standing as tall as my fifteen-year-old frame would let me, I said, "Yes, sir. Of course, sir."

His eyes shone, knowing what I'd finally agreed to do.

I wished I could kill myself. After this, there would be no one left.

I just agreed to kill my brother.

The final step to finishing the transformation from human to Ghost.

Zel suddenly stopped scratching my arms and twisted her body. Her left leg scissored outward, kicking as high as she could go. Her hand flew to her tangled hair.

I squeezed harder.

She grunted with the last few dregs of oxygen in her lungs; her fingers erupted from her hair, clutching something.

The thick pulse of blood in her veins chugged harder, inching closer to cardiac arrest. My eyes smarted, wishing I didn't have to be such a coward. I just wanted to be free. I didn't want to kill this woman. I liked her. I cared for her. I wanted to keep her.

But just like everything I wanted to keep, I wasn't allowed. They all had to die. Every single one.

I bellowed as something sharp plunged into my calf, followed by a slick withdrawal. Another hot, burning slice joined the symphony of agony as Zel plunged the serrated weapon into my thigh.

A Ghost prided themselves on working through pain—nothing would stop our objective, but the flash of torture brought clarity.

What the fuck am I doing?

I scrambled off Zel and scuttled back. Far, far away. Away from touching distance. Away from killing distance.

The white fog from my eyes withdrew, helping me to focus on the present and not the past.

I'm out. They won't know if I don't kill her. I no longer belong to them.

The sudden tsunami of relief crushed my lungs. My head fell forward as I let my hands drop to my sides. I didn't have to kill her. She was safe. The conditioning ebbed away, popping into nothingness in my blood.

I didn't care about the crimson gushing from two gashes in my leg. I didn't care about the red-black stain pooling quickly beneath the wounds. All I cared about was ending my miserable life.

I didn't deserve to live. Not after the atrocities I'd committed or the lack of strength I had to ignore a lifetime of training. I was ruined, and there was no way I could change.

Zel had guessed everything right about me, but she'd also shown just what a lost cause I was. There was only one way to end my suffering, and it wasn't through the gasping, wild-eyed woman slouched in front of me.

Zel squirmed into a lopsided upright position, one hand rubbing her tender throat. Her lips were bluish-white from lack of oxygen; she watched me with tears glassing her eyes. "Don't touch me, you asshole!"

My eyes dropped to her bloody outstretched hand, smeared from stabbing me. She brandished her skinny blade in my direction. "That's twice you've tried to kill me. I'll murder you if you try for a third." Her voice wasn't soft and melodic; it rasped and croaked from strangulation.

"Do it, operative."

"Finish it."

My hands clenched as the commands siphoned through me. I shook my head, trying to clear the conditioning. The need to kill throbbed just out of reach, making me wish I could peel off my skin and find the switch to deactivate it.

I needed serious fucking help. She'd never forgive me. *I'd* never forgive me.

I deserved an eternity of purgatory.

Zel climbed onto her knees, double-fisting the knife. "Who the hell *are* you?"

I dropped my eyes, looking detachedly at the wounds in my legs. The red seemed to twist and helix into shapes. I became entranced watching the droplets spread into a larger stain on the carpet, turning black to deep red. *Who am I? I don't know. I'll never know who I was before they broke me.*

I deliberately poked the oozing wound in my thigh with an unforgiving finger. I winced, hissing through my teeth. The cut wasn't big, only a centimetre in length, but it was deep.

I'd been stabbed, beaten, and tortured more times than I could remember, but Zel was the first female—the only woman—to ever inflict harm on me.

My eyes flew up at the thought. Every injury had been given by a man. Either sought out by fighters or retribution from my handlers.

My anger toward Zel changed to deep respect. Something untangled deep inside me, unlocking long forgotten needs. I wanted companionship, friendship—someone I could rely on to never let me get out of control.

It was as if the sun entered every recess of my brain, chasing away the darkness and despicable past leaving me to see clearly for the first time in my life. Hazel was strong enough, brave enough, stupid enough to put up with me. I could suddenly breathe easier, and the hatred for myself ebbed just a little—leaving me suspended, tingling with hope.

I drank her in: her fire, her temper, her amazing strength.

She was fierce and quick and smart. She'd prevented a Ghost from killing her. No one had been able to stop me mid-mission.

I opened my mouth to say something, anything, but what could I say? How could I put into words the epiphany Zel gave me from stabbing me in the leg? She'd knocked more sense into me with one action than anything she'd screamed at me in passion. She may never forgive me, but I'd fallen more under her spell and had no chance in hell of letting her go.

Panic raced in my veins with a compulsion to tie her up and never let her out of my sight again.

"What's wrong with you, Fox?" Zel snapped me out of my thoughts. She sat braver, slightly recovered. Her lips were parted, eyes wild, and the buttons in her shirt had torn open revealing lace-cupped breasts.

I couldn't tear my eyes away. "Everything's wrong," I murmured. My heart thudded with lust, so different to the driving throb of taking her last night. This was different. It was laced with something deeper, more profound. I wanted to be deep inside her. I didn't want to come fast or search for a quick release, but just feel her heat and rest a while.

Rest.

Sleep.

A chill seeped into my bones, and I dimly wondered how much blood had spewed from my body to floor.

Perhaps it was best if I just let go. Let death finally take me.

Anything would be easier than the constant fight—even if Zel had shown me hope.

A rustling caught my attention and I craned my neck to look at Zel standing above me. "You move and I'll stab you." Her green eyes glowed and the knife stayed pointed in my direction. "Stay there."

The incredible urge to say 'yes, sir' filled me with amazement.

Oh, my fucking hell.

By earning my utmost respect, she'd somehow earned a top

hierarchy in my mind.

I'd done it. I'd found what I'd been searching for and constructed a replacement for my handlers. If I could learn to obey Zel's every command—to find that sweet surrender of never thinking, always obeying—I might find freedom.

I would belong to her body and fucking soul. She could order me to do anything and I would, regardless.

That's not freedom.

I wanted to laugh. I wanted to curse. I hadn't found freedom. I'd just replaced one prison with another.

My head swam as I closed my eyes. *I'm fucked.*

The sound of the door locking gave me something to latch onto, but I let myself drift—welcomed the vagueness, the coldness, ignoring the intermittent shivers and lightheadedness.

Sighing, I let myself tumble back into memories.

The stars above glittered in the black velvet sky. A small flurry of snowflakes made their way into my pit when the wind blew from the northeast.

Frostbite was my only friend and I lay on the icy ground with only leaf matter and mud for insulation.

I made a promise.

The first opportunity, I would kill myself. This wasn't a life. It was servitude. I would be better off dead than alive and doing the devil's work.

Crossing my seventeen-year-old fingers, I swore on the moon.

"I will kill myself to avoid more orders. I'll put myself down like the predator they've trained me to be."

My eyes flew open. I'd forgotten that promise. It'd been pushed to the depths of my mind as more and more travesty was layered upon me.

But I could keep that promise now. I didn't have to search for someone to obey, so I could fall back into old patterns. I could control my own fate for once.

The pill.

My head flopped to the side, looking toward the wardrobe. I couldn't keep putting people around me at risk. I was too messed up; I needed too much help. To think I could change was a fairy-tale. I wasn't the handsome knight who won the girl—I was the scarred troll whose only purpose was to be killed.

It was time to end it.

The day my handler tossed me out, he'd given me a goodbye gift. His parting order had been to swallow the pill and erase myself from existence. I fought the command for days, not wanting to die.

But every day I suffered a slow death of misery.

Zel wasn't my cure after all. There *was* no cure for my disease.

Rolling onto my elbows, I hoisted myself up amongst multitude of aches and spasms. The beating from Poison Oaks made my muscles stiff and unmovable. More blood gushed down my calf and thigh as my heart pumped harder with exertion.

Putting pressure on my leg hurt like a motherfucker, but I walked like normal, forcing my body to move around the injury. I'd worked with worse. I'd gone days with a broken femur or collarbone to finish a mission before I was given any medical care.

The two slashes Zel gave me were nothing.

I left a trail of red behind me as I entered the wardrobe and shoved aside rows and rows of black attire to reach the safe hidden in the back. Squashed into the racks, hidden by cashmere and cotton, I punched in the fourteen digit code and cranked open the door.

My old life greeted me in a gust of memories.

"It's complete. Do you feel the brotherhood, the shared power and awareness?" my handler asked, stepping back and surveying his handiwork. He passed me a mirror. I held it up, angling to see over my shoulder.

My back had been transformed from adolescent skin into a canvas of disaster. Every symbol closed my throat in fear—they'd marked me forever. I would never be free.

Keeping my despair hidden, I nodded. "Yes, sir." Those two little words. The only conversation we were allowed. Every response required nothing more than 'yes, sir.'

"You did good. You took a while to see reason, but you obeyed in the end." He slapped my burning shoulder, smearing fresh blood from the tattoo. "Do you agree?"

My eyes flickered to the small boy's corpse in the corner of the room. Lifeless, blue, starting to smell. I'd done that. It'd taken me weeks to break, but they'd done it.

I was theirs.

"Yes, sir."

The gun lay like a sleeping enemy, resting beside five hundred thousand in cash, and a small medicine bottle with one word on the label.

Konets. Russian for 'end.'

This was the end.

Unscrewing the lid, I tipped the innocent blue pill onto my awaiting palm and stared. What would hell be like? Would I survive more unhappiness?

I'd passed up all rights to go to heaven on my seventh birthday. I knew I had no chance of finding the pearly white light people spoke of.

Looking down at my leg, I frowned at the soppy wetness of my trousers. The blood hadn't stopped. I could just bleed to death.

Take the pill.

It would be fast. Hopefully not too painful.

Working my throat, I tried to create enough saliva to swallow without needing water. My dry mouth refused to cooperate.

I couldn't do anything right.

The weight of everything was suddenly too much, and I bowed my head against the edge of the safe. I would rest for a moment, then find a glass of water. A few more minutes before I died.

I slipped into a semi-trance state and didn't hear the footsteps until it was too late.

My reactions were compromised. I no longer cared.

Something hard cracked against the back of my skull, and I plummeted like a rock.

I was out cold before I hit the floor.

I came to with the sharp prick of someone stitching my leg. I recognised the pull, the tightness. It'd been over two years since I'd been stitched back together, and I found in my fuckedupness that I missed the sensation of being repaired.

My head hammered with every sluggish beat of my heart, and I couldn't swallow the foul taste in my mouth.

Maybe this time I could be put back together the right way.

My gut twisted. The pill! Did I take it and this was hell? That didn't explain the swelling on the base of my skull or the soft murmur of voices. Someone knocked me out, and I guessed they'd used one of the smaller statues sitting on the tables around the room.

My eyes shot wide and I sucked in a breath. Zel bowed over my leg, her forehead furrowed, lips pursed in concentration. Two fingers pinched my skin together while she pulled a needle and surgical thread through the wound.

My hands clenched as the rush of conditioning doused me with violence. My labouring heart beat faster as Hazel touched my thigh. I wanted to scream at her to run, but the sharp pinprick of pain from the needle helped me retain my self-control. Shame filled me. I was addicted. They'd turned me into an addict of agony.

I clutched the bedspread, panting with heat, shivering with chill.

Her eyes rose to meet mine, bright green filling my world. "I have no idea what I'm still doing here. But I couldn't walk out the door when I saw you holding that pill. I know what you were going to do." Her eyes flickered to a medic sitting on the other side of the bed. Masked, dressed in white, his blue eyes never stopped looking at us. She'd brought a bodyguard? Or was the medic supposed to be the one sewing me up?

I blinked, trying to understand.

"The minute this is done I'm leaving, and I never want to see you again," Zel muttered.

My heart tripled its beat, but I nodded. It was the only way.

Zel stabbed the needle in my skin, deliberately punishing me. "He wanted to numb the area while I worked, but I thought you might like the pain." Her eyes held a silent conversation.

I know you self-harm, and I figured this would be what you wanted.

I nodded, battling past my headache. "Thank you." I couldn't say it out loud so I forced the message silently. *I didn't mean to hurt you.*

Apologizing wordlessly wasn't enough. She deserved a heart-felt apology. She deserved me on my fucking knees begging for forgiveness.

Keeping every part of myself on high alert, I captured her bloody glove-covered hand and squeezed. Swallowing hard, I murmured, "I'm so sorry. I have no excuse for what happened, and I know there's no chance you'll forgive me. Just..." I met her eyes, staring hard. "I need you to know you've helped me more than anyone, and I'll never forgive myself for hurting you. I didn't mean to."

She pulled her hand away. "You could've fooled me. The look in your eyes, Fox. You weren't all there. I think you need to find proper treatment."

I wanted to tell her everything. Then and there. I didn't care anymore about secrecy or what they'd do to me if they found out. I just needed it to be freed from inside me.

There's a witness.

I looked at the medic. His masked face was blank; body tense. I shut down. I couldn't discuss what I was in front of him.

Zel caught me looking at him. "Don't worry. He won't touch you."

I frowned, gritting my teeth as she poked me with the needle again. "Why are you the one sewing me up? Do you have medical training?"

Zel's lips flickered into a tiny smile. "He's not doing this as I don't want him in danger. You tried to kill someone who you knew—what would you do to a stranger?" Her eyebrow raised. "I have basic CPR and what I studied to earn a receptionist job at a doctor's practice. But I'm not flying blind. Before you woke up, he helped." Nodding at the medic, she added, "He checked your wounds while you were out and agreed nothing internally is damaged." Her lips twisted into a wry grin. "I'm a good sewer. Ask Clue. I can crochet with the best of them, and I figured this couldn't be much different."

My eyes popped wide, flaming my headache. "Stitching a leg is completely different than stitching a damn pillow."

Her eyes narrowed. "Well, I think I'm doing a damn good job and considering I'm battling the urge to stab you multiple times with this tiny needle for what you did, you can fucking sit there and let me finish." Fire lit her eyes. "If you think you can stop me, or if you move too fast, that lovely gentlemen over there will dose you up with anaesthesia so fast you'll be out cold, and when you wake, I'll be gone forever."

The needle stabbed me hard, deliberately rough. "Understand?"

Instead of being cowered by her tirade, my fucking cock thickened. My heart pumped lust thick and fast, and all I could think of was kissing her. I wanted so fucking much to be normal so I could hug her and kiss her, and thank the universe for giving me an angel.

"As long as you're inflicting pain, I can keep it together." The admission made Zel look up. I lowered my voice, throwing an annoyed glance at the medic. "I want you to know. Everything about me. Maybe then you can understand. I want you, Zel. The thought of you leaving fucking kills me."

Her hands shook—the only sign of emotion. Her eyes tore away from mine, and she resumed her stitching.

We didn't speak again as she finished sewing me up. Her touch was light and gentle, but every stab of the needle gave me what I craved. Somehow, she created a new sensation. Mixed with pain and sweetness, making me surrender to her hypnosis, giving me the strength to ignore the conditioning just for the moment.

I fell into a trance. When I next opened my eyes the medic was gone and Zel had stuck crisp, white bandages over the stitched-up wounds. It was only then I noticed she'd cut off the leg of my trousers.

Her eyes met mine before she ever so carefully, ever so hesitantly, touched a large scar on my shin bone where they'd snapped my leg and then pinned it back together after a mission.

I sucked in a breath, clenching my fists. Without pain the conditioning echoed in my brain.

"Did you do this snowboarding as a child? Or perhaps falling off a motorbike when you were a teenager?" Her voice stayed low, none of the anger and heat from before.

She wanted to know.

Joy lit my heart. She wouldn't leave until I explained. I'd answer any fucking question she had if it helped her forgive me.

For now emotions between us were pure, almost as if the fight had cleared the air for utmost honesty. "No." My own voice shocked me. I'd never spoken to anyone about my past. Ever. Cold chills darted down my back.

She won't forgive you. She'll hate you even more when she learns the truth.

"I'm waiting, Fox. Tell me who you are."

She'd look at me with terror and loathing. She'd feel it was her duty to report me. I'd be locked up in another cage and made to stand trial for what I'd done. Overwhelming fear cracked my heart. "No." I couldn't do it after all.

Her face darkened and her eyes dropped. She focused on her finger trailing around my kneecap. Small X shaped scars decorated the joint where they'd stuck torture devices so I couldn't bend when I walked. They said I had to learn how to run and move in any condition, including being almost disabled.

"Did you fall off a horse, or perhaps were hurt in a car accident?" Her voice whispered. A threat more than a soothe. Her entire body hummed with tension—anger barely contained.

"No."

Her touch crept upward, ticking my thigh, brushing through hairs and tracing old injuries. Every inch she travelled, my stomach tightened. Confusion smothered my brain. The conditioning grew stronger with every sweep, but I clutched the bedspread, reactivating the pain from my bruised knuckles.

I wanted her to stop. My body wanted to kill her because that's what it'd been taught to do if touched. But for once, my brain wanted more. It wanted the softness, the gentle caress.

I wanted more of the sweet torture of being stroked.

Such a novelty. Such a rare gift.

Zel never stopped her feather light touch. "Did you have a boating accident, or fall off a skateboard?" Her voice painted pictures of a carefree kid who'd had a normal upbringing. Had loving parents and a fun-filled childhood. She painted a lie. A lie I desperately wished was the truth.

"No."

Her fingers flattened against my thigh until her entire palm pressed against me.

The conditioning increased its ferocity until I trembled, trying so hard to ignore it. Her body shifted as she moved higher, following the contour of my thigh until her hand disappeared under the torn material of my trousers and brushed against my cock.

I jerked. I gasped.

My brain had too much to filter.

Don't hurt her. Don't kill her. Please keep it together.

All I wanted to do was surrender to the sweet agony she invoked. My hard cock swelled to the point of pain, summoned to life by one innocuous touch.

I groaned as her hot hand clasped me, squeezing firmly. "Does that hurt?"

I couldn't speak, but it did. It killed me from the inside out. I'd never felt such fucking pleasure. Such branding awareness. Nodding, I moaned again as her hand released me, dropping to cup my balls.

All my life I'd avoided touching it, looking at it. The one and only time I'd brought myself to release had come with dire consequences.

Zel grasped me firmly, squeezing with a mix of authority and temper. Her touch sent me spiralling into a cesspit of memories.

"What is this piece of meat, Fox?"

"Nothing, sir!"

"Then why were you jerking it like it was your favourite toy?"

My fifteen-year-old cheeks flamed. I forgot there were cameras in my room. I hadn't meant to touch myself. I hadn't meant to chase the delicious tightness building in my balls.

I didn't mean to get caught.

"If this is proving to be a distraction, we can remove it. Can't we, Fox?"

My heart ceased to beat. "No, sir. You don't have to do that. Never again, sir. I swear, sir."

Sir. Sir. Sir. I couldn't stop begging.

His hard grip on my dick squeezed before letting go. "You touch yourself again, and we'll rip it off."

"Fox. Fucking stop. You're hurting me," Zel snapped. Her palm slapped my cheek, bringing a sharp sting.

My eyes flew open and I jerked my fingers away, releasing her wrist. The moment I freed her, she rolled her hand, bringing blood circulation back into her hand. Her eyes glassed with tears but they weren't sad tears—more like rage. "Why the hell am I trying to help you? You're beyond help!"

My heart stuttered and I grabbed her hand again, massaging life back into it. "Fuck. I'm so sorry. Are you okay?"

The mixture of uncertainty and fear in her eyes undid me, and I'd never been so close to breaking down. After everything I'd done, she still hadn't left. She hadn't given up, and I thanked the fucking universe for whatever connection existed between us. She persevered with me, not because of the money, but because she couldn't walk away.

"No, I'm not okay. Everything about you tells me to run, yet I ignore myself and end up getting hurt again. I hate myself for needing to help others—it's a compulsion that's driving me insane."

She squeezed her emerald eyes before looking right into my soul. "You're driving me crazy but I'm learning and because I'm learning it makes it harder to leave. "

"What are you learning?"

She sighed heavily. "How to help you."

I sucked in a breath, hoping, praying she was right. I'd had my moment of weakness and contemplated suicide, but now I was ready to embrace a cure. I would do anything. *Anything.*

I didn't know what to say.

We stared for an eternity before she whispered, "Do you trust me to do something? I want to see if it works. If it doesn't, I'm done. But if it does, I'll stay and honour our agreement."

Whatever the fuck she wanted to do, I hoped it worked.

"Yes. Do anything you want."

She braced her shoulders and said, "Don't ask questions. Lay back."

I obeyed instantly. She waited for me to rest against the pillows and settled herself on her knees between my legs. My entire body thrummed from having her so close, and I forced my hands under my hips, pinning them beneath me.

"I'm going to touch you now," she whispered.

Before I could reply or prepare, her hand disappeared up my cut-off trouser leg and wrapped boldly around my cock.

"Holy fuck," I groaned. My brain capacity zeroed in on her hot, captivating hand. Every cell in my body gushed with need so sharp I felt like she flayed me alive.

"Concentrate on me touching you. Never stop focusing on my grip."

I struggled to keep my eyes open as my stomach fluttered and my quads tensed to granite. Her gaze locked with mine, clouding with desire.

Another groan erupted from my mouth as her fingers tightened, moving up and down in an endless rhythm determined to shatter my brain. "Tell me what you're feeling, Fox." Her grip twisted around my dick, adding a new sensation.

My eyes wanted to slam closed, but I didn't dare lose myself completely. I might hurt her. I might kill her. "I can feel how hard I am. How much I want to fuck you."

"No. Focus inside. What do you feel?"

Fuck, I didn't like delving into feelings. And I sure as hell didn't want to share them with Hazel.

"Do it." Her hand cupped the tip of me, pressing down, swirling moisture that appeared from nowhere. Shooting stars and earthquakes took up residence in my stomach, needing to release.

"Oh, my God, woman. I'm going to come."

Her grip immediately softened, letting the orgasm fade. "Not till you tell me how you feel."

Goddammit. "I feel torn into pieces that will never fit together. I have so much inside, I just wish I could hit a reboot button and forget about everything until the second you started jerking me off. I was taught to ignore right and wrong. I'm a fucking mess."

Her hand increased its pressure, rewarding me. "Do you want me to stop?" she murmured.

I wanted to say yes. Tell her it wasn't safe, that she'd pushed me too hard, but I had no willpower left. None. Gone.

Non-existent. "No."

Her fingers wrapped harder, stroking me, pumping me. Blood flowered thicker, filling my cock with an eager heat until I blazed for more. I shifted my hips, giving her better access. I wanted to be inside her. I couldn't take much more of her possessive grip.

Zel didn't move or touch me apart from my cock, and I was eternally grateful she kept her distance. But at the same time I was pissed off, annoyed, and wanted so badly to take control.

With her free hand, she inched the waist band of my trousers down my hips, never stopping her mind-bending stroking.

I raised my hips for her to pull the material off. Inch by inch, she slid the ruined trousers further. I didn't care about her touching me. I didn't care that more scars were on display.

All I cared about were the sparks and tingling tightness in my lower belly and dick. The conditioning lost its power over me. Everything ceased to exist but her.

The moment the trousers slid off my ankles, she knelt lower between my legs and squeezed. "I'm going to kiss you."

My eyes shot wide, shattering the spell she'd put me under. The urge to grab her neck pulsed behind my eyes. I couldn't handle her kissing me. I'd lose it.

"No. Don't."

Her tongue darted out, pink and wet. "Not on the lips," she whispered. Her thumb caressed the highly sensitive tip of my cock, pressing against the hot flesh. "I'm going to kiss you. Here."

Oh, my fucking God.

Never in my life had anything sounded so good. So fucking deliciously good. Never before had lips ever come close to that part of my anatomy.

I ceased to know how to speak. I nodded once, eyes wide, muscles tight.

She licked her lips, sending a thrill right through my heart.

The anticipation of her licking me, tonguing me, made my

cock lurch in her fingers. Dropping her eyes, she bent over. The anticipation was too much. I couldn't suck in a proper breath.

I waited endlessly for the first sweep of her tongue.

But then she stopped.

Sitting upright, she released her hold on me. My heart bucked in my chest as she stood up and moved to the side of the bed where I'd placed the leather cuff.

Holding it up, she said, "I'm going to put this on you. I want to give you pleasure but I refuse if I can't restrain you." Her voice wobbled; her body flushed with lust, same as mine. Her eyes fell to my straining cock, standing stiff and hot and begging for her mouth. The connection between us throbbed with rightness. Whatever we were doing was perfect. Whatever she was doing was working. I was healing.

I nodded.

Without a word, she padded back and waited for me to put one arm against the metal tree headboard. Doing her best not to touch me while securing the leather, I risked everything by leaning forward and placing a simple kiss on a darkening bruise on her neck. "I'm sorry," I whispered, breathing in her subtle scent of Lily of the valley.

She pulled away. "I know." Disappearing into my wardrobe, she came back with a belt. Her eyebrow raised, looking at my other hand. I kept my palms curled, hiding the III tattooed in the centre.

I obediently placed my wrist against the bedhead, hissing as she straddled me, deliberately brushing her jean-clad pussy against my extremely hard cock.

She tightened the belt before resuming her kneeling position between my splayed legs. Her hot breath tickled my upper thighs, and I didn't know how much longer I could wait.

I wanted her mouth. Terribly.

"Tell me what you want," she said softly.

I shook my head. It was one thing to accept what she wanted to give, but I couldn't tell her what I wanted. Not after

197

everything. I owed her more than I'd ever be able to repay.

"I want to hear you say it." Her eyes flashed and her fingers squeezed me in warning.

A flush of heat threatened to paint my cheeks. After a lifetime of being told to forget about sex, she now wanted me to dive in and embrace it. Swallowing hard, I growled, "I want to feel your mouth around my cock. I want to feel your heat and hear you moan from my taste."

Fuck me. I could've come just from talking dirty. It turned me on—sent comets exploding in my cock.

Zel smiled. "As you wish."

Keeping eye contact, she bent over me, and without any warning, slid her hot, wet, *exquisite* mouth over the tip of my erection.

My world went from black to prismatic. I'd never felt such wonderment, such freedom, such deep seated primal happiness. My heart swelled; my limbs locked. I couldn't focus on anything but her. Her. *Her.*

I groaned with gratefulness and thankfulness and joy. Her fucking amazing mouth sucked my length deep, deep inside. The swirl of her slippery tongue licked and adored, giving me no chance of remaining sane. I lost myself to Zel. I willingly gave everything to her.

"Like that?" she breathed against my lower belly. "Do you enjoy my tongue licking you, pleasuring you?" She trailed kisses from base to tip, always stroking.

I groaned, trembling with a mixture of furious conditioning and heavenly pleasure. "Yes. Fuck yes. Don't stop."

She laughed softly and descended once again. Her hand slid up and down, lubricated by saliva, feeling out of this world. A bonfire built deep in my balls.

I flinched, testing the restraints as Zel cupped me, massaging sensitive flesh. I couldn't keep track of her mouth and fingers and touch.

My brain tried to revert into Ghost mode. My muscles shuddered with orders that would never be fully ignorable.

Then Zel swallowed my length and hummed. The vibrations smashed through my conditioning, bulldozed through my thoughts, and I regressed to a simple creature. A man chasing pleasure for the first time. An animal with the only intent of coming in this beautiful seraph's throat.

The bed jangled and shook as I fought against the restraints. I wanted to touch her, thread my fingers through her hair and thrust into her mouth. I wanted to give her everything.

But the cuff and belt held me captive, leaving me completely at Zel's mercy.

Her mouth sucked harder, dragging more and more fire into my groin. My spine tingled with need; my eyes snapped closed.

Zel was magic. She was a witch. I wanted to come forever.

The last of my undoing came in the form of her hair cascading onto my thigh. The tickling amplified my awareness of her hot, slippery mouth and her tongue swirled harder, building me faster, sending me hurtling toward the edge.

I had no choice but to let go.

I completely forgot who I was and the disaster my life had become and dropped all my walls to my soul.

I came like a fucking garden hose.

Spurt after spurt I jerked in her hold. She lapped up every thrust, swallowed every drop. No amount of prose or literature could describe the intensity, the visceral sublimity of my release.

It changed me. It gave me warmth for the very first time. It gave me fucking hope.

I opened my eyes as her tongue flicked out, washing me clean from the last of the most intense orgasm of my life. She'd taken a part of me into her. She'd completed the bond that I'd felt ever since I set eyes on her.

No one had made me feel like Zel. No one held me hostage like Zel.

She'd successfully done in ten minutes what I'd tried to do in two years.

She brought me back to life.

Eleven

Hazel

Life has a way of lulling unsuspecting victims into a false sense of security. Providing answers to problems that seem too hard to fix. Giving love to combat loneliness. Sending a kind word in a moment of doubt.

But it was those moments that made you weak, and that was when life struck the hardest.

I thought in my naivety I'd found a way to help Fox. That I'd done the impossible and made progress with a man so psychologically damaged. I thought I'd find a cure for Clara thanks to Fox's money. I thought so many happy, hopeful things.

But just like everything.

I was wrong.

A week passed after our fight and the unfortunate incident of Fox trying to strangle me. After seeing his naked legs and sewing the stab wounds I inflicted, I'd hoped he'd get over his issue of clothing and nudity.

But not once did I see his legs again, or his chest or back or arms. I'd catch myself watching him, tracing his muscles beneath his black shirt, wishing I could touch and taste.

The longer he remained elusive, the more my mind went wild with what he kept hidden. What if he was so badly mutilated under the clothing that I'd burst into tears, grieving for a little boy who'd never had a hand laid on him in friendship or love? What if he hid something even more sinister?

The morning after our fight—after I made him break apart with my mouth—things changed between us. He accepted my need to return home in the evenings. And we silently agreed to start from scratch.

We never discussed the contract—we didn't need to. As far as I was concerned, the agreement was void. What happened gave us something deeper than a piece of paper. Fox would still pay me, and I would still accept it for my daughter, but we'd evolved past exchanging one commodity for another.

We became friends.

A few days after the incident, I tried to change his bandages to inspect the stitches in his leg, but he flatly denied me and moved as if he had no injury. He was the master at masking pain.

As strange as it seemed, we understood each other and time moved forward. Fox knew I wouldn't put up with his violence, and I knew he wouldn't tolerate being touched.

It was a whole new world full of wanting and fearing.

During the day, I stayed with Fox. We explored his house, or went for walks in the semi-wild gardens around his property. He showed me how to help with the paperwork of Obsidian and most days I sat beside him at his desk filing receipts, sending out monthly invoices for membership, and offering suggestions on how to improve productivity.

Instead of being possessive of his company, Fox listened intensely, nodding to advice, and softly answering questions about the legal aspects of his club.

Our minds found even ground, laying the foundation for a topsy-turvy friendship that seethed with chemistry and need, but was never acted upon.

Fox opened his life to me—every avenue of his business, every account and password on his computer—but not once did he let me touch him, or ask anything about his past.

The smiles he gave were tinged with shadows; the laughs echoed with loneliness. My heart screamed for him to recognise the gift I wanted to give him. I wanted the honour of healing him. I wanted the joy of bringing him true happiness.

But it didn't seem possible.

I'd catch him watching me as I bent over his books or walked silently by his side. His smoky eyes were so damn expressive he didn't need words.

The message was loud and clear.

Why are you still here?

Why waste your time on me?

I'll only destroy you.

I ignored those messages. I also ignored my own thoughts.

Lying in bed at night, listening to the soft breathing of Clara, I rifled through my feelings toward him.

I'd told him I hadn't forgiven him for the bruises and terrible fear he'd instilled in me. Even though I lived a dangerous past, facing pain and not-so-perfect choices, I'd never been so petrified before. The thoughts running through my head when his fingers crushed my windpipe had been full of Clara. She'd never know how much I loved her. She'd never understand I'd do anything for her.

But then, thankfulness layered my horror. Thankful that I would die before my offspring—I wouldn't have to see her wither and beg for help I couldn't give.

Fox made me assess every inch of my life and I hated him for it. I didn't think I'd ever truly get over what he'd done, but at the same time, he was the most real and unapologetic man I'd ever met.

Fox never told me where he went on the night he took me,

but the bruises around his eye and cheek bone had faded to a muddy yellow. I didn't think I'd ever get used to his joints clicking or his back creaking whenever he moved after sitting for a period of time. He sounded like an old tin solider badly in need of some oil.

At five p.m. every night, I would leave Fox and catch a taxi from his home to mine. He'd given me the one hundred thousand cash he promised, and I was able to afford another trial inhaler for Clara. He tried to drive me, but I flat-out refused. While I admitted I had a fondness for him, an insatiable need to fix him, and a craving for him physically, I was still afraid of what he was capable of. He was an undetonated hand-grenade, and I had no intention of letting him near Clara. He had his secrets, and I had mine. That was the way it had to be.

Clara would launch her warm, squirmy body into my arms and we'd eat together, watch television, do her homework, then giggle and talk in the dark until she fell asleep. I hoarded those moments like gold dust, locking each memory into a safe inside my mind, knowing each recollection would torture me when she was gone.

Every morning, I woke with the hope that doctors had diagnosed wrong. Clara seemed too healthy and vibrant—her hair glossy, eyes bright and mind inquisitive.

At ten a.m. every day I would return to Fox and climb into his bed. He'd wake, smile, then go back to sleep, leaving me to sunbathe in bright sunshine, keeping vigil until midday when he woke.

For a week, I balanced my two lives perfectly; I began to think it could work.

But of course, life liked to prove me wrong.

"Holy crap, you scared me," I said, clutching the folders tighter against my chest. It was early afternoon, and I'd been working on ordering more supplies for Obsidian's fighters. Fox had disappeared an hour ago, saying he'd be back.

I didn't expect him to be silent and lurking against the black walls of his office—completely unnoticeable until he moved.

His lips twitched but he didn't fully smile. He never did. Just once I'd like to see him let go and be happy.

If he knew how to, of course.

"Sorry. I was waiting for you." He moved forward and took the heavy files from me, placing them on his desk. I'd been down on the fighting floor with Oscar taking note of the dwindling supplies that we needed.

He'd asked for more hookers, and I slapped him playfully. As much as I didn't want to admit—I liked Oscar. He'd called me a whore and grabbed my boob, but beneath the brash exterior lurked a fun-some surfer whose blue eyes caused one or two wings of attraction in my stomach.

He was so different to Fox. Sun to dark. Happy to brooding. But I wouldn't stray—not that I had any relationship obligations to Fox apart from a money transaction—but my feelings had grown from lust to something deeper.

I no longer thought about our time together just for a month. I would stay until Fox smiled with his soul. I would stay until he could make love to me like I wanted him to.

And if he hurts you again?

I'd leave and never look back. I had feelings for him but I didn't have a death wish.

"I want to go outside. I need some sunlight," Fox said, spinning back from placing the paperwork on the desk. "Come with me?"

Such a simple request. A walk around his property in the sun.

I smiled. "Are you asking me on a date?" Tapping a finger against my lips, I said, "Could this be seen as an improvement to the kidnap by knife routine?"

His hand suddenly captured my elbow, pulling me forward. He kept a small buffer of space between us, but his breathing altered from relaxed to shallow. "Do you know why I've avoided you for a week? Why I haven't begged for your mouth, or dragged you into my bed?" His silver eyes scorched me with acres of pent-up lust.

I bit my lip as a wave of desire spread like wildfire. My core grew liquid at the memories of sucking him: his salty dark taste, the way he came apart in my hands. I liked the power I had over him. I loved bringing him to a body shuddering climax. But for the past week, I walked on knife blades. My body wanted Fox every second of every day and not being able to touch him—to let him know I wanted him—had been torture.

"Why?" I murmured, hypnotised by his bottom lip.

"Because I want to give you what you gave me. I want to make you come so fucking hard that you fall into my arms. I want to be able to catch you and tell you everything you want to know."

I swayed forward. "Do it then." My heart raced like a rabbit.

His head dropped, bringing his lips temptingly close to mine. "I would if I could. But I don't have the strength. I'm a walking battleground between my past and the future I want. And I'm so fucking scared of hurting you again." His fingers tightened around my elbows. "I just want to be quiet inside. I want normal thoughts and the luxury of just fucking hugging you."

Fox was unlike any man I knew. I couldn't hate him. Not with his gigantic heart and the sweetness lurking in his violence. But I did hate that he spoke the truth. It wasn't a game he played. He honestly couldn't control whatever lived inside him, and my life would be forfeited if he lost control.

Our eyes locked, green to grey. I stood on tip-toes to kiss him.

He froze as my lips moved on his, and I waited to see if he

would push me away. I wasn't stupid. After what happened before, I now carried a knife in my hair and in my back pocket. I fully intended to deliver my threat if Fox ever overpowered me again and made me choose who lived or died.

His mouth opened beneath mine; he moaned low and deep as my tongue entered and swept over his bottom lip.

My arms wanted nothing more than to wrap him in an embrace and crush myself against him. I wanted friction between us. I wanted his hands on every inch of me.

His head tilted to deepen the kiss, following my lead with his tongue. It was the contradiction that made me hot for him. A dominate male through and through, but beneath that lived a man who only wanted approval. A man who had never had affection or love or a simple kiss.

And that broke my fucking heart.

He pulled away, looking deep into my eyes. "Walk with me?"

I nodded.

Leaving the office, we made our way down the steps and through the fighting rings to the front of the house. Only two fighters had arrived for a morning session and no one disturbed us.

Fox didn't stop when we reached outside. He lifted his face to bask in the golden warmth. His black clad body looked like a misplaced shadow as we made our way across his gravel driveway to the grass beyond.

He waited for me to walk beside him and gave me a gentle smile. "My life would be a lot easier if the sun shone twenty-four hours a day."

I played with my fingers, rubbing the need away to hold his hand. I hated that I couldn't touch him. There was intimacy just waiting to be claimed between us, but without touch it ebbed and faded, leaving a trace of awkwardness. "If you hate the dark so much, why do you wear all black?"

His jaw clenched but we kept walking. "It's a stupid reason and doesn't even make sense to me. I should dress in yellows and whites—avoid black completely, but I don't."

"Tell me," I whispered.

He stopped and faced the house. Glaring at the huge gargoyles decorating the mansion, he growled, "I'm free. So why did I build a house on the *exact* replica where all the hell and evilness occurred? Why do I wear the only colour we were allowed?" His eyes met mine. "Because it's all I know. The only place and colour that I trust to keep me safe. Everything else terrifies me because I'm not worthy of forgetting my past."

My heart splintered, the shards poking through my lungs. "You are worthy. Every day I spend with you, you're improving."

He laughed darkly. "Only because I keep my distance and don't touch you. Believe me, if you knew my thoughts you would run."

"Do you want me to run?"

His eyes narrowed. "You should."

"But do you *want* me to?" I stepped forward, cursing the inability to grab his hand and hold him. "Focus on what you're feeling."

He shook his head, striding off toward the back garden. "What I want doesn't matter. It never did."

I trailed after him, wishing I could crack him open and pull every bad thought from his memory. We didn't speak again until he led me toward a large greenhouse at the back of his extensive property. The large stone wall barricaded anyone from accessing the space and the sun glinted off the glass walls and roof, warming the budding plants within.

Fox opened the door, and a huge gust of heat slapped me in the face.

"Go in. I have a few things I want to show you." His voice was rougher, sending my stomach twisting.

Entering the large greenhouse, I glanced around at the seedlings and exotic flowers. Spread out down two aisles with a large chair at the end rested vegetables, herbs, and bonsai. Orchids, in vibrant blues and purples, hung from elongated stems. Tomato plants cast a sharp pungent smell into the space.

Fox walked down the right aisle and stopped in front of a tray of pretty white flowers—tiny, like snowflakes hanging off a bright green stalk. "Do you know what these are?"

I moved closer. Of course, I knew what that was. As a mother, I'd meticulously catalogued every plant, household chemical, and poison that could harm Clara. I also spritzed on the scent every morning. My one luxury.

"It's lily of the valley." Staring at the little, innocent plant, I murmured, "Why are you growing it amongst edible and non-toxic plants?"

Fox rolled his shoulders. "We used to take turns maintaining the greenhouses at the compound. Lily of the valley, deadly nightshade, foxglove, all plants that can be turned into weapons."

I froze, picturing killers tending to such delicate things like flowers all with the intent to murder.

Fox grabbed my hand suddenly and dragged me down the aisle toward the single large chair. It looked well used: a cracked brown leather.

"Do you come here often?" I asked, noticing a few discarded water bottles.

"Yes. I come to sit in the sun. The heat punishes, but also saves. It's so different from where I'm from. I never want to be cold again."

Letting me go, he dug into his pocket and held out another chain.

My heart did a weird swoop. He wanted to restrain me and there was only one reason why. He wanted sex.

His shoulders tightened. "This is a modified version. Hold out your hands."

I didn't want to, but I obeyed. His fingers whispered over my skin. First my right wrist, securing a separate bracelet, and then my left, repeating.

Once they were clasped, I held them up to inspect. My heart clenched at the dangling silver star on both. "Why did you do that?" I looked up, furious. I didn't want the precious star necklace I shared with Clara to be anywhere near this world with Fox.

His eyes darkened. "Because it means a lot to you and I wanted to." Capturing my cheek, he held me firm as he dropped his mouth to mine.

For a second, I wanted to bite him. I needed to argue and tell him it wasn't okay that he'd trespassed into my life beyond him, but his tongue speared my lips, and I lost coherent thought.

Every shred of lust I'd been living with exploded into life, and I didn't struggle as he pulled me forward. He sat in the chair, dragging me down until I stood over him.

Breaking the kiss, he murmured, "I need you, Zel and I want you fast. I'm not asking. I'm telling. I paid for a service, and I want you to sit on my cock."

I should've been repulsed, but I was the total opposite. My skin hummed with sexual need; my body boiled in the heat of the greenhouse.

Fox reached forward and pulled my white t-shirt up a little. With a separate thicker chain, he looped it around the jewellery running down my front and brought my wrists to secure it. Once my hands were bound, his fingers fell to his buckle.

My mouth went dry watching him strip. I sucked in a noisy breath as he arched his hips and tugged his trousers down to his quads.

My eyes couldn't feast fast enough. Fox never wore underwear and the hard equipment between his legs sprang into freedom. Countless silver scars decorated his upper legs. Everything about him enticed me. I'd never been so hungry or physically attracted to anyone as much as him.

"Come closer," he ordered.

I did as requested, moving between his open legs. I stifled a moan as his fingers brushed my lower belly and dropped to caress my thigh. Trailing down my floaty turquoise skirt, he never broke eye contact.

I surrendered to his snowy gaze; goosebumps scattered over my skin as his touch moved down and down and down until he grazed bare leg. His hand trailed my kneecap, turning inward to begin the journey in the opposite direction.

Every inch was torture and heaven. His fingers were strong and dominating on my inner thigh, creeping higher and higher and higher.

I was panting by the time his knuckles brushed my pussy. His hand cupped me, holding me firm. I jolted in his grip.

He sucked in a heavy breath, eyes flaring wide as he felt how damp I was. "Fuck, you never fail to surprise me, Zel. I'll never get enough of you. All I can think about is you riding me—of your mouth around my dick again."

His other hand disappeared up my skirt to ease my knickers down my legs. He removed them quickly, his actions speeding up as his need compounded. The minute they hit my ankles, I kicked them away, thrilling at the hot air against my nakedness.

Sitting forward, Fox grasped my hip with one hand while his other disappeared under my skirt again. There was no hesitation when he reached my pussy. With clenched teeth, he pushed one long, delicious finger inside me.

I wanted to collapse at his feet. He moved his finger, stroking my inner wall.

I shuddered, unable to keep my eyes open. All I could concentrate on was his wondrous touch deep inside. His digit moved again and my pussy rippled around him, begging for more.

He froze. "Fuck, do that again."

I looked up, a smile teasing my mouth. "Do what?" I tensed around his finger, loving his sharp hiss and wide eyes. He could lie all he wanted, but his wonderment at finger-fucking me told me this was a first for him. My heart pounded at the thought of what I could teach him—what we could learn together. How could a man like Fox be so sexually innocent? It was as if he'd been a recluse all his life.

"Show me. Tell me what to do," he said in a strangled

whisper. "I want to make you come on my finger."

My hands shot up, desperate to capture his face and kiss the hell out of him. But the chains jangled, keeping me prisoner.

Fox smiled wryly. "See? You naturally want to touch. Did you think you could avoid the urge while I fingered you intimately? This is the only way." His digit worked deeper and I moaned. "Tell me. Let me know how to make you shatter."

I swallowed hard, cheeks flushing with excitement and nerves. I'd never had to explain sex. I barely knew the mechanics myself, but I had learned my body. I found the trick to exploding in the dark beneath my covers.

"Put another finger inside me," I whispered.

His hand clutched my hip harder, and I dared look at his cock. It stood proud and so, so hard between his legs. My mouth watered to lick him again.

Slowly, he withdrew his finger and brushed my clit as he pressed two digits together. I stumbled as he very carefully and oh so teasingly pressed two fingers deep. I banded around him. I was more turned on than I'd ever been in my life.

"Shit, you're the prettiest woman I've ever seen," Fox growled as his finger worked me, pressing deep and withdrawing in a perfect rhythm.

Seen.

Oh, God.

I looked up, freaking out. "The glass. Anyone can see us." I wiggled, trying to free myself, but he held me firm. "Let me go. I agreed to sleep with you not give the world a show."

He chuckled. "We're too far away from the house to be seen through the windows and there's a lot of grass to cross before they'd get an eyeful."

His fingers dived deep and possessive, forcing my attention back to him. "Now tell me how to make you come."

Everywhere he touched, I incinerated into smoke. My hips began a slow dance, rocking on his hand. I didn't need to think, only listen to what I needed. I honestly didn't know if I would be able to come while standing and giving instruction to a man who consumed my thoughts, but he wanted to try; I wanted to give in.

"Keep thrusting with your fingers, and swirl your thumb around my clit."

Fox obeyed immediately. His thumb pressed the sensitive nerves, and I bucked in his hold. His forehead furrowed as he concentrated on perfecting his rhythm. Thrust, swirl, thrust, swirl.

With every stroke I forgot where we were, how strange our relationship was—I forgot my own name as heat gathered and rushed between my legs.

My knees wobbled wanting to crumble to the ground.

"Like this?" Fox asked, his voice so deep with lust I could barely understand.

I no longer possessed the gift of speech and ground myself onto his hand in answer.

"Fuck," he groaned. His own hips began to pulse just slightly, a natural urge to join. "What else? Do I have to do anything else?" His hand left my hip and ascended to capture my breast. His fingers squeezed my nipple and I suffered a full body tremble.

"Yes… like that. Umm hmm." My vision went black as all my senses turned inward, focusing on where he touched me.

His hand increased pressure until he rocked against my clit. "Come for me, Hazel. Fucking come on my fingers."

His crude commands sent another wave through me, and he groaned. He lost the finesse of easy thrusting and grabbed my hip to hold me in place. "You're going to fucking come." He drove into me hard and deep. I cried out as intensity level went from hot to scorching.

"Come for me. Come for me. Fucking come for me." He never stopped ordering and every stroke wound me tighter and tighter until I couldn't wind anymore.

My lips parted, and I threw my head back as I rode Fox's hand. The first wave of release shattered me just like he wanted. He growled low in his throat as I gripped tight around his fingers.

"Fucking hell," he grunted, increasing his pressure and sending my orgasm into another realm entirely. I lost all mobility and became nothing more than an exploding firework.

Wave after pleasure wave I surfed. I'd never come apart so completely.

The moment my orgasm faded, Fox ripped his fingers from me, spun me around, and pulled me down fast.

I moaned long and low as his cock pushed up and entered me in one thick invading impale.

With nothing to hold onto and my hands chained to my stomach, I couldn't fight or twist. Fox controlled every inch of taking me, and he'd stolen even my right to look at him.

His body was hard and hot behind me as his drove upward, taking me ruthlessly. I was so wet. His invasion slipped and stroked, sending yet more waves through my system.

I bounced in his lap, our only contact his erection deep inside me and his hands on my hips. Jerking me back to meet his thrusts, he breathed loud. "Goddammit, it's like heaven being inside you. I never want to. Fucking. Leave." He thrust with every word, shaking the chair until it scraped on the floor.

"Oh, hell," he groaned. "I'm going to come. I can't—I wanted. Fuck."

He sounded like a wolf intent on shredding his prey alive as hot jets of wetness filled me. His thrusts turned feral as if he wanted to split me in two, delivering as much of himself as he could.

When the last band of his release left him, he slouched back into the chair. His cock twitched inside and I wanted nothing more than to lay back and have him wrap his large strong arms around me.

We didn't move. The only sound was our breaths panting in the stuffy heat of the greenhouse.

After a minute, Fox patted me on the back, murmuring, "Thank you."

I struggled not to laugh. Such a formal touch and verse.

Nothing like what we'd just done. We'd just owned each other in a fit of fucking, and he'd already withdrawn.

There was no afterglow or tender-hearted cuddling. Instead of being hurt, I smiled.

However strange our interlude had ended, he'd been an eager lover and hadn't tried to kill me.

Progress.

Two days later, I reclined on Fox's bed watching television.

The episode displayed a sexy sun-bronzed man arguing with a pretty redhead. The undeniable tension on screen amped up my own need until my core grew wet. Being around a male like Fox without being allowed to touch was a daily agony of unrequited pleasure.

He hadn't come near me since the greenhouse, and we hadn't spoken a word about it. That night when I went home to Clara, she'd had a coughing fit, and it was all I could do to not break down and scream at every entity for making her sick.

Every day I suffered more and more guilt. Guilt for living another life away from her. Guilt for finding small smidgens of happiness thanks to Fox. I felt like a traitor and a bitch.

Clara grew sicker despite the new pills I made her take every morning and the exorbitantly expensive trail drug in her inhaler.

Fox stalked toward me, wiping his face with a black towel, panting and sweaty from his session in the gym down the hall.

Not only did he drive his broken body to failure by endless fights and working long hours, he also worked out religiously every morning when he woke. Wearing the same black trousers and long sleeved shirt, he came back drenched in sweat.

"I'll just have a shower, then we'll head out. We haven't left Obsidian since we met, and I need to run a few errands. I'd like you to come."

Not waiting for my reply, he disappeared into the bathroom and closed the door. I waited for the shower to turn on, imagining Fox naked and wet.

My tummy fluttered with the thought. Pushing Clara from my mind, compartmentalizing my two lives, I scampered off the bed and tiptoed toward the bathroom.

What if he catches you?

With my heart in my throat, I turned the handle. I expected it not to turn—after all, Fox was so private I figured he would've locked it—but it unlatched.

I stopped breathing as I cracked open the door and peered inside.

Fox stood trembling and tense in the centre of the shower while hot water hissed and fizzled on his skin. He stood side profile, hiding his back and chest—the two areas I most wanted to see. With one hand, he held a razor and pressed the blade hard against his inner thigh.

His eyebrows drew together, knitting tightly as a small trickle of blood erupted from the wound and sluiced down his leg with boiling water.

I wanted to run in and stop him, but he cut himself again— one more perfect line. Tossing the razor to the side, he switched the water from scalding to freezing and tension siphoned from his muscles down the drain.

Resting his forehead against black tiles, he groaned with every sadness and fucked-up emotion inside.

I couldn't watch any longer.

Closing the door, I drifted back to the bed in a daze. I felt as if he'd dragged the blade down my heart instead of his leg.

You're so stupid, Zel. You thought you'd broken through. You thought he was on the road to recovery.

I was idiotic to hope he wouldn't self-harm anymore. I'd searched for evidence, but saw none. Now, I knew why.

His inner thighs had an array of marks and cuts, decorating his already scarred legs. He'd even taken out the stitches on his thigh and calf, causing the wounds to gape a little, not fully healed.

Fuck.

I rubbed the heel of my hand into my chest, trying to dispel the aching agony. I hated seeing someone in pain. I hated not being able to help.

There was no helping someone with a mind so scrambled like Fox's.

The shower switched off and a few minutes later, Fox strode into the room dressed in his usual wardrobe of black.

His eyes narrowed, running hands over his wet hair. The strands of colour captured sunlight, looking bronze, cinnamon, black, and gold. The Sydney sun bounced through the large windows, turning the black interior into a sun-soaked paradise.

"What the fuck, Zel? You look like you just witnessed a murder." Scowling, he headed to his wardrobe and came back with a black blazer.

I blinked, forcing the unhappiness away. "Nothing. Just a sad program on television."

He dropped his arms, the blazer dangling by his side. "Don't you dare lie." His eyes flashed white, looking around the room, searching for some hint at what switched my mood. "Tell me. What did you do?"

"I didn't do anything. It's what you did!" *Shit.*

He prowled forward, then stopped, keeping a careful distance. The air around him crackled as the calmness he'd reached from inflicting harm in the shower disintegrated.

My skin quivered with need; my core throbbed—stupidly turned on by his anger.

For a moment all we did was stare, then knowledge exploded in Fox's gaze. "You watched." He threw the blazer across the room. "You fucking watched!"

My muscles locked down in fear before rupturing with adrenaline. I flew off the bed, keeping it between us.

His eyes never left mine, hands curling in rage. "What did you want to see, *dobycha?*" He inched closer to the bed.

"Perhaps you're looking for the mark? Maybe you've figured out who I am after all." Sneering, he added, "You're too fucking intelligent not to have guessed by now what I am."

I didn't have a clue what he was, but once again, I knew I had to push him. I had to shove him so far past his comfort zone I broke another small part of him—all in the name of making him whole again.

Reaching for the hem of my grey t-shirt, I yanked it over my head, standing tall in my jean-shorts and bra.

Fox slammed to a halt. "What the fuck are you doing?"

My hands trembled as I pulled the small knife from my pocket and tossed it onto the mattress, keeping it in easy reach. My heart roared in my ears as Fox rolled his well-formed shoulders, eyes locking onto my exposed flesh.

The sun bounced off my chain, glittering a silver path from collar to waist. "I'm done dancing around you like you're a precious piece of china. What good is it to be bought for sex if you never deliver?" My voice filled with breathy trepidation as well as billowing lust. "You taunt me by never touching. You make me wet by never coming close. You self-harm instead of turning to others. You're dying inside when I'm trying to help you live."

Planting hands on my hips, I snarled, "You always think of yourself and never about me."

His mouth hung open as his eyes narrowed to silver slits. "I take it back—you're not intelligent, you're fucking suicidal. Don't push me again, Zel. Remember what happened last time?" He took an angry step toward me, closing the distance between us. He fisted his hands. "You know why I can't touch you! Stop fucking pushing me."

"No, I don't! All you've told me is nothing. Secrecy on top of hidden agendas on top of a multitude of half-truths. Why can't you touch me, Fox? Who made you like this? Who stole every basic right from you?" My shaking fingers went behind my back, pinging the clasp on my bra. I moaned as the material whispered off, kissing my nipples on its fall to the floor. I'd never felt so exposed or empowered. Stripping for a man who didn't even want me. Who couldn't come within a metre of me without locking his jaw and inching into murderous rage.

"Do you want to die? Is that what you're trying to achieve here?" Fox growled. His hand dropped to cup between his legs. "You want this so damn much you'd be willing to die for it?"

"No, I'm not willing to die for you. I thought I proved that before." My eyes shifted to where I'd stabbed him. "I'll never forgive you for hurting me. I'll never forget the madness living inside you. I will gladly kill you if you ever try to end me, but I need human connection, Fox. And you're not giving it to me. You need to get over your issues. Forget your past, so you can touch me. Make love to me."

It was too infuriating spending so much time with someone who I desperately wanted to help. Any minor progress we made was swallowed back into his deep-seated problems. For someone like me who existed to save others it was persecution, and I refused to be a martyr anymore.

Fox snorted. "Make love. I don't even know the meaning of it. How can I do something I'll never understand?"

I'll make you understand.

My eyes flew open. Somehow my need to help him became tangled with the desire to make him fall for me. To keep him, so I could always be there to bring him back from the dark.

It didn't matter that I'd be shackling myself with more problems than support—or that I never wanted him near Clara. It was a stupid fantasy.

It didn't stop my skin burning for his mouth or my pussy growing wet for his cock. I wanted. I wanted. I *wanted.*

Yet he never came near me.

Angry tears glossed my eyes. "If you can't give me what I need, then this deal is done. I told you I agreed to your terms not just for the money, but because I wanted you. Well, try wanting someone who can never give anything in return."

My fingers dropped from pebbled nipples to my button and zipper. Undoing my shorts, I pushed them down in angry jerks—nothing sensual or alluring. I was fucking angry, and I needed to get rid of the insane need in my blood.

Fox made a tortured noise in the back of his throat. "Stop it. I'm not safe. Put your clothes back on and give me time to get my shit together."

I should've heeded his warning. I knew how dangerous he was. But it didn't stop me. I snapped, "I want to see you naked. I want to run my hands all over you. I want to lick your chest and trail kisses down your stomach. I want—"

Fox froze. His entire body locked down. "If you think you can touch me like you did when you stitched my leg, forget it. I was in pain—that same pain helped distract me while you stupidly touched and provoked me."

"*Provoked?* You call sucking you until you exploded down my throat, provoked?" My body flushed with heat. "You *wanted* me to touch you. You craved my tongue and the warmth I could offer your frozen soul. You let me *own* you in that moment, Fox."

"I was fucking weak and stupid." Dashing a hand over his face, he growled, "You were lucky I had enough control to obey. But I'm done obeying anyone. I want to obey myself. I don't want you to tell me what to do." He punched himself in the chest. "No more, you hear me! No more fucking orders. I'm out."

His tone had changed from pissed to belligerent like a child speaking to an authority figure. He didn't talk about our fight; he spoke of yet another issue inside him. Something I would never understand.

"I'm not asking for your compliance. You don't have to obey me. You were strong enough to seek pleasure. *You* were the one who controlled *me* in the greenhouse. Your fingers, your touch, you consumed me. You can do it again."

A smidgen of fight left him and his shoulders sank. "I—" He looked away before gritting his teeth. "I don't trust myself to try again. No matter how much I want to." His eyes flew up, locking on my naked breasts. "Fuck, how I want to."

My heart fluttered with delicate wings. He wanted me. He wanted what I did.

He wanted me all the while keeping his distance to protect me. My heart thudded harder, forcing more lustful blood through my system.

Fox stood glowering, chest pumping, the front of his trousers tenting with arousal. "Put your clothes back on."

I shook my head. "I want to fuck you, that's why I'm taking my clothes off. You should try it. It makes the whole experience that much more enjoyable."

Picking up the knife on the bedspread, I deliberately cut the lace on my hips, letting my knickers flutter to the floor. Standing naked before him, I murmured, "Let me undress you. Let me touch and kiss you. Let me see what you're hiding beneath all that black."

He shook his head. "Not going to happen. Your bruises are only just fading. What if I kill you next time? You've forgiven me for so much. Don't ask me to hurt you more."

Annoyance chased my need and I kneeled on the bed, crawling toward him. "I haven't forgiven you. I'll never get over you strangling me half to death. But I don't care because you owe me. You owe me another orgasm. You owe me to let me try and help you."

I reached the side of his bed, and he backed away. I climbed to my feet, advancing.

Keeping the same amount of distance between us, Fox moved backward, heading toward the seating area by the windows.

While we danced across the room, I gave myself over to my insanely foolish plan. My feet moved toward him as I began my idiotic seduction. "Working beside you makes my heart pound…" I swirled my fingertip on the swell of my breast, directly above my heart. "Here."

Another step toward him. "Talking to you makes my breath come faster, dragging your smoky scent into my lungs…" I pressed my fist against my solar plexus. "Here."

Fox waged a battle, his face flickering with so many thoughts. Every step that took me closer to him, I feared he'd snap and kill me, but I never stopped.

"Staring at your lips makes me fantasise about you kissing me." I trailed my finger across my parted mouth. "Here." Every part of me sparked and fizzled and pinpricked with need.

Fox shook his head, eyes shadowing with urges I didn't comprehend.

Dropping my fingers, I tugged on the bar bell through my right nipple. "I want your mouth here." My hand drifted lower, trickling over the chain, darting over my caesarean scar from Clara, and boldly going between my legs. "I want your tongue here." I gasped as my finger swirled my clit.

The back of Fox's knees connected against a chair; he slammed into it. His hand clutched at his erection, almost unconsciously, his gaze raking over me greedily.

My vision darkened as bubbles of lust sprang into a wrecking ball of desire. "I want to feel you deep inside me. I want to hear you groan and pant and moan as you plunge deeper and deeper."

He swallowed hard, his throat contracted with fear. "I'm—you're, fuck me, Hazel." His snowy eyes flinted to dark grey, erupting a flurry of need in my stomach. "I want you so fucking much. Do you know how hard it's been keeping my distance and then you go and practically beg me to plunge inside you? I have self-control but I'm not a saint."

Wetness trickled at his confession; my heart burst with hope. "Please, Fox. I *am* begging. I need you to make me come again."

His jaw locked as his hands fumbled at his fly. In a matter of seconds, he undid the material and shoved them around his thighs. His glistening, rock-hard erection sprang free, only to be captured by a brutal unforgiving hand.

He pumped himself demonically, eyes wild. "Touch yourself. Make yourself come."

My fingers turned harsher on my skin, adopting the same

violence Fox used on himself. "I'll do anything you want if it means you'll get naked and make love to me."

He groaned, hand slowing to a tantalizing stroke on his hard length. "I can't."

Biting my lip, I slid two fingers between my legs. My eyes swam with passion; I breathed, "You have to get naked at some point. That's what sex is, Fox. The joining of two bodies. The joy of exploring each other, touching, stroking, licking, tasting—"

He cut me off. "I don't need to be naked." His gaze fell to his lap. "Only this." His face darkened as his hand stroked defiantly. The glint in his eye looked like he expected me to tell him to stop pleasuring himself. The tilt of his chin spoke of bravado for rubbing the silky hot flesh between his legs.

I couldn't take my eyes of his cock already glistening with a bead of pre-cum. My heart raced as his breathing picked up.

"Imagine your fingers are my fingers. What would I do to you?"

My nipples tingled at the power in his voice. The domination laced with uncertainty and harsh desire.

A blush warmed my cheeks at the thought of acting out my fantasies. He watched me with such scrutiny. My body wasn't perfect. I'd carried a child. I'd lost weight from stress and couldn't hide the silver lines of stretch marks on my lower stomach. The list of my insecurities raced in my head, dousing my arousal.

"Stop thinking and do it." Fox ran a thumb over the top of his cock, deliberately taunting me, smearing the drop of moisture.

I moved forward till my knees almost brushed his. His eyes fell to my pussy; his face etched with stress, the scar livid on his cheek.

"You'd push two fingers deep, feeling my heat, loving my wetness," I whispered. "You'd work me just like you did in the greenhouse. You touched me like an expert. I want you to do it again."

His throat moved as he swallowed. His quads tensed, cock rippling in his hand.

I couldn't breathe. I couldn't move. I stood transfixed, never taking my eyes off his slow assault on his erection, entranced by the small edge of control he had left on his violent nature.

The element of real danger dampened, but also accelerated my teeth-clenching need for him. If I touched him now, I doubted my tiny knives could fend him off. Obeying him was a matter of life and death.

"What else," he murmured. "What else would I do to you?"

My blood thrilled, nipples hardened painfully. "You'd lick my clit and taste how wet I was. You'd kiss my inner thigh and bite." I pinched my clit, so, so close to giving in to the spindling orgasm pulsing in my blood.

"I want to watch you come apart. I want to see you pant and tremble. I want you to imagine me sinking deep inside. Hard and fast and taking everything from you." His voice rasped, sounding like pure sex.

Brazenly, I cupped my breasts, rolling my pebbled nipples. I forgot about being a mother or being responsible. I focused only on the sexy dangerous male watching me as if I could ruin him with one word.

I gave myself to him.

I lost myself to sin.

"Fuck, you're beautiful. Sweet and utter fucking perfection," Fox grunted, working his cock harder.

The fire in my blood raced like an inferno, incinerating my core.

My throat slammed closed; my eyes fluttered shut on their own accord. Fox successfully intoxicated me—made me drunk on desire for him. Feeling lightheaded, I swayed forward, craving his hands on me.

I loved holding his complete attention. Too often his eyes swam with ghosts and demons, never fully centred in the present.

Everything I'd agreed to, everything that I was, disappeared. It was just me and him—the world stood still. The connection between us grew.

Friendship.

Companionship.

But I wanted more. So much more.

Trailing my fingers from breasts to pussy, I cried out as Fox suddenly sat upright. His heavy hands landed on my hips, holding me still. The way he devoured me with his gaze didn't make me conscious. It empowered me. It enriched me.

His eyes glowed white as, with no hesitation, he forced my legs apart and thrust a finger deep inside. I moaned loudly, shivering with need.

"Come for me. Fuck my hand, Zel. Fuck it." Fox inserted another finger, and with his grip on my side, forced me to ride his hand.

I didn't know what to do. I wanted to collapse onto his lap. I wanted him to fill me, but all I could do was stand there and preform a miracle by coming and not touching him for balance. I'd enjoyed what he'd given me in the greenhouse, but I wanted more than that. I needed full body contact. I *craved* it.

But he gave me no choice.

His finger twisted inside, focusing on the extra sensitive area. His thumb pressed and swirled on my clit and every atom in my body self-imploded. He was a fast learner and the orgasm tore through me, rupturing my heart, seizing my muscles, shredding my womb with every pulsating release.

On and on, he fucked me with his fingers until the last ebb squeezed my entire body dry. I forgot where I was. I forgot who I was with. I tumbled forward into his arms and touched him.

Life went from heaven to hell in an instant.

Fox shoved me to the ground, tearing his fingers from me. I bounced off the carpet, my eyes flying wide as he loomed above me.

Gone was the lust and need and softness, replaced with

sheer trembling rage. Cold calculation filled his eyes until he looked blind from everything else but the urge to kill.

"Fox. Wait." I tried to scramble backward toward my discarded knife.

He fell to his knees, and with excruciatingly strong hands, flipped me onto all fours. Pushing my shoulder blades, he forced my cheek against the carpet and captured my arms behind my back. I squirmed, trying to get free, but it was impossible. "Fox. Stop. Please."

"Shut up. To be inflicted is to inflict." His voice was programmed—robotic. "I must obey. I must—"

My heart bolted, bringing with it terror and trepidation. His tone was military cold, remote and unfeeling. He'd relapsed and there was nothing I could do.

Tears sprang to my eyes. I begged, "Please… do—"

Then, he fucked me.

His hard cock plunged deep inside, filling me, distorting me. The wetness from my orgasm prevented searing pain, but the fierceness of every thrust made me ache instantly with bruises.

He grunted and rutted like a fucking beast. Fingers digging deep into my hips, jerking me back to meet his every surge.

I didn't want him like this. Not again. It was like a horrible flashback of the first time. The violence, the way he seemed to hate that he needed me—hate the weakness of wanting to join.

My back bowed as he thrust deeper and deeper. My eyes leaked, adding salt to my stinging carpet-burned cheek. I hated him. Hated the brokenness inside him.

"I told you. I warned you. You didn't fucking listen. Now look what you made me do. I can't stop it. Goddammit, I can't stop." He drove into me like a monster. He was big. Too big. It wasn't erotic or fun. It was purely punishment and nothing else. My heart broke, hating his coldness. Hating him for making me hope that he could be fixed.

Fox cursed in a foreign language. His hipbones dug into my ass, faster and faster.

I sniffed back my tears and hardened my heart. I was wrong

to think we had anything special. Fox had eloquently shown me how stupid I truly was. It was over. I was done. This would be the last time he hurt me.

Shutting my emotions down, I let him fuck me. I switched off every sensation and waited for it to be over. I preferred to ignore what was happening and pretended none of this existed.

You brought this on yourself.

I told myself to shut up. I'd only done what I thought might work. I poured all my effort into him only to be thwarted in the worst possible way.

His hips thrust harder and instead of trying to get away, I pushed back, deliberately impaling him harder.

He gasped. "Fuck. Fuck. Oh, God."

Wanting it over, I squeezed my inner muscles around him, rocking back, giving him everything I had left.

His breath came faster, harsher as he thrust again and again. He was violent and cruel, every stroke measured for pain rather than pleasure. He bumped against the top of my pussy, hurting me with urgency.

Curling over me, his back smothered mine as he sunk teeth deep into my neck. I screamed as he thrust again, filling me completely.

Then he came.

Hot, wet streams spurt deep inside. On and on and on.

His hands on my hips clenched hard and teeth bit down on the sinew between my neck and collarbone.

And then it was over and his ragged pants turned to agonized curses. "Fuck."

He pulled out, stumbling to his feet in a rush. The sound of his zipper and belt were the only noises apart from our harsh breathing. Everything ached. Bruises throbbed.

"Fuck!" he roared, prowling around me with his trousers undone and desolation in his voice. I didn't dare move, but I did flip onto my side and curl up into a little ball. Hiding my nakedness, nursing my shame.

Fox dropped to his haunches in front of me. The veins in

his neck stood out as he breathed hard through flared nostrils. He reached out to touch me, but then stopped. His groan held every sadness and regret in the world. "I'm so fucking sorry, Hazel."

I didn't say a word. I had nothing to say.

I was done.

Fox stood up and moved away. Looking back at me, I knew without a doubt he would find some way to fuck himself up with pain. He looked lost and terrified. He looked like a man ready for death.

I tried to make myself care. I tried to find compassion deep inside but I was empty.

I'd already given him everything and had nothing left.

Fox stepped into the bathroom and closed the door behind him.

The instant he was gone, I sat up and let the torrents of tears run down my cheeks.

Gathering my discarded clothing, I dressed, and turned my back on Obsidian Fox for the last time.

Twelve

ROAN

No one knew.

No one.

Not my handler or my contact.

But it was the thing that granted me freedom.

It was nature bringing down a predator. It was life giving me a second chance.

It didn't happen overnight, but slowly, gradually, as if the atrocities I'd done stained my eyes until they no longer wanted to witness my sins.

It took a victim to uncover my one weakness. And I would be forever grateful.

I fucked up a mission, and my target showed me I suffered a handicap.

Something I hadn't even noticed.

The news spread, and my handlers booked me in for Lasik and other supposed miracle cures. But it was no use. The doctors said there wasn't anything wrong with me. It was all mental.

I was going blind.

I bashed my head against the back of the bathroom door, willing away the cold lecherous orders; ignoring the overriding urges I'd never be free of.

Fuck.

Fuck.

Fuck.

My mind wouldn't stop whirling with images of Hazel on her knees while I drove manically into her. The red burn on her cheek from pressing her face into the carpet. The sounds of her cries and pleas.

I'm a bastard. No, I'm worse than that. I'm a soulless machine.

Today was not a good day. I woke to a strong wave of conditioning. The first of every month had been a special recap for operatives. A day we were made to cement our training with yet more grotesqueness.

I warned her!

I fucking warned her to keep her distance and yet she kept pushing and pushing and *pushing.*

I spun around and smashed my fist against the door. Gritting my teeth against the pain licking my knuckles, I glanced in the mirror.

I was fucking wild. Out of control. A rogue operative who should've taken the pill two years ago and ended his miserable life. The scar on my cheek itched with memories, hurtling me back to then—to a place I never wanted to return.

"Hold him down."

My twenty-one-year old heart tore itself into pieces as my handler held up a short crescent moon blade. I'd forged it. I'd hammered the steel into creation. I was well-known for being one of the best metal smiths in the society. And now it would be used against me.

"I obeyed. I did what you said."

My handler paused beside me, looking down with eyes devoid of emotion. "You didn't though, did you, Fox. You think you can flaunt the rules. You can't. You belong to us, and you kill whoever we say you will."

The two men holding my shoulders against the table grunted as I fought. But it wasn't any use.

The sharp tip of the knife entered my mouth, moving to rest behind the soft smoothness of my cheek.

"Every time you look in the mirror you'll see what happens when you try to fight the control."

His wrist flicked up and pain exploded in every crevice of my body. I screamed and choked on my own blood as my cheek gaped in two.

I hated him. I wanted to fucking kill him and every Ghost here.

Throwing the knife to the floor, he ordered, "Sew him up. No morphine."

The bathroom swirled around me; phantom pain ached in my badly sewn up cheek. The flesh inside my mouth felt rough and foreign. Infection after infection had turned a neat line of stitches into a tattered mess.

I'd forgotten the message they'd scarred me with. My thought patterns weren't my own; my body obeyed no one but the programmed rules and commands.

Why did I ever think I stood a chance? I wished I could rewind time and never look at Zel. I wanted to erase myself and all the pain I'd caused from her life.

My white eyes met my mirrored image.

How could you hurt her?

You're so weak.

You've lost her.

You don't deserve her.

I sighed heavily, hanging my head.

I never wanted to see Hazel again—not after hurting her so fucking much. Every time she came near me, I was the crux of every bad thing that happened to her.

It wasn't fair. I wouldn't do it anymore.

I wanted her gone.

Whatever progress she made the night she stabbed me had disappeared. Whatever sweetness we might've found in the greenhouse disintegrated. I'd hoped she'd broken through and set me on the road to recovery, but it'd just been a moment. One brittle moment that shattered the second it was over.

She'd turned me from killer to man—licking me so sweetly, giving me a gift no one had before and all I did in return was revert back to a useless miserable operative with no chance in hell of living.

I couldn't ask any more of her. I couldn't expect her to stay. Not now.

Minutes ticked by. I wanted to leave but I couldn't risk returning to the bedroom.

Grabbing a small hammer from the vanity, I stepped into the shower. Kneeling, I searched for the seam of the secret escape hatch I'd designed. I would never again go into a room with only one exit. After a life time of cages, I knew the value of having two ways out. It meant the difference between surviving and dying.

The custom-made bench seat looked as if it was tiled and part of the shower, but with a few carefully placed taps of the hammer, the mortar cracked, breaking the false seal.

The escape hole only led to the next bedroom's closet, but it gave me the freedom I needed.

The minute I crawled through the small space, I stood upright and buckled my trousers.

My cock still throbbed with the fading orgasm. I cursed the sensitivity of my balls—hating the tingling from being deep inside a woman who I couldn't help but destroy.

She'd never forgive me, which was fine as I would never forgive myself.

Opening the door to the corridor, I checked to see if Zel was around before charging toward the opposite end of Obsidian.

I wanted no chance of running into Zel. Jogging down the stairs, I entered the section of the house I hadn't shown her.

The foyer held most of my creations. Birds and horses and every creature I'd ever met in the Siberian forests of Mother Russia. It was a zoo made out of bronze and copper.

When I lost my sight, the thing I missed most was sculpting—bringing animals to life even though they'd never draw air.

The contract I'd signed when my blindness had been discovered roared back to mind.

There are only two ways an operative may leave the Establishment.
Death.
Disability.

Upon leaving, the agent promises to never speak of said Establishment to anyone at any time for any reason. They solemnly swear to never talk about missions, details, or history. They must have their affairs in order and swallow the last instruction of duty.

Sharing of secrets is not permitted and the Establishment will not hesitate to carry out orders to erase both ex-operative and person who knows intimate knowledge.

The operative has exactly five weeks from removal to swallow his final task.

If this is disobeyed, the Establishment has full right to hunt, interrogate, and kill.

We are always watching.
Invincible. Impenetrable. Invisible.

Like the fucking schmuck I was, I signed it. I wanted out. I *needed* out. Every day, I lost more and more of my vision until I relied on a cane to move around. I already lived in hell, but now I lived in complete and utter darkness. I hated every moment of it.

Every day I begged for freedom—and fate finally listened by taking away my sight until I was useless to them.

I signed it.

I learned to read braille.

I left and never looked back.

For two years, I lived a life adrift from others. I opened Obsidian and hired Oscar to oversee it. Using my inheritance from my slaughtered family, I began a new life. I worked during the witching hours and slept while the sun protected me, basking my skin in warmth and safety my eyes couldn't see.

And slowly, my vision came back.

The pressure of my past stopped crushing me; I believed

the illusion that I was free—regardless of the fact that I was supposed to put myself down like a dog. I had everything I ever wanted apart from the privilege of indulging in another human for comfort. I thought I didn't want it—that I was above such frivolous desires. But I wasn't.

I wanted Zel like I wanted my next breath. I was dying to touch her. I'd give up my vision all over again if it meant I could kiss her and wrap my arms around her and be sure I'd never hurt her again.

I would undergo any operation or therapy if it meant I could just be normal. All I wanted was to provide and care for a woman who gave me all of herself. I hadn't given anything in return, and I was sick of taking. Sick of being a mess. Sick of every damn thing.

I wanted to be a man for her. To shelter her, nurture her...learn to love her.

You're a fucking idiot.

I'd just proved how wistful and fanciful such dreams were. I took Zel by force all because she touched me briefly.

You don't deserve her.

Damn right I didn't. I didn't deserve anything more than a hole in the fucking ground.

The switch inside had flicked on and drowned out everything else. I was inflicted—therefore I had to inflict. Simple. Powerful. Unfightable.

Moving through the house, I didn't know where I would go. I doubted Poison Oaks would indulge my needs so soon. I'd have to resort to more rudimentary methods and lurk in an alley once again.

The anticipation of a fist to my jaw gave me the willpower to keep moving and not bash my head in with the small rabbit statue sitting on the side table.

Wrenching open the door, I sucked in the early afternoon air. Gulping in freshness, I tilted my head up to the sun.

The sun.

Shit. No clubs would be open to fight at this time. No alleys would be dark enough. I had nowhere to go to purge my body and punish myself. I needed a physical release, not just a few lines of a razor blade. Even the tools in my workshop wouldn't give me the wallop I hungered for.

Where could I go to find redemption?

My brain filled with images of Zel again as I stalked around the side of the house toward the garage and my black Porsche.

Her beautifully firm ass as I drove into her. Her gorgeous cascading hair and heart shaped face. The way she looked at me afterward told me exactly what she thought.

Her eyes screamed the truth: I was diabolic. Not fit to be around others. And definitely not worthy of her.

I'd never forgive myself for drilling murderously into her like she was an enemy I needed kill.

Squinting in the glare, I stopped short.

Shit, I hated what I'd done so much, my vision was compromised. A slight film covered my gaze. I'd contaminated myself with horrendous actions toward a woman who deserved a kingdom.

I needed to leave that instant. I didn't want to watch her go. I'd severed the connection between us, and there was nothing but the cold-hearted mistress of conditioning.

It was over.

I'd wanted to know so much about her. She could see the truth through all my bullshit and knew so much more about me than I did about her. The secrets she kept hidden were so deep inside I had no chance of deciphering them.

All I knew was the driving force behind everything she did was grief.

Sadness, heartache, despair.

I hated to see her so unhappy and not have anyone to lean on.

"Um, hi." A soft, high pitched voice jerked me to attention. I looked around, searching the large expanse of pebbled driveway. I frowned. In my rush, I hadn't noticed the white car parked at the front of Obsidian.

All members' car parks were at the rear of the property. Who the hell had the nerve to park in front of my residence as if they owned the fucking place? I moved forward, wondering what the hell was going on.

"Um, mister? Do you have a key to the big door? My auntie and her friend left me to go talk to my mummy, but I don't want to wait. I said I'd be good and sit in the car because little kids can't go inside, but I want to see her."

I spun around, kicking up gravel.

A perfect replica of Hazel stood behind me.

A child.

A girl.

A daughter.

Fuck.

A flashback grabbed me with its gnarly claws, dragging me deep and dark.

"Congratulations on your promotion, Operative Fox. Tell me again how many family members you had."

I hated this part. The mind games. The constant mental torture. He knew how many family members I'd had because he made me kill them all.

"I had a mother. Vera Averin. She was a whore, a traitor, and a thief, and deserved to die. I had a father. Alex Averin. He was a womanizer, a cheater, and a liar, and deserved to die. I had a brother, Vasily Averin. He was the spawn of Satan, a heathen, and only evil lived inside him, and he deserved to die."

The moment the vile lies were spoken, I hastily thought the truth. Silently, I undid the heinous things I said. Vera, my mother, was kind and generous. She didn't deserve to die. Alex, my father, was a great provider and protector. He didn't deserve to die. Vasily—

My heart ceased to beat as grief crippled me. Vasily, my brother, was a proficient artist, kind and smart. He didn't deserve to die.

"Good. And did you know you had a sister?"

My gut churned, threatening an explosive reaction. A sister? No. No, please no. I couldn't handle killing another sibling. A girl. An innocent, little girl whose only crime was to share my blood.

"You killed her, too. Don't you remember?"

*I blinked. White noise hissed in my ears, drowning out my panic.
"Excellent, sir. I do not recall that mission." Like so many others, I'd
wiped them forever from my memory. I wasn't surprised I couldn't recall
killing yet another sibling. I would rather pull my brain out through my
ears than remember.*

*"Yes. Your mother was pregnant with a girl. A double murder and
you didn't even know." The pat to the shoulder came with an electric
shock. Every muscle seized as the current passed through my body.*

"What do you say?" the handler asked, once he'd let me go.

*My brain screamed, die you motherfucker. My mouth said, "Thank
you, sir."*

I returned to the present with a bang, stumbling as vertigo
hit me hard.

Goddammit. I fucking hated them. Hated. Hated. *Hated.* I
wished I could stick a cattle prod in my brain and short circuit
my entire system. The flashbacks were the worst they'd been in
a long time—brought on by the stress of hurting a woman I
cared deeply for.

Zel.

Her daughter.

I knew without a doubt the little girl standing in front of me
was hers. There was no mistaking the long mahogany hair, the
perfect cheekbones, the shape of her chin. The only difference
was eye colour. Green had given way to soulful liquid brown
eyes that looked right into my fucking soul.

My breathing accelerated; my heart pumped like a demon. I
backed away as fast as my legs could motor.

Don't come near me. I couldn't do this. I couldn't have more
blood on my hands. Her blood. Zel's little legacy.

Pebbles skidded beneath my shoes as I practically surfed on
gravel in my terror to run. I needed to get far, far away from
this miniature replica of Hazel. Before I hurt her.

Her dark eyes met mine, and I lost touch with reality.

"For the third and final time, kill him!"

"No!" Wetness splashed on my eighteen-year-old cheeks and it took a

while to realize it was tears. I'd never cried before. Not even when I killed my mother and father. But this...I couldn't do this.

"You made me take care of him! You brought him to stay with me. I thought you wanted me to train him to be like us!" My voice broke as I looked at my small nine-year-old brother, Vasily. His cheeks were still chubby with youth, his blue eyes wide with terror. A dark stain on the front of his jeans signalled fear had hijacked his bladder.

For three months, we'd slept in the same room, ate together, laughed together. I thought my handler rewarded me for good behaviour and given me a friend. Given me my brother to train and integrate into this new way of life.

I never suspected this.

"Roan. Pl—please help me. Don't kill me. Please?" Vasily's soprano voice brought fresh tears to my eyes; my body heaved, fighting against years of conditioning and the wrath of my handler.

"I. Won't. Do. It," I snapped, sucking in large gulps of air. I refused to kill my last blood relative. A boy I cared for more than anyone in the world.

"Yes, you will, Operative Fox. Otherwise we'll torture him until he dies, then cripple you as you're no longer viable property."

I couldn't stand anymore.

My handler grabbed Vasily by his neck, bringing him closer to me. "Do it."

Vomit exploded from my mouth, splashing onto the concrete floor.

My brother stopped crying, squirming out of the handlers hold. Instead of running away from the man destined to murder him, he ran toward me and wrapped his bony arms tight around my waist.

"Mister? Hey, mister?" A tug on my cuff removed me from my horrible memories, slapping me into reality. "Are you okay?" The high, lyrical voice pierced my throbbing brain.

I charged back, breaking her hold on my shirt. "Don't touch me."

The little girl looked down and scuffed her shiny black shoes in the gravel. "Oh, sorry." Her eyes met mine again, wide and worried. "Are you okay? You were mumbling things I couldn't understand." She cocked her head. "What language was that? My teacher said we should learn a language. I'd like to learn, but I don't know what. Maybe I could learn what you just spoke." She stepped forward, her little lips never stopping. "Can you teach me? I'd love to learn and mummy would be really proud of me. Would you teach me, please?" Her eyelashes flurried and my fucking heart shattered into pieces.

I sucked in air, locking my muscles, conjuring all the self-control I possessed. If I ever needed complete and utter discipline, it was now. I'd avoided children since losing Vasily. I couldn't look at them or listen to them or even watch them on television.

To me, children were the embodiment of everything I tried to preserve: innocence, fragility, trust, and unconditional acceptance.

I deserved none of it, therefore I wasn't fit to be around them.

The little girl inched forward again, encroaching on my space. I didn't know how most children should behave, but she was forward—so fucking brave and inquisitive. Shouldn't she be timid and meek? Too frightened to talk to a scarred stranger?

"You look scared. What happened? You can tell me. I won't tell anyone." She drew a cross over her heart. "I promise. I have nightmares sometimes. Do you?"

Everything about her intoxicated me until I couldn't move an inch. She came forward another step. "You're not like the other adults. You look like one, but I don't think adults get scared. You shouldn't be scared. My mummy taught me to not be afraid of anything."

Her tiny fingers flew to her lips. "Oops. She said I wasn't allowed to talk to strangers. Um, you won't tell on me? She gets real mad when I talk to people. I don't know why. I know when they're bad, and you're not bad. Mummy also gets mad when I cough which is so silly." Her eyes met mine. "Do you have a mummy who tells you off for making friends with strangers?"

She moved until she stood directly in front of me. My body shuddered and vibrated. Memories of Vasily and my past kept battering me all the while this perfect angel chattered on—seeing deep into my black-ridden soul further than she had any right to.

"Whoa. What happened to your cheek?" Her little hand pointed upward, eyes squinting in the sun behind me. "It looks like a bad man hurt you." Her eyes narrowed. "Did the bad man hurt you? I hope you made him pay. Those sorts of people shouldn't be allowed to go around making other people ugly."

Every word lacerated me until I felt like a large tree being hacked at with an axe. Every syllable and consonant chipped away at my already crumbling foundation, and my roots began to snap.

My left leg gave out, slamming hard against pebbles. My right leg joined until I kneeled before the one thing in my world I couldn't fight.

I toppled to the ground before her, undone by her pristine innocence.

Every organ howled against conditioning, every bone bellowed in agony—my refusal to inflict anymore pain brought mind-numbing orders, amplifying and amplifying, enraged by my disobedience.

I no longer needed fists to find redemption. I found punishment just by staring into the eyes of someone so pure.

"Do you understand English?" the girl asked, moving to stand right in front of me. Her eye level was slightly higher than mine, making me feel as though I should bow to her, obey her, worship her.

I didn't know what compelled me to reply, but I couldn't stop. "Yes. I understand English."

She smiled, clapping her dainty hands. "Great. I thought you did seeing as you told me not to touch you. What language were you talking just now?"

"Russian."

"And your cheek. Did a bad man do that?"

"Yes."

Her smile increased and a flash of anger that shouldn't be seen on a little girl's face crossed her features. "Did you kill him? I would've killed him."

Who was this child? This perfect, brilliant, brave, little child.

I hung my head. "No. He's still alive."

She tutted. "Well, I would kill him." Flicking her hair over her shoulder, she announced, "I like you." Her face scrunched up as if I'd passed her test of likeability and stuck her hand out. "I'm Clara. What's your name?"

A lazy, warm wind drifted across the driveway, rustling the trees ringing the perimeter. I gawked at the little girl dressed in a purple sweater and black leggings. Her hair hung loose, strands kicking in the breeze. A single purple ribbon twirled around her jaw.

My vision blurred around the edges.

This girl was everything I needed. Everything I was running from and to, and I didn't even know it.

Her sweet fearlessness clutched my heart and in a matter of moments, she'd monopolized my every thought.

My gravity shifted.

I fell madly fucking in love.

I knew I shouldn't do it.

I knew I should run and never look back.

But I didn't.

Holding out my hand, I moaned when her little fingers squeezed around mine. Tears sprang to my eyes in overwhelming gratitude. Gratitude for being able to retain my self-control and gratitude for this perfect creature.

Her touch shattered me.

Her touch awoke me.

Her touch destroyed me.

"Hello, Clara." I looked up into her liquid eyes. "I'm Roan."

Thirteen

Hazel

I'd always known life had its favourites. Like a parent sometimes has a favourite child, life lavished attention and gifts galore on the ones it favoured. The ones it didn't care for were forgotten. Allowed to survive, but given no special treatment.

I was one of the ones allowed to survive—to carve my own journey with no help.

But Fox, he was someone else entirely.

He was the child that every parent hated. The one no one understood. The one everyone pretended didn't exist.

Not because he was evil or awkward or cruel—but because he was damaged and needed too much repairing to be feasible.

Ignorance and hatred pushed that child into the dark and their only chance was to turn inward, suffer silently.

I wanted to hate him.

I wanted to despise him.

He hurt me.

He used me.

Again and again.

But ultimately, I understood him.

I forgave him.

But I would never be able to save him.

Three life changing events came in quick succession.

The first happened when Clue charged through the doors of Obsidian's fighting floor and almost knocked me on my ass. I'd been on my way out—about to leave Fox's world forever—when she burst in out of nowhere.

I whirled backward, only to be caught by Corkscrew as he appeared right behind her.

One look from her tear-swimming eyes—I knew.

Something had happened to Clara.

"Is she okay? Tell me!" Panic lashed in my blood, flaying me alive. "Tell me, Clue! Now!" Nightmarish scenarios crushed my brain.

Clara dead.

Clara in a coma.

Clara gone forever.

My eyes grew wider; heart pounded harder. "She's de—dead?"

Corkscrew's fingers dug into my elbow, keeping me steady as Clue captured my cheeks and shook her head. Her almond eyes were red from crying, but she seemed calm. "No! She's fine."

She's fine. Thank fucking God.

Panic gave way to undiluted anger.

"You gave me a fucking panic attack to come and tell me she's *fine?*" I shrugged Corkscrew off, clutching my rapidly thudding heart. "I don't understand."

Clue shot a look at her backup support. Ben was the one who swallowed and said, "She collapsed at school." His voice was soft and smooth, keeping me calm even as my body felt as if it exploded with shrapnel. "She suffered a seizure for three minutes. The school called an ambulance who took her to the

ER."

My brain swam. My worst nightmares were coming true. Too soon. *It's too soon!*

Her coughing fit the other night and now this? Her symptoms had increased rapidly.

I'd have to ask Fox for the money now. I'd have to come up with a story that warranted him parting with another one hundred thousand dollars.

Clue stroked my shoulders, her warmth and support doing wonders for my scattered thoughts. "She's alright. The doctors don't know what caused it—"

I snarled. "Of course they know what caused it. Fucking idiots for not catching it sooner." I clutched my chest as a huge ball of agony lodged in my heart. "They didn't catch it, Clue. Because of their mistake, they sentenced my daughter to death."

I'd always held such tight rein on my grief, but in that second I wanted to explode. I wanted to tear through the globe like an angry typhoon and wreck as much destruction as possible.

I wanted to destroy the doctors who ruined my life and my baby's.

I didn't want to put up with anything anymore. Fox had hurt me. Life had slapped me in the face. My past had almost ruined me. I just wanted out.

I'm not strong enough!

A massive sob bubbled in my chest and I bent over, sucking in gulping breaths.

If you start crying now, you'll never stop.

"It's okay, Zelly. It's going to be okay." Clue stroked my back, murmuring, "It's a bitch of a situation, but she's alright. Honestly to look at her you'd think she faked it just to get out of school. You don't have to worry."

I threw my hands up. "I don't have to worry?" Tears shot up my spine in a tingling wake. "How can you *say* that? Every night I lie in bed, counting her breaths, making sure she's still with me. One day, there will be no more breaths, Clue! Then what? What the hell do I do with my life?"

The regret and hatred for myself crashed like a tidal wave. Where had I been while Clue picked up *my* daughter from the ER? Instead of soothing *my* child, I was being fucked by a man who I had no hope of saving.

Your priorities are all screwed up.

I hate myself.

I'll never forgive myself.

Everything that happened with Fox seemed trivial. So what if he hurt me? So what if I had some saviour complex? So what if it was my fault he'd snapped?

I'd pushed him too far, and I could only blame myself for the consequences. He hadn't meant to hurt me—beneath the scariness, he was just a man looking for a way out—same as me.

His issues were vampiric, sucking my soul and energy dry until I was empty and shrivelled and on the very ledge of my wit's end.

I had nothing left to give, but I had to keep going. I didn't have the luxury of forgetting or indulging in tears.

Clara was the one who needed me.

She was all that mattered.

A whimper escaped, and Corkscrew gathered me into his large midnight arms. His body heat helped burn some of my unhelpful thoughts, granting me a moment of lucidity.

He and Clue barely knew each other, but he'd become a huge part of both our lives. Every night I'd return home, and he would be there. A fabulous cook, considerate houseguest, and completely besotted with Clue.

His deep voice vibrated in his chest. "It's okay. We're here for you if and when that happens. For now...Clue. Tell her."

I went from slouched to stressed again in a second. "Tell me what?"

Clue took a step back. "After the ER, we headed home, but Clara threw a huge tantrum and made us come to you. She refuses to go home without you. I'd never seen her so upset or stubborn. She was a little spitfire."

My ears rang, clanging with loud, terrifying bells. *Please don't say it—*

Ben cleared his throat. "I know it's not the best idea to bring a kid to an illegal fight club, but…well, she's here."

"What?" I screeched, attracting the attention of two burly men warming up in the boxing ring.

They brought my dying daughter to a monster's house!

"She's in the car waiting for you. Corkscrew came with me to get into the club. I figured we could all go home together." Clue stroked my arm, trying to calm me. "It's okay, Zelly. We'll have a quiet night—just the three of us—like old times."

I didn't listen to a word she said. "You left my daughter in the car in front of an illegal club. How stupid can you be?"

My body was consumed with the thought of Clara being so close to the devil inside Fox. Two parts of my life I wanted to keep separate. Two parts that should never *ever* mix.

"It was the only way. We couldn't exactly bring her in here," Clue said.

No amount of hands could restrain me. I charged.

Slamming open the large, metal doors, I winged my way down the corridor toward the exit.

Please don't let him be anywhere near her. I balled my hands, praying Fox was still in his bathroom, doing God knows what to bring himself back under control.

I couldn't stomach the thought of him being around such a precious, breakable thing.

If he so much as looks at her.

Rage, hot and brewing, geysered in my blood. Every single motherly instinct vibrated on overdrive.

The second life changing thing happened when I threw open the front door.

My heart bucked as I charged from inside to out and skidded to a halt.

Oh, my God.

No. Please let it be a hallucination.

It couldn't be true. It couldn't.

Clue swerved to a stop beside me just before Ben hurtled to a standstill next to her. "What the hell?" Clue muttered. "Care to tell me what the—"

I swallowed a scream, and I charged like a hundred cavalry. My arms were muskets. My legs were cannons. My voice was trumpets warning the enemy they were about to die. "Get *away* from her!"

Fox looked up, white eyes wide as I skidded to a stop. He didn't move an inch as I bared my teeth like a feral cat and yanked Clara away from him.

Their hands snapped loose and Clara tripped, stumbling against my body. "Ow!"

I'd never felt so sick, so violent, so absolutely ready to draw blood. Panting, I shoved her behind my legs, barricading her tiny frame with mine. I faced the man I thought I could care for, the man I secretly wished I could love, and released all my animosity and capsized emotions.

"Don't you dare touch her! What were you thinking? Just because you weren't able to hurt me you thought you'd hurt my daughter? Shame on you!"

Fox flinched as if I'd slapped him, bowing his head.

Clara squirmed, breaking my hold to position herself in front of me. My eyes flew between her and Fox, counting the feet between them—assessing the risk if he were to tackle her to the ground.

Her bright, expressive eyes met mine. Fear and confusion painted her cheeks. "What are you doing, mummy? He wasn't hurting me! We're friends. We shook hands as that's what new friends do. Remember? You taught me." Her little foot stomped in the gravel. "He didn't do anything wrong. Leave him alone!"

Her temper was alive and well. In a moment, I assessed her skin colour, her ease of breathing—searching for any sign she was closer to death than she was to life. But she practically glowed, looking rosy cheeked and fierce.

She'd never been a normal child. So bold and into everything; endless questions and no fear when it came to talking to everyone.

I looked over her head at Fox. He hadn't moved. No matter how many times I blinked, I couldn't remove the image of Clara's tiny hand swallowed up by Fox's large one. The same hand that'd strangled me and held me firm while he fucked me ruthlessly. The same hand that'd been scarred countless times doing things even he couldn't live with.

Ignoring Clara, I hissed, "Fox. You heard me. Don't you go near her again. This wasn't part of the deal."

His eyes came up slowly as if the weight of his crimes crushed his shoulders with a heavy yoke. "I'm sorry." He blinked, shaking his head. Comprehension and aliveness filtered into his silver gaze. "I couldn't help it. I—" His eyes flew to Clara. Immediately they swelled with adoration and awe. My heart stopped with how—consumed he looked—how completely different. He'd been transformed from angry warrior to soft giant who hung on every word of a child. "She—she's perfect, Zel."

Slowly, he creaked upright, running hands through his hair. He shook himself as if he was a bear coming out of hibernation. "You'll never understand how much I hate myself for what happened between us today. No amount of apologies will ever redeem my actions, but please believe me when I say I would *never* hurt your child." His mouth twisted and he punched himself in the chest. "I give you my oath."

Clara tugged out of my grip, darting to Fox's side. My heart ceased to beat as she wrapped her tiny digits through his monstrous ones. Fox shuddered, locking into place.

"Can't you hear? He's sad. You've told him off, now forgive him. That's how punishment works, isn't it? When I do something bad, you yell and then you hug me." She came forward, unsuccessfully trying to drag Fox toward me. "Hug him and make him feel better."

Both Fox and I jerked back, leaving Clara stranded between us. Our voices blended in a loud combined, "No."

We stood staring while Clara planted her feet firmly in the pebbles. "He's mine. I introduced myself, and we're friends now. I like him, and you're silly to think he'll hurt me. He wouldn't do that, mummy. He's not a bad stranger, so stop being mean."

A noise of half laughter, half panic exploded from my mouth. How had I raised such an eloquent tyrant? So stubborn and old beyond her years.

Clue arrived, jogging to a careful stop beside me. Her body was poised for a fight, eyes flying between Fox and me. "Everything okay here?"

Corkscrew appeared behind her, his ebony skin absorbing the sunlight like black marble. "Mr. Obsidian. Everything alright?"

Fox looked toward him, clearing his throat. "Yes. Fine. Everything's fine." His voice held no sign of what happened, or any of the pain I'd heard when he swore he wouldn't hurt Clara.

His eyes dropped back to Clara, filling once again with amazement—bordering on obsession. My heart skipped a beat. Almost unconsciously I moved forward and wrapped an arm around Clara's shoulders, bringing her tight against me.

She squirmed, pushing away. Her strength made me rock on my feet, and my attention shot to her. Her cheeks were pink, lips red, and eyes full of fire. The only sign of her episode was paler than normal skin.

She looked ready to go to war for a scarred stranger she'd just met.

She's just like me.

The thought both thrilled and terrified. I'd been so stubborn when I was young. I wanted to wave a magic wand and make everyone happy—save kittens, rescue homeless children, cuddle puppies, and grant world peace. I'd been so stupid to think I had the power to change anyone's life. And

Clara wouldn't live long enough to learn that lesson.

Needing to touch her and remind myself she was safe and unharmed, I ducked down. Smoothing her favourite purple jumper, I asked, "Are you okay? Auntie Clue told me what happened at school."

She looked toward Fox, giving him a small smile. He seemed in a trance, neither returning it, nor even acknowledging anyone around him.

He was completely and utterly besotted.

I hated the intensity. The single-minded connection he had with my daughter. It freaked me out, but also filled me with a small thrum of hope. For the first time, I saw yearning in his gaze.

Yearning to be better. Longing for something I didn't know.

"I'm fine." She scowled, her bright eyes meeting mine before flying back to Fox. "I just felt tired from coughing, that's all. I had a nap, and the stupid school called the hospital."

"Clara. You know you're not allowed to use the word stupid." I tapped her on the tip of her nose. "Use silly or don't use it at all."

She sighed, eyes flashing. "Don't embarrass me, mummy. I'm not five anymore."

My heart flopped out of my chest remembering her as a tyrannical five-year-old with more energy than a megawatt battery and flossy brown hair.

Clue came forward, putting her hand on my shoulder. I stood upright, not letting go of Clara.

Fox hadn't moved a muscle. His eyes were full of memories I could never understand, his jaw slack, body slouched as if Clara had stolen the life out of him.

Despite what had happened between us, I hated the desolation in his gaze—the lostness, the sadness.

Tucking Clara behind me once again, I moved forward and waved a hand in front of his eyes. "Fox."

It took a second, but he blinked and refocused, dragging

himself out of somewhere dark. His shoulders straightened. "Sorry. Thinking of someone else."

Someone? Who?

Clenching his hands, he kept his eyes on mine, not looking down at Clara. "Look, I have to go. Work. I forgot—urgent business."

My stomach fluttered at his obvious distress. He didn't need to work. The accounts were in order, all supplies filed and delivered. Opening time wasn't for another six hours.

He was running.

Two conflicting emotions filled me. I wanted him to run. I wanted him as far away from Clara as possible. But my heart wept at the thought of him alone. Running from a little girl who already adored him. Sprinting from a woman who'd used her short fuse of anger and now just felt endlessly sad.

Sad for him.

Sad for us.

Just sad.

I wanted to blame him for his actions before—for once again proving he wasn't normal and couldn't be tamed. But if I had to cast blame, I was tainted myself. He would never have hurt me if I hadn't pushed. He'd warned me, and I didn't listen.

Despite what happened, he had made progress from when I first met him. The difference was he *wanted* to change whereas before I didn't think he thought he had that option.

It just wasn't enough.

He was beyond dangerous—entirely unpredictable—and I couldn't afford to let him into this part of my life. If I offered another chance, he might hurt me, or worse, hurt Clara.

My first commitment was to my daughter, and they just didn't work together. Delicate and dangerous. Fragile and frightening. No, I wouldn't let it happen.

"Yes, good idea. You better go." I didn't want more blood on my hands, and I knew I'd end up killing him if he so much as looked at Clara wrong.

Fox took a step back with a heavy nod.

Corkscrew moved forward. "Hey, you want some help? I came for a quick session when Clue told me she was heading over, but I'm more than happy to run a few errands if you need anything." His black eyes flickered back to Clue.

She nodded with a slight smile. It seemed all three of us had banded together in operation get 'Fox away from Zel's daughter.'

Clue said, "That's a good idea, Ben. I'll come back and pick you up when I've dropped Zelly and Clara off at home."

Clara's little hands shoved my hip, bumping me out of the way. "I don't want to go yet. I like it here." Her lips pouted and she pointed at Fox. "I want to know more about the bad man. He scarred my new friend, and I don't like it."

Before I could grab her, she darted across the small distance and stood so, so close to Fox. Too close. Dangerously close.

My heart fucking clawed into my throat when she placed her hand on Fox's hip, looping her finger through a belt loop.

Fox's eyes snapped closed, and he sucked in a huge lungful of air.

Everyone froze.

Clue and Ben had no idea the risk Fox presented, but they sensed it. They tasted my panic, and we all moved at once.

Gravel kicked as I rushed forward and grabbed Clara's hand, jerking her away.

"No!" She clutched Fox's belt loop, fighting me. "I want to stay."

She'd never pulled a tantrum in her entire life. Never. She knew better, so what the hell was she doing? Twice in one day!

"Clara Hunter you obey me right now." I slammed my hands on my hips, glaring at my disobedient child. The same child who held onto a monster as if she found a new pet.

Fox tumbled suddenly—he went from standing to kneeling in a second flat. The same position I found him touching my daughter. The same position that put him just below Clara's full height.

His snowy eyes opened, locking onto Clara's. "You need to

listen to your mother. She wants you to go."

Clara pursed her lips, colour dotting her cheeks. "I don't want to go. You have stories. I want to hear stories. I want to hear about the bad man. I want to stay." Her huge brown eyes welled with tears.

A few times in the past, Clara used crocodile tears to wrap me around her little finger. I was immune to her wily ways, but Fox...he wasn't.

He groaned and hung his head, clutching his skull in his hands. I never thought I'd see such a violent threatening man come undone by a few glass tears from a child.

Clara stopped instantly and did something that turned my dark hair grey.

Her little arms wrapped around his head, pulling his face against her tiny, breakable, oh so vulnerable chest.

"No!" I rushed forward, but Clue jerked me back.

"Zelly, you'll frighten her. It's okay. Ben's here if anything goes wrong."

She didn't know what Fox was capable of. She didn't know!

I wriggled in Clue's hold, tears springing to my eyes as Fox ever so slowly pushed my daughter away. Every move was precise, controlled, seething with discipline and strictness.

Clara didn't stand a chance at holding onto him. With his large hand splayed on her stomach, Fox pushed until an entire arm length separated them.

Her arms unravelled from around his head, and she stood with wide hurt eyes. "You don't like to be hugged? I like to be hugged if I'm not feeling well or hurt myself." She fidgeted, never taking her eyes from Fox. "You're hurting, so I wanted to hug you. It'll make you feel better. I promise."

My legs trembled. I had no idea how I remained standing.

Fox looked at her as if she was the only thing in the world. His entire body trembled; his hands clutched his thighs, digging hard into muscle. "A hug isn't the same for me as it is for other people, Clara."

She inched closer again. "So...how do you make yourself

feel better?"

Fox's eyes rose to latch onto mine. The power of his silver gaze untangled the rest of my emotions, and a small moan trailed from my mouth.

"Well, your mother has been helping me a little." He smiled, his eyes looking more like soft snow than harsh blizzard when he looked back at Clara. "She's amazing. You're very lucky to have her."

Clara looked back at me and shrugged. "She's okay, I guess." A small giggle escaped her.

Ben laughed and my legs gave out. I had no choice but to sink to the floor and kneel just like Fox. The two of us stared across the gravel; my daughter in the centre.

His eyes shot silent promises.

I promise I won't hurt her.

I give you my word.

Please…

I didn't know what the final plea was for, but I shut my eyes, blocking him off. I'd never known a man who could frustrate me, terrify me, and undo me all at once.

My heart, bruised and torn thanks to Fox, shed the armour I'd conjured against him. A fissure broke the hardened shell, and something twisted deep inside.

I wouldn't be able to help Fox.

But my daughter could.

My tiny, dying daughter who I would miss for the rest of my life.

My eyes flew open, ready to answer his silent beg. He wanted permission to be around Clara. I could manage for a few hours, and then I would whisk her away and lock her behind closed doors. There was only so much tempting danger I could handle.

You hurt her, I'll kill you.

I'll do it with no hesitation.

But okay…

His large shoulders rolled inward and a faint smile kissed

his lips. *"Klyanus' moyey zhizni ya ne budu yey bol'."*

Clue shifted beside me, crossing her svelte arms. "Um, care to repeat that in English?"

Fox shook his head, eyes flaring wide. "Sorry. I didn't know I slipped. I said, I swear on my life I will not hurt her." His answer was for Clue, but he never looked away from me. His eyes resonated with truth. I honestly believed he would kill himself before he let whatever madness inside him hurt Clara.

A small smidgen of worry evaporated; I nodded.

Fox closed his eyes briefly, glowing with thankfulness.

Ben came forward, eyebrows drawing together. "Hang on, what do you mean you won't hurt her?" His tone was sharp. "Of course, you won't. Who the hell says something like that?"

Tension gathered in our small group, causing my skin to prickle. "It's okay, Corkscrew. I know what he meant." Ben looked at me with concern on his face. I nodded. "It's okay. Truly."

Clara bounced in her dusty black shoes. "I know what he means. I do. I do."

My heart stopped, waiting for her declaration. Fox seemed just as anxious as he repositioned his knees uncomfortably.

"He means he doesn't like hugs or being touched. I think the bad man made him hate hugs because bad men don't like love. They're evil and cold, and I don't like them." Her large eyes met Fox's. "I'm right, aren't I? You really do want my mummy to hug you even though she was mean and yelled at you, but you don't know how. It's easy, you know. All you have to do is wrap your arms around her."

An eternity passed before Fox nodded infinitesimally. "You're right, little one."

The sweet surrender in his voice set fire to my blood. I just granted him the right to spend a few hours with Clara, not an eternity. I couldn't have him falling in love with her. She wasn't his to keep.

I hurled upright onto my feet. "Don't, Fox."

His eyes met mine, frowning. "Don't what?"

I glared harder, hoping he'd get my silent message. *Don't you dare fall for her. She isn't yours to fall for.*

He stood too and took a step back. He didn't say a word.

Clara spun to face me, hands on her hips, looking far too opinionated for her young age. "If he gets to be called after an animal I want to, too. Call me Pony…no wait, call me Horse." Her nose wrinkled. "They're not as pretty as a Fox." She spun to face him. "Why does my mummy call you that?"

Fox glanced at me before very cleverly changing the subject. "Why do you want to be called Horse or Pony? I think Clara is a very pretty name."

Clara giggled, moving back toward him as if he was the largest sunflower and she was a hungry bumblebee. "It's because I love horses. My favourite show in the whole entire world is Flick the pony, and I want to grow up and own lots and lots of horses and be a jockey." Her bright, hopeful voice made me want to burst into tears.

She had an obsession with horses—it would be a dream come true to be able to afford her own equine or even riding lessons. In a different world. A different life maybe. A different existence where she didn't have a death sentence hanging over her head.

Fox smiled. "I like horses, too. All animals. I make them if you'd like to see?"

A cloud rolled over the sun, casting us all in shadow. My body tensed, sensing an omen, a premonition of doom. I didn't want Clara anywhere near his house. I would never get her out of there with all the fascinating artwork and statues. I'd agreed to let Fox talk to her, but I didn't agree to more time than a brief acquaintance.

Clue moved closer, whispering in my ear. "I've never seen a man so besotted with a kid before. No wonder you like working for him. Beneath the scary appearance, he's a massive softy."

I snorted. Fox. A softy? Was I the only one who saw past the livid scar, the surliness, and into his soul? His dark and damaged soul?

No, I'm not the only one.

Clara did, too, but instead of being afraid of him, she suffered the same malady I did. She wanted to fix him. She stupidly thought a bit of glue and paperclips would fix him. And it would break her heart when she realized it wasn't possible. But how could I prevent her from trying?

"Do you have horses and ponies…and sheep? Oh, I like sheep." Clara once again moved far too close to Fox.

He pre-empted her touching him and took a step back. "I have many animals, but no sheep."

Clara chewed on her cheek in thought, looking as if that was a deal breaker. Her eyes lit up. "Can you make a sheep?"

Fox smiled softly. "I could make a sheep if you wanted one."

She nodded. "Good. Yes, I want one."

Fox moved away a little more, stress lines and shadows darkening his face. He'd run the gauntlet, and he looked as if his reserves were dwindling. How much longer could he hold onto his self-control?

Moving forward swiftly, I grabbed Clara and pressed her against my legs, imprisoning her with my arms around her neck. She squirmed, but let me contain her.

The third and final life changing event came in the form of Clara's innocent question.

"Mummy, I want to see Roan's animal collection. Don't make me go home yet, okay?"

Roan?

Roan.

His true name.

My eyes shot to Fox's, wide and amazed and slightly hurt. He'd told my daughter, who he'd known all of ten minutes, his first name. He hadn't given me that honour. He'd taken everything I had to give and hadn't granted me a single part of himself.

Fox gritted his jaw, recognising my anger, but not

acknowledging it. Instead, he asked, "Is Clara why you leave every night? Why you don't stay?"

Clue sucked in a breath beside me, finally sensing the sparks and awareness between us. I didn't give him an answer. It wasn't any of his business.

He dropped his eyes to Clara. "Does your mum come home to you every night? Would you miss her if she didn't?"

Clara, happy to be included in an adult's question, reeled off way too much information. "Yes. She goes to work and then comes home and hangs out with me and Auntie Clue and Ben. We watch television. She makes me do homework." Her nose crinkled. "Bleh." Then her little arms came backward and squeezed my legs behind her.

My heart clenched with overwhelming love. "But then we lie in the dark and talk about what we want most, like an ocean full of chocolate ice-cream, and I fall asleep to her telling me lots of wonderful stories. She's really awesome." She looked up, her little nose catching a ray of sunlight breaking through the clouds. "I love her. I would miss her if she didn't come home, because she's my best friend in the whole wide world."

She moved suddenly, rushing to Fox and wrapping her hand in his.

He froze, turning from man to statue. His legs wobbled, but he stayed upright this time. "Is that why you like my mummy? Does she tell you stories and help with your homework?"

Clue and Ben held their breath, feeding off my fear. I didn't dare move in case I triggered a violent reaction in Fox. Ben subtly moved closer to him, putting himself in grabbing distance.

I flashed him a grateful smile. Thank God he was here. I needed a constant bodyguard around Fox. And I hated how sad that was.

Would we ever find a balance? A peaceful moment where we could touch and laugh and stroke like any normal couple?

We're not a couple.

Things between us were complicated, but it'd been

transformed into a Rubik cube with a thousand different colour sequences now that Clara had skipped the line from secrets to Fox's realm.

Fox never let go of Clara's hand, and my heart remained in my throat as he ducked to her level.

"She helps me with my homework, but she doesn't tell me stories. Do you think you can tell me some she told you?"

Oh, God.

I couldn't think of anything worse. Every story I'd ever told Clara was steeped in fact and twisted with life lessons I'd learned the hard way. My trials had become mythical beasts, my defeats evil witches, but every story ended with a happily ever after.

Fox would know—he'd learn my secrets through my open book of a daughter. Nothing from my past would be safe.

Clara nodded, happiness glowing in her brown eyes. "I can. Can you tell me some in return? Do you know any good stories? I bet you do. I bet you got your scar fighting a dragon while saving some pretty princess." She tugged on his hand, excitement flying through her young body.

Fox nodded. "I have a few stories I could share." He bent in half and whispered in her ear. "I've never told anyone, so you'll have to tell me if my stories are any good."

Clara beamed up at him, joy swimming in her eyes. "I'll tell you. I'm sure they're great, though. Can we go see the horses now?"

Fox looked to me. I looked to Clue. Clue looked to Ben. Ben looked to Clara.

There was only one answer to give, but it wasn't the one I wanted. I wished Fox had never set eyes on Clara as I doubted I'd ever get them apart.

"Yes, you can go. But I'm coming, too."

Fox gave me a soul-destroying smile before striding toward the house.

With a heavy heart and my hand clinging to the knife in my pocket, I followed a killer whose fingers were wrapped around my daughter's.

Fourteen

ROAN

All humans collected fond memories. It used to be a favourite pastime of mine: asking fellow recruits what their happiest recollection was. Where did their minds go while they were being beaten or ordered to murder?

Their happy thoughts ranged from cuddly toys, to a pretty girl, to their favourite food. Not once did we include our family.

That was just asking for trouble.

I broke that law by thinking of Vasily.

The three months while we shared a bedroom were the worst and best of my life. I was responsible for his food, water, and shelter. I was his protection. His brother and friend. Knowing he relied on me gave me purpose. He gave me a reason to keep going. He gave me hope.

The day they made me kill him, it ruined everything left inside me. The hope extinguished, all chance of happiness blotted out. All trace of who I'd been erased—just like they'd planned.

I'd lived almost ten years in silent persecution before the walls caved, sun shined, and pain rained anew.

A child was my cure.

The daughter of the woman I tried to kill.

It was time to face my past full of darkness and say fuck you.

It was time to start new memories.

It burned.

How it fucking burned.

Her every touch scraped flesh from my bones, searing me, helping me forget my past.

Her every look peeled away my crimes, offering neither judgement nor compassion.

Her every laugh shaved away my hopelessness, strengthening my will to fight.

But then there was the conditioning.

On top of her miraculous effect, I battled an entire lifetime of orders running fiercely in my blood.

"Kill her."

"Annihilate her."

"We won't command again."

"Do it."

The orders were a constant stream of filth in my head.

I sweated and shook and ached with rapidly increasing urges, intensified with refusal.

Being in Clara's presence gave me all the self-harm I ever needed. Never again would I need to lift a blade to my skin, or coax my blood to flow. As long as I had her near me, I had both pleasure and pain, hope and damnation, sickness and health.

I could never have guessed my Achilles heel would come in the form of a spritely young girl. But every time I looked at her, I felt myself changing, evolving, twisting. My body fought against the lifetime of discipline, shedding its old scales and rottenness.

The transformation gave me fucking wings, but it also

crushed me. What if Hazel was right? What if I couldn't keep my oath and hurt Clara just like I did her mother?

I hadn't meant to snap today. I tried to stop it even as I fucked her. I just wasn't strong enough, and that killed me to know how broken my handlers left me.

This isn't right. Tell her to leave. Run. Never come back.

Looking down at the halo of brown hair surrounding someone so innocent, I knew I could never be a martyr and send her away. That would be a death warrant, and I was selfish—so incredibly selfish—to want both daughter and mother.

My eyes flew back to Zel, trailing after us with a fierce glare in her green gaze. Feelings I'd kept locked away shattered through my walls, swelling in my chest, recognising that whatever bond existed between us wasn't something I could ever give up.

For the first time, I let myself acknowledge how deep my attraction for her went, how badly my body ached to join with hers in lingering lovemaking and not abusive fucking. I wanted her to be my first—my first real connection.

I want her to touch me.

The realization knocked me on my ass. I made a vow right then and there to fix myself. To stand up and stop being a pussy. I wouldn't stop until I was cured enough for Zel to touch every inch of me. I wouldn't rest until I was strong enough to hug her and hold her close.

I thirsted to make the dream a reality.

My cock hardened at the thought of her mouth on me again, of her fingers trailing over my skin. I wanted to give her everything that I was—including my scars and tattoos. I wanted her to understand me, so she didn't have to fear me anymore.

Opening the door, Clara dashed forward. "Wow!" Her bright cherub voice rung around the foyer.

My heart lurched in a mixture of torture and adoration. One thing was for sure: Clara would be my annihilation. She already held the fuse to destroy me completely.

And I didn't care if she did. I would rather be destroyed by her than live the rest of my life struggling. Clara was my wakeup call. I couldn't continue living as I had—it wasn't a life. I wanted more. I wanted her. I wanted Zel.

I was never letting her go.

She was mine.

Her mother was mine.

Mine. Mine. Fucking *mine.*

Clara danced through my house, her tiny fingers stroking every statue I'd ever made. Just like her mother—she had to touch.

She wrapped stick thin arms around toddler sized bears; she shoved tiny fists into howling wolves' mouths. She patted owls on their heads, and kissed the tops of ponies' withers.

Her eyes swam with wonderment, and I wanted to give her everything.

I didn't care that she ruled me. I didn't care how crazy and unstable I came across being so obsessed by a child I had just met. No one would be able to understand the sheer freedom I felt after twenty-two years of living in the dark.

Clara was a walking sun, and I would trail after her through unlimited sunrises and sunsets.

My heart erupted into pieces, shattering with hope. Before I could stop myself, I murmured, "They're all yours. Every last one."

Zel froze beside me. "What?" Her eyes locked on mine. Amazement flickered, followed by annoyance, confusion. "You can't. We have nowhere to store them." She dropped her gaze, her shoulders rising and falling as her breathing accelerated. I didn't blame her for being freaked out—for being on high alert, watching my every move. She had no reason to trust me and no idea what I'd been through to understand I would put a gun in my mouth and swallow a bullet before I ever hurt Clara.

I won't obey. Vasily was the last child I would ever hurt.

Zel straightened her back, keeping her face closed off. "That's very generous of you, but we can't take them."

Clara skidded to a halt in front of me, barely stopping before crashing into my legs. "I love them. Love. Love. *Love*."

My face and ears still burned from when she hugged my head. When her arms captured my face outside, my gut heaved and brain exploded. I very nearly vomited on the driveway fighting the conditioning. Images bombarded me of death and dismemberment. I'd been petrified to open my eyes just in case I found her torn to fucking pieces on the ground.

But I'd managed to push her away.

I'd held steadfast.

I'd survived, and she'd lived.

I gritted my teeth knowing I'd have to guard myself every time she came near. I'd never been around someone who touched so effortlessly.

"Thank Mr. Obsidian for the offer, Clara, but you know we don't have room." Zel placed a hand on Clara's head, running her fingers through her tangled brown hair.

Clara pouted, looking at me then Zel. "But…I love them. I want them all in my room." Her beautiful brown eyes skipped between us, bright with frustration. "They're all alive inside. They need a home. They need someone to love them and stroke them and feed them—" A loud whooping cough interrupted her, causing her to slap a hand over her mouth and whirl to face Zel.

Zel's body went rigid. She ducked to grab Clara's shoulders. The terror swimming in Zel's eyes broke my fucking heart. It was just a cough…wasn't it?

"Breathe. That's it. Do you need—"

The coughing stopped as suddenly as it began, and Clara shook her head. Wiping her mouth with the back of her hand, she stomped her little foot. "I hate coughing. It hurts."

Zel gathered her close, hugging her. "I know. We'll find a way to make it stop. Soon."

I loved watching the two of them together—such a natural love. A family bond I'd lost forever. A small bolt of jealousy filled me. My body ached to take Clara's place—to enjoy the comfort and safety of someone's embrace.

"Do you suffer from hay fever, Clara?" I asked, drawing Zel's attention to me. Her eyes were shut down and unreadable, protecting her damn secrets.

The brightness in Clara had faded a little, but slowly the flame came back. She shook her head. "I don't know what that is? Is it a sickness that horses catch from hay?"

Zel let out a huge sigh, then chuckled. "No, but it makes more sense. Hay fever is when you're allergic to pollens and other irritants in the air."

I expected Clara to ask a hundred questions, but her eyes turned solemn and she nodded. "Okay."

Turning to me, she announced, "I'm allergic to air."

Zel made a small choking sound, and I couldn't explain why my stomach decided to wrestle with my heart in such a painful tango. "You're allergic to air?"

She moved forward to a statue of a badger, her breathing slightly wheezy. "I must be because I cough a lot and I only breathe in air and not pol—pollams."

Zel's arms wrapped tight around herself, her eyes locking on her daughter.

Something wasn't right.

My hunter instincts tried to uncover her secrets, but she suddenly unlatched her arms and clapped her hands. "Would you give Clara one of your statues?" She raised her voice to where Clara had drifted to. "How about you pick one? We have room for an extra houseguest."

Clara perked up and beamed. "Okay." Spinning on the spot, her smile fell. "But there's so many. How do I choose?"

I couldn't stand the pinpricks of pain for making her choose. I wouldn't do it—not when I wanted her to keep every damn thing in my house. They meant nothing to me. If I could share them and earn a smile or two in return—that made me richer than my entire family's fortune.

Taking a step closer to Zel, I murmured, "They're all hers. Every single one."

Zel stiffened and I wanted nothing more than to touch her—to offer some level of comfort. Something weighed her down and I wanted to give support—even if she didn't confide in me.

Touching her cheek, I waited for the onslaught of conditioning. I was prepared for the pain and orders, but instead of being excruciating, it only pulsed and throbbed.

It's bearable.

My eyes widened. Was that the key? To push myself to the end of my endurance—constantly pressing through the pain until my brain either adapted or snapped?

"Why are you doing this?" Zel whispered, so Clara wouldn't hear. "Why do you care? You hurt me again, Fox. You have to understand how difficult this is for me. I never wanted you to meet her."

The flash of rage and agony caught me by surprise. "You think I don't care? That I'm just a monster who's only goal is to hurt you?" I hated that her assessment of me was so low. What the fuck?

"No. I know you're not. I know you're trying your hardest, but it isn't good enough. You can't expect me to put my child in danger just because you suddenly want a kid in your life."

Pressing forward, I hissed, "I don't want a kid in my life. I've spent my entire life *avoiding* them. I didn't ask you to bring her here. I can't change what happened just as much as you. No one could've predicted the way I'd react, so why don't you stop fighting it and fucking trust me." My eyes flew to Clara who was oblivious to our discussion, stroking a racoon statue.

Zel's nostrils flared, and we glared for a tense moment. She was the one to finally back down. Her eyes dropped. "I'm not comfortable with this, Fox. I know it was my fault you snapped today, but it wasn't my fault before that, or when you stole me at knifepoint. Don't think things are good between us, because they aren't."

Stalking away, she stole my chance at rebuttal.

I knew without a doubt if I let her walk out the door today,

I'd never see her or Clara again.

That just isn't an option.

I needed another bribe—another contract to keep Zel bound to me—to give myself time to fix what I ruined between us and most importantly fix myself.

Swallowing my temper, I said loudly, "You don't have to pick, Clara. They're all yours. And you don't have to worry about storage either because you can keep them here. You and your mother are more than welcome to stay with me for as long as you want. In fact, I'd love you to move in tonight."

Clara squealed and charged toward me.

Fear hot and fierce shot through my body as her little arms wrapped around my legs and squeezed. *Holy fuck. Don't lose it. Don't.* The world swam. Infernos blazed. Blood scraped my veins with tiny daggers.

"Kill her."

"Bleed her."

"Do it, Operative Fox."

Zel grabbed Clara and tore her off me, backing away quickly. "Don't touch him, Clara. Ever."

Even though my entire body felt as if I'd been whipped and mutilated after the heavy crush of orders, I was lighter that I'd ever been. I was positively buoyant because I'd held on.

A child had hugged me, and I hadn't broken. She was still alive, and I'd proven to myself I could find freedom.

It was the best fucking feeling in the world.

Clara tried to free herself from Zel's grip. Her little face shone. "You mean it? I can sleep over? And you'll make me a sheep?"

Before I could answer, she threw herself at Zel, almost tackling her to the ground. "Can we, mummy? Please. Please. With a cherry on top?"

Zel smiled, brushing some unruly flyaway strands from Clara's forehead. "How about you let the adults talk? I think I spy a polar bear down the corridor. Just don't go too far."

"Oh really? I want to pet it." Clara took off in a whirl of

purple, sprinting out of hearing distance.

Zel slowly stood upright, and I fought the urge to take a step back. Her eyes blazed with green fire. "What the *hell* do you think you're doing?"

She was so fucking strong. So fierce in protecting her offspring. My heart swelled to ten times its normal size, suffocating in my chest. It'd only been a couple of weeks, but I would always be indebted to this woman for bringing me back to life. And because I owed her my life, I could never let her leave.

"I'm honouring our agreement."

"What fucking agreement? I don't remember signing away mine and my daughter's life to come live in your freaky-ass home. You can't say things like that in front of a child. Now she'll be broken-hearted and disappointed and she'll hate me when I take her home tonight." She stormed forward. "Because that's what will happen, Fox. We. Aren't. Staying."

I balled my hands. "I'm not asking you to marry me for fuck's sake or even stay forever. If you never want me to come near you again, I won't.

"All I want is the right to take care of you. Give me a purpose. Let me provide for you, and be there for you. That's all I'm asking."

Zel's bottom lip wobbled, but her face darkened from angry to livid. "You think I can't take care of her on my own? You think you're strong enough to swoop in and *fix* everything?" She dragged hands through her hair, barely holding onto the tears shimmering in her eyes. "What part of 'I don't want you near her' didn't you understand?"

I advanced, forcing her to take a step back. "I understand perfectly. You're a fucking hypocrite. One minute you're here for me. Healing me. Giving me everything you have even when all I do is take, and the next you want to withhold everything from me and paint me as the devil. Don't think I haven't noticed how much you forgive me. You're a fucking saint to even speak to me after the things I've done. But I warned you at the beginning that I sense things people try to hide."

Grabbing her elbow, I held her tight. "Let me tell you what I've come to know. You're drowning in sorrow. You look at that little girl as if she's the most precious diamond in the world, and you're terrified of losing her. And that cough? You reacted as if she could die instead of it being a simple affliction. I think there's something big you aren't telling me and I want to know."

"Let go of me, you bastard. You think you're so clever, but you don't know anything. You don't know what it's like to be a single parent. To be solely a mother and no longer a person who can chase their hopes and dreams. You didn't have your life turned upside down by an accident only to have that accident be the best fucking thing to ever happen to you."

"Didn't I? Haven't you been listening to anything I've been saying? I've been a fucking prisoner since I was six years old. You're the only person I've been close to in my entire life. Is it so wrong of me to ask for more? To request that you stay with me and give meaning to my fucking sorry excuse for a life?"

I shoved her away. My heart bolted around my chest, and I needed a fight. I needed to throw my fist into something flesh and bone and let out all this rage.

Fuck!

Zel stood glaring, panting hard. Her eyes flew up the corridor where Clara had disappeared. I didn't worry she wasn't visible. There was nothing but statues to entertain and no way out unless she came back this way.

"You're impossible," she muttered.

"No. You're impossible. Shit, I'll give you the remaining one hundred thousand now if it'll help sway you. Hell, I'll triple it if you stay. I'll give you anything you want—just agree to stay for a few days at least."

Zel shifted, eyes darting around the space, searching for answers. "A few days?"

I wanted to sigh in relief. I'd won. This match.

"That's all I'm asking." It wasn't, but she didn't need to

know that.

Zel slumped, all the fight fizzled from her limbs. "What are you trying to do, Fox?"

I ignored the soft defeat in her voice and murmured, "I'm not trying to do anything. I just want the opportunity to share your daughter—if only for a brief while."

A crush of vulnerability filled me, and I dropped my head. I was tired. So tired. "Please…I need her in my life. I need you." Swallowing hard, I captured her hand and relaxed a little when the conditioning stayed blessedly absent. "Please, Hazel. I'll give you anything you want. I'll pay you any sum you desire. Just stay. Give me another chance."

Her eyes bloomed with fresh anger. "You think I'm that shallow? That you can throw money at me and allow you to buy me and Clara?" She snorted. "We don't come with a fucking price tag, you idiot. You could offer me a million, and I wouldn't stay if I thought you'd hurt her."

"I swear on my life I will not raise a finger to hurt her. You have my absolute word."

She shook her head. "It's not good enough. You can't promise that." Her eyes met mine, and I wanted to dig out my heart and slap it into her hands. Then she'd know how much I needed her and Clara and the tantalising hope she offered.

She ran hands through her long hair, her perfect breasts rising and falling with rage. "What you did to me, Fox…that…that's not natural. You shouldn't have such strong triggers that make you a danger to anyone who comes into contact with you. What if you lash out again? What if I'm not around to stop you from strangling her or tearing her into chunks? You don't trust yourself. *I* don't trust you, and I sure as hell don't trust you around the reason for my very existence. Plus we have a life, appointments to go to, school to attend. It's not a simple matter of saying stay for a few days."

Her anger fed mine, and I welcomed the warmth. I growled, "It's obvious you don't trust me in the slightest. You hid her from me. You've kept every part of your life a secret from me."

My temper helped soothe my raging need for pain just a little. "You know a lot more about me than I do about you. Everything about you is a mystery, and it fucking hurts to think I don't deserve to hear a little about your past or who you truly are."

Looking to where Clara had run to, I lowered my voice and took a step closer to Zel. "You said you signed the contract because you wanted me. Because you felt what I did—that you were drawn to me. And yet, I've embraced that bond and relished in finally deserving your attention, but no matter what I do, you look at me as if I'm a pet project. You exploded my mind by sucking my cock. You pushed me until I lost control. And then you condemn me when I don't respond to your crazy form of therapy.

"I need time. I know I need help, but you don't care about me...not the way I care about you." I snapped my lips together, hating my slip—I'd shown my weakness.

Her mouth fell open. "You think I don't *care* about you?" Her eyes flashed with emerald fire; pressing closer, she drove me backward. "You're stupid as well as screwed up. Answer me this. Why the hell do I keep coming back? Why the hell can't I hate you for hurting me, not once, not twice, but three times? Why can't I just walk away and throw your damn money in your face?"

Her eyes glittered with pent-up tears. "I'll tell you why, you moron. It's because whatever you feel, I feel. It's there—pulling us together. You make my heart race every time you look so broken. You make me feel stronger and deeper than I've ever felt for anyone. So don't tell me I don't care!"

Dashing hair out of her eyes, she snarled, "Whatever exists between us is determined to destroy me. How am I expected to ignore something so strong and undeniable? It drives me fucking insane, just like you and your issues drive me insane. All I wanted was a way to save—"

She cut herself off before whisper-yelling, "I want you so damn much my skin screams for your touch and my fingers ache to reciprocate, but I want to *know* you. I push you to break you, hoping you'll find a way back to normality. But it doesn't work, and you end up hurting me. After everything I've done, you have the nerve to tell me I don't care about you?"

She panted hard, cheeks flushed with colour.

I'd never been so alive. So fucking turned on. Her passion, her confession squeezed my heart until I couldn't stay still.

Every angry word stroked my cock, making me harder than I'd ever been in my life. My entire body screamed for hers. I needed to claim her. Mark her. Solidify whatever existed between us.

I didn't care that Clara was down the hall absorbed in my bronze creations. I didn't care that the stress of the day had stolen the edges of my vision or that my body felt like an overstretched rubber band.

I didn't fucking care.

"I can't do this anymore." I launched myself at her, shoving her against the opposite wall. My heart exploded as my mouth crashed hard on hers.

It wasn't sweet. It wasn't planned. It was angry and violent, and everything that I needed.

My hands captured her cheeks, holding her firmly in place. My lips moved against hers, hungry and demanding.

She gasped in shock, then moaned in anger, trying to bite me as I pierced the seam of her lips and plunged a hungry tongue deep into her mouth.

I fucking kissed her like I wanted to so many times before. I kissed her with everything that I was and hoped to be.

Her body went taut, vibrating against mine. My brain sparked and overloaded with too much sensation, but for once I was able to keep it together. I flattened her against the wall, squashing her breasts against me, loving the rapid *thud thud* of her heart against my ribs.

"Fucking kiss me," I growled against her mouth. I wanted to tear her clothes off and take her against the wall. I wanted to sink deep inside her hot dark warmth and prove to her I could give her what she wanted.

It took a never-ending moment, but suddenly the tension in Zel's body switched to writhing passion. Her tongue flashed out to battle with mine.

We didn't kiss. We fought. We poured everything we couldn't say into one timeless action.

I groaned, threading my fingers through her hair, capturing the back of her scalp. I pulled her harder against me.

"I want you to touch me. I want you to break me. I'm yours, Hazel. Fuck."

She swallowed my invitation, kissing me harder, bruising my lips with hers. Our teeth clashed and my skin erupted, *needing* her fingers on me.

But her arms stayed locked by her sides.

She moaned as I left the realm of sanity and poured every apology, every regret, I had into her mouth and down her throat and into her fucking heart. I wanted her to know that she owned me. I needed her to know she'd helped me—more than she knew. More than anyone.

I owed her everything; I couldn't let her leave. It was the one thing I wouldn't do. I would gladly go to hell for kidnapping and holding her prisoner, but she'd given me a cure not in herself, but in her perfect, amazing, life-altering daughter.

Clapping entered my thoughts, followed by a feminine giggle. I crashed to earth and swore under my breath.

Shit. Hardly appropriate for child's eyes.

I broke away, sucking in huge gusts of air, discreetly rearranging my trousers. Clara stood there looking like she'd watched a prince claim his fucking queen. My heart lurched thinking how close to the truth that was. My family tree was royal. My blood supposedly blue.

That made Obsidian my kingdom and Zel my subject to do as I pleased. And what I pleased was to take her behind closed doors and hand myself over to whatever medicine and therapy she had in mind.

"Aww, I knew you liked my mother. She gives the best kisses, but not like that. Those were icky." She rolled her eyes. "You're hopeless. You don't know how to hug or kiss."

Zel swallowed a surprised cough, quickly straightening her shirt. She unobtrusively wiped her red swollen lips, removing traces of my kiss. "You're right, Clara. He has a lot to learn." She shot me a glance, and I couldn't fight the smile hijacking my lips.

"I saw the polar bear. It was awesome. But I want a sheep." Clara radiated happiness and I risked everything by placing a tentative hand on her bony shoulder.

Calming my rapid heartbeat, I smiled. "I'll get started on it tonight. Your mother and I came to a deal. You'll stay for a few nights and then go home. Is that okay?"

Her smile fell a little. "I guess." Looking at her mother, she added, "But if I'm good maybe I can stay longer?"

Zel made a *humph* noise, not moving from her place squished against the wall. Clara moved toward her mother, and leaned her head against her waist. Zel wrapped an around Clara's head, holding her close. She moved slowly almost as if her body was too heavy, too sensitive to bear. I could relate completely. Every part of me felt as if I had a billion needles dancing on my flesh—both pleasure and pain, intoxicating and distracting.

Clara suddenly grew shy and whispered to Zel, "I'm hungry. Can I have chicken nuggets? I went to the hospital today, and you normally let me have them for being brave."

Hospital? *What the fuck?*

My gaze bored a hole into Zel, but she refused to make eye contact. Ducking to Clara's level, she pressed her lips against her ear and said something I couldn't hear.

My stomach rolled, searching for any sign of why such a vital little girl would've been at the hospital.

Zel finally stood and met my livid gaze. "She had her annual inoculations, that's all. But she's right, I do let her have chicken nuggets when she's been. Do you think we can rustle some up for her?"

I had no idea what was stocked in the kitchen, but I would buy a hundred damn nuggets if that's what Clara wanted.

Before I turned chef for the first time in my life, I had to know. I'd announced it to Clara, but Zel hadn't agreed yet. "You're staying?"

Zel pursed her lips. "Will you keep your distance?"

"Yes."

"Okay. One night."

I wanted to argue for more, but I had twenty-four hours to plead and cajole. Right now, I had to do the most domestic thing of my life, and I couldn't fucking wait.

I'd probably burn them. We'd most likely end up ordering in, but I couldn't think of anything else I'd rather do.

Smiling at Clara, I said, "Let's go see what I have in the fridge. I'm sure they'll be something delicious in there."

Clara beamed and bounced away from Zel. "Oh, goodie. And then I want a story."

No amount of sunlight could make me feel as happy as I did in that moment. Life seemed suddenly bearable—more than bearable: joyous.

I motioned for Zel to walk beside me, wishing for the day when I could hold her hand and not battle the urge to destroy her.

Zel nodded and fell into step with me. "I don't think Fox's stories are quite suitable for your ears, Clara. How about we head to the library and pick up a few?"

Clara turned around, wrinkling her nose. "I don't want stories from the library. I want real stories." She danced on the spot, twisting her sweater. "Oh, and mummy. His name isn't Fox. It's Roan."

That was two days ago.

Forty-eight hours that were heaven and hell—perpetual amounts of stress and agony. My nerves were shot, flashbacks of Vasily crept up on me in the worst moments, and I found myself exhausted when I crawled into bed at daybreak.

But I wouldn't change a thing.

Self-harm came in the form of battling my conditioning every time Clara came near, and I grew to understand my triggers better; understand what made me snap and revert to Ghost, and what allowed me to stay sane.

On the first night, after burning a tray of chicken nuggets, I finally got the hang of how to use the oven and had the best meal of my life. Sitting around a kitchen table I'd never sat at, using skills I'd never had to learn, I indulged in normalcy.

Staring at Zel and Clara while eating such a simple meal, I cursed my handlers once again for stealing my life. For giving me a world shut off from love, laughter, and gentleness. Not once had we ever been allowed to form attachments. Our cells were apart, our meals eaten separately. Our only purpose to rest like a stowed weapon until a new contract came through. A new enemy to kill or vendetta to fulfill on behalf of obscenely wealthy men and women.

It'd been worse than a prison sentence, and I felt as if the bars were finally disappearing—I'd found a way to weld myself free, and I would never allow anyone to steal so much from me again.

Zel kept her distance. That first night, I gave her the room next to mine—fully aware she would need her own space with Clara. I didn't push for another kiss, or time alone to talk. I was content to just have them in my home. I may be obsessed with Clara, but I knew I had to tread lightly. To not let on just how fucked-up I was, and how much I needed her.

Every second in Clara's presence lifted the black cloud from around my heart, and I found my lips twitching and stomach clenching in a brand new emotion of happiness. It filled me with sunshine and for the first time since they stole me, I didn't fear the darkness inside my soul. I had something other than death surrounding me. I had life.

Clara didn't go to school the next day. Instead, Zel allowed her to explore my home while I slept till midday. I found them in the greenhouse when I woke and trailed after mother and daughter, drinking in their magic.

I'd wanted Zel the moment I'd set eyes on her in Obsidian, but it was nothing, *nothing,* compared to the ever burning passion I now smouldered with. Every time she laughed at a quip from Clara, or tossed her dark hair over her shoulder, I inched closer to falling.

I didn't know if she'd accept me, or if she'd leave in a few days and that would be the end of it, but she owned me more than anyone. More than my handlers, more than my own self-worth, I belonged completely and utterly to her.

I did the right thing—the only correct thing in my life by keeping my hands off her. I didn't know how I managed. My cock had a mind of its own, and my eyes weren't content unless she was centrefold, but I refused to hurt her again. I meant what I said when I agreed to never going near her if that was what she wished.

I ignored my thoughts of taking her and hoarded the sweet, unsullied companionship Zel and Clara gave me.

The next time I took her—if there was a next time—I wanted to give her everything. I wanted to make love to her. I wanted to learn the difference. I wanted her to know I belonged to her.

Every now and again, Clara would cough and tears would fill her little eyes. Zel would administer an asthma inhaler and the coughs would dissipate. Whenever I asked why Clara was coughing, Zel would snap and tell me it was only asthma—nothing to worry myself about.

But I did worry. A lot. Something wasn't right. Her lies stank, drenched in grief, and the sharp tingle of fear never left my skin.

Seeing the love Zel had for her daughter almost brought me to my fucking knees. I'd give anything to have her look at me that way.

Her sorrow tainted everything she did, though. She thought I didn't notice; she thought Clara didn't notice. But we did. Often Clara would catch my eye over Zel's shoulder mid-hug, her little eyebrow raised in question.

Zel carried sadness inside, heavy and aching, and she never uttered a word about it.

When Zel and Clara went to bed, I oversaw Obsidian. Once the last fighter left at five a.m., I headed to my basement and worked on Clara's request.

The second night was spent out on the lawn under the summer sun. Complete with Nutella sandwiches and chocolate dipped marshmallows. Zel had rolled her eyes at how easily swayed I was by the whims of an eight-year-old. She didn't know taking orders was in my DNA. She also didn't know I'd fought my handlers all my life and enjoyed finally obeying such simple, innocent requests from someone so tiny.

I would kill for her without question. I would protect her with my life.

When dinner was over and Zel announced it was Clara's bedtime, she'd pouted and moaned and only settled once I'd dragged three bronze statues into her bedroom—slowly building a menagerie of metal wildlife.

I indulged her. I adored her.

I'd never been so consumed by one person. Every time I watched her liveliness, my heart would break for Vasily and all the children like me who'd been killed because we weren't cold-hearted enough for the warped game of our handlers.

Clara looked nothing like him—where she was dark and pearly skin, Vasily had been dusky skinned and fair. Vasily's eyes had been like mine—an artic white-blue so clear I had a vague memory of my mother calling them icebergs.

It didn't matter Clara looked nothing like him. My brain couldn't stop poking at wounds, invoking pain I thought I'd put behind me.

But the pain didn't compare to the newness and warmth I'd found. Where Clara was my sun—healing and casting my shadows away—Zel was my fucking cosmos.

She was everything I wanted. Everything I needed. Everything I never thought I'd deserve.

Obsidian used to be my obsession, but now I no longer cared about the fighters pummelling each other in my house, or the steady influx of money from eager members. I wanted to rest and step back from violence.

I was done with it.

I just hoped it was done with me.

I woke at my usual midday and worked out for an hour before entering my office. The calendar on my desk blotter told me it was Saturday.

A big night at Obsidian and the weekend. No school for Clara. My heart picked up its beat at the thought of asking Zel to stay another night.

She'd agreed previously not because she wanted to, but because Clara had bounced around like a little lunatic and sealed the deal without her permission.

Ask her in front of Clara again.

I knew it was underhanded to use the excitement of an eight-year-old to keep Zel here, but I didn't mind playing dirty if it meant she never fucking left. My days were brighter and darker, easier and harder, when she was around, and I wasn't ready to give that up.

"Can we go to the beach? I want to go to the beach." Clara's high voice preceded her as she bolted into my office with Zel trailing close behind. I hadn't seen them since last night, and my fucking heart leapt out of my chest and splattered at their feet.

Zel met my eyes, a soft look in her green gaze. "Good morning."

"Morning," I murmured. I couldn't tear my eyes off her. Dressed in a feminine white skirt and pink singlet, she looked too young to be a mother and far too intoxicating for my already strained self-control.

Clara pressed her hands on the front of my desk, jumping up and down. "Morning! We went for a walk. The sun's out, and it's hot already. I want to go for a swim."

I leaned back in my chair, drinking them in. "I can see you had a good walk." I smirked. Her glossy brown hair held foliage and pieces of freshly mowed grass.

Clara darted around my desk to stand beside me. My skin pricked; muscles coiled with anticipation—sensing her will to touch me, preparing itself to battle the imminent urge to kill.

"Yep. Like my daisies?" She shook her hair, showing a long daisy chain wrapped in the strands.

"They're very pretty." I smiled, never relaxing.

Clara grinned. "You're coming to the beach. I've already got my bathing suit on. You need to bring yours, so you can swim."

My throat slammed closed. The idea of going to the beach filled me with horror. How could I explain the thought of being half-naked gave me the cold sweats? How could I explain the tattoo on my back or the scars on my chest?

I couldn't.

"Scars are a mark of pride, Operative Fox. They show how successful you are. Many requests for killers come in based on how many injuries you've endured and overcome."

That's all we were. Evaluated on how efficiently we exterminated another life—how perfectly we obeyed orders.

"Please, say you'll come." Clara's voice shattered the flash back. She moved closer, hands out-stretched, eyes full of determination.

All my strength had been replaced with icy fear. Shoving my

chair back, I kept my distance. I couldn't do it.

Zel made a noise in the back of her throat, rushing forward. "Clara, don't touch Fox right now. He's not feeling well." Her eyes met mine, and I stopped breathing.

Her green gaze glowed, lips parted, face flushed. She stared so intensely at me I swore she touched me, whispering across my black covered body. All her passion and anxiety for Clara's well-being battled with the complex emotions she felt for me. It was as if she whipped me with everything she struggled with: uncertainty, anger, grief, lust, friendship, betrayal. My heart went from sluggish to racing, pumping my blood with need.

I want you. So fucking much. I shot the message as hard as I could, hoping she'd decipher my soundless sentence.

She sucked in a breath, drawing my eyes to her breasts encased in her pink tank top. Her nipples hardened beneath the fabric, and it took all my willpower to stay sitting and not launch myself across the desk and grab her.

Clara ceased to exist as I stared at Zel. Her eyes went heavy with lust.

She made me fucking crazy.

I could no longer operate my body, and all concentration flew out of the window. All thoughts turned to binding her with silver jewellery and fucking her. I couldn't get enough of her. I *missed* her.

Then another thought hit me.

Maybe I've done it the wrong way. Maybe the only way to succeed at never hurting her would be to trap myself in bondage. *Am I always destined to be an animal only fit for shackles?*

Life decided to answer my dumbass question in the form of tiny, breakable hand landing softly on my scarred cheek. Clara chose that exact moment—the moment I wasn't concentrating—to touch me in the worst possible spot.

Life ceased to exist.

Death roared in my brain.

Hands clenched. Body shifted. Zel screamed.

Oh, shit. Oh, shit.

Conditioning tsunamied through me, wreaking havoc on my self-control, reminding me I'd been forged as a weapon, not a human to interact with something as killable as a child.

I blinked, bringing a terrified Clara into focus and a tear-stained ferocious Zel. "No!" she screamed.

My hands clutched Clara's shoulders, digging into her, and it took every single reserve left inside to shove her away. The second she tumbled to the floor, Zel scooped her up and darted backward.

I fell off my chair and clutched my skull, trying to crush the overpowering orders.

Kill. Sever. Bleed. Devour.

I looked up, searching for the letter opener I kept on the desk. I needed a weapon to put myself down—before I did something I would never be able to live with.

"Clara, no!" Zel cried, sounding muffled in the crash of orders in my head. "Stay away."

Amazingly, Clara brought on the conditioning, and she was the one who ended it. Her loud, little voice yelled, "Stop it!"

And...it did.

Just like that. Instant silence, leaving me shaking and eerily empty.

I snapped my head upright, breathing hard. I climbed to my feet, creaking in joints that had no right to move after a lifetime of torture. "Are you okay?" My voice was gruff, strained. Gulping in air, I ran hands through my shaggy hair.

The spell of lust between Zel and me was gone, replaced with appalled horror in her gaze. My heart deflated. *Why can't I be fucking normal?!*

I wanted to tear my office apart and fight. I ruined it. Proved to Zel Clara wasn't safe around me. Fuck!

"Hazel, you know I—" What could I say? I'd made more progress in the last two days than ever before, but it wasn't enough. It would never be fucking enough to deserve them.

Clara squirmed in her mother's hold. Zel seemed to be in livid shock, her face frozen in stone.

Freeing herself, Clara came forward. Not close enough to touch, but close enough for me to witness the fierceness in her dark eyes. "I'm sorry. I forgot. I didn't mean to touch you." Her head hung, sending a curtain of shiny hair around her face. "Don't yell at me, okay?"

My heart lurched. I felt like fucking crying. None of this was fair. Not to Clara, or Zel, or even me. I was and always would be a machine who should remember his place and stay in the dark.

Clara was so innocent. So pure. Everything that I wasn't.

"I won't yell at you, little one. It wasn't your fault." Sighing heavily, I stayed slouched on the floor, keeping a careful eye on her. "I think you and your mother should go."

Zel sucked in a harsh breath, life animating her body once again. I searched her gaze and fucking died when she nodded once. "Yes, Clara. I think Mr. Fox needs to have some time on his own. Let's go to the beach with Auntie Clue and Ben."

"But I don't *want* to go to the beach with them. And stop calling him Fox!" Clara's cheeks grew pink. "It was my fault. Don't kick us out, please. You haven't told me any stories. You haven't shown me a sheep. I don't want to go."

I couldn't stand seeing her bottom lip wobble.

Right there. Right then. My life split, heading into a crossroads.

I was obsessed with finding redemption. Destroyed by love. Possessed by hope. Consumed by a past I couldn't shake. My eyes locked with Zel's. It was time. I couldn't pretend I didn't come with baggage, or issues that I might never be free of, but before Zel walked away from me forever, I wanted her to know the truth.

I wanted to know her. I wanted to earn her trust. I wanted a connection. I didn't want to be feared or hated. I didn't want to be an inconvenience or burden.

It was time to tell her everything, so she could decide for herself.

It was the only way forward. And it would mean I'd lose

both of them because she would never allow her daughter near me again.

"I think it's time I told you a story, Clara." My voice sounded heavy and bleak. *I'll tell you things that'll scar your mind and grant you nightmares for life.*

Zel sniffed, straightening her back. "I don't think that's a good idea." She moved forward, wrapping her arms around Clara's shoulders. Her body trembled with tightly reined emotion; her limbs brittle, eyes tinged with grief. "Please, Fox. You keep forgetting she's a child. You can't tell her what I think you want to. You can't unburden yourself onto such an innocent mind. I won't let you."

"I'll filter. I'll turn it into a fairy-tale. I promise I won't share too much, just…please…give me the opportunity to tell someone. Before you leave."

She bit her lip, deliberations filling her eyes.

I looked at my hands. Holding them up, I said, "I can tell you the story behind every scar, every nick, and every mark on my body. I'll answer any question you want, and then you can cast judgement." My fingers weren't appendages—they were ruthless weapons and held a lifetime of grief. "I'll save the details for you, but give me the chance to tell your daughter one story."

Looking at Clara, I added, "I'll tell you about a boy who lost his life only to have a little girl give it back to him."

Clara smiled heartbreakingly sweet, her dark eyes so wide and forgiving. Her fierceness made me yearn for another child…a boy, who'd been just as tough and perfect.

"I'd like that. But I want more than one."

Zel gave in. Her shoulders slumped. "One story and then we're going home."

I nodded. I could live with that. I couldn't expect anything more.

Clara smiled, happiness glowing on her face. "Tell me now."

Fifteen
Hazel

The day I told the father of my child about Clara, I walked away bleeding and scarred.

Instead of the swarmy, smooth ways that made me spread my legs for him, he glared as if I were scum.

He called me a whore, a slut, a gold-digging bitch.

I didn't know he had rich parents, or that he stood to inherit a substantial empire. We'd met on the streets, hanging around fast food chains. I thought he was an orphan—like me. Turned out he liked to dabble in darkness before going home to his perfect bed. It wasn't until I stalked him to his house that I found out the truth.

His parents heard us screaming; his dad shoved me out the front door and straight into a large flower pot. The rose bush sliced the delicate skin below my eye with its angry thorns.

Blood dripped, smearing my one and only t-shirt, and I knew I never wanted anything to do with them.

The baby was *mine*.

Ever since that day, Clara was mine completely. I wasn't good at sharing, but Roan Fox gave me no choice.

He fell in love with my child with a freaky single-minded determination that scared me more than his underlying temper and violence.

He looked at Clara as if she held the answer to all his problems.

But he didn't know.

He didn't know that one day soon she'd be gone.

The day that happened, his life would be over, and my heart would break, and I would give him back his blue pill.

The day Clara died, she would take both of us.

It was inevitable.

A story.

There were good stories, bad stories, tragedies, and happily ever afters. Whatever Fox wanted to tell Clara, I doubted it would be fluffy unicorns and sunshine.

I wanted to end this—all of it. I couldn't stand my heart breaking every damn day. I couldn't stand lying in bed thinking about Fox and fighting a never-ending war of hating him for making me feel, and despising him for keeping me hostage.

I'd been prepared to walk. I couldn't sacrifice myself for a man who suffered more demons than the devil himself. I'd been through too much to let him hurt me again.

But then he saw Clara.

He fell in love with Clara.

He stole Clara, and she was no longer mine.

The slow burn of rage hadn't left since he fell so obsessively in love with her. I wanted to sneak out the moment he'd gone to bed and leave—but when I took Clara's hand and dragged her down the driveway, it was as if an invisible chain tethered me. Pulling me back, making me stay.

It wasn't obligation or about the money anymore. By falling for Clara, he'd proven he had a heart. He proved he was a man—deep inside, and as much as I wanted to hate him, I couldn't.

Not when he doted upon my own flesh and blood; cooked her food, cut the crusts off her sandwiches, and jumped to her every demand. He became human in my eyes and that made me want to hate him more.

But hate was an emotion that demanded limitless energy. I lost the will to stoke my rage and fan my flames of anger. After all, didn't everyone deserve happiness?

Even men who'd killed. If they repented and acknowledged their sins, wasn't it my job as a human being to help him on the road to recovery?

At the cost of Clara?

No, at the cost of him. It would be Fox who would suffer—not Clara. She was too bold, too well loved and strong, too educated about the world to have long-term effects from Fox. But him? He wouldn't survive her.

And that turned my hate into a sadness, more heavy and all-consuming than ever before. By letting them grow close, I was destroying both of them.

I didn't seem to exist to either Fox or Clara as he picked himself off the floor and stalked toward the exit. He didn't come back to collect me, or offer his hand to Clara. His body was locked down and untouchable.

"Hey, wait for me." Clara shot out of my arms and trotted after him like a perfect puppy. I, on the other hand, trailed after them like a zombie whose world had just collapsed.

Fox led us down the corridor where the high-noon sun beamed through the glass ceiling. The heat warmed my shoulders and top of my head as we climbed down a flight of stairs to the main foyer. We headed along another hallway toward the back of the property before heading deeper downstairs, trading sunlight for shadows.

All the stupid hope I'd had that Fox might've broken through his no touching issues had been dashed into dust thanks to what happened in his office. He was still the same. Still haunted. Still ruined.

I thought my heart would never find a natural equilibrium again.

My skin pricked with goosebumps, and I breathed

shallowly. I hadn't been in this part of the house, and my limbs throbbed with adrenaline. I kept an ever watchful eye on Clara, poised to grab her just in case anything went wrong.

I want a weapon.

The thought popped into my head as Fox stopped outside a massive medieval door with a large lock. Engraved in the wood, looking as if someone took a sharp blade and carved with no finesse, were three lines. III.

It didn't look like it belonged in this century. Just like the house constructed around it, there was something sinister and evil—something inhabitable.

The hair on the back of my neck stood up as Fox inserted a key and pushed open the door. The only door without a keypad lock.

He looked back, his grey-white eyes delving into mine. *You can leave if you want.* His gaze screamed the message glowing with pain.

I wanted to take him up on the offer. I wasn't ready. I didn't think I would ever be ready for what he wanted to show me.

I couldn't give him a reply—either silent or verbal. My thoughts waged with each other, terrified at knowing, horrified at what he had to say. But mostly petrified of the decision I would have to make.

Clara darted inside—no fear or residual surprise with what happened in his office. A brief exclamation of amazement escaped her, followed by a delighted giggle. "It's like a cave. No, it's like a prison cell." She turned to me. "Remember? Those pictures you showed me of those poor people in Tower of London for stealing the crown and all the Queen's money? Remember, mummy, with the things dangling from the walls and the horrible items they used to make the poor men tell the truth? It looks like that."

My heart stopped beating as I moved forward, taking in the room. Clara was entirely right. The space looked like a dungeon—fit only for murderous thieves and men who waited for the gallows.

Fox snorted before moving forward to flick on a row of lights hanging above work tables, tool benches, and paraphernalia. The light helped dispel some of the original cell appeal, but the walls were damp, the floor unfinished and compacted with earth.

The sharp metallic scent of bronze and lifeless metals hit my nose. Mixing with old sooty smoke from the large fire, and the cold dirt around us, the scent reminded me of Fox.

He belonged here more than he belonged in the black decadent rooms above. I couldn't swallow at the thought of him living somewhere like this. Enduring a life in this sort of environment.

Clara skipped around the room, inspecting old-fashioned bellows, and eyeing up two massive anvils. Pliers lay scattered along with hammers and odd bits of discarded metal.

My eyes fell on the silver chain draping off the corner of a table. Fox spun to lock gazes with me. He nodded. "It's the same gauge I used on you. It seems stupid now." His eyes fell to the glint of silver around my throat. I still wore the star bracelets he'd made. The centre piece that secured my wrists to the belly chain had disappeared into his pocket never to be seen again.

"You were never the danger. It was me. I should've been the one to wear that. Not you." His eyes fell from my throat, tracing the metal under my clothes.

"Wear what?" Clara came to my side, her eyes wide and interested. She coughed gently, sending spasms into my heart.

"Nothing."

"You always say that." Snorting in annoyance, Clara dashed off and disappeared through a crack at the back of the work room.

"Clara!" I jogged forward, very aware of how many sharp instruments and dangers this place held. What the hell were we doing down here? Fox could've told her his story anywhere. The garden where the sun was bright would've been much better than a fucking dungeon. "Get back here."

"Shit, I thought that room was locked." Fox moved forward, effortlessly swooping like a shadow on the wall rather than a human. Something about him had changed, almost as if he embraced the side of himself he was about to expose. He didn't have to hide down here—he fit.

I held back, letting him crack open the heavy door that looked like a bank vault. Disappearing inside, he looked over his shoulder. "It's safe. I promise. It's a hobby of mine—that's all."

I frowned, entering the smallish space. Rows and rows of shelves existed from floor to ceiling.

Oh, my God. My heart clouted my ribcage, taking in what the shelves held. How was this possible? *I've stepped through time, or entered a movie set.*

"Wow, this is awesome," Clara said, spinning around in a treasure trove of weaponry.

Fox kept a careful eye on her, but his body faced mine, ready to take whatever I had to say. I glared at him, unable to believe he thought bringing a child to someplace like this was smart.

But as much as I wanted to scream, I couldn't deny he hovered over her like a protective father, ready to snatch whatever danger she gravitated toward out of her reach.

"Holy crap." I drifted forward, eyes bugging at the huge arsenal hidden beneath Fox's house. A secret room full of secret things. Things from his past. Things no one should see. Unless they were a Jacobite, or Napoleon Hill. Every item of death existed from dirks, sickles, swords, and bayonets to sabres, axes, long bows, and nun-chucks.

"Like I said, I don't use them. Not anymore. I just make them. I did it before with—and…well, I find it therapeutic to work with what I know." His body vibrated with tension, filling the small space with masculine energy.

My face went slack as I drifted around the room, drinking in the sight of blades and killing apparatus, breathing in bronze and iron, metallic and sharp.

Clara piped up, dragging her damageable fingers along a wicked looking spiked mace. I almost had a heart attack before Fox carefully removed her hand and placed it by her side.

"You made this?" Her innocent voice rang around the room—a huge contradiction of purity compared to the barbaricness of what she touched. "Are you going to war? Who are you fighting?" She stilled, biting her lower lip. "Ohhhh, I get it. Is that how you got your scar? You've *been* to war."

My heart glowed for my bright little girl. "Stop asking such prying questions, Clara. His scar is personal, and I doubt it's a story he can tell easily."

I glanced at Fox, and he unconsciously stroked the puckered skin on his otherwise perfect face. He had a five o'clock shadow which was unusual for him, and no hair grew where the skin had been damaged.

He blinked, shaking whatever memories haunted him away. "I might tell you that story another time, little one, but not today."

Ducking to her level, he added, "I didn't go to war, but I did serve time and obeyed orders I wished I didn't have to."

Clara's face fell. "I'm sorry."

Fox's lips twitched into a small smile. "It's not your fault." His face darkened. "If you want to hear my story, Clara, you have to promise me you won't be sad. It isn't about fairies or mermaids, it's about a little boy who had a family and was made to do bad things to them. It's about a teenager who did things he'll never be free of, and it's about a man who wished he could rewind the past and start all over again."

Clara nodded, blinking big soulful eyes. "I promise. I know bad things happen. I'm big enough to hear."

He looked up, grey eyes delving into mine. "I'll censor, but it's still going to be hard to tell." He stood up, coming toward me, but not reaching out. "Is that okay?"

Was it okay? Not really. I didn't like the thought of Clara's head being full of sadness, or things that might give her nightmares. I didn't like that Fox had chosen my daughter to share his past with—but I also…

Shit, I trust him.

I trusted him not to go too far. To filter the gruesome and spin a story that Clara would believe would be fanciful and fantastical. Something released in me, some of the anger I felt disappeared, and I found myself falling once again for the damaged man before me.

"I trust you." Three simple words, but they resonated with a new beginning. Somehow, I'd forgiven him yet again. I'd granted absolution for him stealing my daughter and turning my life upside down.

He sucked in a massive gust of air, eyes boring into mine. He didn't need to say anything, I could read him clear as day. He vibrated with thankfulness.

"Just… be gentle," I whispered.

He grimaced. "I'm trying damn hard to embrace that word every day."

Clara moved closer to Fox, and I tensed, hoping she wouldn't touch him. She must've been affected by what Fox did in the office more than she let on because she kept her tiny hands to herself. "Why don't you like to be gentle? Did you never have a pet to learn how to be nice? I can teach you to be gentle. It's not hard."

I laughed softly. "It's not that easy to teach a man to ignore a lifetime of training, Clara."

Her face shot to mine, sadness tugging her mouth down.

I rushed to add, "But I know you help Fox a great deal."

Clara scowled, one dainty foot stomped the floor. "His name is Roan, mummy. How many times do I need to tell you?"

Fox chuckled, smiling sadly in my direction. "I never told your mother what my first name was. She's not used to calling me by it." His large hand moved to ruffle her hair, but dropped just as quickly. "My first name is precious to me. I told no one, not even the men I grew up with. You were the first one I told."

My heart burst. I never thought about a name being sacred or something to be hoarded. In my past, I traded names like I stole new clothing, never attached, always changing.

Fox sensed my train of thought and murmured, "My first name was the only thing I had left of my past before they stole everything from me. I kept it hidden, first in defiance, then in desperation. Only my little brother, Vasily, was allowed to call me Roan. And now Clara. And now... you."

I swallowed hard, picturing a younger version of the scarred man in front of me. "You want me to call you Roan?"

He captured my heart and soul with his look. "Yes. It would mean a lot to me."

Fox suddenly moved forward.

My back straightened, stomach flurried. He was close, so close, his white-grey eyes staring mournfully into mine. "Please forgive me for what I'm about to tell you. But if you can't...I understand."

Tearful prickles raced up my spine and I couldn't speak. I nodded, aching to hug him, offer solace in my arms. For two days I kept my distance, harbouring my anger, not wanting to be weak when my first duty was to Clara, but it was no use. I wanted to help this man. I couldn't stop—just like I couldn't stop my feelings for him.

Fox's nostrils flared, his lips parted, and every part of me throbbed for every part of him. Even though Clara would never be safe around him, I had a hard time ignoring practicality in favour of my heart.

And my heart wanted Roan.

Desperately.

I didn't just want him physically; I wanted him mentally, emotionally, spiritually. I wanted to own every part of him and trade his life for mine.

Clara broke our moment with a cringe worthy question. "You have so many weapons. Have you used them?" She stroked a huge sword that looked as if it should be stuck in a rock in some storybook myth. Her voice was faint, but her question turned Fox to a statue. "Have you killed people before? Did they deserve it?"

Every question sent a dagger into my heart. Who knew that a kid with no life experience could have such perception? She read everyone like a picture book. All our sins and secrets might as well be tattooed on our foreheads.

Fox closed his eyes, an expression of deep regret and pain etched his features. Finally he opened them again. "I wish I didn't have to answer your question, but I promised myself I would tell the truth." Sighing, he added, "I've taken lives before. Some bad. Some deserving. But most were kind and gentle and didn't deserve to die." He looked up, freezing me in his stare. "But I didn't do it willingly. You have to believe me."

I couldn't catch a proper breath. The room closed in, swords and daggers loomed like nightmares, filling my head with horror.

Clara moved closer to Fox and it wasn't until she put a hand on his leg that I noticed she clutched a tiny dagger with an intricate gem inlaid in the hilt. Fox sucked in a breath at her touch, but didn't move.

I backed toward a shelf, blindly groping for a blade just in case.

With ease and brittle gentleness, he pried Clara's fingers from around the dagger before placing it back on a shelf. "I don't think your mother would want you playing with knifes." He shot me a look. "How about we get out of here? You've seen enough."

Clara shook her head, her eyes never leaving the pretty ruby inlaid dagger. "I don't want to play with them. I want to make them. They're so pretty and shiny, and I want to know how. Can you show me? Please? Can I have that?" She pointed at the knife.

"You're not having a knife, Clara. No matter how much you beg." I glared my 'do-not-mess-with-me scowl.'

Fox didn't smile. His face remained serious as he said,

"Maybe when you're older I can teach you. You should only have a blade if you know how to use it. It's dangerous to wield something you don't understand."

I balled my hands, fighting the painful squeeze on my heart at the thought of Clara growing up. I wanted that to happen. So much.

Clara moved to the other side of the room, brushing her fingers along a particular sword that'd been polished until the blade turned into a mirror. Her delicate features bounced back, contorted by the shape of the metal. "I suppose I can wait. But don't be too long." Her eyes darted up and latched onto mine with intelligence far beyond her years. "Being allergic to air is hard. I don't think I have too much time."

My knees buckled and the heavy shroud of faintness almost stole my sanity.

A strangled noise sounded low in my chest, and Fox looked up to glare at me. How did she know? Did she sense her lifespan would be shorter than most?

How does she know?

Tears wobbled in my eyes at the thought of her lying in bed at night afraid and alone. She never asked about her coughing fits, asthma attacks, or constant lung infections, never once questioning what it meant, and why she was different from other kids.

Ignoring Fox's confused and angry glower, I held my hand out for Clara to come to me. Dropping to her height, I whispered in her ear, "I love you so incredibly much. You'd talk to me if something was worrying you. Wouldn't you?"

She nodded, rolling her eyes. "Of course. But nothing's worrying me, so I'm all hunky-dory. Can Roan tell his story now?"

I wanted to scream. To demand she tell me why she thought she had less time. I wanted to know her every thought and conclusion, but I forced my fingers to unclamp around her shoulders and breathed deep.

I couldn't crush her enthusiasm, but didn't know if I had

the reserves to listen to such a dark and sorrow-filled story Fox obviously had to share. Not now.

Fox seethed with temper; his eyes burned a hole into mine. The energy in the small room was full of questions. He heard truth in the cryptic comment from Clara. His perception was too highly tuned. But that made sense now. After seeing his workshop, weapons, and finding out he killed people; he transformed into more hunter than man in my eyes. Of course, he would have the instincts of a true predator—after all, they relied on their instincts to survive.

I looked up, shaking my head. *I'll tell you, but not yet.*

I hoped to avoid the subject to spare him. I hoped to avoid it, because I wasn't strong enough to voice it. If I told another person, it made it real. I didn't want to make it real.

Fox scowled and came toward me. Grasping my elbow, he lowered his head to mine. His breath sent shivers down my back as he whispered harshly, "Be prepared to talk after this, Hazel. I'm done being kept in the dark. I want to know. And you're going to tell me every single thing you've been keeping secret."

Before I could reply, he left the vault and disappeared.

My heart couldn't calm down at the furious restraint in his voice. He was pissed and no way in hell did I want to deal with a pissed off Fox.

Clara and I followed, hanging back as Fox spent a few minutes dragging dinged up leather chairs toward the central fireplace. Grabbing a poker, he viciously stabbed the coal embers until happy yellow and orange flames came to life.

Pinching the bridge of his nose, he sucked in a heavy breath before deliberately shedding his anger and re-centring himself.

Holding out his hand, he ordered, "Come here."

My heart couldn't cope; I shuffled after Clara toward one of the chairs and sat heavily into the soft, springy cushion. Clara lost her fierce independence and instead of taking the other chair, she plopped onto my knee and snuggled. Together we sank into the leather, looking up at Fox. His scarred cheek danced with firelight; his body echoed with pain. Pain given to him by his past. Pain given to him by telling the truth.

His eyes locked with mine, and I didn't know what he searched for. Acceptance, understanding, willingness to listen and not judge until the end? I didn't know, but at least he no longer looked as if he wanted to tear me apart for keeping secrets from him. For now Clara's impending demise was safe.

He held up his hands, bracing them like a traffic warden, displaying fleshy palms and callused fingers. "See that? The marks directly in the centre?" He leaned forward, so his hands were only a foot away from our faces.

Clara spotted the greenish-grey lines before me. "Yep. They're faded. Do they mean something?" Her voice was timid and I cuddled her closer.

Fox curled his lip, bringing his hands back to him, glaring hatefully at them. "Invisible, impenetrable, invincible."

The hair on the nape of my neck sprang up as he added in a low timbre voice, *"Nevidimyy, nepronitsayemyy, nepobedimyy."*

He looked up, eyes glinting with remembered hatred. "The three things a Ghost must be. I've scrubbed my hands with abrasives; spent hours scouring them with sand to remove their trace, to forget, but they never leave, just like the conditioning will never leave."

His voice turned inward, full of memories, echoing with agony. "That's all we were. Ghosts to do their bidding and obey their every request. We were told to kill and we did. We were told every murder would slowly turn us immortal like gods. And just like gods, we had power. We were the law and nothing could touch us."

He shook his head violently. "But that was all a lie. We were just humans, tortured within an inch of our psyche to become what they wanted us to be. A mindless machine for hire. Mercenaries of the highest order who anyone could buy to complete a task."

His body shuddered, bowing his head. His hands clenched and every turmoil he felt lashed at me, bleeding me dry. He battled so deep, suffered so much, sucked backward where nightmares still ruled.

Minutes passed while Fox stood motionless, only his lips moving soundlessly. I'd seen a few people have flashbacks, their present overcome by an overpowering memory. Clara squirmed on my lap, her little body tensing with every minute.

As sudden as the flashback took him it was over. He looked up, blinking once. He rolled his shoulders. "Sorry."

Clara shifted. "What were you thinking about?" Her warm, comforting weight helped keep my panic at bay, retaining my utter horror for the pain Fox had lived through.

"I was thinking about a little boy. You remind me of him so much, Clara. He was bright, funny, brave. His name was Vasily—it means kingly, of royal descent. He was nine when he died."

Clara sighed. "I'm sorry. I like his name. What does yours mean?"

Fox smiled. "It means redhead, even though my hair turned darker as I grew older. A false name really."

"I like it better than Ghost or Fox. I don't believe in ghosts and you're not see-through and can't fly, so that's just stupid. Those bad men who made you do bad things know nothing."

I smothered a chuckle under my breath. I didn't mean to laugh—the tension in the room had no space for humour—but Fox cracked a smile, too. Some of the overwound tension left his body. "You're right. I'm not a Ghost. Not anymore. I'm just a man searching for a way to be human again."

My heart squeezed to death.

Clara leaned back into me, her dark eyes riveted on the licking flames dancing over Fox's face. "You may have killed, but you aren't a bad man."

Fox froze, drowning in her gaze. "What makes you say that?"

She broke eye contact, kicking her feet, looking anywhere but at him. "Because only bad men are lonely because no one can love them." Her little lungs strained, sucking in courage.

She burst out, "And I love you, so you can't be a bad man otherwise how could I love you? I would know. I would be able to tell you were naughty, and I wouldn't want to love someone like that."

Fox went from standing straight and tall to looking ancient and frail. He sucked in a heavy breath, and for the briefest of moments, moisture filled his eyes. But then it was gone, and the fragility was replaced with power once again.

His throat worked hard. "If it's okay with you, I'll start the story now." Gripping the hem of his black t-shirt, he tore it over his head.

What in the living daylights is he doing?

I squeezed Clara so hard she squeaked. For weeks I'd wanted to see Fox naked. I'd wanted to understand what he kept hidden. But now he stood before me and I wanted to shut my eyes.

He didn't need to verbalize his story. It lived in his skin, engraved into muscles, and imprinted into flesh.

Balling the t-shirt, he threw it away.

My eyes were transfixed by his ripped muscles. They were too defined, too angry, too lacking nutrients and a healthy layer of fat. Every sinew, every vein, every thread and bunch of muscle seethed beneath the thin membrane of skin.

My fingers ached to touch him, to run along the long swooping scar on his rib cage and whisper over the small uniformed marks just below his collarbone. There were circular scars and oblong scars, square scars and scars that looked as if they still retained gravel and dirt from however they hurt him.

His stomach was so toned every ridge looked too harsh, too unforgiving to cuddle or sleep against. He didn't look man. He looked like stone. Forged from granite and marble, carved from obsidian and slate.

"Fox...I—" My voice deserted me. A flare of connection and lust sprang to a fever pitch between us. Fox tensed, highlighting yet more scars in the light of the fire.

"Now you know why I don't like for people to see."

Clara stayed mute on my lap, either unimpressed by the show of male brokenness, or overwhelmed by the violence living on his skin. I shouldn't allow this. I should take her far away, so she didn't have to live with such atrocities in her young mind.

But she knew things she shouldn't know. She knew her time was limited. She acted far beyond her age, yet she dealt with everything with such fine edged decorum and sensibility.

Tears tracked silently down my cheeks for both Fox and Clara. Two people who connected and were drawn to each other; two people who would destroy each other.

"I don't want people to know. I don't want people to guess my story, or display my crimes. Every day I try to forget, but every day I remember thanks to a body that will never erase or heal. But if you want to know, I will tell you the story behind every mark and cut. I've never forgotten—the memories are vivid and never ending in my head." His voice dabbled with self-hatred and pleading.

I shook my head. I never wanted to know. I thought I did. I thought I wanted to uncover his secrets, but I couldn't make him live through his past—not while it lived so deeply on his skin in the present.

Clara had no such scruples.

Her little hand darted up, pointing to a scar above his protruding hip bone. "That looks like a ce—cee—caesarean scar. Mummy has one, and she said she loves it because it reminds her of me." She swirled in my arms to plant a gentle kiss on my cheek. "I didn't mean to scar you, you know."

I gathered her close, squeezing hard. "I love that scar. I'm thankful for it every day as it brought you into my life." She sighed and squirmed closer while looking up at Fox.

Dropping his eyes, he traced the scar with a finger. "This is from a knife similar to the one you picked up. It was a test—weeding out the recruits who would operate in intense pain compared to those who couldn't."

My hands wanted to slam over Clara's ears. I shot Fox a

warning look. "Perhaps we've had enough story-time for one day." I shot another message with my eyes. *Stop it. You'll scare her. She doesn't need to know details.*

Fox nodded. "We'll avoid the scars for now. I'll tell you the story of this." Sucking in a breath, he turned away from us.

My mouth fell open, jaw slack in shock. If I thought his chest was impressive with its relic of memories, his back was a piece of parchment with history inked into every crevice.

Clara bounced off my lap, tearing my arms off her. "Wow." She moved forward, transfixed on his tattooed back. The golden hue of licking flames highlighted the ridges of his muscles and flickered over the silver of his scars like some expensive imbedded jewellery. "What happened to you?" Clara leaned forward, childlike wonder shining bright in her eyes.

"Life happened to me, little one."

I didn't know if I wanted to laugh or cry. In one move, Fox gave everything that he was. He bared his soul; he dropped every barrier, so we could understand him better.

I hated myself in that moment for keeping so much from him. For judging him. For not understanding or granting more compassion.

His tattoo wasn't something he wore with pride. It wasn't an achievement or earned. It was a plain message of ownership. Every design spoke of proprietorship and control.

My heart swelled for this broken warrior. My eyes burned with tears.

Looking over his shoulder, he murmured, "Ready for your story now?"

Clara nodded, dumfounded, eyes flittering all over his inked back. Fox bent his knees and crashed to the floor, presenting himself at my feet. Clara moved closer, breathing hard. "Can I—I want to—"

Fox clenched his fists, digging them into his thighs. "You can. I'll tell you which to touch, and I'll tell you the story."

A large smile broke her face, then she frowned. "Is it all sad? I don't know if I want to listen to something all sad."

Fox laughed softly. "Life is sad, little one. It's full of heartache and bittersweet hope, but you are my happy ending. You are my happiness, so remember that when I tell you."

Clara reached out to touch.

My throat dried to a husk as Fox muttered, "Go slowly. Start at the top."

My muscles were ready to spurn forth and snatch my daughter away. This was the worst possible place for her to touch him. Weapons lurked in every corner, a fire billowed beside them. He could bludgeon her and burn all evidence in a matter of moments.

Clara nodded, her fingers trembled as she gently laid a hand on the base of his neck where a Celtic-like knot had been drawn.

Fox said, "That one—that's the symbol of never-ending battle." He stopped, clearing his throat. "Once upon a time, a boy who was born to royal blood strayed too far from home. He didn't listen to his mother's warnings and thought he knew best. Their castle rested on the edge of a mystical forest where bears and wolves played in the snow. The little boy explored for hours, searching for them, but he didn't find any bears or wolves. But he did find something else."

Clara dropped her hand to the next tattoo, willing Roan to continue.

Roan.

I'd slipped and thought of him by his first name.

He flinched as her finger circled an angel bowing over a sword across her legs with three words in a circle. "That's the mark of a Ghost. The angel of death and our three promises: Invincible, impenetrable, invisible. It was a pledge, a curse, our destiny."

Fox sucked in a breath and continued with his story. "The little boy found two men and thought they were there to guide him back home. So he went willingly and didn't struggle when they shoved him into a van and drove for miles into the wilderness. They told the boy his old life was over and to survive he must follow every rule without question."

The atmosphere in the room thickened with anticipation. I sat forward on the chair, inching closer, my skin tingling.

Clara stuck her tongue out in concentration, dropping her hand to the next symbol. It depicted a swarm of angry swirls, never ending.

"That one represents evil. We were the weapons of righteousness. Our only purpose was to obey our master—if we did as we were ordered, we would be safe from evil." His back tensed as he continued, "Years passed for the boy as he grew from child to teen to adult. As he completed stages of training, exams were given and to pass he had to hurt his beautiful mother, courageous father, and talented little brother. The boy was brainwashed every day. He was told he was no longer human, but a Ghost whose job was to exterminate vermin. Out of fifty other boys and girls who lived with him in this new castle, only thirteen graduated. The rest disappeared, stolen by the snow to never be seen again."

I winced as my nails dug hard into my palms, drawing blood. My heart thumped in heavy pain for all the children who'd been forced to kill. All the children who'd been murdered by the sick, twisted men who kidnapped and tortured young innocence.

Clara shook her head in sadness. My heart seized at the thought of her wrapping her arms around him and hugging. The longer Fox told his story, the further his voice sounded—swallowed up by the past. It lost its intensity, drifting off into a soft, hypnotic tone.

Clara dropped her fingers, tracing a pretty snowflake on Fox's spine.

He growled, hands clenching. Clara lost her balance a little before steadying herself.

"That's the tattoo I hate the most. It was punishment. If we failed to do exactly what they wanted, they'd make us spend nights alone in the forest. The once mystical bears and wolves I wanted to find were now my enemies in the dark. Hungry and looking for a tasty snack—" He cut himself off before continuing, "The little boy spent his eighth birthday in the pit. The worst place to go if you disappointed your handlers. Day and night with no shelter. No warmth from dusting snow, or blankets to stop frostbite from turning your limbs into ice. The little boy hated the pit, and his deep-seated fear of the dark stemmed from those nights. Endless blackness only punctured by a weak moon and the glowing yellow eyes of wolves."

Clara skirted over the Roman numeral III and went straight to a flame with an anvil.

Fox sighed, releasing some of his recalled fear. "When the little boy obeyed orders, he was allowed to work in the smithy. He loved the heat and brightness of fire and his skills grew. He threw himself into turning hunks of metal into weapons of destruction—it was his happy place. Despite the daily toils and gruesome tasks he was given, the boy never forgot who he truly was and always remembered the truth. They broke him again and again, but he knew in his heart he wasn't what they said he was. It wasn't until a fairy godmother granted him the loss of sight that he was able to find freedom."

What? Fox had been blind?

Clara whispered, "The last tattoo of the fox. That's you?"

Fox smiled. "Yes, when the little boy graduated he was told to choose a code name. Something he would wear with honour for his achievements. He liked to think he was smart enough to win in the end—wily and cunning like the small, red-coated fox. It reminded the little boy of his mother's red hair, and his father's bushy moustache."

Clara leaned back, waiting for the end of the story.

"The moment the little boy was free, he made a new promise. To never kill again and that he'd find a way to break the brainwashing and make up for his sins. But it wasn't until a little girl with long dark hair entered his life that he was finally able to believe he could achieve his promise." Fox looked over his shoulder, grey eyes blazing into mine. "Now life is good for the little boy, and he can finally start to put the past behind him. Every day he strives for forgiveness, chasing an unfamiliar emotion. He has something else to fight for."

"What's that?" Clara whispered, her face glowing from the fire.

Fox spun around, hiding his back from view. His lips twitched into a soft smile, causing a flurry of butterflies to erupt in my stomach. "Family."

I didn't think I was capable of feeling so wretched or so hopeful all at once. He hadn't just stolen Clara from me, he'd stolen my heart. I wanted to throw myself into his arms and tell him I'd do anything to bring his dreams to life.

Then my heart shattered. *What will he do when I tell him about Clara?*

The thought made me want to run and never come back. He'd hate me.

Fox stood up suddenly and headed to a table beneath a bright halogen. He tucked something under his arm and came back. Placing the dirty rag-wrapped present on the floor by Clara's feet, he yanked the material off. Resting on the floor was the fattest, woolliest, perfectly created metal sheep I'd ever seen.

My heart cracked, splintered, shattered in my chest. And I knew without a doubt I would love Roan until I died.

Clara's eyes bugged and her little mouth fell open in a huge grin. "My sheep!"

Fox nodded. "Your sheep."

That night, after an afternoon of heavy contemplation about Fox's story, I put Clara to bed. Hugging her tightly, I breathed in her fresh apple scent, praying with all my soul she would survive beyond all doctors' predictions. That she wouldn't have to leave me.

After hearing Fox's tale, I wanted to tell him mine. I wanted to be as open and honest, but at the same time I didn't want to. I had no happy ending to offer him. I didn't want to break the little boy's heart and kill him, so soon after he found a way to be free.

Clara coughed quietly, drawing my attention. Her beautiful liquid eyes shone from the bedside light. "Something's wrong with me. Isn't there, mummy?" Her high lyrical voice was hushed, almost as if she didn't want to say it aloud.

My world crunched to a stop, but instead of wailing and cursing life for such unfairness, I clutched hard at calmness and hid my tears. Strength I didn't know I had filled my limbs, keeping my voice steady.

Inside, I felt like a cracked china doll with broken pieces that would never be glued together again, but externally, I was a strong mother who would be there for her daughter till the end.

Running my hands through her hair, I murmured, "There's nothing wrong with you, Clara. You're perfect in every way." I sucked in a breath. "And that's why you'll be leaving me soon. You're too perfect for this world. Too precious. You'll be called to somewhere much better than here." I clamped my lips closed as a wave of grief threatened to make me break. "You have nothing to be frightened of. Promise me you won't be scared." She looked up, her large, dark eyes looking like an eclipse blotting out the light. "Why do I have to go? I don't want to leave you."

I had no answers for her. My mind was blank and worthless. "We never know what life will bring. But we won't be apart for long."

"Did I do something bad? Is that why I cough so much?"

Oh, God.

"You didn't do anything bad. Nothing. It's just your lungs, sweetheart. Some people are born with a different life path, but it doesn't mean you won't be happy and healthy. You're just going to somewhere better."

She lay quiet for a time before tugging on my fingers. "Will *you* be okay? When I'm gone, I mean?"

I gave up the battle to stay dry-eyed and kissed her soft forehead. "I'll be fine. I promise. I'll talk to you every day. You'll be with me always."

She sighed, pressing her face against mine. "Even though I might leave, I won't ever truly leave you, mummy. I'll find a way to come back and be with you. But you have to promise me you won't be alone. I would cry to think of you sad because I left you."

I couldn't reply.

She squirmed upright, placing her slightly sticky hand on my cheek, just like she'd done to Roan. "Promise me you'll fix him, mummy. He needs you."

I didn't want to promise something I couldn't achieve, but looking into her urgent eyes, I found myself nodding and swearing on my life I would fix the man I was falling for.

Only after I'd told Clara a story, and unwrapped her sleeping figure from my arms, did I slide down the bathroom door and cried wracking sobs with a fist in my mouth. On and on, wave after wave of crashing sorrow.

I purged myself until no more liquid existed in my body.

Only once my body quietened from sobs, did I stand up and look in the bottom of the rubbish bin where I'd hidden yet another complication.

The two pink lines mocked me from the home pregnancy test. All my life I believed I had one chance at motherhood. That the brutal attack in my teens left me barren. All the doctors concurred I was too badly mangled to conceive again. The nurses stroked my hands and consoled me. I'd been offered counselling to come to terms with never giving Clara a brother or sister.

At the time, I didn't care. Clara had been a mistake—a wonderfully joyous mistake, but one I probably wouldn't do a second time—but as time passed, I found myself sad to think I would never bring more life and wonder into the world.

But just like everything, life had a way of knocking me on my ass with surprises.

Conceived by a forceful lover and a man consumed by demons.

I was now pregnant with his future.

Sixteen

ROAN

The truth shall set you free.

That was bullshit.

The truth made me a monster and placed fear and sadness into a little girl's heart. But it helped with one thing: it gave me Zel. The way she looked at me changed from wary to wanting, from fearful to needful.

The night I told my story, Zel came to me and broke my walls. She smashed my conditioning, and I hoped life permanently changed for the better.

I hoped I was cured.

But hope is a fickle thing. It made the future look bright and pure when really it did nothing but camouflage the dark and dirty truth.

Truth Zel kept from me.

Truth that ruined my hope.

Truth that undid all my progress and hurtled me back from human to weapon.

That night, after Zel retired with Clara to bed, I spent a few hours overseeing Obsidian.

The time had just struck midnight, and the club heaved with eager fighters. Men swarmed in packs, discussing strategy, sharing war wounds, eagerness on their faces for a chance to excel in a fight. Every cage, mat, and ring was occupied with a long waiting list hanging beside the rigging. Seats held blood-hungry spectators. Girls circled the crowd delivering drinks and offering themselves for entertainment while private rooms were in hot demand.

Another busy day at the office.

I couldn't stop thinking about the way Zel had looked at me or the need throbbing in my blood. It took all my strength to stay there and not storm back to Zel's room and drag her out of bed to take her. I'd never needed sex so badly—never needed the affirmation that I hadn't ruined the chance to be together.

You may have told her the truth tonight, but she's keeping something from you.

My hands gripped the balustrade harder. Her secrets were driving me insane—especially seeing as one revolved around Clara. I wanted to know. I *deserved* to know.

"You alright, Fox?" Oscar appeared at the top of the stairs. His blond hair was spiked tonight, dull with wax. His tan deeper, browner, as if he spent the day in the waves under a beaming sun.

"Yeah, I'm good." And despite everything, I was. I'd survived telling the truth. It hadn't been as terrible as I imagined—not that I'd gone into detail. By speaking of it, memories swarmed my brain, pushing and shoving for space. It was hard to ignore since I invited the past back into my life.

I looked away, focusing on two men brutally hitting each other in the boxing ring. The urge to fight filled my stomach. It'd been days since I'd entertained the thought of a session. I missed it.

Being around Clara gave me pain to ignore most of the

conditioning, and the small self-harm I did in the shower gave me the extra edge I needed, but I wanted the joy of my fist crunching against something hard. I wanted the thrill of taking someone down. I didn't want the shame of being a pussy and cutting himself like an addict.

You'll never be fully free.

I'd never be tamed or soft and gentle. Violence was as much in my DNA as my brother and past. It was fruitless to pretend otherwise.

"I didn't think you'd be working tonight. Ever since that little girl arrived, you've been distracted." Distracted by chasing a better life. Focusing on other things to turn me into a better human being.

I flashed him a half-hearted smile. I wanted to ignore him. I was in no mood to chat after spreading my life's history at Clara's and Zel's feet. My entire body was bruised, my brain bleeding from remembering, my throat sore from speaking about such atrocities.

"Yeah, had a few things on my mind lately."

Oscar came to stand beside me, carefully overseeing the men below us. "I hope you know what you're doing."

I glowered. "Why? What's it to you?"

He faced me, giving me his full attention. His bright blue eyes pinned me in place. "You don't seem yourself. You're frankly freaking me out. One moment you're untouchable and slightly crazy, the next you're brought to your fucking knees by a kid—and not just any kid—but a kid belonging to a woman you're falling for." He sighed, running a hand over his face. "I know it's not any of my business, but are you truly okay?"

I bared my teeth. "I'm fine. Drop it." I turned my attention to two feral fighters who'd left etiquette behind and turned into royal uproar in the MMA cage. The crowd salivated at the brutal punches and the first spray of fresh blood.

The angst and love of pain filtered into my body, feeding my tiredness with unhelpful rage.

Oscar muttered under his breath. "She's falling for you,

isn't she?"

I balled my hands, ignoring him. I hated sharing my private life. It wasn't any of his business.

When I didn't say anything, he added, "She's good for you, Fox. I got it wrong when you first brought her up here. I thought she was another floozy only after your money, but she's strong." His blue eyes stopped trying to read me and returned to the fighting floor. "She's got iron flowing in her veins and blades for fingernails."

Despite myself, I was intrigued. "What makes you say that?" I knew the second I met her how strong she was. Her courage was the reason I chased her. Her strength was the reason I was in this mess. Obsessed with a kid and falling for a woman who I couldn't read. One moment, I thought she cared like I did, the next I couldn't tell.

Oscar's eyebrow rose. "Well, for one thing, she doesn't put up with your bullshit. Thanks to her help with the paperwork, she's increased margins and the club is running smoother than ever." He smiled. "She keeps her mouth closed about some of the not so legal things we're doing, and she's loyal to you. If you think she's the one, then I agree—she's perfect."

I searched his eyes, wondering if Zel had ever spoken to Oscar about me. He seemed to have changed his tune since the first night. I never saw them together, but that didn't mean they didn't have time to chat. Apart from the hostility at the beginning, Oscar had softened and welcomed Hazel. Even smiling when Clara appeared in my office at odd times in the day.

Oscar grinned. "I'm happy for you." He shrugged. "In any case, she's intelligent as hell. I'd watch her if I were you."

The secrets she was hiding once again filled me with annoyance.

My back tensed. "Watch her why?" Suspicion rose. Maybe they *had* talked behind my back. My hands clenched.

"Because the quiet ones are always one step ahead of you. They have everything all figured out while keeping an entire lifetime behind their kind and gentle thoughts." His eyes gained a wistful look, remembering someone from his past perhaps. "The quiet ones run deep, and no matter how much you think you know them—you never truly do."

His words struck me. *He's right.* No matter how I wished differently, Zel never gave me all of herself. She remained aloof, mysterious, entirely too closed off. And I was done being kept in the dark.

I wanted sunlight and answers and truth.

I wanted to know everything.

I'd been truthful; it was time for her to give me the same fucking courtesy. My eyes scanned the fighting floor one last time before I shoved away from the balcony. "I'm leaving."

Oscar nodded. "Thought you might. See ya later. I've got this."

Not looking back, I stalked away and headed toward my bedroom. My heart pumped heavily as I unlocked the door and entered. My thoughts full of fists and bruises—contemplating if I could risk another appearance at the Dragonfly.

"Hello."

My mouth promptly fell open, drinking in the apparition on my bed. All the angry, blood thirsty needs headed rapidly south. My cock tightened, thickened, hardened.

Bare skin. Bare breasts. Bare everything.

My feet moved forward, compelled toward the woman I wanted to fuck so badly. "What are you doing in here?" My voice was gruff and gravel from my previous temper, threading with the exploding lust unravelling in my blood.

I cleared my throat, inching forward another step.

Zel never took her emerald eyes off me. Sitting primly like a fucking princess in the middle of my bed, she looked unconquered and entirely regal. Her long, dark hair cascaded over her shoulders, teasing me.

Naked.

Gloriously fucking naked. The only thing she wore was the silver barbell through her right nipple and her star necklace.

The chain I'd made was gone, along with the custom designed bracelets. My eyes narrowed, searching for the missing jewellery.

My temper rose once again, pissed off she'd removed it. I put it on her—I marked her as mine. She had no right to take it off without my permission. It was a slight against me—as if she no longer wanted me.

"Where's the silver?" I crossed the bedroom, prowling toward the warm glow of light beside the bed. "Why did you take it off?" *And why are you here?* She should be in bed with her daughter, barricaded by a door, so I couldn't hurt either of them.

Zel sat higher on her knees. "I took it off. It's not me who should be chained. It's you."

Even though I'd come to the same conclusion, it didn't sit well with me. I couldn't stomach the thought of being captured against my will—just like all those days in Russia. I shook my head. "I'm done being bound and owned."

Zel dropped her head, soft locks drifting over her face. "Tonight will be the last time. I promise." Taking a breath, she murmured, "If you do what I say, I think I can help."

Shifting sideways, she gathered a length of chain from the covers around her legs. I couldn't see where she'd pried the links undone, but I stood transfixed as she crawled on her hands and knees toward me. Her breasts swayed erotically, and the gentle clink of metal set off a warning in my muscles. She cast a spell over me so effortlessly. I didn't want any part in being bound, but I knew I would say yes. Whatever power I had was useless against this woman.

My muscles locked as Zel reached the end of the bed, sitting on her heels. "I've seen your back and chest so you don't have to hide anymore. You let Clara touch you. It's only fair to let me do the same. I'm going to break you, Fox. I'm going to stroke you and touch every inch. I'm going to take you and show you how to love me properly, and I'm not going to accept no for an answer."

Her throat worked as she swallowed hard, hinting at the fear she kept locked away.

The tension in the room thickened until I breathed it deep, clogging my lungs with need. "And if I don't agree?"

She shrugged, drawing my eyes to her exposed perfect breasts. "Then you don't get what you want."

"And what do I want?"

"Happiness."

She couldn't have toppled me with any other word. *Happiness*. The one thing I hungered for and the one thing I didn't think I'd ever achieve. Even with her and Clara, it still felt fleeting—as if I'd wake up one morning and find it'd all been a dream. Snatched away and burned, leaving me with cinders and grief.

Despite all that, I might've believed her if it wasn't for the glitter of sadness in her eyes. My stomach rolled; I muttered, "I know you're hiding something from me. Clara knows it, too. She senses whatever you're trying to mask, and I'm done waiting for you to tell me. I want to fucking know."

She shook her head, hair whispering over perfect skin. "There is something you should know. Two things, actually. And I promise I'll tell you. But not tonight." Her eyes captured mine, filling with need. "Not right now. Tonight is for us. For you. For our future." Passion resonated in her voice, drawing me closer, drugging me until all I saw was her.

I didn't know I moved until my knees crashed against the edge of the bed. I nodded, allowing her one more night of secrecy.

Breathing shallowly, Zel moved closer. Her body heat struck me first, along with her sweet, exotic scent. Her mouth came within a millimetre of mine, her breath feathering over my lips. "I want to kiss you, but I need to tie you first. I don't want to run the risk of what happened before."

I groaned, balling my fists to stop from reaching out to grab her.

Her eyes trailed down my front, scorching me with fire.

"Strip."

The command made me shudder, made me drunk on the anticipation of sex. I gawked at her nakedness, revelling in her flat stomach and perfectly formed breasts. Her nipples pebbled, bunching into tiny buds, reacting to my gaze. My mouth watered to suck. I wanted to lick her all over, rain kisses, and bite. I wanted to give her the same explosive pleasure she gave me the other night.

I growled, "And if I agree to you taking control, what then? You'll refuse to let me touch you? Will you prevent me from fucking you? From claiming you and making you mine?" I leaned forward, so, so close to kissing her swollen lips. "I've been dreaming of being deep inside you, Hazel. No matter what restraints you put on me, it won't stop me from taking what I want, from driving deep and hard, stroking you with my cock until you disintegrate around me."

Zel panted; her arms twitched at her sides. She sucked in a fluttering breath. "If you can prove to me I can touch you without you killing me, then you can take me however you want." A shaky hand raised, dangling silver from her fingers. "But for now…I'm going to make love to you. I'm going to teach you the difference." She spoke with such control and strength, sending a riot of conflicting confusion through me.

I loved she was strong enough not to fear me—to allow me close to her—to be vulnerable around me, but I wasn't comfortable with her taking full control. It was too similar to my past. My stomach rolled at the thought of being chained by my ankles and hands and throat.

"See this collar, Fox?" My handler tugged on the leash attached to the leather cuff around my neck.

"Yes, sir."

This is so you know who you belong to. You carried out your assignment last night, but you took two hours too long. Next time, if you're not back in time, I'll attach one of these to you and hang you from the fucking ceiling. Got it?"

My heart bucked, but there was only one answer I could give. "Yes, sir."

I shook my head, dispelling the short flashback. "You can bind my wrists, but that's all."

She narrowed her eyes, dropping them to focus on my hands by my sides. Uncertainty and fear swarmed in her gaze. She'd had first-hand encounters with how deadly my fingers could be.

I cursed myself for not having the strength not to hurt her, but no matter what she asked of me—I couldn't give her full body immobilisation. It would kill me.

"I promise I'll keep it together this time. Just don't—don't push me too far."

She shook her head. "But that's the point. I need to push you to help you past whatever barriers are in your mind." She glanced at my hands again.

She didn't know I'd killed men with my legs, elbows, ankles, even my skull. Every part of me, not just my hands, were fatal. I had no wish for her to know either. I'd let her tie my hands, but the real chains would be self-imposed. Only my willpower could stop me from killing her. Ropes and restraints wouldn't work if I wanted to snuff out her life.

But I didn't.

Never.

Hazel was mine.

After a long pause, Zel nodded. "Fine. I'll bind your wrists and nothing else." Her gaze dropped to the hard bulge in my trousers. "Now, strip." She licked her lips, a flash of passion glazing her eyes. "I'm wet for you."

My cock lurched, cursing the restriction of my trousers. I wanted to slip inside her that very fucking second.

My hands trembled pulling off my shirt. The moment the material landed on the floor, I tensed. Hating my skin, the scars, the memories. Even though I'd stood before her and Clara and allowed them to see what I hid from the world, it still didn't stop the overpowering urge to cover up.

Rejection and self-hatred were fellow emotions as Zel's eyes swept over me, lingering on some areas, coasting over others.

"You're so beautiful," she whispered.

My stomach flipped and my heart no longer beat—it strummed for her. Only for her. Breathing hard, I brought my hands up to unbuckle my belt. Her lips parted as her eyes followed my every move. I inched the zipper down, feeling air kiss my nakedness beneath. Kicking off my shoes and socks, I let the material fall to the floor.

My cock hung heavy between my legs, begging for her touch. It felt alive with want, filling almost painfully with the urge to come all over her. I wanted her to wear my scent—to see my mark all over her white breasts and soft curls between her legs.

"Goddammit, Zel, you have no idea how much you fucking turn me on." My hand skidded over my stomach, cupping myself, easing some of the tension throbbing in my length.

She sucked in a breath. "Hold out your hands."

Heat and a small flare of panic rushed my blood as I slowly unlatched my fingers from my cock. I obeyed.

Locking my elbows, I steeled myself against her gentle touches as she wrapped the entire length of chain around my wrists. Not once or twice, but three loops before gathering a small padlock from the black bedspread and securing me.

I tested the tightness, already feeling sick to my stomach, battling residual recollections of being bound.

This wasn't a shit hot idea. Not only did I have to fight the conditioning, but now I had to battle the memories of being controlled and bound. I shook as my muscles bunched and quivered. *What if I'm not strong enough?*

My lungs stuck together as Zel exhaled a small sound of relief. Did she fear me that much? She didn't look turned on by securing me, more like less ready to bolt out the door.

You're doing this for her.

"Climb on the bed. Lie on your belly."

My eyes flared. "Why on my stomach? A vital part of my anatomy isn't useable unless you intend to teach me how to dry hump a mattress." I tried to joke, to dispel some of the tense anxiety between us, but Zel's lips only twitched. I'd mistaken any sense of relief when she secured the padlock—she hadn't relaxed at all, shaking with tension.

"I want to do something. You let Clara do it. Now, it's my turn."

Fuck. She wanted to touch my back. She wanted to look deeper at the tattoos, see beneath the ink to the lash marks and countless other scars hidden beneath the Ghost designs.

I shook my head, about to refuse, but Zel leaned back, inadvertently flashing me her delicate pink flesh between her legs.

All thoughts detonated out of my head. I followed like a lovesick teenager, mouth-watering, wanting so fucking badly to taste her.

I'd never kissed a woman down there. Never brought a woman to climax, or enjoyed the privilege of thighs quivering around my ears.

I wanted her. On my face, in my mouth, down my throat.

My already hard cock lurched painfully. "I'll only lie down on my stomach if you do something for me in return."

A barter system.

Something from her in return for something from me. And I knew exactly what I'd ask for.

Zel moved to the side as I awkwardly made my way high enough up the bed. With my hands locked together, I threw myself onto my back, rather than my stomach.

She scowled. "What do you want?" Little spots of colour danced on her cheeks, her lips growing pinker.

Instead of answering, my eyes dropped down her body, coming to rest between her legs. I stifled the groan, noticing for the first time the streak of glistening wetness on her inner thigh.

Fuck.

She wanted me as badly as I wanted her and the waiting was driving us both crazy.

It would take one good yank of my hands to break the three loops of chains. My arms tensed, preparing to release myself, so I could pin her beneath me. But I swallowed the need. Right now, there existed an equality between us. Zel believed she was safer and in turn might let me do more things to her than if she feared for her life the entire time.

I knew no matter what happened, I would sooner kill myself than her. My self-control would prevail. It had to.

Raising my eyes to lock with hers, I murmured, "I want to lick you."

Her eyes flared wide; her toned tummy tightened.

When she didn't move, I cocked my head. "Let me taste you, and I'll gladly let you touch my back. But I'm not going anywhere until you obey me. Come here."

She shook her head, a blush covering her cheeks. "I can't. How would you—"

Logistics seemed simple to me. "You have to sit on my face, Zel." I couldn't stop the small smile and the thrill in my stomach at the thought of her presenting herself to me. She'd have to willing expose herself and hold herself in place while I pleasured her.

"Move. Now. I won't ask again."

The order in my voice made her slowly slink up the bed, eyes filling with shyness. Her body heat scorched mine, but she carefully avoided all contact. When her knees were parallel to my shoulders, she looked at me. "I can't. It's just—too graphic."

"You want to touch me. I want to taste you. Straddle my mouth, Hazel."

Her eyes snapped closed before a hesitant leg branched out and she positioned herself above me.

She towered above me, looking like my ruler, my queen. Her breasts sat perky and perfect while the contours of her stomach guided me to the sweetest looking pussy I'd ever seen.

My voice thickened and my cock jerked, expelling a small bead of pre-cum, desperately needing more.

"You look fucking stunning." I couldn't tear my eyes away from her pink flesh or her toned thighs, keeping her hovering just out of reach.

Her skin was flushed and she jumped a mile as I quickly stretched up and lassoed my bound hands up over her head, letting my forearms rest on her thighs, imprisoning her.

Her eyes flashed with trepidation as she reared back, ready to fight.

I pressed down, forcing her legs to splay, closer and closer to my face. "I promise I won't hurt you." My voice rang with brusque sincerity. "Please. Trust me."

It took a moment, but her legs relaxed and she closed her eyes. Obeying, but not believing.

I licked my lips, putting possessive pressure on her hips with my forearms. She allowed me to pull her down. Down and down until her legs spread to deliver her wetness to my tongue.

The moment her heat touched my mouth, I forgot who I fucking was. I forgot my name, my family, my past, my trials. I was completely fucking hers through and through.

It didn't matter I didn't know what to do; the instant my tongue swept along her folds Zel arched forward and her hands slammed against the bronze bedhead behind me. A moan tore through her throat almost making me come with no other stimulation.

Her musky sweet taste electrified my mouth, and I had to have more. Spearing my tongue, I flicked her clit, dragging more pants from her.

I adored making her tremble. I loved every second of bringing her pleasure. The conditioning stayed at a bearable level thanks to her wrapping her hands around the gnarly tree of the bedhead.

"Fuck," I growled as I swept my tongue downward and entered her. The wetness short circuited my brain until I couldn't stop increasing my rhythm. I tongue-fucked her with no remorse, groaning, thrusting my hips. I craved her in every inch of my body.

My world swam with completely new sensations. I'd never tasted anything like it. Never felt the urge to turn feral, but sweet. With a questing tongue, I swept upward again, swirling around her clit.

Her entire body jerked. She went from tense with stress to trembling with need in a second flat.

"I'm going to touch you, Fox. I can't help it," she panted.

I shook my head, rasping my unshaven cheeks against her delicate inner thighs. I nipped her sensitive flesh, thrilling at the low mewls escaping her.

"I have to. Please," she moaned loudly as I tongued her entrance again, diving deep and hard.

Breaking away, I looked upward, my vision hazy with lust. My voice was hardly recognisable as I groaned, "I wasn't saying no to touching me. You can. I was saying no to calling me Fox."

Her eyes flew open, and I drowned in her green perfection. Confusion and questions darted like minnows in her gaze.

Pressing on her legs, I brought her entire pussy to my mouth and sucked hungrily, savagely.

My tongue delved deep, deep inside her and my cock lurched—hurting with the need to fuck her. I wanted to climb inside this woman and never fucking leave.

Her thighs quivered as I nipped possessively on her clit. She threw her head back, moaning, "I'm going to come. Oh, my God, I'm going—I'm coming. I'm coming."

Gathering my stomach muscles, I arched upright, pressing hard into her. My tongue drove deep, plunging in and out of her delicious taste. The first ripple of muscle caught me completely by surprise, but then her hands landed on my head, clutching fiercely at my hair, pulling, yanking as her hips rode my mouth.

White noise hissed in my ears. My muscles burned with the need to obey.

My eyes snapped closed as a roar of conditioning held me hostage. My body twisted, preparing to shove her off and away, but I battled through it. I concentrated on other things—better things. I concentrated on her coming undone in my hands, liquid flowing while I kissed and worshiped her. The release seemed to transfer from her to me, making me throb harder, wanting the same explosion she'd enjoyed.

On and on her muscles contracted around my tongue. Only once the final tremor settled did she open her eyes.

"Wow," she whispered, eyes fogged with passion.

I smiled, loving the feeling of her wetness on my lips and chin. "I owed you. What you gave me the night you sucked me off was amazing. I hope I returned the favour okay."

She laughed once. "It was more than okay."

With aching shoulders, I brought my bound hands up her back and over her head, freeing her, but her hands never left the sanctuary of my hair. She dug the pads of her fingertips into my scalp, sending tingles down my spine.

I used the energy and strength of the conditioning for my own purpose this time. In a move too fast for Zel to fight against, I toppled her from my chin to my hips and captured her face in my chained hands.

She sucked in a shocked breath before I slammed my mouth against hers, bruising both of us in a ruthless kiss.

My tongue darted past her lips with fierce hunger. Her body went from rigid and ready to fight, to liquid and malleable.

I bit her, forcing her to surrender. With a shudder, she sprawled on top of me, her straddled thighs unlatching around my hips.

We both froze as her wet heat brushed against my rock-hard cock.

Our eyes locked. I couldn't wait any longer.

"Fuck it." I thrust upward, filling her in one stroke. My eyes lost all ability to see as I sank deep into her heat. My head swelled with pressure, my body went taut with overwhelming need.

She cried out as her forehead crashed onto my shoulder.

Her entire body lay on top of mine. The white noise grew louder, filling with screeches and shouted orders. My legs jerked as I tried to ignore.

No.

My hands opened and closed, desperate to wrap around her throat. My feet scrabbled for purchase on the sheets ready to propel her off me, so I could kill her.

But her sharp teeth sank into my shoulder as her hips went from stationery to rocking. She brought me back to her—she brought me back from the dark place and gave me fucking light in the form of connection and sweet, sweet emotion.

My muscles churned. I focused on the heat of her around my cock and the taste of her inside my mouth. I stayed grounded. I stayed with her.

"Fuck, Fox. Yes. Oh, God." Zel kept her eyes tightly closed, riding me as frantically as I thrust into her. We both chased a goal, intent on arriving as fast and as explosively as possible.

"Call me Roan, goddammit. I want you to call me Roan."

Her eyes flew open, lips dancing with a smile. Her hands delved back into my hair, holding me in place to kiss me just as hungrily as I'd kissed her. "Roan," she whispered against my mouth.

My cock lurched as my heart cracked wide open and presented itself on a golden fucking platter for her to take. There was nothing left. I was hers.

"Roan. God, oh..."

My heart pounded, loving my first name on her lips. It felt as if it opened another part of me, and I forgot for a moment that I wasn't cured. I wasn't normal, I wasn't safe.

My hands jerked, breaking one link.

I opened my eyes, terrified that I'd gone too far. I wrangled the conditioning into submission. Zel sat upright, placing her hands on my chest. The pressure of her touch sent my brain reeling into darkness, but I gritted my teeth, forcing myself to stay with her.

"Concentrate on me. On us. Don't leave me, Roan. Don't leave me." Her hips rocked harder, her pussy stroking my entire length.

"I'm with you," I groaned, throwing my head back as the first line of fire shot up my cock and spurted into Zel. The instant I started coming, Zel unravelled.

A surge of power grabbed my muscles and I yanked my wrists apart. Silver links strained, fighting my strength, but they didn't stand a chance.

With a gentle pinging, the chain snapped free and slithered off my wrists.

"No—wait." Zel froze.

Grabbing her waist with fierce fingers, I pressed her hard, driving upward. "I'm fine. Really. Don't stop. Don't stop fucking me, Zel."

Her face held two battling desires: wanting to continue and wanting to run. Eventually wanting to continue won and she allowed me to rock her hips, propelling upward.

Together we thrust and ground against each other, taking and giving and fucking. The last band of release gave me something new. Gone was the violent urge to fill her, now I wanted to wrap her in clouds and protect her from everything. I felt almost weightless, buoyant.

Complete.

I gathered her to me in the gentlest hug I could manage.

Her arms came around my neck, pressing her breasts against me. My heart exploded with tenderness. I never thought I could receive such a sought after gift.

Such a simple thing, but it changed my world.

The first time I'd hugged anyone since Vasily.

The first time I'd allowed anyone to hug me back.

"Tell me why you're naked, operative."

I hung my head, avoiding looking at my dangling cock. "Because I fell asleep with no clothes on, sir."

"And now you'll preform the mission with no protection while your white ass glows for your victim to see. You're a prime target. I doubt you'll make it back alive tonight."

"Yes, sir. Sorry, sir."

The rest of the cadets looked at me with a mix of smugness and pity. Six of us had been selected for tonight's mission. All of them wore black. Everyone but me.

The commander presented us with our customary hunting knife, half-moon blades, and gun with silencer. He pointed toward the awaiting van that would drive us to the kill site.

I fumbled with the three weapons. With no place to store, I had to figure out a way to hold them.

My handler smirked. "You were always too bold, Fox. Tonight you'll learn the hard way."

And he was right.

That night I was shot in my ass running away from the security guards of the diplomat I'd murdered. His blood covered my bare skin, mingling with my own from the bullet wound.

Vasily was the one who helped clean and dress my wound. Only eight-years-old, but adapt at triage already.

Never again did I sleep naked. I would never make that mistake twice.

I shot upright, blinking, panicking.

No light.

Nothing but compressing, smothering darkness.

My eyes flew to the window where the stars and moon mocked me. *You fell asleep before the sun was here to protect you. It's our turn to make you suffer.*

I fell backward, screaming as the memory of killing my brother—the one I tried so hard to avoid—crashed over me with a tidal wave of misery.

"Roan. Please—" Vasily's face was streaked with tears, his nose

streaming with mucus. My handler marched beside me, digging a cattle prod into my side while I dragged my baby brother along with a hard grip around his neck.

"Let me go. I promise I won't say anything. I promise, Roan."

My black heart had died back at the training camp, and my eyes were dry as a bone.

I knew where we were going, and I knew I would die beside my brother—either tonight or tomorrow or the day after. It didn't matter. We were both doomed.

The moment we arrived at the pit, my handler pressed the trigger and sent a huge bolt of electricity through my body. My fingers locked involuntarily around Vasily's neck, and we plummeted to the floor of the three metre deep pit.

My body weight crushed Vasily's leg, breaking it in two places. His wails and screams scared wolves and owls far away from our grave.

They left us there for three days.

Starving, freezing, huddling together for warmth and catching snowflakes on our tongue for hydration, Vasily grew weaker every day. His lungs rattled with liquid, coughing and rasping with pneumonia.

Even if by some miracle I found a way out of there, he would die anyway.

So I did the only thing I could for my brother.

I kissed his cheeks and tasted his tears and we hugged goodbye with promises of finding each other in another life.

And then I broke his neck.

The crack of his spine heralded my handler as if he'd been waiting all along.

They hauled me out and patted my back and walked me back as a hero.

"Fox! Fox! Roan! Wake up!"

I jolted awake again, sucking down huge gulps of oxygen. My heart raced as if I'd been drowning, my eyes wild as I looked around the room. Zel had turned on a false sun in the form of a bedside light.

I'd done two things I swore I would never do again: fall asleep naked and sleep with no sunlight.

My skin crawled, and I lurched backward, crushing the pillows against the headboard.

Zel held out her hand, fear and sorrow misting her eyes.

I looked to her hand and shook my head. "Don't touch me. I can't guarantee I'll be safe." My voice was hoarse as if I'd been screaming in my sleep.

Her arm dropped and she plucked the sheet covering her legs. Her naked breasts glowed with warmth from the small bedside light.

I needed silence, and I needed time. Time to put myself back together.

I hated that Zel had seen me weak. Seen how truly fucked up my brain was. I frowned as panic clenched my heart. "I didn't say anything—did I?"

She'll never trust me around Clara if she knows what I did to Vasily.

She shook her head. "You spoke in gibberish or Russian. All I heard was your brother's name, but that's it."

Fisting my hands, I forced my body to relax. She didn't know the worst of it—she would never know how many children I'd been forced to dispatch. I would take that secret with me to my grave.

Minutes ticked past as we stayed on opposite sides of the bed. Zel didn't say a word, but her eyes yelled never-ending questions in my direction. Every part of my body wanted to get up, to punch something, to fight.

My eyes dropped to my scarred torso. Every burn, every punishment mocked me and I couldn't stay naked another minute. I felt too exposed, too vulnerable, too weak.

Black. I need black.

Throwing my legs over the side of the bed, I went to stand, but Zel murmured, "Wait. I'll help you." She crawled toward me, ignoring the sheet twisting around her legs. "Lie on your stomach."

My heart exploded. "You think you can touch me?" I shook my head violently. "Not going to happen. I—"

Zel kept advancing. "You're close to breaking. Let me push

you. Lie down, Roan." Her voice danced with coaxing and commands.

I didn't want to obey; I didn't know how much I could tolerate, but if she was right, it might mean I could be free.

When I didn't move, her face twisted into sadness. Her hand fell to her stomach protectively, her gaze turning inward. For one insane, wild moment, I imagined her carrying my child. Giving me redemption in the form of a new life. Granting me immortality in the form of my own creation. Her voice was barely a whisper. "This is important. You *need* to do this."

The brutal honesty snapped my willpower and I muttered, "I broke the chain." My eyes searched for the ruined silver gleaming amongst the black bedspread.

Without a word, Zel got up and strode naked to the end of the bed. Scooping up my trousers, she tore the belt from the loops and held it up. It looked like a snake—a snake about to sink its fangs into my flesh and poison me to death.

My breath rattled as she came toward me.

"I know you need this, but I don't have the strength. Don't ask me to do this."

Her forehead furrowed and a harsh glint entered her green eyes. "You promised me you'd be safe around Clara, but you almost lost it in your office. I need to make sure that doesn't happen again." Holding the belt in two hands, she presented the taut length to me. "Put your hands together."

Scenarios of hitting her, striking her, and running out the door filled my brain. I didn't want to fall over the edge. I didn't want to succumb to the rage and pain of the conditioning. I didn't know what existed on the other side. What if my mind exploded—what if I couldn't cope?

What if I kill her?

One day you will if you don't break it.

The thought compelled my hands forward, and I rested my joined wrists over the loop of the belt. Without a word, Zel wrapped the leather twice around my hands before securing the buckle tightly.

Leaning down, she kissed me ever so gently on the corner of my mouth. "Lie down. Focus on me."

I obeyed. Sliding up the bed, I hesitantly pressed my chest against the sheets. The moment I was horizontal with my bound hands above my head, I wanted to roar with rage. I hated she'd put me in such a compromising position. I hated being at someone's mercy yet again.

Silently, Zel climbed beside me before throwing a leg over my hip and straddling me. The softness of her ass against the small of my back was the first sharp shock to my system. My hands curled as the familiar urges built behind my eyes.

Her hands landed on my shoulders, grasping hard, digging into muscle.

The urge behind my eyes spread to my teeth and jaw and spine. I went from frozen to trembling with deep-seated aggression.

Kill. Sever. Devour.

I groaned, pressing my face harder into the mattress.

"I won't hurt you. I'm here. I'm with you," Zel murmured, all the while massaging my shoulders with a firm mind-splintering touch.

The brainwashing spread fast until every muscle locked, writhing with the need to obey the simple decree to kill.

"Close your eyes," she demanded.

Was she insane?

"I can't. All I see is death and mutilation. If I close my eyes, I'll be consumed by darkness. I need to focus. I need to focus on the light and you and this room."

Zel didn't say anything as she smoothed her hands from my shoulders to the centre of my back. "You have to give yourself to me for this to work. You have to be completely at my mercy. No holding back. If it gets too much to bear, tell me and I'll add more restraints." Her voice wobbled, but then strengthened. "You have to tell me if it gets too much. I won't let you hurt me again."

I nodded, the sound of fabric from the bedspread loud in

my ear. The shooting pain of disobedience darted through my body. Gritting my teeth, I rode through it, trying so hard to do what Zel said and let myself go.

The silence rushed with the voices of my handlers.

Why are you disobeying a direct order, operative?

She's inflicting you, therefore you must inflict back.

Sweat broke out on my brow as Zel's hands dropped further. Her hand landed on my ass and my back arched in surprise. "Stop—" I growl-panted, my skin scorching with unrequited orders.

"No," she whispered. Meticulously, she traced a finger from the crack in my ass upward to the base of my spine. Deliberately taunting me with a mixture of firm and soft, prohibited and allowed.

"You spilled some of your secrets today. I loved hearing more about you even though your past is so sad. Focus on my voice as I touch you. Try and relax. Try not to fight and I'll tell you some of mine." Her hand splayed on my spine, massaging the tortured muscles below.

A headache swelled, throbbing with my rapidly beating heart.

Kill her, Fox.

We won't command again.

Her fingers feathered over the fox tattoo on the base of my spine. "I'll start with my necklace. I've seen you looking at it— the star. The single silver star." Her voice turned wistful, full of happy memories. "I bought two necklaces with my meagre savings the day Clara turned four. She was obsessed by all things galaxy and drew stars on everything she could get her hands on."

Her fingers continued their maddening assault, calling more conditioning, more pain. I glued my lips together and bore through it.

"I bought her the necklaces for her birthday. Her face lit up as if she'd swallowed the moon. Her tiny hands tickled my neck as we took turns clasping them on each other. The moment they were on, she announced she would never take it off. She's my star in more ways than one." She sighed, her voice turning sad. "I bought the necklaces for another reason, too. But that isn't a tale for tonight."

My brain skipped between her voice and the inner commands only I could hear. It took all my willpower to focus on the present and stay lying flat.

It would be so easy to flip her off.

Her neck will snap if you use your legs around her throat.

Zel continued, fingertips pressing deep into never before massaged flesh. "I've had so many jobs I can't remember them all—most of them weren't legal. I bounced from foster family to foster family, always an outcast. I thought the world hated me—that I'd be forever alone, but then I learned I could create the life I wanted by lying."

She repositioned her legs, straddling me higher to work deeper on my shoulders. "I have authentic looking documents from colleges around the country. But none of them are true. I forged a past from a runaway no-hoper to proud aspiring mother.

"I'll never apologise for lying or stealing because it was the only way to survive. It allowed me to give Clara a better world." Her voice caught before continuing in its smooth lullaby. The more I listened, the more she entranced me, and the more the conditioning didn't hold centre stage.

Every touch was torture—stroking seized muscles, prolonging the utter madness of crashing orders, but it didn't overpower me. I didn't lose myself to blackness.

Her hands moved higher, thumbs digging into hard muscle on either side of my spine. "I have blood on my hands. I've stolen two lives."

My back bowed as the shock of her confession slapped the conditioning away, leaving me clearheaded for a wonderful moment. "What? How did they happen?"

Her hands trailed higher, turning from therapeutic massage to gentle petting. My breathing turned heavy and rasping; my bound fists ached from clenching so hard. The conditioning came back, simmering in the back of my brain.

"I was twelve the first time I turned a man into a corpse."

So fucking young. Like me.

The connection I felt toward Zel blistered my heart, strengthening my will to ignore the orders.

"I was between foster parents. Up till then, I'd been placed with decent families, kind and generous—I was the one messed up and didn't let them help me. But that one…it was different. I wasn't prepared for the jolly overly-touchy uncle to come into my bedroom once everyone had gone to bed. I wasn't prepared for the pet-name 'baby-doll' to become such an irrational fear thanks to him crooning it. I wasn't prepared to watch him strip or the grotesque erection between his legs. But I *was* prepared to defend myself.

"I wasn't innocent, even at that tender age. I'd stolen a kitchen knife from a previous family, and bided my time as he climbed into my bed. His beer breath was rancid in the dark while his foul hands tried to fondle me.

"One touch was all he got before I plunged the sharp blade into his groin. It was pure luck I severed his femoral artery. He bled dry before the ambulance arrived."

Zel's hands never stopped their relentless stroking. Her touch twisted my head with needs and urges all while I tried to concentrate on her story. My body sparked with sensitivity. The tickling of her body hovering above mine drove me insane.

"The second time I killed, I'd just turned twenty-one. I slit the throat of a man trying to rape Clue. I didn't even think. I wasn't desensitized to hurting people—I avoided it at all costs—but seeing him hurting someone half his size, I stopped thinking and reacted.

"I'll never regret saving her. She saved me in return."

Her voice trailed off as she leaned forward, rubbing her hands all over, wrapping me in the fragrance of lily of the valley. Every part of my body ached from fighting an unseen war; anticipation heightening my senses until all I focused on was my rabbiting heartbeat and monstrous curiosity about the woman on top of me.

Slinking forward, Zel climbed my body until she sat on her heels over my ribs. Her hands smoothed my shoulder blades, rubbing with delicious pressure.

Listening to her helped me stay sane, but silence sucked me back into the dark. My headache roared out of control, and I did the only thing I could to avoid falling into the pit. To avoid obeying and hurting her.

I was done having her in control. It was my turn.

In one sharp move, I flipped Zel off my back and rolled over. The belt around my wrists wasn't escapable, but it didn't matter. In a second, I pulled my naked body onto hers, pinning her beneath me.

Her eyes flared wide and panic etched her face.

"Don't worry. I won't hurt you. I'm still in control." *Barely*.

I wanted to lick, nibble, and bite. I wanted to run my hands over her body and touch, just like she touched me. I needed to sink deep inside her to ignore the stronger urges, the more insisting orders.

She'd tried to accustom my body to gentler touches— reprogram my brain from two decades of training in one massage session. I didn't want to shatter her hope. She'd helped, but not enough. The only thing keeping me from killing her was the tiny remaining thread of my self-control.

I was proud of my strength, but disillusioned at the same time.

Eventually, I would snap. And I couldn't have her touching me when that happened.

I tested a wrist, wincing as the leather bit into my skin. Zel had buckled it so tightly it bruised my bones beneath.

"Get off me. We need to finish," she ordered.

Instead of obeying, I wrapped my bound arms around her and arched my back, thrusting gently, searching for her.

I groaned as I found her wet heat. "You've touched me and I've obeyed, but now I need to fuck you. Don't deny me, Zel."

Her ass wiggled, trying to dislodge me. Her breasts rose and fell against my chest as I settled deeper into the apex of her legs.

"But it didn't work. I'd hoped to fix you. I'm not finished." Her gaze searched mine even as her legs spread, giving me room to sink between them.

My eyes slammed shut as I pressed into her heat. Deeper and deeper. I shivered as her pussy took my full length. "It worked enough." Opening my eyes, I smiled. "You owe me a reward for behaving."

She snorted. "Behaving by not killing me you mean."

"Exactly." I dropped my head to kiss her. Her mouth opened; her tongue rose to meet mine, and we began to move. Digging my elbows into the mattress on either side of her face, I rocked hard and possessive, claiming her slowly, deliberately.

Her hands landed on my ass. Instantly the headache swarmed with pressure almost buckling my control. My body froze while I focused on how delicate, how breakable, how much I did *not* want to kill her. "Don't," I whispered. "Stop touching me."

Immediately, her hands dropped.

Rearing back, staring deep into her eyes, I said, "I give you my word I won't hurt you, but I really need to fuck you, Hazel. Give me your hands." I thrust upward.

She raised her hands above her head allowing me to capture her wrists with my fingers. The moment she was secured, I dropped one barrier inside my mind. Harnessing a small taste of violence, I surged into her.

She cried out with the brutal thrust, panting as I drove into her. My heart drummed with angry conditioning, fighting with sexual need.

Her legs came up to imprison my hips, pulling me deeper inside.

I growled as a fresh burst of urges filtered through my blood, almost stealing me from reality. But I held on. I focused. I concentrated. I never reverted to Ghost.

"God you feel so good. So tight. So perfect." I rocked harder, filling her with everything I had. She was mine, and I wanted to mark her to prove it.

Releasing her wrists, I dropped my hands, forcing one finger into her mouth. "Suck it," I ordered.

Her eyes flared and lips latched around me, dragging me into her mouth. The matching wetness and heat drove me wild. I pumped harder and harder.

"Do you feel me?" I growled, loving the sparking orgasm building in my balls.

She nodded, sucking my finger, biting with sharp, little teeth. Her legs spasmed around my hips. "You taste of metal and smoke. You feel fucking amazing, Fox."

I groaned. I couldn't hold off any more.

The sparking release exploded in my belly and I came, filling her with everything left inside me.

She tensed beneath me, throwing her head back as her internal muscles rippled, wave after wave, squeezing my length with delectable strength.

Her body went from rigid to floppy and a small smile twitched her lips.

Cursing the headache and the still insistent conditioning, I kissed Zel on the tip of her nose. "How can I get you to remember?"

She frowned, a sated glow flushing her cheeks. "Remember what?"

Lowering my head, I bit her neck. "To call me Roan."

Seventeen
Hazel

Happiness.

Such a farce.

I'd been happy—blindingly happy only twice in my life.

The first was when I held Clara just after she was born. She unlocked emotions and joy I never knew existed.

The second was when I landed a job at a prestigious company thanks to a forged resume. I might have earned the job with lies, but I earned a bonus in the first month thanks to my work ethic.

Both showed my life improving, both hinted at pleasures to come.

Then I met Fox and I dared to hope I'd have a third moment of happiness.

But just like everything, it was the brief interlude before the main event.

The eye of the storm.

The beginning of the end.

I'm pregnant.

Not a whoopsy daisy I was stupid and forgot to use contraception. Not a I was sick and didn't use other precautions while on the pill. Not a I forgot to update my shot or my coil didn't work or the condom broke or I forgot to take the morning after pill.

Nothing like that.

No, life found a way to create something from nothing, cementing a marvel inside a womb that'd been confirmed as sterile forever.

I didn't believe in miracles, but I did believe in second chances.

And this was Fox's.

Roan's.

For three days, I nursed the news. I sat awake at night, running my hands through Clara's thick hair, imagining a future where she'd survive and grow up with a baby sister or brother. I painted a fairy-tale where Fox could be touched and loved, and we created a wonderful family from a very dysfunctional beginning.

I wanted to tell him. I went through every scenario of how to announce the news.

Every time he looked at Clara with smitten eyes the words *I'm having your child* danced on my tongue, waiting to be said.

But I cradled the news with utmost secrecy.

You're avoiding it because you don't know how you feel.

My hand fell on my flat stomach. I would never terminate a pregnancy, but I couldn't wrap my head around holding another child. Loving another child.

It felt traitorous to Clara. I felt unfit and unworthy, and it tore me up inside. I couldn't love another cherub-cheeked baby—it was a betrayal to her.

Wasn't it?

I threw up twice—not from morning sickness—but from guilt. Guilt for loving another child as much as I loved Clara. Guilt for replacing her.

That was my true issue.

My firstborn will be dead, but I'll have another. I wouldn't have the time to mourn, or the luxury to forget about life. I wouldn't have the privilege of ruining my own world once Clara left me.

I would have to go on surviving, smiling, living, all for a baby I'd never thought I'd have.

And it made me fucking angry.

Angry to recognise how weak I was—knowing I would love this baby with everything I was, which wasn't fucking fair to Clara. She owned my heart, body, and soul, and she would be dead.

I was dizzy, tired, and nauseous trying to come to terms with gaining a life just before I lost one.

Ironically, I kept my secret because of my own regret, but Clara was the one who made sure I'd never tell him.

It was Tuesday, and the club was quiet.

After a trip to the bathroom to yet again scream at myself to consolidate my stressed emotions, I entered the office where we were finishing some paperwork.

Fox sat at his desk, dressed in black, surrounded by black; he looked like the son of a scarred kind-hearted shadow.

Clara lay on her stomach, little legs flying, hands cupping her chin as she watched *Nemo* on the large flatscreen.

Fox looked up; a gentle smile graced his lips. "I'm done here. I was thinking we could all go out—maybe grab takeaway and watch the sunset?" He laughed. "Listen to me—never thought I'd say such a domesticated thing."

Clara looked over her shoulder, grinning. "I want fish and chips. But I don't want to eat *Nemo*, so make sure the fisherman doesn't kill him."

Fox shook his head, eyes glowing with love.

He'll make an amazing father.

I flinched, taking in the domestic bliss in front of me. Despite his touching issue, Fox was perfect. Strong enough to protect, wealthy enough to provide, fierce enough to love with everything bared.

His snowy eyes met mine, and my stomach tripped over itself. The message he sent was lust. He wanted me. For the past three nights, I'd sneaked into his room once Clara was asleep, and I let him tie my hands before giving me all of himself. He fucked me, but made love to me. He gave me sweet and gentle wrapped up in brutal violence.

My heart fluttered, responding to his unspoken request. I wanted him, too. Not just now, but for always.

I want this. All of it.

Forever.

My heart switched from fluttering weightlessly to plummeting like a stone. My eyes fell on Clara. I hated my sad thoughts. I despised the weakness and perpetual grief.

Nothing lasted forever. I just had to embrace every moment I could and prepare myself for pain at the end. I would miss her like I would miss my own soul, but I would live on.

I would be the universe for another child who needed me.

The pregnancy had thrown my world off balance, and I hadn't found my feet in this new gravity.

Fox deserved to know about the new life inside me—perhaps it would be enough for him to keep his sanity when Clara was gone.

You know that's not true. Not possibly true.

Clara would rip a chunk of our hearts out, and we'd never be the same. My shining star would burn out and leave us in the dark.

Roan stood, pushing his chair back. The energy in the room increased as he moved toward me. My skin sparked in anticipation of his touch; my body warmed, preparing for his possession.

And then it shattered.

Clara coughed. Nothing huge, nothing scary or major. I thought nothing of it.

But the silence afterward sent icicles stabbing into my flesh. My eyes flew to her, almost in slow motion.

More icicles stabbed my limbs, drawing forth agony and

terror.

Clara's legs went from kicking in the air to sprawled, her little elbows gave way, and her head thunked against the carpet.

"No!" *Shit.*

Shoving past Roan, I threw myself onto the carpet and gathered her rigid form into my arms. Her little body was a plank of rigid wood. Her eyes rolled back, white and vacant. Her lips opened and closed fruitlessly trying to drag oxygen into her body.

"What the fuck?" Fox slammed to the floor beside me. His large presence crowded me, making me claustrophobic.

"Get back. She can't breathe!" I hoisted her torso upright, willing her to suck in a breath. "Come on, sweetheart. Come on. You can do it. Please. Not yet. Come on." Her lungs wheezed and clattered as a smidgen of air got through.

"Give her to me," Fox demanded, shoving me aside to spread Clara onto her back. I toppled sideways, tears distorting my vision. "Call 111." His blazing blizzard eyes met mine. "Go!"

Scrambling to my feet, I ran back to the room I shared with my rapidly fading daughter and upended the bag Clue had packed for us. Clothes, toiletries, and cuddly toys went flying. "Where is it? Where the fuck is it?"

I shoved aside items frantically until my fingers latched around the asthma inhaler. Charging upright, I raced back to the office.

Fox had one hand pinching her nose while he breathed a lungful of air into Clara's mouth. Her chest rose, then fell as he leaned back and pressed the heel of his hand against her bony chest.

"That won't work. She needs this. She needs the medicine." I shoved his shoulder, causing him to shoot a hand out to stay upright. His back tensed as he fought whatever urges he dealt with.

Positioning my hand behind her neck, I looked into Clara's rolling, panicked eyes. "Suck in, okay? You know how to do this." A flicker of life returned to her gaze, and I pushed the inhaler past her blue-tinged lips.

Fox looked like a black-hole beside me, trembling with rage and dread.

"What's happening to her?" he growled.

Ignoring him, I pressed the trigger, administering a cloud of medicine into Clara's mouth. She wheezed, gulping what she could.

But it wasn't enough.

Hot scalding fear replaced my blood as her little hand clawed at her throat. Her lips turned from blue to indigo.

"Lay her down," Fox snapped.

"She can't breathe like that!"

"Just do it!" Fox yanked Clara from me and placed her on her back again. Planting his massive scarred hand over her chest, he pushed down hard. Glaring, he ordered, "Do it again."

With shaking hands, I placed the inhaler in Clara's lips and stabbed the plunger. Fox slowly removed the pressure from Clara's chest, effectively dragging the medicine into her lungs by manual force.

A second ticked past, then another.

"One day, when I grow up, I want to be a doctor, so I can stop people coughing like me."

The memory came and went so fast, I barely acknowledged it. But my heart died with terror—I couldn't let her go. *No!*

I couldn't stand it. I had to give her another dose. I had to save her.

Then the silence was broken by her spluttering and sucking in greedy lungfuls of oxygen. She lurched off the carpet like a drowning survivor, drinking in air as fast as she could.

I slumped in massive relief, then sucked back tears as a bout of coughing hit, reminding me this time she'd stayed alive. But the next or the next...

Don't think about it.

All I cared about was that she was alive and breathing again.

I needed to stay strong and not focus on the unchangeable future.

Awareness filled Clara's eyes and tears welled. She reached for me, and I dragged her into my lap. "I don't like it, mummy. When will it stop?"

My stomach clenched. I sat rocking, peppering her forehead with kisses. "You're okay. It's alright. Breathe."

Clara's breathing slowly changed from rattling to smooth, and she rested her heavy head on my shoulder. Her body heat comforted me—reminding me I hadn't lost her yet.

I didn't know how much time passed as I drowned in memories of her. The joy on her face when I painted our bedroom with purple horses, the way her face screwed up when she sneakily stole a sip wine. Everything about her had been three dimensional animation. And it killed me to watch her fade to crackling black and white.

A lone tear slid down my face as I rocked and stared into the past. I lost track of where I was. I lost track of Fox. All I focused on was my slumbering daughter, balled tight and fragile in my arms.

My arms couldn't hold her hard enough. I wished all my health and strength could filter into her through osmosis. I cursed God that I couldn't trade my life for hers. The lump of terror that'd replaced my heart hung heavy and unbeating in my chest.

I jumped a mile when a shadow prowled in front of me. Fox dragged his hands through his hair, pacing with fury that sparked in the gloom around him. "I've given you time. I've sat here for the past hour watching you rock your sick child to sleep. I told myself to leave. To let you have time together. I've told myself I shouldn't care this much for a child that I've only just met. I've told myself so many fucking things…"

He stopped and faced me with furious features. "But then I stopped telling myself things and decided I would stay. I decided that no matter what happens, I belong to you and that little girl, and I have the right to know what the *hell* is going on."

Pointing at Clara fast asleep in my arms, he growled, "Start speaking. I know there's something wrong with her, and I know you've been keeping it from me. Fuck, Hazel, even the kid knows she's on limited time, yet you thought you could hide it from me?"

Clara made no move to wake, but I pressed a hand over her ear. "Keep your voice down."

He scowled. "She's not going to hear me. Can't you tell the difference between normal sleep and sleep so deep you wouldn't hear an atomic bomb explode? No? Well, why would you after your perfect life instead of being a prisoner where every sleep you rested like the dead hoping, *praying*, that you'd never wake up."

His anger whipped me until I felt sure I bled from lacerations. He cut my soul just like Clara tore out my heart. "Don't make me tell you. Not with her in my arms."

Please.

I knew it was coming. I knew it would happen. I'd tried to prepare, to face the end with strength and even a trace of bittersweet happiness at the thought of her no longer being in pain. But I hadn't been strong enough.

Sucking in a breath, I muttered, "I'll tell you, but give me time."

Keeping his voice low, he whisper-shouted with pent-up rage. "No more time, *dobycha*. Now. I want answers. *Now.*"

What could I say? I knew this day would come; I had hoped I could pick the opportunity and circumstance, which was ridiculous considering Clara had so very little time. I had so much to tell him.

Time had run out. For all of us. It wasn't fair. None of it. A man I loved hated me. A child I adored was leaving me. I just wanted to lie down and indulge in waves of self-pity.

He'll hate me.

But he deserved to know. I should've told him the night he shared his story. That would've been the correct thing to do.

I waited for the crushing guilt of keeping it from him, but a chill entered my bloodstream, granting an eerie peace instead. I was numb. Numb to the new life inside me. Numb to what Fox would say.

The only thing that entered my self-imposed numbness was my anger and grief about Clara.

"I'm going to own a horse when I grow up. Lots and lots of them. Including Pegasus." Clara's sweet voice ran around my head.

I looked up into his blizzard eyes. It was time for the truth. Time to break Fox's heart.

He leaned over me, looking menacing and cold. His energy slapped me with seething anger. "Tell me."

Before I could open my mouth, he stormed away and dragged another hand over his face. "Look, I'm sorry for being so fucking angry, and I want to console you and fucking support you—but you've been keeping this from me and I'm pissed."

Spinning around, he faced me like a black hurricane. "So tell me the truth. What the fuck is wrong with her?"

I tried to stay strong, but angry tears leaked from the corner of my eyes. Making sure my hand was tight across her little ear and her eyes remained closed in sleep, I snarled, "She has PPB."

"And what the fuck is that?" Fox growled.

Don't say the C word. Don't say it. It'll make it true. Pretend. Forgot.

"It's short for Pleuropulmonary Blastoma. She's—"

Fox froze. "Cancer?"

I hung my head, fighting the tears, cursing my wobbling frame. Sucking a deep breath, I spat out the entire truth, the history, the fear, reeling it off as fast as I could. "I told you I bought her the star necklace on her fourth birthday. I couldn't afford it, but I had to buy it. That was the first day she was admitted to the hospital from a coughing fit. She was so scared. So freaked out. After she was discharged, I would've done anything to battle away the terror in her eyes from almost suffocating to death.

"The next time was only a few months later. She'd gone from a healthy toddler to active child who would suddenly collapse in a coughing fit. She was diagnosed with severe asthma. We were given inhalers and oxygen purifiers and told to avoid certain foods. And for a while, it seemed to work.

"A few years went by with the occasional episode and two more journeys to the ER. Clara was a trooper. Never complaining, so strong willed and amazingly happy considering she had an array of tablets and inhalers to take and use every morning."

I stopped. My lip wobbled, and I bit down on it, drawing blood, focusing on the pain. It helped mask the agony of remembering that day only a month ago.

Fox dragged his hands through his hair. "Go on. Don't stop. I want to know all of it."

"A month ago, Clara collapsed and the usual emergency inhaler didn't work. She was announced clinically dead in the ambulance as we tore to the hospital. They managed to bring her back, but stole her from me for hours to perform tests. I had no idea what they were doing with her. I threatened to burn the hospital to the ground if they didn't let me see her."

I shook my head, remembering the exact afternoon as if it replayed in perfect detail before me. "Clara sat up in bed slurping on red Jell-O. She was awake, rosy cheeked, and happy. All my debilitating fear disappeared, and I felt as if life had finally given me good news. I'd done endless research on asthma in children and a lot of them grow out of it as they get older. I stupidly thought that the episode signalled the end, and she would never have another one again.

"That was before the doctors took me into another room and told me my daughter was dying." My hands clenched and all the rage I'd bottled-up exploded.

I glared at Fox, not caring my cheeks were stained with tears. I wanted to kick and punch and kill. "That was the day they told me they fucking misdiagnosed my child. That she had

Pleuropulmonary Blastoma and the tumours had grown so big they were suffocating her day by day. They said operating wasn't an option as it'd spread to other parts of her body. They said the only choice was chemo, and that would only extend her life by a few months. They said they were fucking sorry and offered me counselling. They spoke about her as if she was already dead!"

Fox hadn't moved. His body looked immobile, locked to the carpet. His eyes flashed with such livid anger I feared he'd track down the doctors and kill them himself.

"That was the day I died. I accepted your contract for a stupid fantastical dream of a trial drug in America. Something that has the power to reduce white blood cells and stop the cancer from spreading. But even if it worked, Clara is riddled with it. It lives in her blood. Killing her every second. That's why I agreed to sell myself to you. That's why I kept coming back. And that's why I didn't want to tell you. I didn't want to admit my daughter was dying and I couldn't save her. No matter what hope I chased I would fail."

Fox tore his eyes from mine, pacing to the mural of the black fox on the wall. His hands opened and closed by his thighs. "How long?"

My throat closed up.

"Mummy, when I'm old enough, do you think I can have a puppy?"

Everything Clara ever wanted was in the future. When she was old enough. When she'd grown up. I never had the heart to tell her that there would be no Pegasus or puppy or university education.

Shit, I couldn't do this. I would never be ready to say goodbye.

He spun to face me. "How fucking long, Hazel?"

Steeling every muscle in my body, I voiced Clara's death sentence. "A few months."

"Fuck!" Fox whirled around and punched the wall so hard his fist disappeared through the painting. "And you didn't think to tell me? You didn't think I ought to fucking know? For fuck's sake! I'm in love with that little girl! You allowed me to fall head over fucking heels knowing full well I was about to lose the one thing curing me. She's the key to fucking healing me, and you tell me she's about to die!"

"Shut up!" I glared at him almost suffocating Clara in my arms. "Enough!"

Fox ignored me. Thumping his chest, he winced in agony. "You gave me everything, and I stupidly thought I had a future. A fucking family. I had something to strive for. Something to fight for. I was doing it all for her!"

He charged toward me, the harbinger of death and destruction.

I braced myself for his wrath. *Kill me. Then I don't have to watch her die.*

He glared, looking so strong and invincible. Then something cracked inside him. He transformed from a broken, livid male to an unfeeling, unthinking machine. He willingly gave himself to the ruthless conditioning of his past—shutting down his hard won emotions.

The ease of which he regressed terrorized me. I screamed, "Don't go back. Don't give up. You love her. Don't abandon her when she needs you the most." *Don't abandon me.*

Fox laughed coldly. "You think I'm abandoning her? Goddammit, I'm protecting her. You've torn my fucking heart out. How am I supposed to trust myself feeling so empty and alone? It's Vasily all over again. Everyone I fucking love dies!"

"Mummy?"

My heart dropped into my toes, and I looked down to see a groggy Clara blinking in confusion. "Why is your hand over my ear?"

I laughed through the sudden onslaught of tears. "No reason, sweetheart." I removed my palm, clenching my fingers around the heat residue from touching her. She looked worn out, pale, and entirely too thin. Her lips had never lost their blue tinge and she felt frail, unsubstantial, as if her soul had already begun the journey to leave.

My body seized. *No…*

"When I grow up, I want a sister. I want to dress her, play with her, and teach her all about horses."

I couldn't breathe past the rock in my throat.

Clara's brown eyes flickered upward to Fox. "Were you fighting?"

Fox immediately dropped to his haunches, reaching out to take her tiny hand. "No, Clara. We weren't fighting." His eyes swirled with hurricanes and snow, glistening with rage and misery. "Just talking. That's all, little one."

She sucked in a wheezy, unfulfilling breath. Another cough bombarded her small frame. "Good. I don't want you to." Her eyes closed again, and we stayed frozen. I dared to hope she'd fallen asleep, but her little lips parted and a darker tinge of blue returned.

My heart ripped itself out, vein by vein, artery by artery as my body prickled with foreboding. She'd never looked so wraith-like, so ghost-like, so…

You can't have her. Not yet. Not yet! I yelled in my head, wishing I could go head-to-head with the powers that be. *I need more time. I'm not ready.*

Her liquid eyes re-opened. "Mummy?"

A gut-wrenching moan escaped my lips, before I cleared my throat and forced my terror away. The part of me unbound by earth—the spiritual part—knew the doctors had my daughter's lifespan wrong once again.

There would be no more months. No more days.

"When I grow up, I want to be just like you, mummy. You're my best-friend forever and ever."

I couldn't explain the crushing, debilitating weight that took up residence in my chest. Horror scattered down my spine as tears prickled my eyes. "Yes, sweetheart." I kissed her forehead, threatening away tears, drinking in her fading warmth.

"Do you think Roan would like my star? I can't take it with me."

Ah, fuck.

No. No. No.

I gathered her closer, rocking, choking on relentless tears. I hated everything in that moment. Every doctor. Every hope. I hated life itself. "You can give it to him when you've had a good night's rest, Clara. Don't fret about it now." I kissed her again, inhaling her apple scent into my lungs.

"When I'm older I'll look after you, mummy. Just like you look after me."

Her eyes suddenly popped wide, looking intelligent and almost otherworldly. She stared right at Roan as if she saw more than just a scarred man, but a broken boy from his story.

A large cough almost tore her from my arms. Once it passed, she gasped, "Don't fight with mummy, okay? And you can have my star."

Roan cleared his throat; his entire body etched with sorrow. His jaw clenched while his eyes were blank, hiding whatever he might be suffering. The scar on his cheek stood out, silver-red against the paleness of his face. "Okay, little one." His large hand came forward and rested on her head.

Clara smiled and her eyes held Roan's before coming to rest on mine. Something passed between us—something older and mystical than an eight-year-old girl. I saw eternity in her gaze and it shattered me as well as granted peace. She truly was a star. A never ending star.

"I love you, Clara. So very, very much," I whispered, kissing her nose.

She sighed. "I'm tired. I'm just going to go to sleep now." Clara shifted in my arms as another cough stole her last bit of air.

"When I grow up, I'll never be sad or lonely or hungry. And I'll make sure no one else suffers either."

I had never held anything as precious as my daughter as her soul escaped and left behind a body that'd failed her. Something deep inside me knew the very moment she left, and I wanted nothing more than to follow.

My own soul wept and tore itself to smithereens at the

thought of never hearing her giggle or see her smile again. There would be no more talk of growing up or planning a future that had barely begun.

It was like a candle snuffing out. A snowflake melting. A butterfly crashing to earth. So many beautiful things all perishing and ceasing to exist in one cataclysmic soundless moment.

I didn't shout. I didn't curse. There was nothing to fight anymore.

It was over.

My daughter was dead, and Fox hadn't moved a muscle. His heavy hand stayed on her head, fingers playing with strands of faded hair.

Silent tears glided down my cheeks. I never stopped rocking, holding the last warmth of my daughter's body.

"Mummy, would you be sad if I left?" The memory came from nowhere and I curled in on myself with pain. *"Yes, sweetheart. I'd be very sad. But you know how to stop me from feeling sad, don't you?"*

Her little brow puckered. "How?"

I scooped her up and blew raspberries on her tiny belly. "By never leaving me."

I traced her every feature, from her heart-shaped face and full cheeks, to her dark eyelashes and blue lips.

"You left me," I whispered. "You made me sad."

Fox made a heart-wrenching noise in his chest and stood quickly. Staggering, he looked as if he would pass out. "This can't happen. It can't."

His entire body trembled, hands open and closing, eyes wide and wild. He looked completely and utterly destroyed.

He needed soothing. He needed to let his grief out. He needed to find healing not just for Clara's death but his awful past. But I had no reserves to console him. I had nothing left to give.

Fox looked at Clara one last time and every ounce of humanness, every splash of colour that Clara had conjured in him faded to grey, to black. "It isn't fucking fair. It wasn't supposed to happen. Not like this. Not so soon. Not like this!"

His rage battered me like a heavy squall and I couldn't do it. I needed to remain in a little cocoon of serenity where I could say goodbye to my wonderful daughter. Hunching over Clara's body, I shut him out. I opened the gates to my grief and let myself be swallowed by tears.

"I don't want you to be sad, mummy. So I'll never ever, ever leave you."

The memory brought a tsunami of tears, and I lost all meaning of life as I tried to chase my daughter into the underworld. My ears rang as Fox howled and every good and redeemable thing in him died.

There was nothing left to say. Nothing I could do to change what had happened.

Turned out, I couldn't save either of them.

"I can't do this. I can't—" Fox snapped with the brittle rage. He left in a flurry of shadows and sin, leaving me to pick up the broken pieces of my completely shattered life.

Eighteen
ROAN

I thought my darkest hour was the moment I killed my brother. It took the agency months to break me. I withstood hours upon hours of torture, all so I could drag out my brother's life.

But in the end, I'd done what they asked—not to prove my cold-heartedness and obedience, but because death was a better existence for him. Frostbitten, drowning with pneumonia, he'd wasted away from a bright, intelligent boy to a bag of rattling bones.

I'd put him out of his misery, hoping someone would do the same for me.

But I'd live that day a thousand times over to avoid watching Clara die.

She stole my will to live.

She stole my humanity.

I no longer wanted to fight.

I wanted to go Ghost and forget.

About everything.

I needed to inflict pain.

I needed to be inflicted.

I needed the sweet salvation of agony.

I needed to fucking die.

Anything. I would've accepted anything to be free of the revolving horror in my head.

She's dead.

It's over.

She hadn't fucking cured me. She destroyed me. She took every good part left inside and stole it when she took her last breath.

I couldn't handle seeing Zel come apart wrapped around her daughter. I couldn't fathom the intolerable agony I would inflict if tried to console her.

Fuck, this conditioning!

Every part of me hummed with confusion. I wanted to fight. But I wanted to hold Hazel and wipe away her tears. I wanted to murder. But I wanted to scoop up the body of Clara and share my life with her. I wanted a miracle. I wanted to be fucking free so I could be there for the woman I loved.

But you're a machine. Love and touch aren't permitted. They would never be fucking permitted.

As much as I wanted to fall to my knees and wrap my arms around the two most important people in my life, I couldn't. One touch and I'd kill. My mind wasn't strong enough to override my training. And that shredded me, stole all my hope, and plummeted me into the dark.

Kill. Sever. Bleed. Devour.

Violent anger squeezed my muscles until I shuddered with the need to kill. I'd been around death—it reminded me of my past and my true identity.

I gripped my skull. I refused to regress. I refused to slip down the slide back into Ghost.

"My sheep!" Clara's voice sprang into my head, making me howl in heartbreak. She'd gone. She'd left me. She'd taken all

my progress, all my happiness with her.

I was nothing without her. *Nothing.*

I skipped over sadness and went straight to rage. My life was a fucking joke. Full of injustice and unfairness and every fucked up circumstance. Time and time again fate played with me—granting me a sliver of hope before crushing it completely and leaving me in despair.

I couldn't stop thinking about Clara. Her collapsing. The wheezing. The sweet innocent taste of her as I forced oxygen into her failing lungs.

She broke my fucking heart, looking at me with terrified eyes, begging me to help her.

"Please, Roan." Vasily's blue eyes met mine, swimming with tears and fear. "I'm so cold, brother."

The flashback exploded as my ears echoed with the sounds of Clara choking, gasping, dying.

She'd been the colour my life was missing. She splashed me in yellows and oranges; she turned my black soul into a riot of rainbows. And now her light was gone, leaving me in the dark once again.

"That's it, Operative Fox. You know who you are. Fight us no more."

Hazel.

After everything she'd given me, I couldn't go back. I wasn't strong enough to ride through the storm of sadness—I couldn't be there for her.

Everything I'd worked so hard for didn't matter anymore. What was the point when all the good things in my life were stolen anyway? No matter how much I tried, I couldn't cure illness or bring loved ones back to life.

I couldn't change the past—just like I couldn't change the future. It was written in stone, crushing my bones, wrapping me in chains that I'd only just begun to shed.

"What is a Ghost, Operative Fox?" My handler stood above me, pacing my cell.

I clenched my teeth. I didn't want to answer.

He kicked me, growling, "Answer me. What is a Ghost? What is your only purpose?"

Huddling into myself, I answered, "To kill."

"Kill who?"

"Anyone who our clients wish to die."

"And that makes you?"

"An assassin."

My handler clasped his hands in front of him. "That's right, Operative Fox. You are a highly trained, highly specialized assassin. Your life is ours. Your only task is to carry out orders from governments, individuals, and anyone else rich enough to buy your services. You are ruthless. You are merciless. We made you this way. You are a Ghost."

The conditioning I'd been running so hard from opened its sinister arms, welcoming me back. It was like slipping into well-worn clothing, still warm from when I had shed them. I hated how easy it was to revert. How all my struggles meant nothing. They were right. They fucking owned me. Always had. Always would.

Kill. Sever. Bleed. Devour.

The urge to kill returned with a vengeance. There was nothing I could do to prevent it. Seeing Clara die had reminded me of my purpose. My one and only purpose.

I need to fight.

I need to draw blood.

I need to kill.

I needed a victim. If I didn't kill and accept my heritage, I'd explode into a billion fragments, raining blood and bone.

"You thought you were free?"

I looked up at the walls of the dank pit I'd spent the last two nights in. I'd tried to run like a fucking pussy, but they caught me. Just like every time.

"You know there's no escaping us, Fox. The sooner you give in, the easier life will be for you." He kicked some snow from around the hole, landing on my freezing body. "Say you'll obey, and you can come back inside."

The thought of warmth and food almost broke me, but I was a stupid, stubborn ten-year-old—I wouldn't give in.

I turned my back and didn't look up when he left.

That night was the first time I dragged a sharp stick across my arm, trying to find freedom from the impossibility of my life.

The flashback ended, and I bolted.

I couldn't be anywhere near Hazel. I wouldn't have the self-control. She'd already lost her daughter I didn't want to steal her life.

Kill. Sever. Bleed. Devour.

I had no control left. I was a machine. A Ghost. I'd been stupid to try and change my life path. I needed to purge. I needed pain. Agony. Torture. I couldn't live in a body while my soul tore itself into pieces.

Throwing myself down the stairs onto the floor of Obsidian, I searched the early arrivals.

You won't find redemption here.

My mind darted into the unknown, feeding me alternatives that I'd never thought of.

Go back. You've accepted who you are. Go back. Go home.

My hands clenched at the thought of returning to Mother Russia. Returning to the place where my life was ruined. I would renounce everything: turn my back on Hazel, admit I could never heal. Everything I'd fought so hard for was a complete fucking joke.

Ghosts didn't have families. Ghosts felt no pain.

So why am I in so much fucking pain?

My vision went hazy. I couldn't do it anymore. Hating myself for my weakness; flaring with shame for my needs, I grabbed a pen from my pocket and stabbed it into my palm.

The agony washed through me with a wave of heat, followed by prickles of release. It granted a small spotlight of rationality in the chaotic storm of confusion.

I knew what I had to do.

Kill. Sever. Bleed. Devour.

Zel owned me more than anyone, and I wouldn't survive without her. Clara had gone. Hazel was all I had left. I'd kept secrets from her. So many fucking secrets.

I wasn't worthy. I wasn't safe.

But I could change all that.

Kill. Sever. Bleed. Devour.

My heart died in my chest at the thought of betraying her. She would need me. She deserved a shoulder to cry on and another person to share the burden of grief. But I couldn't. Not yet. Not while I existed on the border of Ghost and sanity. I couldn't hug her. I couldn't console her pain.

The moment I let my guard down, I would snap her neck.

I couldn't give Zel what she needed. I wasn't whole.

And I meant to fucking deserve her.

My anger turned outward, focusing on the handlers who'd fucked up my life.

Kill. Sever. Bleed. Devour.

The conditioning throbbing in my brain was right. I needed to kill. And now I had my victim. I was done being an outcast. I was done not being normal.

I thought Clara had been my cure.

I was wrong.

The fucking cure was inside me all along. I held the key to fixing myself by returning to my past and annihilating them.

Kill. Sever. Bleed. Devour.

"Fuck this." I let down all my walls. I welcomed the ruthless conditioning with open arms. I smiled as the ice entered my limbs and filled my head with fog. I allowed my muscles to remember exactly what I'd been programmed to do.

I went Ghost.

And I lost myself.

Mother Russia.

The Iron Fist of a past I couldn't out run. Bleak and barren and home to my misery.

I only vaguely remembered how I got here. I bought every ticket in the first class cabin to ensure no one touched me. I locked myself into the freakish persona of an assassin and no one—not even the air hostesses came near me.

The moment I landed, I stole a 4WD to drive into the snowy wilderness. I said goodbye to no one. I just disappeared.

Kill. Sever. Bleed. Devour.

The conditioning throbbed harder and harder, recognising its place of origin. I was returning to my handlers and the training was fucking ecstatic to embrace the true machine I was.

I had no belongings apart from some cash, passport, and my memories, but that's all I needed. The establishment stole me when I had nothing, and I would return with nothing.

And then I'd make them fucking pay.

Over and over again.

I was ready to go rogue and dance in blood. The ice was back in my veins, howling like a Siberian winter. I'd embraced who I truly was—who they made me become.

"You're not a bad man. You can't be a bad man because I love you and well, I couldn't love a bad man." Clara's voice whipped around me with the artic wind.

I shook my head as a fresh, crippling wave of grief threatened to overshadow the rage. I couldn't let myself mourn. Not yet. Not when I had so much to do.

Kill. Sever. Bleed. Devour.

Sucking in a deep breath, I deliberately pushed Clara from my thoughts.

I stood on the perimeter of the establishment, hidden by thick trees. Thunder rumbled above, chasing jagged lightning, illuminating the compound in flashes of white.

My skin crawled beneath my black attire. Home. Hell. My place of birth from child to killer.

Snow flurried like icy tears—glistening in the dead of night, raining over the landscape and hiding a multitude of sins.

Russia was just like I remembered—frigid, ruthless, uninhabitable.

Kill. Sever. Bleed. Devour.

Australia, Hazel, Clara,—all of it seemed like a dream. I felt as if I'd never left this terrible wasteland and everything in me said to *run*.

Beneath the pulsating conditioning all I wanted to do was run far, far away and never look back. I didn't want to be here. I wanted to be fucking free from all of this.

My muscles tensed. *You will be free. Kill them all. Make them give you freedom by taking their fucking lives.*

Straightening my back, ignoring the howling wind and jagged teeth of frost, I prepared for battle. I would win tonight. I would take back what was mine.

"You always were a weakling, Fox. Got to beat that compassion out of you."

The flashback came from nowhere as I stared at the gargoyle embellished facility—so similar to the building I'd erected at home.

"You're no one to anyone anymore. You're an orphan, a drifter, an unknown. We are now your family, your shelter, your owners. Never forget that."

Rows upon rows of windows, containing cell upon cell of new recruits and old, glowed dimly in the night. My heart thundered to think how many more they'd ruined while I'd been gone.

"Time to work, Fox."

I rolled over, clenching my teeth against the broken radius in my left arm. I couldn't remember a thing.

My handler laughed. "Trying to recall what some dickshit paid you to do last night? You won't, Operative Fox. We programed you to forget. You're brainwashed to suffer short-term amnesia whenever you complete a mission. That way you cannot compromise yourself or us if you're ever caught. You cannot lie if you don't remember."

I wrapped my hands around my head, trying to squeeze the flashbacks from my thoughts. I couldn't go to war compromised. I had to stay clearheaded and be the ultimate Ghost.

A sudden image of Clara consumed me, almost bringing me to my knees. Her innocent smile, her intelligent eyes—all gone.

"Roan, don't fight with my mummy. She needs you."

My stomach snarled, tangling with my heart. I was a fucking bastard for leaving her. Abandoning her and Zel when she needed me most.

I couldn't breathe at the thought of never seeing Clara again. I'd never fight the horrible urge to kill such innocence again all while falling madly fucking in love with her.

Hazel replaced her daughter, taking me hostage. Her tears, her grief gripped my heart while the haunting sound of her wails danced on the wind. I hated that I wasn't there for her. I hated I wasn't man enough, strong enough.

Kill. Sever. Bleed. Devour.

Blinking, I forced them both from my thoughts. They had no place here. Nothing else existed but the machine I was and the bloodbath I was about to indulge in.

Balling my hands, I took a step out of the tree line. Exposed in the cleared snowy moat of land around the house, I shed everything but my mission. I ceased to be Roan. I ceased to be heartbroken by a little girl's death. I ceased to hate myself for not being there for the mother.

For this mission, I was nameless.

I was Karma. I was Fate.

I ran.

The backdoor, fortified with iron that I helped maintain, and a lock I helped design, barred my entry. Scraps littered the snow from dinner and trails of blood drifted off into the distance where local wolves took recruits that hadn't made the cut.

I might have turned blind from a psychological issue to avoid more horror, but others—they just shut down. Nothing reached them. Not even the threat of death.

Picking up a rock resting by the door, I smashed the hinges

with all my strength. I'd never be able to crack the lock, but the hinges—they were old and weather-worn. Wood splintered and groaned mixing with the howling wind.

By the time the door creaked open, my hands were bloody and I shook uncontrollably from ice.

I weaved through shadows, breaking into the one place I'd always tried to break out of. It was dark and late and no one was around. Dancing around tripwires and avoiding alarms, I moved deeper into Hell.

I infiltrated an operation so cocky and arrogant, they never thought to fear one of their own coming back to end them. They were so self-assured, believing their human weapons were subservient and loyal to the end.

They had it wrong.

No one wanted to be there.

No one wanted to serve in purgatory.

Kill. Sever. Bleed. Devour.

My first stop was the armoury. A range of knives, blades, and other equipment lay as I remembered from two years ago. The anvil was the same. The stench of sweat and metal the same. But there were new items, too. The finesse not as refined, the lines not as straight. The smithy had been the only place where I'd found a smidgen of peace.

"I want you, Fox. I want to touch you." Hazel's voice rang in my ears, buckling my heart. I wanted so fucking much for her to touch me, to not have to deal with the shit inside my head.

The fucking bastards had to die. It was my only chance at freeing myself forever. My last hope for a cure. My last chance at happiness with a woman I desperately wanted to hug and protect.

I stood over a pile of weapons, taming my rapid heartbeat. I wanted to inflict pain. After all, I was a fucking Ghost.

I collected crescent moon blades, a silenced pistol, and a hammer I used so often to beat metal into submission.

That was all I needed.

My breathing calmed, my muscles bunched in preparation,

and I slunk like the demon I was down unforgotten corridors. No spike of emotion. No residual humanity. I embraced the ice.

Kill. Sever. Bleed. Devour.

The witching hour was mine and I snuck into the first unseen bedroom, morphing with the dark. I didn't know who'd created the society of Ghosts, or who bought our services. Some missions had been politicians, other movie starlets. There was no rhyme to who we killed—if they had money, they could buy us. We were purely guns for hire and it was time to burn the fucking place to the ground.

The first man I stood over wasn't significant. I wasn't in his realm of minions. He was handsome, well-built, and fast asleep like a fucking angel. But he was a ruthless dictator just like the rest—profiting on others pain and misery.

I pressed one hand over his mouth.

His eyes flew wide, confusion smothering.

He squirmed and his hands came up to touch me.

It was instantaneous. To be inflicted is to inflict.

Kill. Sever. Bleed. Devour.

I bowed to the command for the first time in two fucking years.

With precision and an emotion almost described as serenity, I dragged the sharp blade over the gristle and tendons of his throat.

Instantly, warm, coppery blood sprang from his body in a brutal cascade. His eyes wrenched wider, his mouth snapped below my palm, and he thrashed around in death throes.

His heart pumped rapidly toward death and the stench of his bowels loosening serenaded him from living to corpse.

I left his grave and returned to the hunt. The hunt for evil. He was the first to die, but definitely not the last. I gave myself completely to the sweetness of killing. I threw myself into my task and everything else ceased to exist. Time blurred, blood flowed, and men died like fucking flies.

Room after room, I entered and dispatched. Five with the

silenced gun. Seven with a blade. Two with the hammer. Four with my bare hands.

The night belonged to death, and I was the executioner.

The eighteenth handler died just before daybreak. His final cry petered out, smothered by my hand, and I stood upright rolling my shoulders.

The conditioning pulsed behind my eyes and I could barely feel my extremities. My body had become an instrument of carnage and I didn't focus on the splatter of blood or other human tissue covering my clothing.

Stalking down the corridor, I knew I wouldn't find my handler in this wing. He always slept alone on the opposite side of the compound. He was the next to die. He was my final trophy.

I savoured the anticipation and prowled through the dwelling, suffering blending memories of Obsidian and here. Every door looked the same, the length of corridor the same. I kept expecting to see Oscar appear or Clara bolting toward me.

"You're not a bad man."

Clara had that wrong. I was the worst sort of man: I was a murderer.

Instead of rushing to finish my mission, I stopped to look at the cells. I couldn't let them die behind locked doors when I snuffed out the final handler. Retracing my steps, I headed to the heart of the house where the alarm system rested along with the security mainframe that kept every keypad lock secure on the cells.

With my blade, I stabbed it into the main console and severed power to the rest of the compound.

Instantly, alarms erupted, screaming a warning, shredding the silence of the dawn.

Rushing back upstairs, I passed children, teenagers, and adults as they shuffled out of their rooms. Recruits and operatives, all in different stages of training looked bewildered but with a small spark of hope in their eyes.

The ones who knew me nodded in silent respect before

charging down the stairs and out into the freezing wilderness. The ones who didn't were coaxed by others to leave.

It only took a few minutes before the entire establishment was an empty tomb.

Another minute until the person I was on my way to see, found me. I didn't hear him arrive, but I sensed him.

Kill. Sever. Bleed. Devour.

The hair on my neck stood up on end as I spun to face my nemesis. My handler stood behind me, hands on his hips, his perfect face looking like a flawless sculpture. He was blond and beautiful, but beneath his perfection lurked oil and ink and filth for a soul.

My heart bucked, sending thickening fear through my blood. The conditioning stuttered and failed when faced with the one man who was king over me.

"If it isn't Operative Fox. I see you disobeyed orders once again and didn't swallow your last task." He cocked his head. "And you're no longer blind. Interesting."

I didn't say anything. Clamping my lips shut, I swallowed my terror and stood my ground.

This man had hurt me more than anyone and the conditioning crunched my spine, ordering me to bow to him. To grovel for forgiveness.

"I love you, so you can't be a bad man." Clara's sweet voice pierced through my fog, giving me something to latch onto. I wouldn't let him win. Not this time.

He suddenly laughed. "How did you pull that trick, Fox? I must say. Very inventive."

I clenched my hands around the hunting knife. "No trick. You warped my mind so badly, my brain decided it no longer wanted the gift of sight. You drove many of us mad with what you made us do."

Clucking his tongue, he shook his head. "Always so dramatic." He paced forward a couple of steps, closing the distance between us. Holding out his hand, he growled, "Give me the blade, Operative Fox. Return to your cell immediately.

Punishment will be absolute after this heinous treason."

My legs spasmed with the compulsion to obey. I took a step back unable to ignore the conditioning forcing me to my old cell. It crippled my mind, took my limbs hostage. It was like fighting a puppet master holding all my fucking strings.

Closing my eyes, I thought of Obsidian and the man I'd become. I'd struck fear into the hearts of others. I'd become more than just an operative. That man wasn't afraid of this blond asshole.

I'm not afraid.

I forced my foot to move, followed by another.

"Obey me, Fox. Stand down."

I groaned, clutching my stomach as a wash of sickness filled me. *Obey. Obey. Obey.* Once again, the conditioning buckled my body, making me groan. I belonged to him and it hurt— fucking ~~hurt~~—to disobey.

Gritting my teeth, hating the white smog settling over my eyes, I pressed forward another step. "Not this time."

Every shuffle rebooted my heart from thrumming with terror to thudding with an entirely different beat. One that craved blood. I had violence running in my veins and another's life-force on my hands. He might have butchered and tortured me, but ultimately he made me stronger. Strong enough to withstand him. Strong enough to end him.

"I'm fucking warning you, operative. Take one more step, and I'll slaughter you where you stand."

The conditioning rushed me like a swarm of wolves, tearing savagely at my body. *Obey. Obey. Obey.*

I locked my legs into position. Fighting. Battling. Winning. Then I took another step.

My handler bared his teeth, eyes livid. "One more fucking move and I'll let the bears have you."

Only a foot between us. Our heights were even, our body size mirror images of each other. However, unlike the past, I was no longer his slave.

He was mine.

I struck.

Grabbing his neck, I squeezed with everything left inside me. "You no longer have the right to tell me what to do. You never had the right. You're the fucking devil for making me destroy my family, and it's time you returned to hell."

With cold eyes, he lashed out and a hot laceration erupted down my side. "It's not me who will die tonight."

I dropped him, and he scuttled back. Hunching into a crouch, he bared the knife still red from slicing me. "You don't stand a chance against me. I own you. Give up now and die like the traitor you are."

I snarled, "Never." Exploding forward, I threw away my weapons, and tackled him to the floor. We rolled and fought, grunting and growling. He struck twice with his blade, sending heat spilling down my side. I didn't feel the pain. I didn't acknowledge anything but the objective of killing.

"Pity you don't have any more family, Fox. We'd make them pay for your disobedience." He punched my jaw as we rolled. He got the upper hand and slammed my skull against the floor. Whispering in my ear, he said, "You always were a little bitch, Fox. Maybe I should fuck you and remind you of your place."

His hand slapped my ass, and my mind stretched to breaking point.

I snapped.

I hated this man. Hated. Fucking *hated*.

Kill. Sever. Bleed. Devour.

In the moment of choice between stealing a life and torturing a soul free from its mortal body, I switched from human to machine. I didn't want to dispatch him quickly. I wanted to make him pay. Pay for everything he'd done to me, to my loved ones, to countless other victims.

He would fucking pay for his trespasses and then he would burn in hell.

My mind shut down.

And I vanished into ruthless revenge.

I watched her.

From my place in the shadows, I watched the woman I wanted more than anything.

I didn't mean to stalk her. To follow in secret and witness her private sorrow, but I couldn't go to her. Time and time again, I tried to move my legs and walk to her, but I didn't trust myself. I wanted to wipe away her tears, and hold her. I wanted to rock and console her, but although I'd found hope, I hadn't found a cure.

My jaw gritted as my heart raced. Anger and frustration had replaced the iciness of the conditioning. After I'd finished with my handler and the massacre of three nights ago, I'd showered and dressed and bandaged my wounds. I'd boarded a plane and returned from frost to sunshine and hoped it was over.

Whenever I tried to recall that night, only fragments returned. I couldn't remember in detail what happened. I remembered walking over body parts and opening the doors wide so local scavengers could clean up my mess. I remembered a red cascade of blood sluice down the drain in the shower. Some of it mine, but most of it from my handler. I remembered the stench of fear coming from a man who'd brutalized me all my life. I remembered his screams, and the blessed relief I felt as the obedience of my past slowly unbound its tight web around me.

My conditioning weakened the moment he died. It was as if the orders in my head melted from blizzard to softly falling snow, granting a reprieve from the agony of ice.

I wanted to rejoice at my newfound freedom, but then I mourned because instead of being completely unhindered, I was only marginally free. The Ghost persona hadn't fully gone.

And I grieved everything I would lose because of it.

I would never be normal. I would never be able to fully relax and sleep harmlessly beside Hazel. I would always have to monitor my thoughts and actions.

I was fucking exhausted, and there was no respite in sight.

Behind my sunglasses, and hiding place by the cafe across the road, I watched as Hazel and Clue disappeared into a second-hand shop. I hated having her out of my sight.

For three nights and two days, I followed her. I slept outside her flat in my car. I had countless conversations with her in my head. I acted out exactly how I would go to her and how I would apologise. But every scenario didn't end well, and my confidence deserted me.

How could I say sorry for leaving when her daughter died? How could I beg forgiveness for being a man who would never be able to hold her?

So, I stayed in the dark and watched her go through the motions of life. She barely left the apartment and it gave me plenty of time to figure out how to do something—not for Hazel, but for Clara.

I used her love of horses as inspiration for her final resting place and I called the one person who I knew would execute my plan flawlessly all while being there for Zel.

When Clue answered the phone, I almost broke down and asked to talk to her. To murmur condolences and tell her how I felt, but I stayed focused and stuck to the plan. Clue had taken my offer with eager arms and within a day, she'd dragged Zel out of the house to make preparations.

With my heart racing, I charged across the street. Entering the second-hand shop, I made sure Hazel didn't see me and ducked behind shelving groaning with knick knacks and paraphernalia. A whiff of dust and ancient belongings filled my nose.

Clue and Hazel were at the back of the shop. I moved closer, staying hidden so I could hear what they said.

"How about this one, Zelly?" Clue held up a bright pink,

plastic pony with see-through wings.

Hazel smiled softly. "Yes. She always wanted a Pegasus."

Clue laughed quietly and reached out to hug her. "That's true."

They clung to each other.

My heart squeezed with jealousy. I cursed the unfairness—the fucked-up mind I lived with. It should be me holding her and sharing tales of a little girl taken too soon. But I was also grateful that Clue was there for her.

The two women parted, before rummaging around in a bin full of toys. Glittery ponies, bright blue and rainbow ponies—they came out and were placed into a basket.

"You know, I bet she's watching us right now and laughing."

Zel looked up, her skin dull with grief. "What do you mean?"

Clue smiled. "Well, she probably has a real Pegasus and unicorn by now. And she'll be laughing thinking how much we're missing out on. How silly these plastic things are." She flicked the tail of one glow in the dark horse.

Zel looked down at the yellow pony in her hands. "I like to think of her like that—surrounded by things she loves." She sniffed, giving a watery smile. "I know I've had time to prepare for her passing. I know the doctors told me what to expect and what stages of grief I would go through, but nothing fully prepares you for it."

Clue stopped rummaging and gave Zel her full attention.

"I keep thinking she's just around the corner. I'll see the tip of her hair disappearing around a building, or hear her voice on the breeze." Zel's eyes welled up and my heart shattered. "I keep hoping she'll come bounding home from school, or trail bubble bath all over the floor." She rubbed the centre of her chest as her voice turned thready with sadness. "I miss her so fucking much it hurts. It hurts in my head, my eyes, my back, my soul. It doesn't matter that I know she's in a better place. It doesn't make it any easier knowing she's no longer in pain."

Her eyes met Clue's, lost and in pain. "I don't—don't know how to go on." She hiccupped as a torrent of tears flowed down her cheeks. "It's so damn hard. So unfair to be the one left behind."

Clue scooted closer and gathered her into a huge hug. "Aww, Zel. It's okay." She stroked her hair, rocking just like Zel had done when Clara died. Clue began to cry silently. Even though she cried, she never stopped being strong for her friend. "You need to give yourself permission."

"Permission?" Zel pulled back, smashing at the tears on her cheeks.

Clue nodded. "The reason why you're hurting is because you're clinging to the past. You're not ready to face a future without her. And that's okay. It's okay to miss her, Zelly. You'll miss her every damn day, but you can't forget to live either."

She shook her head. "Clara wouldn't want you killing yourself with grief and I don't want it either. We both knew this was coming. You just need to find acceptance and rejoice in her life, rather than drown yourself wishing for a different outcome."

Zel blinked, sucking in a cleansing breath. "How are you coping? You're so strong. You're letting me lean on you so much."

Clue pulled away, rubbing Zel's arms. "I have Ben when it gets too much. He's been amazing. And even though there'll always be a hole in my heart where Clara used to be, I can't begrudge or scream at life for taking her. She taught me so much—she taught you so much. Hell, she even taught that asshole from Obsidian so much. Something as amazing as Clara doesn't last long. You have to come to terms with it; otherwise you'll never be happy again."

Zel sniffed and anger filled her eyes, muting out the sorrow. "I can't believe he left. He left me crying over my dead daughter and couldn't even bring himself to stay." Zel balled her hands, clutching the yellow horse. "Clara may have died that day, but he proved to me I can't rely on anyone. I survived on my own and I was stupid to let him in. He made me hope. He made me rely on him. He made her death so much harder because I thought I would be able to share it with him. Find comfort together. But he was a spineless coward."

Clue bit her lip. "Don't judge until you know the full story, Zelly. He might have a good reason."

Zel laughed coldly. "Of course he has a good reason. He can't touch. And I can't blame him. But it doesn't mean I can forgive him. I'm done with it all. I need to say goodbye to Clara, then find a fresh start."

I couldn't listen anymore. I backed away feeling as if my veins were open and spewing blood. She'd flayed me open, leaving my beating heart unprotected.

She would never be able to forgive me.

"You're not a bad man. I love you, so you can't be a bad man."

I earned the love of an eight-year-old, yet I couldn't earn the love of a woman I would fucking die for.

No matter what I did, it would never be enough to repair the past and give her what she ultimately needed: a man who could hold her and fight battles on her behalf. I was a fighter. An assassin and mercenary. I could be so many things for her. I just had to figure out how to be the rest.

"Stop fighting with my mummy. I don't want you to."

I swore on Clara's life I would find a way to be everything Zel needed. Every touch would still be torturous. Embraces almost a mythical dream. But it was possible, because I wouldn't stop until I made her mine forever.

I'd done everything I could to 'fix' myself, but I refused to face reality. The brainwashing was too deep inside me. Too imbedded in my psyche to ever let me go. However, the intensity had faded just enough. I had more power. Power over myself. Power over my thoughts. It was a beginning.

I will find a way.

I would fucking love Hazel and share her future and be there for her always.

Fox died the night of the Russian massacre.

Roan had been reborn.

Zel wanted a fresh start.

And I knew exactly what to do to make her wish come true.

Nineteen

Hazel

I thought I had space in my heart to love two people. To share my life with another. I thought I could love another child to ultimately replace the one I lost.

I thought Roan would change—that Clara would show him a way to be human. I thought even though a tragedy had happened, I would be able to cope.

I thought so many, many things, and they all turned out to be bullshit.

Turned out my heart wasn't a living, beating thing. It was made of concrete and lead and rock, destined to never love another or ever beat fully again.

Part of me died that day.

I wished I *had* died that day.

But I couldn't.

So I kept going.

Alone.

The funeral was held on a large piece of land just outside of

Sydney. I didn't know whose property it was. All I knew was horses existed everywhere. Paints, palominos, thoroughbreds, and Arabians. Their long noses and velvet soft ears squeezed my heart until I couldn't breathe. Clara would've loved it here. She would've hugged every horse, slept in the open fields, and begged never to leave.

It was the perfect place.

God, I miss you. The burn of tears that were never far away stabbed my eyes.

The rain that'd been a constant companion for a week stopped the moment we arrived. It was as if the mourning period had been put on hold to celebrate the life of one taken so young.

I'd existed in a fog all week. I didn't like to dredge up excruciating memories of Oscar finding me still holding Clara, or the hearse that came to take her away. I didn't like to recall the agony and tears of telling Clue that our little trio had been broken. I'd been terrified Clue would resort to self-harming again—to find a release—but I hadn't factored in the comforting presence of Ben.

Clue had been so amazingly strong. She'd held me while I broke. She'd cried with me and laughed with me. She kept me sane. And it was all because Ben was her pillar, feeding her strength, giving her the safe haven she needed.

Ben did for Clue what Fox should've done for me. I had no one to bury myself in or cry myself to sleep in their arms. I would always love Clue like a sister and could never have existed without her, but I needed…him. I needed his strength, his fight. I needed his anger and even his fuckedupness. Instead, he left me to fumble all alone and proved just what an asshole he was.

Ben kept me alive the past week. He held us until we almost passed out from tears. He gathered us close and gave us a rock to cling to while grief threatened to wash us away from this world.

He fed us when we forgot to eat, and he began our therapy

early. Instead of letting us wallow in sorrow, he found every painting Clara had ever created, every picture of her, every macaroni glued statue she'd done at school and made Clue and me tell him stories of my daughter.

He reminded us she would never be gone as long as we kept her alive in our thoughts, and we had to remember the good not the bad. We had to keep living for her.

A few days after Clara's death, Clue received a phone call that shot life back into her. She went from couch potato to a whirlwind of efficiency and threw herself into arranging the most perfect funeral any little girl could want.

I looked over at my non-blood sister. The breeze ruffled her straight black hair and tears glistened in her eyes. She nodded, feeling the same bond, the same need to remind ourselves we were there for each other.

"Thank you," I whispered. "For this. For everything."

"Don't thank me. There's someone else you should thank, too."

I looked over my shoulder at Ben. He looked regal and dapper in a black suit, black shirt, and the requisite My Little Pony badge over his heart. The funeral was in Clara's honour—and My Little Pony had been her favourite.

My heart squeezed hard, threatening to send me keeling over.

I can't do this.

I wrapped my arms tighter around myself, gathering the black mournful dress I wore and holding the shattered pieces of my heart.

Don't cry.

I'd shed more tears the past week than I ever thought possible. I should've shrivelled into a husk with the amount of water I expelled. But no matter how much I wailed and cursed, I didn't feel better. The tears escaped, but my sorrow didn't. It sat festering in my soul, mixing with loneliness and slow building hatred for the man who'd left me when I needed him the most.

After everything I'd sacrificed for him. After everything I'd given him, he couldn't bring himself to even attend Clara's funeral. I'd not only lost my daughter forever, but him, too. I would never forgive him for leaving me to face this without him.

Not once did I think about the baby inside me. Not once did I turn to Clue or Ben and tell them the news. I wanted to forget. I wished I wasn't pregnant. I wanted life to stop and leave me the fuck alone. Nothing else existed but the death of my daughter.

"Don't feel sad, mummy. I don't want you to feel sad."

Sunshine suddenly pierced through the rolling grey clouds like a giant spotlight. The bright ray landed on a beautiful horse with a red-speckled coat and pink mane and tail. A roan.

My heart flopped thinking of a little red-haired boy who'd lost his entire family only to turn around and watch me lose mine. Where had he gone? What the hell was he doing?

What was more important than being here to say goodbye?

More rays of sun beamed through clouds, turning the rolling meadows into glittering green blades, swaying gently with the breeze. The horses glowed like equine jewels, and I knew this was the right place for Clara. Nowhere else would've fit.

I didn't know how Clue managed to find such an idyllic spot. I hadn't bothered to ask. If Clue hadn't helped me arrange everything, I would probably be mummified lying on Clara's bed staring at the ceiling.

"Come on, Zelly. It's about to start." Clue wrapped an arm around my waist. I gave her a watery smile and let her guide me to a small semi-circle of black-shrouded people.

Everyone wore a My Little Pony item and the flowers dotting the small group were arrangements of ponies of different colours. Some unicorns, some with wings, some glitter-filled, some glow in the dark.

Clue and I had scoured all the toy shops and second-hand sellers for as many My Little Ponies as possible. There were so many I had no idea what I'd do with them afterward.

The reverend began to talk, and I tuned out. Ignoring the small huddle of children from Clara's school and a few teachers who'd come to say goodbye, I stared at the horses. So powerful but delicate. So strong but gentle.

They hypnotised me as the service droned on and on. I didn't need to know how miraculous Clara had been. I'd lived it.

"I'm tired. I'm going to sleep now."

Finally, the reverend's sermon came to an end and arms went around me. I shut myself down, focusing only on the animals my daughter loved more than anything in the world. I couldn't stand people touching me, consoling me.

Once the final stranger had hugged me and a hushed expectation filled the air, I panicked.

I wasn't ready. I couldn't do this.

I'm not ready!

The reverend walked toward me, and I took a step back, shaking my head. He took my arms gently and laid the hand-painted urn in my hands.

It was cold and lifeless and my façade broke. A single tear streaked down my face knowing I would never hold Clara again. Never see her smile or laugh or grow.

"Don't be mad at him, mummy. He needs you."

My sadness switched to anger. Him. He did this. The man who loved my daughter so fiercely, he made the clock tick faster—take her quicker than I ever wanted.

My mind tried to tell me it was a blessing. That she'd gone before being paraded through hospitals or prodded by merciless doctors. She was free now. But the mother in me couldn't see it that way. It didn't matter that she was in a better place and eternal. All that mattered was she was dead.

And Fox ran.

Standing in the patch of sun, hugging the urn of my daughter's ashes, I tried to cry. I wanted to rain tears on the field just like the sky had before. I wanted to let every crushing thing inside out.

But nothing happened. I just existed in hell.

An image of a new child filled my mind. Instead of a little girl, I pictured a boy. An innocent infant who would never know his big sister. The picture stabbed my heart. I didn't want him. I didn't want the responsibility of loving something more than life itself only to run the risk of losing him just like Clara.

I didn't have the strength. My life had hit rewind and replay, leaving me at the beginning again with endless heartache, no future, and a baby growing inside me.

A horse flicked its tail and cantered forward. The burst of life cast away my worry of the future, and I turned inward. I wasn't ready, but it was time to say goodbye.

Closing my eyes, I whispered, "I wish you hadn't left me. I wish you were still here. I can't go on without you. I can't live without you near. How am I supposed to go on, Clara? How am I supposed to survive?"

The build-up of emotion crushed my head until I thought I'd explode. Opening my eyes, I stroked the urn, tracing the explosion of stars on the glazed porcelain.

"I'll never forget your perfect laugh or your smiling face. I'll never stop loving your silly jokes or your warm embrace. I'll always be here for you even though you're gone. Until the day we meet again, until my life is done."

Clue came to my side, jerking me back to the present. I looked behind me. Only Ben stood sentry. The rest of the congregation had gone. How long had I been standing there, hugging the last remains of my daughter?

"Don't be sad, mummy. I don't like it when you're sad."

"It's time to let her go, Zelly." Clue laid a hand on the top of mine. "We can do it together."

A low moan rose in my throat, but I allowed Clue to unlatch my arms and share the weight of the urn. I wanted to stop her. I wanted to curl up on the ground and petrify like a fossil curled around Clara's ashes, but Clue didn't give me a choice.

Her eyes met mine, spilling with tears. "She'll be happier with the horses, Zel. Don't make her stay in such a small, dark place." She sniffed as a fresh wave of tears trickled down her beautiful face. "It's time."

It took everything I had not to break down and unravel. To tear the jar from her and leap onto a horse's back and gallop far away. Run from this reality. Pretend it wasn't true.

Placing one hand on the bottom of the jar and the other cradling the top, I waited for Clue to do the same. She leaned in and kissed my cheek before nodding.

My heart stopped beating as together we tipped the urn upside down.

A grey cloud fell like icing sugar, and my heart went from dead to thudding like crazy. A gust of wind captured the fine dust, whipping it upward in a delicate dance. I bit my lip as Clara embraced the wind and soared toward the horses. The breeze swooped between the legs of a palomino before spiralling upward in a mini tornado and scattering in all directions.

Clue sucked in a shaky breath, and we squeezed each other, both feeling awed rather than sad. Awed because for one tiny second, I swore I heard Clara's laugh.

"You're too precious for this world. You'll be called back to somewhere far better than here."

My heart squeezed with never ending love for a soul I would see again when it was my turn to join her.

"She'll be happy here," Clue said.

I turned my face toward the sun, letting the warmth thaw my chilled and grief-stricken heart. A horse nickered. And I found a small smidgen of peace.

For the first time since she died in my arms, I stopped being crushed by pain. I could breathe a little easier. Handle life a little better knowing that her body might've left but her goodness and rightness and perfect little innocence would be with me always. "I know she will."

I didn't know how long we stood there, but eventually the

sun returned to hide behind the clouds and the chill of the breeze bit through my black dress.

Together, Clue and I turned to go back to the car.

Ben enveloped us in a hug when we reached him. His masculine smell of Old Spice hurt my heart thinking of another man. A man who hadn't shown up to say goodbye.

How could he? I'd nursed hope that he'd show. That he would put aside his wrongness and issues and come to honour Clara's life.

He was never normal and I fell in love with a fraud.

Ben kissed my cheek, whispering, "He's here. Been here the entire time."

I froze, looking into his dark eyes. My body sparked, throbbing with energy after a week of dullness. "Where?"

He conspicuously cocked his head to the small hill to the right. Sure enough, a black splodge broke the perfection of green sweeping grass.

My hands balled and I wanted nothing more than to run up the hill and punch him. I wanted him to feel the pain I did. The knife clipped in my hair could find another home lodged in his lifeless heart.

I gritted my teeth. "I don't want to see him."

Clue shook her head. "You need to talk."

"There's nothing to talk about."

"You need to listen to what he has to say, Zel."

I frowned, pissed at her. "Why are you on his side all of a sudden? If I told you what he's done—"

"Maybe *I* should tell *you* what he's done." Clue grabbed my arm. "Zel, he was the one who found this piece of land. He was the one who called me and told me he'd pay for all the arrangements, including the exclusive use of the fields."

My heart ceased to beat. Confusion swirled making me feel slightly sick. He'd meddled. He'd contributed to her funeral all without my knowledge. I couldn't untangle how that made me feel. "What? Why?"

She sighed. "I thought it was obvious. He loves you."

My eyes widened as a sharp shock travelled through my heart. A tug, a bolt of aliveness reminded me I couldn't live with the ghost of my daughter. I couldn't live in a world of tears and sorrow. I belonged with the present and it killed me all over again at the thought of walking away from Clara and moving on without her.

"He needs you, mummy. Don't be mad."

I shook my head. "That's not possible." *He doesn't know the meaning of love.* How could a man who couldn't even be touched understand the meaning of unconditional love? *He loved Clara.* I hated that I stabbed a hole in my own conclusions. He was capable, and beneath the issues, he was kind and sweet and eager to please.

Shit.

Fire filled my body, making me steam with rage for everything I couldn't change.

Clue scowled, temper staining her cheeks. "Well, if you feel that strongly, you need to say goodbye. End it properly. Otherwise it will haunt you. And you owe him a thank you at least."

Ben captured Clue, dragging her against him. "No need to get upset, little fortune cookie. I know you're hurting, but you can't force Zel to be with someone just because you don't want her to be alone."

My eyes shot to Ben's. He gave me a small smile. I didn't know how to react. I liked that he had my back, but I didn't like that he saw me weak and needing someone to 'save' me. Did they think I'd do something stupid now Clara was gone?

I wanted to scream: *I can't do anything reckless. I can't forfeit my life to sadness because I'm fucking pregnant.*

But I couldn't. I didn't want to focus on that hiccup yet. My thoughts belonged to Clara. It was treason to think and make plans without her. I couldn't do it. I couldn't be so heartless and forget her so quickly.

Pursing my lips together, I looked over Ben's shoulder and flinched.

The black spot on the hill stood upright and came toward us. I cursed the flutter in my stomach. I threatened to cut out my eager heart. I shouldn't love someone who ran when I needed him most. I couldn't condone his actions. I wouldn't live with a man who couldn't touch. He needed serious help, and I wasn't the woman who would heal him. I wasn't strong enough.

Clue and Ben drifted away, leaving me exposed and waiting for Fox to arrive.

"Don't be sad, mummy. I don't like it when you're sad."

I wished Clara's voice would stop. She sounded so wise. Pushing me into solutions I wasn't ready to accept. I wanted to be sad. I wanted to cry. I wanted her to come back to life so I could pretend the world was perfect and never cruel.

He stopped a foot away, grey-white eyes as bleak as any snowstorm. "I had to come. I had to say goodbye to her."

I stayed silent, not trusting myself to be able to speak without screaming or crying.

He moved forward a step. "Zel. I'm so unbelievably sorry. I can't ever express how much I wish I could rewind time." He looked like a black mountain, shuddering occasionally with grief. "I know you'll never forgive me, but I had to see you. Had to talk to you and explain."

I studied him. His face held shadows of bruises, his jaw slightly puffy. He'd been in another fight—searching for a way out of this hell. His black jacket and trousers swallowed the brightness of the day. He'd always favoured black and now I knew why. He was death incarnate. Everything he touched turned to ruin.

I flinched, dropping my gaze. I couldn't look at him.

"He needs you. Don't be mad."

Even now, Clara was driving me insane.

Fox came forward. "Please. I know how hard this must be for you. Let me explain."

Anger exploded out of me. "Explain? *Explain?*" My broken heart rallied in my chest, throwing off melancholy and thrumming hot and furious. "How about *I* explain? You. Left. Me. You ran when I needed you the most." I waved my hand, wanting to hit him. "Your promises of wanting us—of working to deserve us—it was all bullshit. You never changed. You watched my little girl die—the same girl you'd hoped would cure you—and you ran because there was nothing else for you to stay for."

All the greyness and sadness inside me suddenly erupted into gold sparks. I shoved him back with a finger to his sternum. "What do you want me to say, Fox? That I'm sorry you're hurting. That I'm sorry you fell in love with her only to have her gone so soon?" I threw my hands up. "Do you want me to forgive you for leaving me shattered and all alone in your office? That it didn't fucking ruin me that I had to cry into Oscar's arms, or Ben's and never yours? How about the fact that no matter what you promise you always break them! You'll never be able to give me what I need. You'll never be able to hold me or even sleep beside me."

Everything angry and crazy inside suddenly simmered, like a hurricane that ran out of puff. I sighed heavily. "I don't know what you want from me, Fox. And frankly, I don't care."

"Don't fight with him, mummy. He's hurting. Same as you."

I hated that Clara's voice had become my conscience. I hated that what she said was true. And I hated that no matter what I said or did, I couldn't ignore her. I would never be able to ignore my daughter.

The image of the little boy came again, and I knew I owed it to Fox to tell him. He deserved to know. I couldn't steal another family member from him—I wasn't that cruel. He may have destroyed me, but I wouldn't be responsible for ruining him further. He didn't need my help with that.

Fox dragged a hand through his bronze hair, looking up the hill to where I'd scattered Clara's remains.

"Fuck, this is all so twisted. I hate myself for everything I've done to you." His jaw clenched, and moisture glistened in his eyes. "If you only knew how much I hate myself. How much I want to sacrifice my entire life just so you never have to feel such pain."

His big body shuddered; his shoulders rolled and his destitution turned my spent rage into wistful longing. Clara was right. He was hurting. Badly.

He'd been alone—dealing with Clara's death without anyone's support. He'd done who knew what to find some sort of peace and I couldn't be angry anymore. I couldn't hate him for the sins he'd caused because ultimately, he wasn't responsible.

Forgiveness.

It was like a drug, warming me, soothing me. Turning all my anger into grudging acceptance. I knew if he reached out to hug me, I would forgive him. If he could wrap his arms around me and give me a sanctuary to cry in, I would forgive him for everything.

A hug would grant me hope.

A hug would show me promise.

But asking him to hug me was like asking for the moon. It wasn't possible, and he couldn't be who I needed him to be. The vicious circle was complete. It was time to share the news I hadn't told anyone and walk away. If he wanted to be part of the child's life, I wouldn't stop him. But I couldn't share anymore of mine with Roan Fox. I couldn't set myself up for more heartbreak.

Bracing my back, I said, "Fox, I'm—"

Fox launched forward, bringing the scent of smoke and metal. He smelled of salt too—of tears and sadness. My heart squeezed into a small ball at the thought of him grieving all alone.

His eyes flashed. "Stop calling me that, goddammit," he growled. "How many times do I need to tell you to call me Roan? Clara did. She understood why I needed her to call me that." He dragged hands through his hair looking weary and worn. "Fuck, Zel. Fox is gone. He's dead. I killed him three nights ago when I tried to change my past. I never want to hear you say that name again."

Anger bubbled over again. He'd ignored my heartfelt confession and jumped straight back to what he needed. The selfish bastard. "What *you* want? What about what *I* want?" I laughed harshly. "You left me when I needed you the most. You. Ran. Away. You can't touch, you can't love, you can't even be there for me. Why should I remember to never call you Fox when I have no intention of ever seeing you again?"

He moved suddenly. His large hands on my shoulders detonated my skin with bolts of power and awareness just like when we first touched. It crackled, it burned—whizzing through my nervous system, keeping me locked beneath his grip.

I sucked in a breath, humming with so many different things. My shocked gaze met his haunted icy eyes. His skin was ashen, cheekbones standing in stark relief. He looked like he hadn't slept in days. But beneath the haunted pallor, he shone with the connection. He felt it, too. He burned the same as me. "Feel that? It's fate. We're meant to be together. Please, Zel. Don't you know? Don't you know how much I fucking care for you? How much I miss you? I didn't run; I went to find redemption. And I can touch. I'm touching you now." He sucked in a breath, leaning in close, sending more jolts through my blood. "I'm here. For you. For her. Forever if you'll have me. Just please—forgive me."

"He's not a bad man. I love him, so he's not a bad man."

My knees wobbled and thoughts flew out of my head. I rolled my shoulders under his grip, wanting him far away. I couldn't handle what he invoked in me. I couldn't succumb yet again. He wasn't safe. To my safety or my sanity. "How can you say that? Do you honestly think I could come back to you? Even if I could forgive you for running, it doesn't stop the fact that you can't give me what I need. You're a danger to everyone who gets close to you. Every adult, child, and baby— if they touch you wrong, you'll kill them."

I couldn't tell him. I couldn't let him near his child as I

would never be able to trust him. My heart hammered against my ribs in horror. *I'm having your child and I can't tell you as I don't trust you not to kill it.*

His face twisted, darkening with anger. "I can't live without you, *dobycha*."

My eyes flew wide. "Don't call me that. I'm not your prey. I'm your fucking equal and—" I didn't know what else to say. My shoulders rolled and I muttered, "Even if I did want—" I slashed a hand across my face, so heavy and tired. "You destroyed me, Fox, and now I want you to let me go."

How could love be so wrong?

How could it all be for nothing?

Raising my head again, I shut myself down. I needed to get away from him so I could go back to mourning Clara. "Leave me alone, please. I don't want to discuss this. Today isn't about us. It's about Clara. And you have no respect to her memory by making me fight with you."

Fox bared his teeth; his hands clamped harder on my shoulders. I shivered as another wave of tension and rain of energy lit me up from the inside out.

"Respect? You don't think I have respect? I have so much fucking respect for you it scares me. You have a power over me that you don't even know. And today is a perfect day to clear the air because Clara didn't want us fighting. She wanted us to be happy."

"Don't you dare *use* Clara against me!" Furious tears sprang to my eyes. I couldn't believe his nerve.

He shook his head. His thumbs rubbed my shoulders; every sweep was like a tiny bomb restarting my heart, reminding me what he had was unique and way too special to destroy.

Fox pressed his face against mine, giving me no choice but to see the soul deep pain inside him. "I'll never be able to tell you how much I loved your daughter and how much she cured me. I'll never be able to show the depth of my hatred for myself for leaving you when you needed me most. I'll never have the words to beg for your forgiveness and be worthy. But

I *need* you, Hazel. I thought I could walk away and let you go, but I can't. I need you too damn much. You make me feel alive. You make my fucking heart beat for the first time, and I'm not going to give that up.

"No matter how you fight me, I will never stop. Every day, I'll try again and again. Every hour, I'll touch you, just to prove I'm willing to be everything you need and deserve. You'll never be free of me because I can't live another day without you in my fucking life."

I wanted.

I desired.

I wanted to buckle and let him sweep me away.

He'll kill your unborn baby. He ran when Clara died. You can't do this.

My entire body vibrated; I couldn't control myself. Snarling, I hissed, "You used us. You bought me, and you fell for Clara, but it was all to fix you. It was all about you. Fucking you. You, you, you.

"All your talk of never letting me go because you can't live without me. All your promises that you can be worthy. It's all still about *you*!

"What about me and Clara—what we needed? I gave you everything, including my daughter, and what has it done for me?"

I tore out of his grip and shoved a finger in his face. "I'll tell you what it's done for me. It's shown me I'm better off on my own. You have no choice in the matter. I won't allow you to touch me or chase me or hope for a second chance. It's over!"

The image of the little boy swamped me again. I knew in my bones I carried a son. His son. The son I would raise on my own. The son he wouldn't know about as he was too volatile, too fucked-up to trust.

"You're not safe. I'm not going to put myself in harm's way anymore. I'm done, Fox. You need to forget about me."

I hated every word. Half of me believed them, the other half wanted to wash my mouth out. I spun lies just like my past, mixing with truth until I didn't know what I wanted anymore.

"Don't fight, mummy. I don't want you to be sad."

I almost folded in two as my heart tore itself into pieces.

"Fuck, Hazel." Fox sucked in an unsteady breath, dragging shaky hands through his hair. "Please. Let me show you. I've changed. Let me tell you where I went. I'll never hurt you again. Just please—don't walk away and make me lose you, too. I won't fucking survive it. And I've survived too much to let you give up on me. I won't fucking let you!"

My heart wanted to believe him. I wished I could forgive and trust him, but I was empty. He'd used up all my reserves. The fight had drained me. All I wanted to do was crawl into a hole and cry myself to sleep. There was nothing left. I couldn't fall back into old patterns and keep hoping he was safe. I didn't want to live in fear of touching him or never having sex without bondage.

I'm pregnant.

I had to think of the fragile life inside me, not just his needs and my own. I had to be strong.

Straightening my back, I said, "You don't have the choice. You lost me the moment you left."

Swallowing hard, I looked at him, committing him to memory. He looked like he'd been to war and not come back. With bronze hair and a body scarred with tales, he'd proven too broken to fix. I could've spent an entire lifetime trying to piece him back together and never figured out the complete picture.

Boundless grief squeezed me.

"Stop fighting. Forgive him."

Fox lost the element of fighter, letting me see the truth for the first time. Beneath the scar and anger he was terrified, lost, and all alone. My heart broke all over again.

"Zel. Please. Tell me how I can fix this."

I couldn't do this anymore. He was like a black-hole sucking all my energy until I swayed in the wind.

God, Clara. I miss you so much. I need you here. I need you to repair the mess I've made.

"Fix it? How can you *fix* it? Are you a necromancer and can bring back my daughter? Can you heal my broken heart? Can you stop this awful eclipse inside me?"

He hung his head, gritting his teeth. His muscular arms wrapped around himself, holding tight.

My fingers twitched to reach for him, to wipe away the lone tear that trickled down his face. He looked so broken. Throbbing with agony, living with the twin of my pain. We were two halves of a shattered circle. Microscopic pieces that couldn't survive without the other. And I wouldn't survive if I gave into him. Fate had screwed us over.

It was time to end this once and for all.

With shaky hands, I pushed aside my long hair and unclasped the necklace from around my throat. Clara's star sat above my own, clinking together ever since the hospital gave me back her belongings.

"Can I give Roan my star? I can't take it with me."

I sucked in a breath, battling my tears. She wanted Fox to have it. I would honour her wish.

Pooling the silver into my palm, I held my hand out. "Here. She wanted you to have this."

Fox's eyes fell on the necklace and a feral, heart-wrenching noise erupted from his chest. Something exploded inside him and he hurled himself at me. Large arms wrapped around my body, squeezing me tight.

Life ended.

Then began again.

Noise ceased.

Then came again.

Heat froze.

Then enveloped again.

Sorrow disappeared.

Then settled again.

I left behind Hazel Hunter the second his arms clutched me against him. I became nothing more than a woman adored by a man so deeply destroyed he would never be perfect.

Every spark that existed between us fried my brain, kick-started my heart, and consumed my senses. I breathed in smoke and metal. I pressed against firm muscle and body heat. I was nothing but his.

His.

His.

His.

I was alive, wanted, worshipped. I believed his promises. He would never run again. He would fight beside me and love me always.

I broke.

Tears cascaded into a soul-grieving waterfall. I stood mute and frozen in his arms as Clara filled my thoughts.

"I don't want you to be sad. I don't like it when you're sad."

The breeze twirled around us and I swore I heard her whisper, *"I'm glad you're not fighting anymore. Don't fight, mummy. Save him."*

"Hug me back," Fox murmured, pressing a kiss on my ear. His lips sent tingles and love right into my heart. It didn't feel right falling so deeply only moments after my daughter's funeral. Propriety and heartbreak tried to stop me from reeling into a future where I might just learn how to be happy.

Fox squeezed me harder, kissing the salty tears running down my face. "Hug me, goddammit. I need you to touch me. I need to show you I can be who you deserve. I need to know I haven't ruined everything."

"He needs you, mummy."

With Clara in my thoughts, I tentatively raised my arms and looped them around his back. The moment I touched him, he tensed.

I froze, battling hope and fear inside me. He said I had a power over him. That wasn't true. He had a power over me: he could snap my spine and steal my life and in that very moment I wouldn't have cared. His arms were an aphrodisiac, a heady promise that made me sacrifice my life all too easily.

Fox's body shuddered around mine, feeling like a taut string about to snap. "Hug me harder. I can do this," he whispered. He sounded strangled, out of breath.

When I didn't obey, he clutched me tighter. "Do it, Zel."

Thinking of Clara and how much I wished it was her I hugged, I wrapped my arms harder, banding like a prison around his waist. If he killed me at least I would be with her sooner than I'd planned. I could stop fighting for everything that I wanted and just rest.

Fox shuddered, stiffened, jerked, but he kept his promise and didn't hurt me. His biceps twitched against my arms as he gathered me even closer, as if he could weld us together.

My mind swam with connection; my body sparked and tripped everywhere he touched. Now I knew what it felt like touching your perfect other—the missing half.

Fox nuzzled my neck, his hot breath caressing me. "I'm so sorry I wasn't there. I left because it was the only option. I did it to keep you safe—to give you a future. I want to deserve you, Zel, and never put you at risk again. I know I'll never deserve you, but let me serve you with my life. Let me spend every day trying to be better so one day you can love me."

My legs threatened to buckle as weakness filled me. Weakness for what he offered. Weakness for needing him.

I do love you and that's what cripples me.

With my last reserves, I tried to stop the inevitable. "You were meant to help me save her. You were meant to save me." I sucked in a breath, running out of oxygen as grief took me hostage once more. "You—you—" My voice broke and my heart died all over again. "You were supposed to save both of us, yet you didn't. She died, Roan. She's—she's—she's gon—" I couldn't finish as massive sobs exploded from my lungs.

A week I'd cried but I hadn't found comfort in tears. I hadn't found peace or a place to heal.

But now I did.

It felt caustic and healing and purifying.

Tidal wave after tidal wave.

I let go.

My heart broke, and I crumbled. I let everything free and drenched his black shirt.

Fox held me, giving me somewhere to cling. He smoothed my hair and kissed my cheek and fed me strength just by holding me.

He gave me what I needed all along. He smashed all my reservations that he couldn't give me what I desired and proved love could change anyone—no matter how destroyed.

"It's okay. It's okay. I've got you," he murmured. He rocked me until my legs gave out, then scooped me into his strong arms.

I barely noticed I went from vertical to horizontal as my mind wept for everything I'd lost. Fox cuddled me close just like I'd wanted and dreamed for. His heartbeat thudded thick and loud beneath my ear, giving me an anchor to focus on.

"Don't be sad, mummy. I don't want you to be sad."

"I'm here and I'm never leaving. You don't have to fight on your own anymore, Zel." His voice rumbled in his chest, sending shockwaves through my body.

My eyes filled with fire. A pain that burned and stabbed and lacerated as I cried and cried and cried. The eternity of relief he granted turned me from woman to puddle. The knowledge that my battles were halved; that every high and low would now be shared sent another crash of sorrow over me.

If only I'd met him sooner. If only the doctors had found out about Clara sooner. If only...if only.

"I'll give you everything, Zel. Everything that I am." He kissed my jaw, my temple, my cheek. He worshipped me in kisses. "Please. Don't make me beg. I can't do this. I can't be apart from you. I can't. I need you so fucking much."

My back ached; every part of me was in pain. I was utterly ruined.

Tilting my chin upward, Fox pressed his lips against mine, drinking in the salt from my tears. He murmured against my mouth, "You're mine, and I refuse to live without you." He made me swallow every regret, every sadness he lived with.

"You're mine, Hazel Hunter. And I'm taking you home to heal."

"He needs you, mummy. Go with him. Don't be sad."

My entire body vibrated with a potent mix of confusion, anger, and hunger. Hunger for him. Hunger for what he promised.

He didn't wait for my reply. His tongue speared into my mouth, giving me no choice but to kiss him back. He took and he gave and he consumed, dragging unwilling desire through my blood until it throbbed in my core. He brought me back to life even though I wanted to stay wallowing in my tears. I wasn't ready to face life without Clara. I wasn't ready to say goodbye. I wasn't ready to embrace the world he offered or the baby growing inside me.

I'm not ready.

"Please," he whispered. His breath tickled my cheek and my traitorous body hummed. He helped dull the pain of Clara. He gave me something else to focus on.

Forgive him. Accept him.

I pulled back.

His eyes were glazed and heavy. His body wrapped around mine as if he could protect me from so many other tragic things. Almost every part of me touched every part of him. How was that possible?

Sniffing back my tears, I asked, "How can you stand to be this close?"

He shook his head. "I'll tell you if you come home with me."

I wanted to say no. I deserved to live in misery. I didn't deserve any chance at happiness. Why should a parent outlive her child?

But my trials in life had taught me nothing lasted forever and the best things were fleeting—treasures to be enjoyed for however long they lasted before they were gone. Clara was too precious—too perfect to last. I'd been granted a miracle and it had ended before I was ready.

"Don't be sad. I don't like it when you're sad."

I looked over Fox's shoulder at the horses in the field. They tossed their manes, and pawed the ground, welcoming my daughter and granting her immortality. *"Okay, Clara. Okay."*

Clara taught me precious things were worth fighting for. And the ultimate prizes of life demanded payments that sometimes seemed too high.

"Okay," I whispered.

Fox looked as if the sun had finally found its way into his soul. "Okay?"

I nodded. "Okay, I'll come home with you. For Clara. For us."

This was the man I was in love with.

The father of my unborn child.

The man I wouldn't give up on.

It turned out Clue and Ben knew my decision before me. They'd left, leaving me stranded and pissed off at their blatant disregard for my choices. Clue didn't know what Fox was capable of. I doubted they would've been so keen to abandon me with a man with such a tangled past had they known.

I glared at Fox's innocent look as he carried me to his Porsche. I had no doubt he had something to do with Clue and Ben leaving with no qualms to my safety.

Then my heart melted at the thought of him securing such an amazing place for Clara to find peace. He'd been thinking of her, even when he'd left.

"Thank you," I said as Fox placed me ever so gently into the expensive car and buckled me in. A gust of chocolate caught me from his hair; my stomach fluttered with how attentive and caring he was.

"For what?" He stood upright, the grey clouds framing his black-clad body.

"For this." I nodded at the field and the horses. "For caring enough. For giving her a piece of yourself."

He rolled his shoulders and sniffed. Avoiding my eyes, he said, "I wanted to make her dreams come true. I thought if she was placed here, she'd eventually become part of the horse, evolve into…more. Become what she always wanted."

My throat closed up, and I dropped my eyes. Who was this man? This damaged, scarred, enigma of a man? I loved the thought of Clara evolving—always happy. I loved his reasoning behind his choice of resting spot.

I didn't take my eyes off Fox as he walked around the front of the car and climbed into the driver's side. He moved with a heavy blanket of sadness around his shoulders—muted and solemn.

The engine roared then purred as he turned the key. He glanced over. "Ready?"

Never.

Panic clawed back and it took all my willpower to stay in the car.

The rock lodged in my throat again but I nodded. "As ready as I'll ever be."

Fox grimaced and put the car into gear.

We didn't say a word as he negotiated the dirt track down to the road. Every metre my heart suffocated more and more. *I'm leaving her behind!*

Fuck, it was hard. So hard.

At the end of the field path, Fox climbed out and undid the gate. His back flexed as he dragged the barricade across mud. Returning to the car, he drove through, shut the large metal behind us, and turned left onto tarmacked highway.

Tears glazed my eyes as the sun broke through the clouds again, shining light on the hills behind us. I never wanted to leave. Never wanted to think about Clara all alone in a field with no shelter. I should've built a tent, a shrine, something to grant her safety.

She doesn't need anything. She's gone.

Tears pressed again. As much as it killed me—I had to remember she was above physical needs. She was free.

Fox smiled in my direction, but we didn't say anything. Both too raw, too hurt knowing that the little soul that'd brought us closer together would no longer be with us.

Speeding toward civilization, I balled my hands and tried to keep my nerves to a minimum. Every kilometre, I slunk further and further into my seat. I didn't want to return to Obsidian. I didn't think I would survive walking into the house where Clara had drawn her last breath. I never wanted to step foot in that place again.

The tension in the car throbbed and my skin was hypersensitive for his touch. After staring death in the face, I needed reminding of life. I needed to believe that Clue was right and there was such a thing as reincarnation or a better life. I needed Fox to remind me that I couldn't give up.

Fox slowed for a traffic light. His hand disappeared into his pocket and pulled out Clara's star necklace.

I sucked in a huge breath. The tinkling pieces of my heart rattled in my chest as he reverently clasped it around his neck. He stroked the silver, a look of love and misery on his face.

I looked away, unable to bear the sharp arrows of sadness piercing my soul. The pain of her death was shared—by a man who'd known her for such a little time. A man I still didn't really know.

The light turned green and Fox sighed heavily. Throwing the car into gear, we zoomed down roads and through suburbs I didn't recognise.

Kilometre after kilometre, we remained in silence. Either too wrapped up in Clara to risk speaking or figuring out if our argument had cleared the air enough to start anew.

He looked so odd, so fierce, wearing a simple silver star. Up till now, the only adornment he wore were his scars and tattoos, but I knew in my heart he would never take it off.

Every time I looked at him wearing it, I would remember her. Just as it should be.

"Where did you go?" I asked as we travelled down roads and through city mania.

He glanced at me, his knuckles turning white around the steering wheel. "I went to deal with something."

A chill sent goosebumps down my back. "You were in another fight."

"What makes you say that?"

I shrugged. I couldn't explain the change in him when he fought—the ease, or relief from whatever demons he suffered. Yet, this time, he seemed lighter—more grounded than I'd ever seen him. "You seem different." He was...softer. His grey-white eyes weren't as haunted, as if he'd decided finally to put his past behind him.

"Do you know why I fight? Can you understand the need to find an outlet from internal pain?" He looked over quickly before focusing again on the road.

"Yes. I can understand that."

"Can you understand when I say fighting to me is a medicine? But it's the pain that's my salvation. I self-harm because I haven't found any other way to free the darkness inside."

He reached across and stole my right hand, squeezing hard. "I've self-harmed for a very long time. I hate it. It fills me with shame, but as much as I want to stop, I can't. I can't promise I'll be able to give it up entirely, but from now on, I'm going to try and find some other way."

He smiled. "Clara helped with that, too."

"How?" I barely whispered, too captivated by learning more behind his mask.

"Because her death has given me an unlimited supply of pain. I only need to think of her, and the urge to self-mutilate disappears."

I didn't know how to reply. I hated the thought of him using Clara's memory to avoid hurting himself. Was he tainting her memory by using it for selfish reasons? But then again, I was pleased she continued to help beyond the grave.

"Don't fight. He needs you."

Clara's lyrical voice came and went. I asked, "You didn't just go to fight, though. Did you?" There was a difference in him. A tightness and barely found tranquillity.

"No. I went to see someone. To say goodbye to a past I never wished I lived." Fox squeezed my fingers once more, before placing his hand on the wheel. "I went back to Russia."

My heart raced as my mind filled with images of snow and ice.

"I killed the men who made me like this. I decided to stop relying on others to fix me and find a cure myself."

Had he done what I'd hoped all along? Had something snapped and fallen from his mind? Hope blazed, chasing away the black cloud of mourning for a wonderful moment. "Is that why you could hug me? You can touch?" I ignored the voice telling me he'd tensed and vibrated with energy when I'd hugged him back. "You're free?"

His shoulders slumped; he smiled sadly. "Not free, but better."

I hated the desolation in his eyes. He looked guilty, as if he'd done something wrong by returning to me only marginally repaired. He couldn't be further from the truth. The fact that he'd tried to heal meant wonders.

"Can I touch you?"

His eyes flew to mine. His jaw clenched but he nodded slowly.

Very carefully, I laid a palm on the hard heat of his left thigh. "I'm so proud of you. I know that sounds strange to say, but you took control and you should celebrate your progress rather than hate that it isn't cured completely."

His eyes flashed and he leaned over to press a gentle kiss against my lips. "I swear I could live a thousand fucking years and not deserve you." Pulling away, he turned into a driveway of a gated property right on the esplanade of Narrabeen. The suburb boasted huge modern architecture, all new and sparkling, and right across the road from the beach.

I blinked as he pressed a remote and the gate rolled open. The house was a two-story white and glass design. The ocean crashed behind us, sounding like muted thunder, welcoming us onto the property. The large double garage door opened, granting shade and a huge concrete home for Fox's Porsche.

"Where—where are we?" The Northern Beaches were on the opposite end of town to Obsidian. I'd lost all bearings while driving through the city.

Does he own this, too?

I flicked a glance at the man I'd agreed to return home with. How much did I truly know of him?

Nothing.

I didn't know his favourite foods, or pet peeves, or even his birthday. I didn't know if he was allergic to anything or how many assets he owned. I'd given him my life all because he proved he could love so fiercely.

And I'm pregnant with his child.

"See, mummy. He needs you after all. He needs someone to love."

Clara's voice once again suffocated my lungs. She'd taken up residence in my head, and I never wanted her to leave. Even if it was me telling myself what I needed to hear.

"This is incredible."

Fox smiled, pulling to a stop inside the garage. "It couldn't get any more different from Obsidian. I never want to see another gargoyle again."

I nodded, eternally grateful that I wouldn't have to enter the dwelling where Clara had died. There was nothing foreboding about this place. It looked welcoming, pristine. A fresh beginning.

Turning off the ignition, Fox said, "We're home."

I froze in my seat as a rainbow of emotion filled me: happiness, heartache, hope—all overshadowed by grief. Clara would never see this. She'd never know the massive impact she had on this man.

Turning to face him, I whispered, "I don't understand."

Fox gave a half smile and climbed out of the car. Coming around the bonnet, he opened my door and helped me clamber upright. "There's a lot you won't understand until I grow some balls and tell you. What I shared in my basement is nothing compared to the involved story—but for now, all you need to know is I bought this two days ago. The moment I found the piece of land for Clara, I found the perfect house for us. I couldn't return to the club. I need to get away from violence—to try and fix myself once and for all."

He'd done so much—all behind the scenes while I'd cried myself into a stupor.

"What did you do with Obsidian?"

He smiled. "I sold it to Oscar. He practically ran it himself anyway. I've sold it to him for a rock bottom price." He laughed. "Let's just say he got a steal."

My eyes widened at the joviality—so odd coming from Fox. "What steal?"

Aliveness flashed in his eyes for the first time. "I made him give me ten dollars and an oath that he will never talk to me about it, or mention the name Obsidian Fox again, and the club was all his."

My mind whirled. How could he do that? How much wealth did he have? My eyes narrowed, trying to decipher the conundrum in front of me. "Just who *are* you?"

He shrugged. "Do you want the long story or the short story?"

Oh, God. I didn't know if I should be terrified or excited to find out every skeleton in his closet. "Short story, for now."

"I'm wealthy. From an inheritance." His jaw twitched—the only sign that it was a painful subject for him. "I can take care of you. I *want* to take care of you."

I swallowed.

Fox reached out and dragged me close. His arms wrapped around my waist, forcing my hands to rest on his chest to keep my balance. Every part of me froze; my fingers itched to grab my hair-clip knife, just in case.

His nostrils flared and his face darkened, but he didn't regress or terrify me. Bowing his head, he pressed his forehead against mine. "You asked me who I am. My name is Roan Averin. Forget you ever knew a man named Fox. He wasn't a man. He was the product of a past he hated. I never thought I'd be able to use my full name again, but I want to. I want a new beginning. With you."

My heart broke open and grew wings.

"Roan Averin." The name sounded sweet on my tongue. A world apart from Obsidian Fox. "I like it."

He huffed, body tensing as I trailed my fingertips up his chest to his throat.

"Can I?" I murmured, very aware of every muscle tightening inside him.

He squeezed his eyes, nodding.

Slowly, I grazed my fingers along his smooth jaw and cupped his cheeks. He trembled in my hold. Standing on tiptoe, I brushed the lightest of kisses over his lips. His forehead furrowed; teeth clenched.

The innocent kiss reminded me of how delicate he was with Clara, and I struggled to hold onto the moment where grief didn't interrupt.

I dropped my hands and backed out of his grip. "It will get easier. You'll see. I'll help you."

Am I talking about missing Clara or his condition?

He nodded. "I know. As long as I have you, I can get better. Just please, remember to call me Roan. It will help."

I knew it would be hard to stop calling him Fox. It was the name of the man I fell for. But I saw how important it was to him. Fox had died with whatever he'd done in Russia, and I needed to obey his wishes to put the past where it belonged.

My eyes fell to the star in the hollow of his throat. "She could always see who you really were. She was so much better than me. Always saw the best in people. So trusting. *Too* trusting." I had to stop as my throat closed, and my heart thudded a painful staccato.

Fox's eyes glowed. "You were the same. I recognised something I needed in you the second I saw you. I didn't know what it was, but stealing your knife and marching you up those steps was the best fucking thing I've done in my entire life."

I laughed softly, trembling as he captured my chin. "You'll never lose her, Zel. We'll never stop talking about her or keeping her alive in our thoughts."

Pulling away, he shoved a hand into his pocket and pulled out a folded piece of paper. Handing it to me, he said, "Seeing as I've put so much in the past, to begin anew—this belongs to you."

I took it, frowning. I opened the handwritten contract between Obsidian Fox and Hazel Hunter. My heart swooped and I met his eyes.

Roan murmured, "Tear it up. That man no longer exists."

He was asking me to rip up the past. Walk away from everything bad that had happened and embrace a future together.

With trembling fingers, I obeyed. The sound of shredding paper echoed off the garage walls.

Roan went to take my hand, but I pulled back. "Wait."

I bit my lip as I reached into my dress pocket and pulled out the thing I was terrified of. The thing I'd stolen from Fox the day I knocked him out with the small wolf statue on his side-board. Nestled in a piece of tissue paper sat the blue pill.

I didn't know what it was, but I knew it was poison. I also knew Fox had moments of weakness where he might've done something irreversible.

I stole it to prevent him doing something recklessly stupid.

"Here. This belongs to you."

Grabbing it, he unwrapped the suicide pill. His face darkened; eyes narrowed. "Why the fuck do you have this?" Anger blazed across his features. "Do you know how dangerous this is? What the hell were you think—" Then panic replaced his fear and his fingers dug into my elbow. "You weren't going…please tell me you weren't thinking of using this. For fuck's sake, Zel. What were you going to do?"

I jerked back, hot temper filling me at his wrong conclusion. "You thought I'd be weak enough to kill myself? How could you think that? I may have lost my daughter, but I haven't lost my mind!"

"Then why do you have it?" Roan bundled up the tissue, clenching his fist.

"Because I didn't want to walk in on you dead. I hated the thought that you couldn't stomach living and would rather commit the biggest treason of all and kill yourself. I stole it from you as I didn't want you to die!"

He moved forward a step, crowding me. "It still doesn't explain what it's doing in your fucking pocket."

I shouted right in his face. "Ever since I took it, I've been terrified of it. I didn't know what to do." The relief that came with no longer being responsible for such a dangerous thing quietened my anger. "I kept it taped to the underside of my bed to prevent anyone finding it by mistake. It haunted me, and I don't want the responsibility anymore. I want you to destroy it."

Without saying a word, Roan grabbed my hand and stalked toward the door leading into the house. He jangled a set of keys, trying to find the right one, never letting go of my hand. The moment he unlocked the door, he dragged me down the corridor and to a bathroom off a room that looked like a shadowed cinema.

The immaculate ensuite looked like a show home ready for viewing. Fluffy turquoise towels with sparkling silver tiles were so different to the black facilities at Obsidian.

"Can't believe you've been walking around with this in your pocket." Flipping open the lid of the toilet, he threw the tissue and pill into the basin. Flushing it, he snapped, "There. Gone. Now Fox is really dead, and it's about fucking time you met Roan."

I squealed as he scooped me off my feet and carted me up

the wide white stairs to the second floor. I couldn't see much in the whirlwind of speed, but everywhere I looked was white. Not one inch of black.

Kicking a door open, he prowled inside and gave me exactly one second to glance around the room.

White king-size bed covered in silky pillows that looked like pristine clouds. The huge expanse of glass welcomed the sand dunes and sea inside. The carpet was white, the bedside tables and small sitting area white.

Everywhere I looked white, white, white.

And then all I saw was black as Roan threw me on the bed and crushed me against the softness of duck down. I moaned as his body heat smothered me and for one joyous moment I let go of my grief and thought only of him. This man who'd turned my world upside down, back to front, inside out.

His hands went to the little pearl buttons of my dress, fumbling with the dainty buttonholes. His breathing accelerated, and he growled in frustration. His touch brought me crawling out of the fog of sorrow and latching onto life.

I grabbed the back of his head, whispering in his ear. "Tear it off. I never want to wear it again."

"Thank God," he groaned. His hands bunched the material and tore. The dress went from encasing my body to being ripped into pieces, laying scattered like death on all the perfect whiteness. His eyes dropped to my black underwear. "You're fucking gorgeous."

He bent over me, biting the swell of my breast with gentle teeth. "I'm going to love you every day. I'll never get enough of these." He cupped my breasts, brushing my pebbled nipples with his thumbs. "I'll never get enough of this." His right hand trailed down my stomach to cup between my legs.

I moaned as the possessive heat of his palm sent mini explosions in my blood.

My body welcomed the energy Roan conjured, but my mind skittered away. It was wrong to focus on myself. So wrong to thrill in life when Clara no longer had any.

I can't do this.

I froze.

Roan's hand dropped from me and he exhaled heavily. "Fuck. I'm an asshole."

"No, you're not." I shook my head, cursing the trickle of tears seeping from my eyes. Would I ever be able to stomach the thought that Clara was no longer in my world?

Roan scooted backward, bringing me with him. I stood on my black dress and something sharp poked the bottom of my foot.

Bending to rub my sole, I found the My Little Pony badge from the funeral. I picked it up; the girlish horse design swirled with my tears.

My insides twisted until I no longer knew how to live. My heart had to relearn how to beat. My mind had to come to terms with loss. My body had to prepare itself to bring more life into the world.

There was too much. Too much sensation. Life was moving too fast, putting distance between me and Clara every second.

I looked up at Roan, begging him to fix it.

"Shit, Zel." He dragged me against him and held me tight. His warmth helped comfort but at the same time reminded me Clara was no longer warm. I'd stolen her heat as she grew cold in my arms in his office.

My heart squeezed until I couldn't breathe.

How can I move on when the guilt will kill me?

I didn't know how long we stood there. But Roan never stopped stroking my hair. "It's okay. You don't have to be so strong. Let go. I'm here." His voice soothed me, rough and masculine. He didn't pull away, despite the damp patch growing beneath his shirt from the stress of holding me.

Finally, when my silent shudders had stopped, he disappeared and came back with a white bathrobe from the bathroom. Wrapping me tight, concealing my half-nakedness, he asked, "Can I show you something? It might make it a little easier." His voice hitched. "Or it might make it fucking worse.

I don't know. I second guessed myself the entire time I did it."

Trepidation prickled my spine. "Show me what?"

Pulling away, he captured my hand and dragged me from the room. We travelled down a short corridor before he turned a doorknob and pushed me into a snapshot of my past. I felt as if I walked through a time machine.

Clara.

Everywhere.

Huge canvases of her smiling, running, dancing. I couldn't breathe. I was sure my heart ceased to beat. This must be the gateway to heaven.

Had I died from sadness?

I could sense her. Hear her laugh. Smell her apple scent.

Roan's strong presence appeared on my right. "Are you okay?"

I barely nodded, too consumed with the blown up pictures of Clara. Her smile radiated, so full of life. "H—how?"

"Obsidian has security cameras. I went back through the footage and saved some shots to remind you she'll always be here. Even if she's gone." He drifted forward, toward the largest picture decorating the walls. It was a portrait of me and Clara walking hand in hand in the gardens. Her purple ribbon had wrapped around my arm and we were laughing, trying to untangle ourselves.

All the air deflated from my body, but instead of collapsing in a waterfall of tears, I sighed with a strange mix of peace and nostalgia. Roan had stolen my daughter by falling in love with her but he'd given her back to me, too.

"I—I don't know what to say." I clutched my stomach, holding in the pain of missing her.

He smiled. His scar looked less angry, making him softer, tamer. "Don't say anything. Whenever it gets too much, come in here and talk to her. She'll always be with you." He hung his head, trailing a fingertip over a horse statue I hadn't noticed.

I spun, taking in the details of the room. In every corner rested bronze and copper horses from Roan's collection at

Obsidian.

"I know it's stupid, but I hear her. In here." Roan tapped his temple, then dropped his hand to his heart. "I feel her. In here."

Oh, God.

Sadness, heartache, and overwhelming tragedy bubbled in my chest. Popping and fizzing until my insides rained with glistening tears. But my eyes stayed dry.

I stayed strong to accept the incredible gift Roan had given me.

"I hear her, too." I moved forward, tracing a finger over a beautiful sun-drenched photo of Clara picking daisies. "I think I'll always hear her."

I couldn't believe the scarred man before me was the same fighter who'd bought me for sex. He'd changed so much—yet still seemed the same.

I needed him. I needed to show him how grateful I was. How much he gave me. "Take me back to the bedroom," I whispered.

Roan's eyes widened. "We don't have—"

I shook my head. "I want to." The grief suddenly receded, leaving me blessedly light. Standing in the room surrounded by Clara, I found the strength to put aside my tears and celebrate what I'd gained rather than what I lost.

You need to tell him.

I needed to make it official and stop hiding from the future hurtling toward me. I needed to tell him about his son.

Roan's shoulders bunched and he came slowly toward me. His lips thinned. "I want you, Zel. God knows how much I fucking want you." He dropped his eyes, glaring at his fists. "But I'm still struggling inside. I want to be gentle. To hold you and make love to you. But…I won't be able to and I don't want to take you violently. Not today."

My heart raced. I didn't reply. What could I say? I accepted that and still wanted him. I wasn't asking to be held while I cried and be rocked to sleep. I was asking to forget—for a short while.

Clara's memory would still be there to mourn once I'd thanked Roan with all my heart.

"I understand. I need what you can give me. I need to be reminded of how to fight. I'm sick of tears." Giving him one last look, I moved toward the door.

I didn't wait for him to follow. Pacing down the corridor, I entered the white bedroom, already prickling with heat and regret. Could I celebrate life and accept everything the new pregnancy would offer? Could I put aside my grief for just a moment to spend time with my future, rather than my past?

My eyes fell on the fluffy, perfectly crafted sheep resting by the large windows.

Clara's sheep.

Sunlight struck the bronze, dancing like tarnished rainbows onto the white carpet.

"Don't be sad, mummy. I don't want you to be sad."

My heart died all over again but this time, it restarted with a slight thread of hope. Hope that I could survive and wouldn't buckle beneath the loss.

Arms banded around me from behind. Roan's hot breath caressed my neck as he nuzzled my ear. "I'll stop. Just say the word and I'll leave."

I arched my back into him. "Take me. Make me come back to life."

Roan groaned, picking me up and carrying me toward the bed. "I'll never stop kissing you or loving you. I'll never stop working hard to fucking deserve you."

Settling me on the mattress, his body collapsed on mine. His knee forced my legs apart as he rested his fully-clad body against me. The bathrobe fell apart and his hand landed on my side, sending electric fire darting all over.

I'd never get used to the ferocious tingles or sharp connection when we touched.

"You'll never be alone again, Zel. I'm all fucking yours." His mouth captured mine. His smoky scent intoxicated me and every taste bud came alive as his sinful tongue entered my mouth. He stole every thought. Every tear. He made me focus on one thing only.

Him.

Passion unfurled in my stomach, heating me, thrilling me. I let myself be selfish and only focused on that moment. Not the future. Not the past. Not anything but the slickness of Roan's tongue and the hard heat of him between my legs.

He angled his head, his lips sliding against mine. His tongue licked mine in a possessive dance echoing in my core.

My fingers itched to tug his hair, scratch his back. Something feral unlocked inside me and I craved connection. Craved a fight. I wanted to know I was still strong enough despite what had happened.

Roan's hand cupped my throat, pinning me to the mattress. My eyes flew open as he stopped kissing me. "Say it. Say you're mine."

My heart exploded at the icy intensity in his silver eyes. I swallowed as his fingers tightened. Instead of fearing him, I accepted it. I willingly gave myself into his power. After everything he'd done for me, he shouldn't need confirmation. It was obvious.

"I'm yours. Through and through."

I'm having your child.

His nostrils flared and he moved suddenly, climbing off the bed. The residual heat of his fingers around my neck sparked with erotic torture.

Grey-white eyes locked with mine as he tore off his t-shirt and stood, letting me feast on his skin. Clara's silver star rested in the hollow of his throat and the spasm to my heart crippled me. I forced myself to stop looking and my eyebrows drew together, noticing the new scars mingling with old. Silver and red, along with purple and blue bruises.

Sitting upright, I traced the two large squares of gauze stuck to his side. "You're hurt." I looked up, asking silently what happened. Small pinpricks of blood had seeped through the bandage.

He shook his head. "Later. If you want to know, I'll tell you." His hands fell to his buckle and I swallowed hard. "But right now, I'm going to take you. I need to know you're mine. So I can give you everything that I fucking am."

My pussy clenched at the raw need in his voice. I couldn't look away.

His stomach rippled, muscles dancing beneath ruined skin as he undid the button and pulled down the zipper. He let the material whisper down his legs before kicking them away. He stood proud and naked. So different to when I first met him.

My mouth watered to lick every inch. To taste him. To drink him in forever.

His hands twitched by his sides. "Take your bra off." His voice was dark, husky, heavily accented—the Russian dialect he tried so hard to hide coming through.

Sitting up, I pulled the dressing gown off and unhooked my bra. It came away; I let the cups fall to the bed.

Roan's eyes fell to my chest, licking his lips. He groaned and cupped himself. His cock jerked in his touch as he stroked sensitive flesh. "You're the only woman my cock reacts to. All my life, I've been alone. I was taught to hate sex. That it would fog my brain—ruin my focus for their missions. But now I look at you and I'm glad. I'm glad my cock only reacts to you. Because it means I fucking own you and you own me in return."

The passion in his tone kept me locked in his spell. My brain kept poking at grief, kept trying to suck me back into tears, but Roan trapped me with him. I needed it. Desperately. I needed to remember how to be myself. How to survive.

"You're the only man I've been attracted to. I wanted you the moment I saw you. You scared me, terrified me, but beneath it all I saw who you are now. I saw a man I could love. I'm yours, Roan."

His eyes snapped closed; his entire body shuddered. "Fuck, call me that again." His voice resonated with lust.

I didn't know if he wanted me to tell him I loved him or call him by his name. So I did both. I threw myself into the truth and embraced my future with this scarred fighter.

"I love you, Roan Averin."

His body, so cut and etched in muscle, rippled with need. His eyes wrenched open and for once I saw a sliver of blue in the white depths. I saw ragged passion and undiluted awe. "You fucking own me, Hazel."

"I don't own you. I'll never own you. You're free. You fought your past and you found your way to me." My voice cracked with tears—but these tears were pride and gratefulness that he'd been able to fight.

"Fucking hell," Roan growled. "I need you so much." Letting go of his erection, he pounced. The bed shifted as he landed on top of me. Supporting his weight on his elbows, his lips crashed against mine, pressing my head into the mattress.

He commanded me to open wide, to accept his brutal kiss. His mouth consumed me. Every slide of his tongue fought and parried. Danced and worshipped.

I moaned as his hand trailed down my ribcage, spreading a wake of fire. Caressing my hip, he dipped inward, pushing my legs apart.

"I want you. I need to be inside you." He kissed me so hard my teeth bruised my lips. "I can't be gentle. I'm—sorry. I can't be—"

My body shattered as he pressed two fingers deep inside me. Drawing wetness and sending exploding pinwheels through my heart. "It's okay. I under—"

His mouth landed on mine again, swallowing my words. His fingers thrust in a perfect rhythm building me higher and higher. An orgasm gathered behind my eyes, in my heart, my chest, my core.

Every stroke and tease from his long, strong fingers sent sweat dewing on my skin. The sun streamed through the windows, capturing us in a spotlight of heat.

"God, I want to be inside you. Hard and deep. I want to

claim every inch of you," Roan panted, biting my ear.

"Do it. Take me."

I wanted him now while I existed in this perfect selfish world where nothing else mattered. I'd put barriers up, segmenting the grief I knew was waiting for me.

He laughed, strangled with hunger. "God, you're too fucking potent. I can't think straight. I can't control myself."

I whimpered as the tip of his cock replaced his fingers, nudging, sliding in just a little.

Turning my head, I bit the billowing sheets, trying to keep my hands away from him. I wanted to pull him deeper, force him to take me fast. The fundamental human need to touch drove me nuts—knowing I couldn't risk it. He strained himself so much already. Every muscle vibrated, his eyes tight and dark.

Roan hovered, teasing me. His hips rocked, giving me a small amount of his erection. He breathed hard, panting with stress. "Make me take you. Make me fuck you." He thrust a little, twisting my mind with want. "Take me, Zel. Take all of me. Let me prove you have nothing left to fear."

I stopped biting the sheets and looked at him. Really looked at him. No more barriers, no more smoke or secrets—he let me see just how hard touching was for him, but he wanted me to do it anyway. Every part of him wanted to kill me. The violence was an aura around him, beading on his brow.

He suffered to protect me.

He willingly battled pain to find salvation that might never come.

My heart couldn't handle his agony. "It hurts you." I shook my head. "I can't. Stop. We can try another day."

He growled, dropping his head to bite my neck. The sharpness of his teeth made me freeze.

Has he lost control?

My fingers itched for my knife. I said goodbye to Clara today and as much as I missed her, I wasn't ready to leave this earth.

The realization that I wanted to continue living—even if it

meant without her by my side caught me by surprise. It shot me with fight and adrenaline. Reminding me that others needed me.

Roan needed me.

His son needed me.

Instead of guilt, peace settled.

Then my back bowed as Roan pressed in a little more, stretching me. "I won't go any further until you make me. Touch me." He kissed my cheek, smothering me in the scent of smoke. "Touch me. Please. You're safe." His voice was ragged and strained.

The offer was too tantalising. I wanted to help him break. I wanted him to stop being in pain.

My fingers whispered over his back and he hissed. Every muscle in his spine locked down.

I dropped my hands.

You can't do this.

I no longer played with just my life. I had another. Barely formed and so, so delicate. I couldn't be reckless or selfish.

"I can't."

His eyes flared wide, holding himself rigid above me. "Why not?"

My heart bucked, racing toward the truth. Fear filled me at how he'd react. Would he still want me? Would he view it as a replacement for Clara? I'd worked through my issues and accepted that I could love another without being a traitor to Clara's memory, but Roan didn't know. He didn't have a clue.

"I can't let you kill me."

"I'm not going to kill you. Fuck, Zel. I need you to push me again. I won't get better if you don't push me like you did at Obsidian."

I shook my head. "I have to think of someone else. It's not just my life I'll be risking to save yours."

He reared upright, glaring deep into my eyes. "Spit it out. What the hell are you keeping from me now?" A terrible glint filled his eye. "So help me, Hazel, tell me. I won't survive you keeping secrets from me again."

I sucked in a deep breath, fortifying myself against his wrath. "I'm pregnant."

The world stood still for a fraction of a second. His face froze, eyes dazed. Then life jolted back into him and he blinked. "*What* did you just say?"

I swallowed, hating the rush of sadness at celebrating a new life when I'd only just said goodbye to a girl who would always hold my heart. "I'm having your child."

I wasn't prepared for the switch in him. The savage hunger that exploded, infecting me just as brutally. "Fuck. Hazel." His mouth crashed against mine, his tongue sweeping deep. I had no clue what was going on in his head.

His hands left my hips to capture my face, holding me captive as he kissed me like a man starved of air. As quickly as he kissed me, he pulled away. "What? How?" His eyes darted all over me, disbelief in their depths.

My head swam. My body sparked and hummed. "I thought I couldn't conceive. I was wrong."

"But—oh, my God. I'm going to be a father?" Love glowed brighter than any sun, then shadowed with fear. "Fuck. I'm not—I can't be around something so breakable." He sucked in a breath. "I—I don't know what to say."

I wasn't scared that he'd reject the idea of his offspring, or that he'd send me away. Confidence ran in my blood. "You made so much progress already. You have nine months to finish curing yourself before he arrives."

He swallowed hard. "He?" His eyes shot to my belly. "You already know what it is?"

Every part of me wanted to hug him. He looked lost. Terrified. Almost angry at me for putting him in this dangerous situation.

I shook my head. "No. But I know. It's a boy. Your son. And you won't hurt him. I won't let you."

His hips moved, withdrawing the small amount of connection we shared. "But—I managed to withstand Clara because she was so brave—so strong. But a newborn?" He panicked, eyes widening. "I can't. I don't want to be responsible for kill—" He stopped and gritted his teeth. "No. I'll look after you till you have it, then I'll keep my distance. It's the only way."

Anger.

Hot, swift anger. I'd forgotten what it felt like, buried beneath so much grief. I welcomed it and did something I probably shouldn't.

Grabbing the back of his neck, I yanked him down. His biceps strained, trying to hold himself up. My legs shot upright and wrapped around his hips, finding his hardness again and pushing myself onto him.

He froze, tension echoing in his joints. "Stop, Hazel. Fuck—"

"No. I won't stop. And I'll tell you why. You are going to be part of this new life. You are going to heal and you're going to get better. If I have to show you you can do this, then so be it." My hands dropped from his neck to his hips, pulling him into me. He wrenched back, fighting the need between us.

He fought, looking positively wild, but then all the fight siphoned out of him and he collapsed on top. His breathing rattled in his lungs and his eyes screwed up tight. "It's too hard. I can't ignore the conditioning."

"Yes, you can. And you will."

I needed him to take me. The thirst ached in my teeth, my bones. I needed to solidify our connection once and for all.

We needed to bruise and ride and claim. This wasn't about sweetness and building trust—it was deeper than that. Something that joined us more holy than marriage or a lifetime of togetherness.

"Take me, Roan. I trust you."

He moaned loud and long. "I can't—I don't want to hurt you. This was a mistake." His body imprisoned me, creating a blanket of lust-filled male.

"Yes, you can." My hands landed on his ass.

He shuddered in my hold—his teeth grinding loudly. "Stop."

"No." I sank nails deep into his flesh and pulled him possessively into me. It was the first time I'd taken him. The first time I'd taken everything he offered and more.

His length sank in deep and wide, bringing heat and waves of desire. Every stretch was delicious. Perfect.

His self-control snapped and he threw his head back. "Oh my God. Goddammit, you feel—" He didn't finish as he thrust in deeper—eternally deep. I couldn't keep my eyes open— overwhelmed by the scrumptious fullness, the complete knowledge he was mine and I was his.

"See. You can. You have more control than you know." Wrapping my legs tighter around his hips, I imprisoned him. "I trust you to love me. To not hurt me. Give me everything you have to give, Roan Averin."

Every muscle stood out in stark relief, vibrating with pent-up aggression and only orders he could hear. He shuddered uncontrollably.

Reaching for his neck, I grabbed two handfuls of hair and yanked his lips to mine. "You can do this. Fight through it," I panted against his lips.

He shook his head, tugging the strands in my grip. "What if I hurt you? Shit, Zel, you're pregnant. Am I even allowed to be inside you like this?" His nostrils flared and his hips tried to wiggle out of my locked legs.

"You're not going anywhere." Grabbing more of his hair, I forced him to kiss me. My tongue entered his mouth and a tremor quaked down his back.

Biting his lower lip, I murmured, "I'll touch you if you take me. I'll stroke you if you make me come. I'll always be yours, Roan. Prove to me you can keep me safe."

I deliberately drove him to breaking point. It was fascinating to feel the change in him. The haunted look swirled in his depths. The violence of his past swallowed him whole. But through the transformation from human to machine he pressed his forehead against mine and locked eyes. He locked himself to me. Soul to soul.

Gone was the fight to protect me. His cock pressed deeper and his body smothered harder. He thrust once, gritting his teeth. "I can't be slow. Don't ask me to be slow."

I nodded, stroking his back, thrilling with terror and want. "Take me however you need."

His body slammed into me once, twice, before he found control and stopped—vibrating with barely held restraint. "I'm so fucking scared." His voice wavered and the plea in his eyes almost made me let him go.

Almost.

"I trust you." I'd keep repeating it over and over again until it seeped into his psyche and freed him. "You can't hurt the baby. Take me. I won't ask again."

He switched from human to animal. He let go of everything.

His hips pulled back before colliding with mine with a ferocity that echoed in my heart. Everything about him switched to possessive greed. His face shut down. Lips pursed. Sweat beaded.

"Don't trust me. Don't fucking trust me," he growled, driving into me. Every stroke of his cock claimed ownership and I let him steal me away.

Nothing else existed but him inside me and his hard heat above me. I locked my legs tighter, pulling him achingly deep.

His mouth latched onto my neck, sucking, biting. Sparks of gold and silver whizzed in my blood, intoxicating me—making me come back to life.

"Yes. Take me," I panted as Roan drove violently into me. Every thrust he lost himself until I didn't know which man I held. Obsidian Fox or Roan Averin.

The bed screeched across the floor, the bedding slip-slided all over the mattress as he took everything I had to offer. He was right.

It wasn't gentle. It wasn't sweet. It was dirty and cruel and broken.

But I couldn't get enough.

His hands landed on my hips, holding me in place as he increased his rhythm. His face twisted until he looked furiously angry.

My heart no longer beat—it hummed like a hummingbird as every thrust unlocked a power deep inside me. A power over this man. Over my fate. Over my sadness and happiness and future.

Love swelled like a typhoon in my chest, evolving, growing until it filled every space and cavity. I visualized love protecting the new life inside me—spreading to Roan and healing him. It kept growing until my body had no more space and it exploded out of me, showering us both in emotion.

"God, I—I can't stop." Roan reared back, his face shiny with sweat. "I'm hurting you. God, I'm sorry. So damn sorry." His eyes were wild, skin ashen. "The baby. Make me stop. Make me fucking stop." His teeth gritted as he drove particularly hard into me.

My body sparked with electricity, static crackled between us. I couldn't stop. Not when I was so close to falling over the precipice of a release I desperately wanted.

This was between me and him.

Life and death.

Possession and ownership.

I threw my head back. "You're not hurting me. I trust you."

"Stop saying that!" He groaned, increasing his rhythm until I felt sure I'd snap in two. "Don't trust me. Never trust me."

His guttural moan vibrated through his chest as the first ripple of need travelled down his cock, massaging me with the fierceness of his impending orgasm.

My body clenched, tightened, wound. Taking me out of this stratosphere and placing me on a shooting star. A comet where everything was happy and perfect and there was no tragedy or sadness.

A star.

Her star.

Grief tried to steal me from his embrace and I clamped my eyes shut. Focusing only on his heat and vitality. The more Roan took me, the more he pulled away. Our bodies were connected but our souls had lost each other.

I needed to find him again.

To finish what we'd started.

"More. Please, more." I wrapped my arms around his shoulders, dragging him back against me. He moaned as his entire body went bow-string tight, landing on top of mine. His hips pistoned as I held on, never letting him go. Our breathing mingled, panting out of control.

Every stroke was delicious; every motion sent me higher up the mountain of claiming the most incredible orgasm of my life.

I relished in the fierceness of him, the absolute ownership of his body on top of me. Full body contact. Something completely new.

I loved hugging him.

I loved being blanketed by him.

The first spindle and body-shivering band of my release teetered just out of reach. I dug nails into his ass, curving into him, meeting his every thrust.

Roan cried out with all the torture in the world—lost in whatever mind-warp he suffered. "I—I fucking love you," he snapped, violence tinging every part of him.

That was all I needed.

The knowledge he loved me gave me the strength to brave the unknown future. Gave me the courage to love another just like I'd loved Clara.

I came.

I unravelled and combusted all in one go. The orgasm wasn't just in my pussy; it existed in every blood cell, in every breath I took, in every part of me. On and on the waves rolled, mimicking the crashing surf outside.

"Yes. Yes. Don't stop."

"I'll never stop." His mouth found mine in a battle of lips. He poured struggle, love, and commitment right into my heart.

I felt complete.

I hadn't even known I was missing something until he gave me everything he was.

I'd never be free of him. Just like he'd never be free of me.

I cried out as the contractions of my release squeezed around his cock. He shivered and thrust harder. "I'm coming. Damn I'm fucking coming."

Roan came apart.

His thrusts lost uniformity, driving relentlessly, seeking pleasure, seeking a release. "Take me. All of me." His orgasm tore down his back, rippling like a powerful wave over his muscles. He spurted deep inside, splash after splash.

My release kept going, intensifying as our life mingled. I found, for one brief second, eternal happiness.

Gradually, Roan slowed before coming to a gentle rock. He collapsed on top, his cock twitching deep inside. His breathing was ragged and his heartbeat thudded through me like a heavy drum.

He sounded as if he'd run a gauntlet and barely survived.

"Are you okay?" I whispered.

He snorted. "Once again you ask about my wellbeing when I'm the one who just fucked you like a beast." He looked up with desolate eyes. "Can you forgive me for taking you like that? Today of all fucking days. I should've kissed you and made sweet gentle love rather than bruise you like the bastard I am."

My hand cupped his cheek. His entire body quaked and his forehead furrowed with deep tracks. Our hearts thudded so hard the bed trembled with every pulse, completely out of rhythm, racing to a crazy beat.

Not wanting to push him any further, I dropped my touch. He'd been through enough. He'd done better than I'd ever hoped.

We'd had full contact naked sex and although he'd suffered

like crazy, he hadn't once frightened me.

"You didn't bruise me and you're not a bastard. You took care of me, Roan. You protected me by battling through whatever you deal with." I smiled softly. "And that's why I trust you."

"Doesn't matter. I still had no control. I still took you harder than I wanted."

The sun had dropped from bright to twilight, sending the room into peaceful shadows. Roan rolled off me and sprawled on the tangled sheets.

Every part of me ached, but it was a good ache. A welcomed ache. It reminded me that life went on. I may have said goodbye to one precious thing in my life that I could never replace, but I'd gained more than I ever thought possible.

I propped myself up on an elbow and looked at him. He lay naked, an arm thrown over his head, his flat stomach pulsing as his heart slowly calmed.

The sweat on my skin began to chill and missed his weight on me. I missed being joined.

Sadness found me once again and I squeezed my eyes, trying to stay in the moment where tears couldn't find me.

A hand caressed my cheek. "Are you okay?"

My eyes opened, locking onto his. "No. But I think in time I will be."

His face darkened. "I miss her so much. It's like a part of me is gone. I feel guilty for wanting this baby with you because I feel like I'm betraying her. I feel guilty for living while she's gone." He dropped his hand, looking up at the ceiling. "When is it okay to let her go? When will the guilt stop?"

My eyes glossed and I flopped down beside him, wanting so much to snuggle into his embrace. "Clara wouldn't want us to feel guilty about living. But it's going to take a long time to move on."

Roan shifted, bringing his fingers to lock with mine. It wasn't enough. I wanted his arm around me. But it had to do— for now.

"Thank you. For what just happened. You gave me something I didn't even know I needed." He smiled gently. "I have no words. It was incredible."

I smiled. "Remember what I told you? Sex is meant to be enjoyed with no clothes and full body contact. You'll get the hang of it."

He laughed, then apprehension etched his face. "I managed to fight the conditioning this time, but next time…I don't know if I can. It was stupid to push so hard. Especially now—" His eyes fell to my flat stomach.

Terror filled his gaze and I rushed to stop him from spiralling deep into himself. "Don't think about next time. You probably didn't think you could achieve what just happened, but you did." I leaned over and kissed him gently. "Stop worrying. Everything will work out."

"He's hurting. He needs you, mummy."

Clara's voice captured my heart and I sucked in a breath.

A few minutes ticked by while we fell into our thoughts. The only sound came from the surf across the road. I wanted to stay in this bubble of time forever—in limbo where I didn't have to face more tears or plan a future that would be full of complications.

Roan scowled. Breaking the silence, he said, "I didn't want to do this, but it isn't about me anymore. I need to know you're safe. From me. I need to know I won't hurt you accidently or put the baby's life at risk."

Ice trickled in my blood as a bleak resolution filled his eyes. He'd made a decision without discussing with me.

Shit.

Sitting upright, I snapped, "What are you thinking? Whatever it is, stop it."

My heart picked up until it raced just as madly as before. I hated not knowing what crazy conclusions Roan had come to. *He won't leave. Will he?*

Horror heated my blood at the thought of him walking away under the pretence of protecting me and his unborn child.

"Roan. You can't—"

Cutting me off, he muttered, "I killed my handler in Russia. I broke the control he had over me. It's no longer his voice inside my head telling me to kill and murder. But the conditioning is too deep. I'll never be free because I've been taught all my life to obey a certain hierarchy." He sighed. "Do you understand?"

Tears pricked my eyes. I didn't have a clue. I'd never be able to comprehend what he lived with.

Roan didn't wait for me to reply. "I can't say I won't ever fight again. I can't say I'll ever be strong enough not to seek out pain to help deal with my issues, but I *can* say I will hurt you. It's inevitable. Sooner or later, I won't be strong enough. You'll touch me when I'm unprepared. I'll lash out and cause untold damage, and I refuse to run that risk."

My stomach pretzeled in fear. "What are you saying?" *Don't say you're leaving. Do not say you're leaving.*

"All my life, I've been controlled. I thought I could find help from you, and…Clara…" His eyes misted, then he carried on. "But I'm taking responsibility for my own condition, and I know what I need to do. You're my life now. My woman and lover. I belong to you absolutely. I can't put your life in danger every second of every day. It isn't fair on you. And I refuse to live in fear anymore."

Rolling to face me, he softened his tone, accepting his decision, whatever it was. "Once I drop the barrier in my mind, I will be yours to control in all things. It's the only way I can think to keep you safe from me."

Grasping my hand, his voice dropped to a deadly whisper. "In order to keep you safe, I need to give you the power. I need to know that I'll obey you in all things. I need an owner who I'll obey explicitly if I slip and hurt you. If I put you in position of my handler, one word from you and I'd stop. Without question."

I tried to pull my hand away, hating the thought of taking away his free will or owning rights to his thoughts and decisions. "No. I won't do it." It was barbaric. "You're not mine to control. You're a human being, not my pet."

His fingers trapped me tighter. "You will do this for me, *dobycha*. Otherwise, you will always be that for me: *dobycha*— prey. I'll never be safe around you and you'll have to be on high alert all the time. One of us will screw up and it will be you who pays. You have to do this."

He shook his head, eyes glowing with ferocity. "Do you want to stay here and raise a family with me?"

I glared. What a cruel question. Of course I did. But not at the cost of his happiness. Angry tears filled my eyes, but as much as I hated it, I couldn't argue against his logic.

It's not fair.

But it's the only way.

I knew that. I knew my knife wouldn't be enough to stop him if he forgot who he was and came after me. I wouldn't hesitate to kill him if he hurt his son. I could end up dead or murdering the man I love.

It was a living hell.

When I didn't answer, Roan said, "It has to be this way. You know it's the truth. Until I can find another solution, this is the best I can come up with. I refuse to live in fear of killing you. I'd never survive watching another person I love die."

My heart broke all over again for Clara.

For Roan's family.

For his past.

I sighed as the fight to argue evaporated. I couldn't deny it made sense. And I couldn't pretend that both mine and our unborn child's safety weren't worthy of a sacrifice to keep us alive. "Only until we can find another cure."

He nodded, smiling, but it didn't reach his eyes. I sucked in a breath at the truth in his gaze. He didn't believe he'd ever be normal. He'd given up hope. He'd accepted that this was the way his life had to be—his last chance to find some resemblance of happiness.

I wanted to kill every evil bastard who'd done this to him.

They'd not only ruined Roan's life but mine and his children's, too.

He'd never be free—always be haunted by ghosts.

"Don't give up. Promise me you won't give up." Squeezing his hand, I vowed, "I will never use the power over you for anything other than protecting myself or our future child. You have my ultimate word. But this is only temporary. I know one day you'll find freedom."

He leaned in and gave me the sweetest kiss. Holding me steady, he licked the seam of my lips. His dark taste danced me away from reality and into a happier place. He kissed me to avoid lying to me.

He wouldn't keep trying because he was tired. He'd fought the battle for too long.

I moaned as his teeth nipped on my bottom lip, sending more fireworks to unfurl. He tasted of freedom and future. I wanted so much for him to find ultimate happiness.

When he pulled back, something had changed. He'd activated the conditioning. I didn't know how it worked but he'd given me power over him. And it fucking killed him.

Sighing heavily, he said, "It's done. You're safe." His snowy eyes glowed with a mixture of hate and satisfaction. Relief and frustration.

My gaze grew wet at the thought of irrevocably owning this man. It wasn't natural. It wasn't human. But he'd given every obedience to me.

I felt as if he'd handed over a leash, pulling him to heel. I lost a bit of him even as he sacrificed so much.

Clara would've hated it. She would've known what he'd done. She would've made him find another way.

"Don't give up. He needs you, mummy. Don't be sad."

Keeping my grief at bay, I nodded, accepting his gift. "I love you."

He smiled, bringing me into the crook of his arm. His touch sent heat and burning embers across my skin. Every time he touched me, it was like he gave a part of himself—shared his energy with me.

That's true.

He just gave me his soul.

Kissing the top of my head, he whispered, "And I love you." Sucking a deep breath, he laughed, forcing merriment rather than sadness into his voice. "You own me heart and soul, Hazel Hunter. You're not just my lover but my handler and I will walk over blades for you. I would kill for you. I will lay down my life for you."

Nuzzling my neck, he murmured, "You have the power over a highly trained Ghost. What is your first command, mistress?"

My heart thumped at the pain hidden in his voice. The gift he'd given me. I swore then and there I would find a cure. I would never stop until I fixed the man who fixed me.

Ignoring the painful tug in my heart, I smiled against his lips. "Kiss me. Make love to me. Make me look forward to our future."

His head bowed, lips captured mine.

His eyes locked with mine as he reverently whispered, "Yes, ma'am."

Epilogue

My life ended three times before I finally had enough.

I'd been a boy, a Ghost, a man fumbling to find his place.

I never belonged.

My past was unchangeable, but my future was unwritten and rule free.

Invincible, Impenetrable, Invisible no longer applied to me.

I adopted three new things:

Resurrection.

Redemption.

Resolution.

All my life, I'd been a pawn. But not anymore.

I was a provider, lover, father, and friend.

In the wake of heartbreak came new life, and I was given a second chance. I accepted my handicap and grew to live with it rather than fight it. It wasn't so bad having the woman I adored being my ruler.

But then came the silver lining. The ultimate dream.

I'd been right all along.

There was a cure.

Clara died in February, leaving us to face life on our own. Zel and I spent the first month doing nothing but healing and walking along the beach. It gave us time to grow and mend and develop a deeper dimension to our unconventional romance.

March came and went undetected—just four more weeks without Clara.

April brought a chill, signalling summer was over, and it was time to say goodbye to flowers and heat and sunshine. I returned to Obsidian to collect my tools and smithy equipment. I wanted to start sculpting again. I wanted to recreate Clara's amazing spirit using bronze and copper.

May Clue announced she and Ben were moving in together and Ben bought a house not far from us in the Northern Beaches. He still went to Obsidian to fight, and he gave me a standing offer to beat me bloody if I ever needed my strange kind of therapy.

I took him up on the offer once or twice.

"I love it when you come home all sweaty." Zel appeared around the corner of the lounge. Her small arms wrapped around my torso. "Don't you get hot running all in black?" Her eyes found mine, smouldering with lust. "I want you, Roan. I watched you on the beach. I missed you."

The swell of her pregnant belly pressed against my abs and I suffered a heinous flashback. It tore me from safety to howling winter and the pit. Snarls of wolves filled my head and I regressed.

It was the first of the month. The day that was worse for me than the rest—the day our conditioning was rebooted—reprogramed.

I grabbed her neck, fingers disobeying my commands. I squeezed her throat with uncontrollable anger. "Don't ever touch me."

I watched my actions as if my soul was unencumbered by my body. A spectator as I wrung the neck of the woman I adored. Screaming silently, I raged to stop but the conditioning pulled me under its unbreakable web.

Zel's eyes filled with glittering terror and her fingers flew to her hair.
I grabbed her wrist—stopping her from going for her knife.
"Not this time, dobycha. *Not this time."*
Her body flailed and she tried to kick and squirm, but it was no use.
There was nothing I could do. I would kill her and I would swallow a
bullet afterward for not being strong enough to save her.
Then Hazel saved both of us.
"Take your fucking hands off me, Operative Fox. Stand down this
instant."
The order sliced through my foggy haze, dispelling the howling wolves
and eternity of ice.
I blinked.
The command took all control away from me and I cowered. Pain.
Torture. Payback for disobeying.
Loathing filled me, crippling my limbs as I skidded away and sucked
in ragged breaths. I couldn't do it. I'd done what I'd been terrified of. I lost
control. If I hadn't given Zel power over me, I would've killed my fucking
family all over again.
I ran.
And Corkscrew delivered retribution.

That was at the start of May. By the end of the month, we'd
settled once again into a routine and Clue popped around
often. She and Zel remained close and for the first time in my
life, I had a network of people who saw me for what I was and
accepted me. Dinners were a bi-weekly affair, and Clue kept
Hazel distracted from her thoughts when they turned sad by
planning a ridiculous baby shower and choosing colours for the
nursery.

June was the first month Zel felt the baby kick. It
effectively did what I'd hoped all along. It showed that Clara no
longer needed us, but a new life did. It helped us stay strong
and granted peace. Hazel wasn't completely happy but more
and more I'd catch a soft smile or contentedness mixing with
her heavy grief. She spent a lot of time in the room I'd made
for her. Talking to Clara, stroking the horse statues that she
loved so much.

July Clue and Ben took us out for dinner to celebrate Hazel's twenty-fifth birthday. It was the first party I'd been to, the only one I'd ever celebrated. I couldn't remember my own birth date, so Hazel let me share hers. We ate decadent food and went on a cruise around Sydney harbour. I gave Zel her present when we got back—another metal sheep to stand proud and perfect beside Clara's. It'd been the best night of my life.

August we finished the nursery. And Zel unpacked boxes full of Clara's toys. She decorated the space with memories of her daughter, ready for a new child to play with. I did fear if the child was a boy, though. The amount of My Little Pony stuff that littered groaning shelves would scare any male.

Every day that passed healed as well as hurt. And I often heard Clara in my head. She'd become my unofficial conscience. My lifeline when the conditioning grew too strong.

September, Hazel went into labour. She'd opted for another caesarean after the complications with Clara's birth, and I watched absolutely fucking terrified as she brought not one, but two lives into the world.

My heart broke, mended, and then shattered all over again to think we'd been given one new life, and Clara had somehow found a way to come back to us. I couldn't thank the universe enough. I became a fucking fool—wandering the hospital corridors in a daze while I waited for the nurses to make Zel comfortable.

It'd been a whirlwind of fear and joy. I hadn't wanted to watch Zel be cut open and two little lives pulled out, but she made me stay and hold her hand.

It was the least I could do.

And I'd fallen head over heels all over again. She was so fucking strong. So brave.

Once Zel had been stitched up and the babies cleaned and weighed, Clue and Ben arrived to coo and blow kisses at the tiny bundles in blankets. Ben had seemed more smitten than Clue. His dark skin flushing with awe and eyes filling with future possibilities whenever he glanced at his woman. I had no doubt he had babies on the brain.

I hadn't gone near the twins. I hadn't lied to Zel when I said I was petrified. I wasn't strong enough. I wanted to see them, touch them, but I stayed away for protection.

The moment I'd set eyes on them, I'd been possessed. The love I'd had for Clara increased as my heart swelled for my children. A family I never thought I would have.

I never wanted to be a father. I never thought it would be in my future. I didn't think I would care for anything or knew how to love. But Clara cured me of that ridiculous notion. She'd taught me what my true purpose was. She brought me back to life and if it was up to me, I'd have a fucking plethora of children.

I sighed, entering the private room where Hazel rested. It was late, and the neonatal wing of the hospital was hushed.

The bedside light glowed softly, pooling around Zel. I stopped beside the bed, drinking in the tiredness around her eyes, her tangled hair spread on the pillow. She couldn't have looked more perfect. She'd fought and won. She'd created two intricate, incredible little lives.

Her forehead furrowed while she dreamed and I wondered what went on behind her mask. Oscar had been right about her. She was quiet but there was so much I didn't know about her. So much she hadn't shared. I didn't know who'd fathered Clara. I didn't know how she got the scar below her eye.

I'd tried to piece together little puzzles of what her life might've been like before Clara, but found I couldn't. She hid her past so well and threw all her attention into her future.

I hadn't pried because I wanted her to tell me on her own terms. But the curiosity never left. Then again, she didn't know much about me. We'd come into this relationship hiding who we truly were and found a new identity in each other.

Our baggage had no room to be aired. And I liked to think nothing in our past mattered. If we kept it sealed and hidden, it would eventually cease to exist. Just a distant memory.

Reaching to cup her pale cheek, I swallowed back the overwhelming love.

Her green eyes opened. Foggy at first, but the moment she recognised me, her smile beamed with affection. Affection for me. *What did I ever do to deserve her?*

She cleared her throat and shifted, wincing a little. "Have you held them yet?" Her voice was hushed in the quiet space only interrupted by low beeps and monitors around the room.

A flash of fear darted down my spine. *Hold them.* I couldn't. The past few months had been torturous. Day by day, the conditioning grew stronger again rather than fading.

I'd hoped it would disappear the more I ignored it, but it was the exact opposite—crushing me from the inside out.

"No. I can love them from afar." I dropped my hand to link with her fingers, tensing a little as her grip threaded with mine. The familiar, unforgiving orders radiated up my arm, coercing with commands to hurt her.

"They're yours, Roan. You have to hold them. They need to see their father."

I swallowed hard, looking over at the twin bassinets. The babies were barely visible in bundled up blankets. They wouldn't be here if I hadn't made Zel my handler.

Not a day passed that I didn't thank my fucking genius plan at giving her power over me.

If I hadn't, she'd be dead.

After the incident in May, I'd had two more episodes. Two more times where she had to leave the realm of my equal and assert command over me. I'd told her how to say it, what tone of voice to use.

"Take your fucking hands off me, Operative Fox. Stand down this instant." She cried every time she had to yell it, but at least she was alive. I didn't begrudge her the power over me. It was the only way to love her and not chain myself twenty-four seven. Sleeping with handcuffs was bad enough.

"Maybe when they're older, *dobycha*. Don't make me. Not tonight."

Her eyes flashed and the strength I loved about her tensed her body. "Tonight, Roan. It's important."

I wanted to scream at her not to push. This was one instant where I didn't want her help. I needed time. Time to get my head straight and hope to God I had control. I stupidly hoped I could wait till the twins could speak and teach them the command to stop me.

That way my family became my handlers and they would all be safe from me.

I'm a fucking Rottweiler on a leash.

"Don't." I glared at her. "Leave me alone. Let me keep them safe the only way I know how."

Her jaw clenched.

I leaned forward, encroaching on her space. "Think for a moment. You want me to hold two very innocent, very tiny human beings. You want me to touch new life while barely containing the violence of my past." I jerked a hand through my longish hair. "You should know not to ask for miracles, Zel. Every night you try to push me to snuggle. To see if I have the strength to sleep with you in my arms."

I leaned further, breathing hard. "Tell me what happens. Tell me how successful I am at holding you tenderly and sweet."

Her gaze skittered from mine, sadness mixing with anger. "I don't need to tell you what happens. We both know you're getting worse instead of getting better. But…" She plucked the bedspread, eyebrows drawing together. Finally she looked back into my eyes. "If it's getting worse don't you think you should hold them now? In case you can't at all?"

I hated that I'd lumped her with half a life. Half a man who could fuck her but never make love to her. A man who wanted nothing more than to give her everything all while my past tried to steal her future. I feared every day that she'd grow to hate me for my shortcomings.

I shook my head. "No."

Zel clutched the covers. "Don't be scared. You can do

this." She played the card that always made me bend to her will. "I trust you."

It was an aphrodisiac to me. Gaining her trust. Doing things to justify that trust.

"You're destined to kill me, aren't you?" I groaned, dragging a hand over my face. She'd won and she knew it.

She smiled softly, her beautiful lips distracting me. "Not killing you—making you live."

"Fine," I snapped. "But be prepared to stop me if I can't control it. I can't handle the thought of hurting them."

She nodded. "You have my word. I'll watch you like an over protective mother."

Ever so slowly, I drifted toward the two small cots. I looked upon two tiny raisin-like faces. One pink hat. One blue.

So tiny. So small.

Vasily and Vera.

Named after my brother and mother. I'd asked Zel if she wanted to call our daughter Clara, but her face had tightened and tears glossed her eyes. She said Clara was unique, and no one could live up to her name.

But then her gaze had come alive and she offered me the world. She proposed to call them after my lost family, I had to walk out of the room and hide my suddenly burning eyes. I'd turned into a fucking sap. I wanted to buy her every fucking jewel on the planet to show how much the gesture meant to me. I still hadn't told her about my lineage, or that the twins were now twenty-fifth in line to an obscure royal family who would never be recognised again.

Zel sat higher in bed, watching me. "Hold them. They're yours, Roan."

She could've fooled me. Both had dark hair, no red in sight. Vera had vibrant green eyes like her mother, while Vasily had ice blue just like his namesake. A small piece of me wrapped up in so much of Hazel.

I wonder if Clara looked so tiny when she was born.

My heart spasmed at the thought of the little girl who I

missed with every part of me.

"Roan."

My eyes darted to Zel; my heart thumped like a crazed animal.

She sat higher in bed, face strained from the delivery and what I was about to do. "You won't hurt them. Believe in yourself."

But I will hurt them.

I was too big, too unpredictable. Some days I was fine—able to contain myself. Others, I was a fucking menace and spent the day running on the beach or hiding in the shower with a razor blade.

I loved my perfect world, but I was exhausted for trying to be just as perfect. No matter how hard I tried, I would never fit in.

"Operative Fox, you will hold your son right now," Hazel commanded in the voice she knew would give me no choice.

Obey. Obey. Obey.

"Goddammit, Hazel." I glared, hating her for a brief moment for using the power against me. "You broke your vow, *dobycha*. I don't appreciate being made to do something that might end up destroying me.*"

Her shoulders slumped but eyes flashed with green fire. "I'm doing it for your own good."

My limbs were no longer mine to control. They'd been given an order and I had no choice but to move forward and obey. Damn her. Damn me. Damn everything.

I rolled my shoulders, trying to dispel my anger. I loved her for wanting to help, but I was pissed.

How dare she break her promise? How dare she force me to do this?

That's why I hadn't wanted another owner. Willpower was never my own. It sucked ass not having a choice over my own fucking destiny.

I stood vibrating, looming over the cots. *Don't do it.*
Obey. Obey. Obey.

I can't!

My muscles hurt with disobeying but they were so *tiny*. So vulnerable.

Zel sighed heavily. The bedding rustled as she moved against the pillow. "I take it back, Roan. Operative Fox, you no longer have to obey."

The release on my body was instantaneous. The crippling urge to scoop up my infants gone in a gust of relief.

I sucked in a breath. "Thank you."

"I'm sorry. That wasn't fair of me. But, Roan. Hold your son. You have to do it eventually. He can't grow up with a father who won't touch him." She looked pointedly at the sleeping boy. "You're the one who committed to this. So do it."

I didn't want to do any of this. I wanted the twins back inside Zel where they could be safe forever.

"Fucking hell," I muttered.

"I heard that," she snapped. "Watch what you say around them. You don't want their first word to be a curse. And watch your emotions around them, too. You don't want them to feed off your anger or frustration."

I whirled to face her. "Then why the hell do you want me to pick him up! Aren't I safer over here?" I stalked to the other side of the room, breathing hard. I hated the way my muscles wanted to obey and pick up the delicate bundle of baby, but I didn't have it in me. I didn't have the strength.

I'll kill him.

I'd be responsible for yet another death. Another murder of a life called Vasily. I. Couldn't. Fucking. Do. It.

Zel huffed, looking like a queen in her blue nightgown. "Don't make me command you again. Don't think I won't do it. You know you'll have no choice and you need to make this your choice, Roan." Zel's face softened. "I trust you; otherwise I wouldn't tell you to do it. As much as I love you, I wouldn't let you near Vasily and Vera if I thought you'd hurt them."

My heart swelled, and I almost fell to my fucking knees. It

never got old hearing that she loved me. She—this perfect woman who put up with all my fucking bullshit. I also loved the way she said their names. It was like conjuring the family I barely remembered. Making me whole for the first time in my life.

Ah, fuck. She was right.

I had to do it. I had to face my fear and win.

Clenching my jaw, I moved back toward the basinets and bent over the tiny newborns.

With my heart in my throat, I placed shaking hands around the thick blue blanket and scooped up the lightest human being I'd ever held.

Kill. Sever. Bleed. Devour.

The conditioning crescendod through me with the power of a wrecking ball.

No!

My muscles locked down as I stood shaking and terrified. My jaw ached, battling the conditioning, forcing myself to hold on.

He was so light and tiny. So fragile. It was utterly dangerous for me to be anywhere near him.

Keeping him far away from me, I looked into his screwed up, frankly ugly, little face. The blue hat made him look like a shrivelled up old man.

You're mine.

He's mine.

The bond that exploded through my heart almost beat back the conditioning.

Kill. Sever. Bleed. Devour.

"Support him against you." Zel laughed quietly. "He'll feel unprotected at arm's length like that."

What was this woman trying to do to me? Fuck this was hard. Turning to face her, I demanded, "You have him. I can't do it."

She pursed her lips. "You're holding him. You can do this."

Kill. Sever. Bleed. Devour.

My head shook wildly. "No. I can't. It's back. It's worse. I don't—I can't—"

Zel didn't say a word, but her eyes gave me the final order. *Cuddle him.*

How the hell could a machine like me cuddle an infant? Cursing my past and everything in my head, I slowly brought Vasily against my body and pressed him into the crook of my arm.

Kill. Sever. Bleed. Devour.

The second his weightless form and barely there warmth hit my body, my world ended.

Wolves howled.

Guns fired.

Swords clashed.

A vortex consumed me, ripping me into shreds, tearing my brain apart. I hurled down and down into dark recesses of my mind, careening me from hospital room to the last clear memory of my childhood.

"Don't go too far, Roan. Dinner isn't far away, and your father will be home soon." I smiled at my perfect mother. Reaching up to play with her red curls, I nodded. "I promise."

I broke that fucking promise and brought the apocalypse on my entire family.

Trees creaked.

The moon shone silver.

My teeth ached as I fought, fucking fought, the conditioning

Kill. Sever. Bleed. Devour.

I'd never be free. I had to die. I had to kill myself.

"Roan! Roan!"

With my free hand, I clutched my skull as clanking bells echoed in my ears.

Louder and louder.

Bells and chimes and trumpets.

Every brainwash, every bar and chain I'd been trapped in started unravelling.

Faster and faster, padlock after padlock.

Every inch of my past and torture ceased to exist. Every switch and order that made me the obedient machine I was disintegrated.

Wind whistled.

Ice prickled.

Freedom fell like rain.

Every shackle and programed obedience slithered out of my brain, thudding at my feet with the sounds of clunking iron. Standing still, barely breathing in case it was all a dream, I burst into life as everything filthy and tainted in my mind erupted into flames and dissolved into ash.

Sun shone.

Butterflies flew.

Laughter filled my ears.

My world spun and spun. Throwing me out of my old existence, leaving me homeless and adrift.

Then a new world began. A world I never hoped dream for. A world where my thoughts were my own and nobody could strip them from me.

The vortex that'd stolen me from hospital to past dumped me back into reality. But it wasn't the same one as before. It wasn't the same subspace or even the same galaxy.

My past had gone forever.

My future was fucking bright and clean.

Birds chirped.

Love swelled.

Blissful happiness filled my heart.

I opened my eyes.

Zel was halfway out of bed, clutching her abdomen where fresh stitches held her together. Panic covered her face with damp sweat while her eyes were wild with terror. "Don't. Stop it! Don't hurt him!"

I raced to catch her before she passed out and fell flat on her face. "Zel, no!"

Holding my son in one arm, I pushed the woman I was

going to marry back into bed and brought the sheet up over her shuddering body. Her face was ashen, waxy with stress.

My heart hadn't known such love. I'd never believed I could feel so fucking happy.

I stood numbly, drinking in how much I loved her. How much she'd given me.

She snatched Vasily from my arms, hugging him close. Tears glassed her eyes.

"Goddammit, Roan. You almost gave me a fucking heart attack." She curved her body around Vasily. He began to cry under her fierce embrace.

His wails were music to my ears because there was nothing else. No orders. No rush of conditioning.

All there was were the harsh shrieks of my son and the ragged pants of the woman I adored.

I felt like fucking laughing.

Livid tears spilled down her cheeks. "What the *hell* were you doing? My God. Can I never trust you? Will you never be free?" Her body shook as shock took over. "How can we raise them together if you can't ever be around them? What hope is there? What—"

It wasn't fair that she was so distraught and I was walking on air.

Grabbing her chin, I jerked her mouth up and kissed her. I kissed her like I'd always wanted to. With my entire soul.

I didn't have to fight anything. I didn't have to watch my thoughts or guard myself against her touch.

It was fucking heaven.

Twenty-eight years and I'd finally found what I'd always wanted.

Happiness.

Her lips froze beneath mine. I tasted salt from her tears and sorrow from her tongue. Pulling away, I murmured, "Don't cry."

Her eyes widened as she rocked a screaming Vasily. "Don't cry? If I can't cry over the fact I love a man who can't be around his children what can I cry about? It's hopeless. Everything—it's over."

My stomach twisted at the desolation in her voice.

"I can't do this anymore. I can't live in fear that I'll find you've ransacked the nursery or stolen our children's lives. I want you gone—"

The dagger went straight through my heart. There was no conditioning to wade through or fog of anger. Everything affected me a hundred times stronger. A thousand times deeper.

It was like exposing myself to a whole new existence where the sun burned my skin, tears dissolved my will, and Zel's sadness ripped out my heart with claws.

"Don't. It's over, *dobycha*. It's over."

She sniffed, dropping her eyes. "I know it's over. It has to be." A sob escaped her lips.

Something monumental had happened. Something I never dreamed was possible. And instead of celebrating she was trying to cut me out of her life.

I'm not letting you go. Ever.

Prying one of her arms from around Vasily's shoulders, I tugged her hand toward me.

Her lips popped open. She fought me. "Let me go. Stop it." Her eyes narrowed. "Take your hands off me, Operative Fox."

I paused, tensing for a wave of conditioning, so used to obeying all my life.

Nothing.

Heavenly nothing.

Blessed fucking *nothing*.

No rush of orders.

No crush of commands.

No debilitating need to kill.

I smiled and unwound her tight fingers. "You said you trusted me. Trust me one last time." My voice even sounded different. Less gruff. Less bound to a past I'd always run from.

Zel froze, then let her hand go slack. She never took her

eyes off me as I very carefully laid her hand on my forearm.

I looked up, drowning in her emerald gaze. "What do you see?"

She shook her head. "I don't understand. What are you trying to do?"

I removed her hand and put it against my chest, directly over my heart. Her body tensed, feeling the racing beat beneath her fingertips. Her fear surrounded me but slowly a trace of hope filled her eyes.

"What do you feel?" I murmured.

She gasped, twitching her fingers against my chest. Her touch sent boomerangs of aliveness and heat through me. Branding me. Making me hers. Always hers.

"You're different." Cocking her head, she narrowed her eyes. "What happened? What's changed? I don't understand."

I laughed, feeling weightless.

Guiding her hand up my chest, I shivered as her gentle touch came up my throat and tangled with Clara's silver star around my neck. Her face spasmed with grief before I brought her fingers up and up, until her entire palm cupped my scarred cheek.

I never let her touch my scar.

I hated it.

It was hotwired to my conditioning.

It ruled my life for so long.

Dropping my fingers from hers, I whispered, "What do you sense?"

The hope she'd nursed exploded into her entire body. Vasily stopped crying and a brilliant smile lit her tear-streaked face. "It's gone?"

My heart expanded until I couldn't breathe. My legs wobbled in sheer gratefulness.

"Oh, my God. Roan… it's true?"

Shivers captured my skin sending goosebumps and every emotion that had been muted all my life over my skin. Love exploded my heart. I nodded. "It's gone. All of it. Every last bit."

Her hand clutched my cheek harder, dropped to cup my chin. "Are you sure?" Her eyes danced with hope and hesitation.

I wanted to scream. I wanted to dance. I couldn't stand still with the joy frothing in my stomach. "Positive. Every bad thing inside. Every fucked-up need to obey. Every mind-twisting command is gone. It's disappeared."

She went from ashen to fucking glowing. Fresh tears filled her eyes, but this time they beamed with happiness. "You're free?"

I laughed, stepping backward.

Every movement was lighter.

My vision brighter.

"I'm free."

"I'm normal."

I'm a father.

My eyes wrenched wide and I spun around. I was a father and I was free. I'd never thought I could have so much.

Striding to the cot, I scooped up Vera in her pretty pink cap. Her round eyes opened, locking onto mine.

Blue to white. I fell madly in love.

My heart expanded to include a little girl I'd lost. A little girl I'd gained. And a son and woman I belonged to.

"Hello, Vera," I whispered.

The little girl yawned, her tiny lips stretching wide. She squirmed in her blankets. I knew right then and there things would be okay.

I brought her to my lips and pressed a kiss on her forehead.

She was mine.

She was my new chance.

My future was bright and safe.

Vasily had broken my curse.

Six weeks later, once Zel had healed enough to return home and the twins were safely absconded in their nursery, I planned a special evening just for the two of us.

While Zel was upstairs kissing the twins and telling them stories of a big sister they'd never meet, I decorated the lounge in a gazillion candles. I ordered a banquet of finger foods and delicious entrees and laid large sheepskins on the floor beside the roaring fire.

Tonight, I was going to make love to my woman.

For the first time.

Every time I thought about how different my life had become, I would stop and lose myself in memories. It felt as if I'd lived my entire life in shadows. Listening to conversations under water, and experiencing joy down a long tunnel with no light. Every since my conditioning broke, I hadn't stopped touching.

I barely put the twins down.

Zel couldn't walk past me without running her hands over my back or trailing fingertips through my hair. We hadn't had sex since the birth, but we'd never been so intimate. So in tune.

I'd never been so fucking happy.

Tonight I planned on seducing a woman for the first time in my life. I'd never bought candles or sourced romantic music. I'd never ordered food based on their aphrodisiac qualities.

Vasily and Vera had given me a brand new world to explore and indulge, and I didn't want to miss a second.

My heart raced at the thought of taking Zel. Of worshipping her with everything I could. I wanted to know what it would be like to hug her and hold her tight with none of the shit I'd lived with.

There would be no past or Ghosts or terror.

There would only be love and lust and hunger.

"Wow, you've been busy," Zel's voice sounded behind me.

I spun to face her, never getting used to the way my love for her sucker-punched me the gut. "Shit, I wanted to have all of this ready before you came down."

I still hadn't presented the food how I wanted. And the statue I'd made her hadn't been covered. Damn it.

I moved to hide it, but Zel sucked in a gasp.

"Oh, my God. Did you make that?" She drifted forward, absorbed by the half metre statue I'd done over the course of several nights. The conditioning might have broken, but I still struggled to sleep in the dark.

After a lifetime of sleeping during the day—those patterns hadn't changed overnight.

"Do you like it?" Nervousness scattered down my spine.

Her gaze landed on mine, full of awe. "Do I *like* it? How can you ask me that? I love it. I more than love it. Roan...it's perfect."

My heart hurt as she stroked the bronze artwork with a shaky fingertip.

I let some of who I'd been return, but I did it willingly. I had the choice. I embraced the hunter side of me as I stalked toward the woman I would spend the rest of my life with.

I'd made it for her. A complex blend of her and me. Our beginning and our future. I wanted her to see how much I cared for her. How much I belonged to her and how much she was mine. All mine. For fucking ever.

It wasn't a clear-cut design, more tribal than certain shapes. Masculine and feminine lines showed a sea-froth full of horses. Five in total with Russian names engraved in their manes.

Clara. Roan. Hazel. Vasily and Vera.

Five points of paradise. Amongst the crashing waves, weaving in with the galloping legs were stars—a million glittering stars inlaid with silver.

Stars for Clara.

Zel sniffed, twisting to face me. "You couldn't have made a

more perfect piece." Her hands landed on my chest.

I jolted with pleasure, still amazed how much her touch resonated through my every cell.

Her eyes lit with worry. "Are you okay?" She swallowed, her gaze darting all over me. "You aren't regressing, are you?"

The fear at the thought doused all my lust in an icy wash. I hoped to God that never fucking happened. I couldn't stomach the thought of living with the conditioning again.

I'd have a brain transplant first. I could never go back.

Shaking my head, I dropped my mouth to hers. She kissed me sweetly, innocently, still slightly afraid.

Pulling away, I murmured, "No. I jumped because I'll never get used to you touching me. It makes me come alive. It makes me want you so fucking much."

A blush coloured her cheeks.

I kissed her, nipping at her lower lip. "Touch me again."

Zel obeyed. Her hands came up and landed on the buttons of my white shirt. Slowly, she unbuttoned it. The room filled with throbbing tension, cracking between us. I couldn't tear my eyes away from her and groaned as she pushed aside the material and placed her hands on my chest.

My cock swelled.

My vision popped with bright lights.

"Goddammit, Zel you have the power to bring me to my knees."

Her lips parted and her touch grew firmer, branding me with fire. Every fingertip was fucking heaven. Hot and gentle, possessive and female. She could undo me with a simple stroke.

I held my breath as she pushed the white shirt off my shoulders. My heart raced. "I was the one who wanted to seduce you. But you're the one in control again."

Emerald eyes shot to mine and I drowned in fucking love for her. "You don't need to seduce me."

I shook my head. "I wanted to remind you that you belong to me. That you may have two little lives to look after, but I still own you, just like you own me."

She bit her lip as a torrent of emotion skittered over her face. Her finger looped around the star necklace at her throat. The same necklace we wore to honour Clara's memory. Every time things became too much for her, she'd touch the silver and find peace to carry on. I always knew when she let sadness take her hostage—the light in her would dim—almost as if she left part of herself in this world to go and talk to a daughter who no longer existed in human form.

My heart hurt, remembering the little girl who would've been the best big sister in the world. I would never stop thinking of Clara and what she did for me, but tonight wasn't about grief. Tonight was all about celebration.

"You don't need to remind me. I know I'm yours. Just like Clara was. Just like Vasily and Vera are. You deserve all of us, Roan. You make me complete."

I couldn't help it. I grabbed the back of her neck and crushed her against me. Her taste exploded in my mouth and something snapped in her—meeting the rapidly building need in me.

Capturing the sash of her cherry coloured dressing gown, I tugged on the cord. I'd watched her take a bath earlier and I couldn't get the images of her breasts floating, covered with bubbles out of my mind. She'd looked like a delectable desert all for me.

"I want you, *dobycha*."

"I'm not your prey."

I bowed my head and bit her neck. "No? What are you then?"

She shivered as I licked her gently and dragged my nose up her chin. Inhaling her lily of the valley and clean smell of soap, I drugged myself on her.

Her eyelids fluttered closed, swaying into me as I yanked the dressing gown off her shoulders and cupped her breast. "What are you, Hazel?"

My cock throbbed to plunge inside her, but I wanted to go slow. I wanted to savour every part.

She dropped her eyes. I raised my fingers to press beneath her chin. Her lips tilted upward, looking plump and tempting.

"Kiss me," I demanded.

Her eyes grew heavy. She swayed forward on tiptoe, pressing her delicious lips against mine.

Holding her chin, I forced her to open her mouth, slinking my tongue inside. She moaned; her fingers twitched against my chest. I loved her touch. I loved her being able to touch me. I loved that I had no urge to crush her or slam her to the floor.

I couldn't have asked for a better gift.

"I love you," I whispered against her lips.

Her arms suddenly flew around me, pressing herself hard. Her curves to my edges. Her flame to my dynamite.

Gone was the need to drag out the night. I couldn't think about eating or sitting across from her and trying to ignore the pull.

The room throbbed with need. My head pounded with hunger to be inside her. I'd run out of self-control.

Gathering her up, I stumbled backward, bringing her with me. "I'm going to worship you, Zel."

She trembled in my arms, her sleek wet tongue dancing with mine.

When my bare feet sank into the fluffy sheepskins on the floor, I lowered us down until I sat upright, and she straddled my lap.

I groaned as her hands dropped from my chest to my buckle. I no longer wore black. I no longer had a compulsion to dress in a colour that offered me some form of safety. I wore whatever colour struck me. I embraced designs and patterns.

I still didn't wear underwear though, and gasped as Zel's hot hand wrapped around my cock.

She pumped me once, causing my stomach to clench. Fire exploded in my balls. I lost all thought and control. I struggled to stay coherent. "Zel. Wait—I want…"

Her every touch annihilated me, not because I no longer

wanted to kill her, but because she brought me back to life.

"Make love to me, Roan."

I no longer had to obey her commands, but I wouldn't turn down the request—the sweet invitation of joining with the woman who gave me everything.

I grabbed a handful of hair and pulled her neck back. The silver star glinted around her neck and I paused. Instead of biting her, I kissed her ever so gently.

She moaned, wriggling against me.

"God, don't move. I'll come if you do." My hands dropped to cup her breast. Shock filled me. Her breasts were swollen and big. Not what I was used to from her smaller cup size.

Zel squirmed away after a second, too sensitive. "I need you, Roan. Now."

How was it every time we had sex it ended being too much to bear. Too wild. Too full of need to take it slow.

I could barely see with need for her.

Wrapping my arms around her back, I squashed her against me. Loving the thrum of her heart against mine. The heat of her skin. "I want to spend a lifetime making you come, Hazel. A lifetime of pleasure and happiness."

She smiled, throwing her head back as I kissed along her chin. "I like that proposal." Her mouth searched mine and she moaned as I plunged my tongue past her lips. I fucking drowned in her taste and my hips surged upward, searching for her.

Her tongue swirled with mine while she gyrated on my lap. She rushed me, rubbing her intoxicating wetness along my cock. I growled with frustration as her eager hand went between my legs and cupped my balls. "Now, Roan. Take me."

I gritted my teeth as a wave of lust filled my belly. "I wanted to lead tonight, but you've taken control once again. You own me so fucking completely, Zel." My vision pulsed as she stroked my cock, harder and harder until all I could think about was filling her. Thrusting into her.

"I'm just enjoying being able to touch you with no fear."

She bent her head to bite my neck. "I can bite you."

She stopped stroking me and shoved the robe away until she sat gloriously naked in my lap. Her arms wrapped around my shoulders, bringing us within breathing distance. "I can hug you."

Spreading her legs, she arched her back and sank ever so slowly down my length. "I can fuck you."

I groaned as she consumed me with hot darkness. "I can adore you." Her arms pressed on my shoulders as she pushed upward. We moaned loudly as she sank back down. Down and down until every inch of me was in every inch of her.

Goddammit, this woman. I would never get enough of her.

I fucking loved her forever.

Throwing all plans for a slow and seductive evening away, I pushed up with my legs and splayed her flat on her back on the sheepskin. She flinched at the speed, then sighed and shivered as I thrust into her.

"You like that?" I kissed her nose, her cheek, her eyelids. "You like me being inside you? Fucking you? Loving you?"

She bit her lip, fingernails scrabbling at my back. "Yes. Don't stop. Don't stop."

The flickering gold and oranges of the fire danced across her skin, making her look like she burned with need.

Keeping my weight on one elbow, I traced down the centre of her body all while rocking into her. I followed the path of where the silver chain used to be. The one I'd fabricated in hope it would protect her from me. I missed it. We hadn't used it often, but now I liked the thought of restraining her just so I could indulge in my fill. To make her come apart as successfully as she made me.

I made a mental note to fabricate another. To bind her with silver, so I could take her completely.

For now, I had an alternative.

Leaning down to kiss her, I fumbled for the edge of the sheepskin and came up with the pair of fluffy handcuffs.

Her eyes flared, but she didn't say a word as I secured one

around her wrist and the other…around mine. Locking us together left wrist to left wrist. The novelty cuffs didn't stand a chance against holding, but I liked the symbolism; the blatant acknowledgment that we belonged to each other.

Her free hand captured the back of my head, dragging me down for another kiss. "Whatever you have in mind, you better hurry. I need you so much."

I chuckled. "You've ruined my plans already. I'd planned on making love to you, slowly, softly."

She moaned and shook her head. "No. I want you hard. I want to sweat and pant and explode."

It was my turn to groan.

I couldn't take it. This witch had successfully stolen everything I was and I wanted nothing more than to obey.

I rolled away and carefully pulled her on top of me. Staying deep inside her, I couldn't tear my eyes away from her perfection. Her full breasts. Her pouty lips. She looked like a fucking goddess.

I couldn't stand it. It was too much.

Gripping her hips, I thrust upward, transfixed by her heavy bouncing breasts and flushed skin.

She fell forward, crushing me with her body.

Before, such a move would've caused an innate reaction to kill her. I wouldn't have been able to control the conditioning—now, I never wanted her to leave. I wanted to stay beneath her like this forever.

We rocked together, finding a rhythm uniquely us. Her soft scent drugged me, and I lost all sense of time as we gave each other pleasure.

"God, you feel amazing," I groaned, relishing in the slow build-up, the tightness in my balls.

Hazel sat up, capturing my cheeks. I sucked in a breath at the love shining in her eyes. "You're mine, Roan Averin. Forever."

I nodded in a sex-filled trance. "Forever."

"Make me come." Her voice turned husky and her hand

dropped to land on my heart, bracing herself as she rode me.

Locking my legs against the rapidly building orgasm, I pressed two fingers against her clit and swirled with a pressure I knew she loved.

Her eyes snapped closed; her hips rocked harder, dragging me closer to the edge. "Yes, like that. Um…"

Shit, I need her.

I needed to be in control. The one taking and giving.

Flipping her over, I rubbed her clit with a demanding hand and drove into her. Her legs hooked over my hips as she panted faster and faster.

"Do you want me?" I growled. "Do you want me to make you shatter?"

She bit her lip, nodding. "More than anything."

"Do you know how much I care for you? How much you brought me back to life?"

Her eyes locked with mine. "Do you know how much *I* care for *you?* How much you've given me?"

The unconditional love in her gaze undid me. There would be no more talking. Only chasing our ultimate goal.

Dropping my mouth to hers, I thrust deep. Finding a pace that sent shooting stars down my back and legs.

My mind fogged as my release built and built.

Zel sucked in a breath as I found her clit again. "Come for me, Zel. Come for me like you did in the greenhouse. Shatter for me."

She threw her head back, hair tangling with the sheepskin below. Her skin flushed and the first band of her release caught me by surprise.

I had no chance against the strong grip of her body.

My orgasm raced from tingle to explosions. And my cock detonated with sensation. I thrust harder, letting myself spill. Ripple after ripple, my cock spurted. "Fuck, you're amazing," I growled as I chased the violent edge of my release.

Zel cried out as I drove harder. Her fingernails scratched my back sending ribbons of heat down my skin.

My legs cramped, my body stiffened and I poured every last drop into the woman who I would spend the rest of my life serving.

When the lightning had passed and we lay exhausted in each other's arms, I pressed a gentle kiss on her lips. "One of these days I'm going to seduce the hell out of you. I'll tie you up and spend hours torturing you with every sexual device I can think of."

She smiled, eyes hazy with desire. "It sounds like heaven. Tomorrow. Book that in for tomorrow." She flopped onto her side, curling into the sheepskin. "And a massage, too. You owe me for the one I gave you."

My mind skipped back to the night she'd tried to break me. The struggle I'd suffered. The conditioning that almost ruined my life.

I shuddered.

I never wanted another flashback.

I never wanted to think about Russia or Ghosts again.

Mimicking Hazel, I lay on my side, then I did the one thing I'd been dying to do for months.

Gathering her inert, well-sated form into mine, I spooned the woman I loved. Locking us together like a yin and yang. The fluffy cuffs adding another element of belonging.

She sighed, snuggling her perfect ass into my front and grabbing my arm to hug her tighter. "This. This is what I always hoped we'd have."

I nuzzled her ear, breathing deeply. "I'll hold you every night as you go to sleep. Every morning, I'll wake up and make love to you. And we'll grow old together in each other's arms."

She sighed in perfect contentedness.

We relaxed in front of the fire for hours. My body wrapped around her. Two sides of two lifetimes coming together forever.

The issues of my past had gone. I had freedom to play with my children and learn to be a father. I had the privilege of learning to be a worthy husband.

My life had started with hope and ended by tragedy, but through all of it, I survived. I survived and fell in love with the woman who saved me, and I had a future I would treasure forever.

One day I would hold my daughter's hand while I walked her to school.

One day I would teach my son how to metal work.

I had everything I ever wanted.

I had more love than I could ever need.

I had a family.

AUTHOR

Pepper Winters wears many roles. Some of them include writer, reader, sometimes wife. She loves dark, taboo stories that twist with your head. The more tortured the hero, the better, and she constantly thinks up ways to break and fix her characters. Oh, and sex…her books have sex.

She loves to travel and has an amazing, fabulous hubby who puts up with her love affair with her book boyfriends. She hangs out on Facebook all day every day, so if you want to pop in and say hi, she's always ready to reply.

If you enjoyed this book or her others, Pepper would love you forever if you could leave a brief review on Amazon.

Her other books include:

Tears of Tess *(Monsters in the Dark #1)* Buy HERE
Quintessentially Q *(Monsters in the Dark #2)* Buy HERE
Twisted Together *(Monsters in the Dark #3 Coming May 2014)* Add to Goodreads HERE
Debt Inheritance *(Indebted Series. Coming Soon)* Add to Goodreads HERE

To be the first to know of upcoming releases, please join Pepper's Newsletter (she promises never to spam or annoy you).

Pepper's Newsletter

You can stalk her here:

Pinterest

She loves mail of any kind: **pepperwinters@gmail.com**

ACKNOWLEDGEMENTS

I find writing acknowledgements harder than writing a four hundred page book. I worry about missing people out, having a brain freeze, and forgetting someone fundamental to my journey. So, this is my disclaimer: I'm eternally sorry if I forget you. It doesn't mean I don't love you any less or appreciate everything you do, it's because I've frozen up and my brain has gone on strike.

Now the disclaimer is out of the way, let's begin:

First, I'd like to thank my husband because without his constant support and endless patience I wouldn't be able to write as much as I do. He's there to discuss plot holes, listen to me rant and rave, hold my hand with bad reviews, and cheer me on while I make my dreams come true. Love that man to death.

Second, I'd like to thank the amazing people behind the scenes. Arijana Karcic from *Cover it! Designs* for all my amazing covers and Kellie Dennis from *Book Cover by Design* for the original tattooed cover for Destroyed. Love your talent, ladies, and, Ari, I would be lost if we didn't chat about meaningless things on FB.

Next, I'd like to thank Nadine Colling for doing such an amazing job running my street team. You and Tamara McRae are truly amazing and I love chatting with you ladies. Thank you to all the amazing women in my street team for your incredible support and pimpage. I know I couldn't do any of this without you.

To all the bloggers and reviewers, I love each and every one of you. I love chatting with you, reading your reviews, and can't thank you enough for your support. In particular, I'd like to thank Becs Glass from *Sinfully Sexy Book Reviews* for just being incredible and so lovely, and Milasy from *Rock Stars of*

Romance for being so incredibly supportive of my work and welcoming me onto their website of hugely successful authors.

I'm indebted to Ing Cruz from *As the Pages Turn* for all her extraordinary help arranging a kick ass blog tour and for putting up with me while I delayed the release of Destroyed to make sure it was perfect. She's an amazing woman, friend, and I don't know what I'd do without her.

To Natalie from *Love Between The Sheets* for putting up with me changing my release day and always being around to answer my questions. To Jenny from *Editing for Indies* for an amazing proofreading job. I love your work and your awesome feedback. You went above and beyond and I can't thank you enough.

I want to thank Skye Callahan for being around for our daily chats and putting up with my breakdowns every day while writing this book. Love our sticker wars and aimless chats.

To Chantal Fernando for being so like me and freaking out about the signings we've agreed to this year.

To Lyra Parish for our ridiculous conversations about randomness and our joy of insomnia.

To Rachel Brookes for being so sweet, generous, and a massive cheerleader despite having so much else going on in her life.

To Ker Dukey for being strong, awesome, and impassioned about all things writing. Love your talent.

To Kristi Webster for talking me through every plot hole in Destroyed and calming me down when I was ready to self-combust.

To Kristina Amit for being an amazing beta reader. I can't thank you enough for being so dedicated and loyal. You're amazing and I value your time so much.

To Helena Reviews for pointing out plot holes with gentleness and such an infectious love of my work. I can't thank you enough for all your support.

To Ella Fox for becoming a friend and reading Destroyed in a few hours so I could stop biting my nails and freaking out.

You really gave me the push I needed to finish.

To all the ladies in the SSIRACG. You're amazing and I'm so glad I met you all. Your truly are a lifesaver.

And last but definitely not least, I have to thank my beta readers. Destroyed turned out to be the hardest book I've ever had to write, and instead of the select few I use to beta read, I had to ask a ton of people for their opinion while rocking in the corner. I owe these ladies every thanks for talking me off the 'delete button' and for keeping me going when I wanted to throw this book away. In no particular order:

Astrid Knowles, Lisa Brookes, Vicki Ryan, Sarah Griffen, Celeste Harrington, Katrina Sincek, NJ Frost, and Tamicka Birch. You ladies were a total godsend and I know without your input Destroyed would've remained on my hard drive destined never to see the light of a kindle. I owe everything to you and all the amazing beta readers and friends I've mentioned above.

I could go on and on but I think I'll wrap this up and finish with a HUGE thank you to you, the reader. Thank you for your trust in me, your kind words, and amazing encouragement. I hope you enjoyed Destroyed and all my other work coming soon.

To anyone I forgot, you mean the world to me and I'm blowing kisses. I love each and every one of you and thank you from the bottom of my heart. I know it's cheesy but I honestly could never have done it without the amazing support network offered by you amazing people, and I'll always appreciate you, more than you know.

xxxxxxx Thank you xxxxxxx

Two upcoming releases

Twisted Together (Monsters in the Dark #3)
Goodreads HERE
Expected Publication May 2014
A modern day Dark Erotic Romance

"_After battling through hell, I brought my esclave back from the brink of ruin. I sacrificed everything—my heart, my mind, my very desires to bring her back to life. And for a while, I thought it broke me, that I'd never be the same. But slowly the beast is growing bolder, and it's finally time to show Tess how beautiful the dark can be._"

Q gave everything to bring Tess back. In return, he expects nothing less. Tess may have leashed and tamed him, but he's still a monster inside.

Debt Inheritance (Indebted Series)
Goodreads HERE
Expected Publication March-April 2014
A modern day Dark Erotic Romance

"_I own you. I have the piece of paper to prove it. It's undeniable and unbreakable. You belong to me until you've paid off your debts._"

Nila Weaver's family is indebted. Being the first born daughter, her life is forfeit to the first born son of the Hawks to pay for sins of ancestors past. The dark ages might have come and gone, but debts never leave.

She has no choice in the matter. She is no longer free.

Jethro Hawk receives Nila as an inheritance present on his twenty-seventh birthday. Her life is his until she's paid off a debt that's centuries old. He can do what he likes with her—nothing is out of bounds—she has to obey.

There are no rules. Only payments.

PLAYLIST

Madness by Muse
Falling away with you by Muse
Your Surrender by Neon Trees
Radioactive by Imagine Dragons
Bring me to life by Evanescence
The Verve by Bittersweet Symphony
Possession by Sara Mclaughlan
Angel by Sara Mclaughlan
Iris by Goo Goo Dolls
Strange love by Depache Mode
Cosmic Love by Florence and the machine
Black hole by Sound Garden
Up in the air by Thirty Seconds to Mars

30326331R00261

Made in the USA
Charleston, SC
12 June 2014